I0736150

Love Love Love

KAMRUNNESSA KABIR

ISBN   978-1-951913-71-7   (Paperback)
ISBN   978-1-951913-72-4   (Digital)

Lettra Press books may be ordered through booksellers or by contacting:

Lettra Press LLC
30 N Gould St. Suite 4753
Sheridan, WY 82801
1 307-200-3414 | info@lettrapress.com
www.lettrapress.com

CONTENTS

Story 1 1
Story 2 14
Story 3 49
Story 4 81
Story 5 124
Story 6 152
Story 7 162
Story 8 182
Story 9 217

STORY 1

Silence

All quiet all dark around the sleepless two eyes of Shanti browsing around for a living sign of life by the end of the night while the tiny beam of light is about to waking up from the veil of the darkness of the night. No sign of life yet out, no birds chirping, no flower is blooming with its beauty to show up to the world, no bugs humming, and no winds blowing. The king of the wind seems to have held his breath within himself to blow all in a sudden right at the day break.

Shanti's bed room is silent too. The faces and the scenarios on the picture frames are glowing in the dark. The light beams while the curtains over the windows blowing by the wind of ceiling fan with a sound to give her a life with sound while all the expensive furniture's in the room are only showing the values they are possessing but not Shanty herself. She is waiting for the day break, another day of her life. Looking outside the window gave her a kind of hope doesn't know for what. At least the night is fading away with the appearance of the shallow beam of the light from the veil of the darkness. As far as she remembers she was up almost all of the previous night waiting for none with any regret, no hope just looking outside the window where there was nothing but only darkness of the night. The famous writer wrote in one of his book that the darkness of the night also has a beauty to receive by the heart and I like say that it has a beauty in at this time also right after the sunset a glowing dim beauty of Nature in a color very light yellow as a glow leaving behind the by the sunset as well as at the sunrise as both are the declining and rising of the mighty power. She wished to sleep to have some dream at least with some contents playing some visions in the morning to hold onto something of the mysteries of the world.

Day break now! No one to see to bid 'Good Morning'. Jiban will be arriving tonight from his business tour a very busy man! Perfect for all in the world. He will 'be arriving with a lot of excuses to express how troublesome was the trip by holding a bunch of gifts for her leaving the luggage behind in the car. Seeing her cold in expressions of any kind he would ask for food cooked by his loving wife saying how much he missed her food and how delicious were they. Shanti came out of her room leaving behind all her thoughts in her silent room to proceed towards the dining an open nice space by the big glass window to look out to see the lake view. A nice house by the lake side with all the Natural beauties around she looks out to think how many people on earth can effort a living like this with an open view of Nature by buying the open beauty of a huge one belongs to the very huge and unlimited beauty of the unlimited bounty of the mighty Nature. She took a chair to sit by the window a bit away from the dining table occupied by Maria setting the dining table occupied by her while setting it for the breakfast.

The water on the lake is still and shallow while all in a sudden she wanted to swim in the waves up and down while there's no waves at all. All quiet around since the morning.

'Madam"! Maria came down to Shanti and while Shanty looked back Maria answered, 'Breakfast is ready Mam!'

'Oh, Yes! Shanty came back from the big window to take a sit at the breakfast table. She was barely eating but still looking out to talk to herself 'Big achievement! A few people can live a life like this. All luxuries around, all the beauty of the aristocracy and of Nature together all around. Jiban took a huge plot to make this home a little out of the city. All nice and quiet a very peaceful place in the quiet natural environment makes her mood doesn't know for what? All she feels is only emptiness a lifeless living in all the living things as all very vivid, full of life in the lap of the very Nature. She took a piece of bread to butter it and took a sip of her coffee looked like that's the only thing she was craving for now no hunger no desires and how can that be while feeling all empty in the emptiness of the very soul or can be said a soulless soul? A big apartment, she looked all around as if seeing the very familiar spot with a new vision but for why? The very specious living room with high glass ceiling top to allow the sunshine through peeping and touching the hearts of the residents penetrating the very souls!

All tidy the big heavy curtains on the walls around covering what doors or windows hard to tell from outside. They are more of a decorations rather than a purpose. Big posters and the paintings covering the walls on the both sides of the fire place which actually has no purpose at all in such a tropical country. All the sofa sets bearing some resembles to the aristocratic society. Some glass shelves on the walls around holding a lot of souvenirs for decorations. The porch area, the dining space attached to the wide and spacious living room presenting a huge decorated and spacious place over all. Still something is missing which doesn't make it a home 'a home sweet home!' All tidy, all nice and quiet with aristocracy, beauty as well as with elegancy which must be the soul? Nope! Can't be! Where is the soul? The heart of the home contained by the love and living of the residents here? Shanty is present but where is the other half of the soul to make it a full? If a couple only living in the house where is the other person supposed to be her partner the life partner? Half of the soul meaning one person can't feel properly without sharing the feel the thoughts *by expressing, by feeling in sharing in the expressions! The monument or the statue of a home is there but no residents together in seen to live in there can't really make it a home. Shanty* doesn't know why? When she finished her coffee to look back to the opposite wall through the dining table where there's a little child smiling *with all his* innocence *of the world. Wish if she could be at least get a child to warm up the house as well as the heart? Shanty turned back again to enter her room by suggesting Maria to make a menu with all her husband's favourites for the dinner tonight to prepare before he comes home tonight.*

Then she went back to her room thinking a lot of things to do. All quiet again in her solitary room. She thought only a bit and quickly got hereby very busy to do things. No sign of a living thing or even a bit of sound from inside or out. Maria's working quiet in the kitchen. A very sound home in a solitary surroundings over all.

ii

Two days back in a far and far land of a dreams a very land of dreams Jiban and his lady secretary are together in a luxurious hotel room together sitting by the luxurious wide window of the room open through the nice view outside relaxing to view the outside making a nice and modern city of the cotemporary world of us, a view of the pretty modern civilization. Pushpa opened up her mouth first asking 'how do you like it here?'

'Great! Especially with you! You're my inspiration you are my 'Good Luck!'

--'really? And Bhabhi? She's your love I know------I know all men are like that'!

'How many you know?' asked Jiban as tend to teas.

---'jealous?' smiled Pushpa.

- 'not at all!

-- 'Come on! Relax! What a beautiful evening! Aren't you happy? Aren't you enjoying? How's the lunch?

--oh! Yea, it's really great. Nice luxurious hotel with a nice view around! What else you can dream of? Jiban got very pleased in his expressions.

Pushpa joined him in enormous enthusiasm said; 'yea!' we are very familiar to view some well-developed civilizations like this one.

----yes! Only some fortunate people around the world can effort all these. Look at that big building almost touching the sky. Look at the shallow lake down bearing the witness of Nature at the feet of human civilizations". Jiban got very excited describing the entire city to express his happiness to share his dreams with his present partner. Also proceeded proudly,' Pushpa, I'm very proud of this day. I can't believe I managed all these with my own efforts!'

Pushpa kept watching his happy face and the proudest eyes with her very keen eyes thought 'definitely this ambitious man enjoying his success in achieving all the success this morning in getting signed their business contract; the luxury tour all around, staying at expensive hotels, the delicious dinners all at the same time loving the time with a very hot woman like her. Needs a Good night sleep for the flight tomorrow then?' And when she got out of the shower after almost 45 min couldn't see Jiban in the room must have been gone for a walk outside for dinner after. The ambitious humans tend to move up following up all their ambitions just like the high rise sky touching buildings as Jiban was describing a little while ago. Our ambitions are sky touching as we give them a concrete figure tend to be the very high rise like our ambitions the same way we leave our lives behind basically leaving down or keeping down our consciences as well as humanity basically by treating us poor as a whole where rich and the poor are the same poor people deprived personalities this way or other in the loss of live and the values in life. Thought her next, 'O, well! Enjoy yourself! Free air free man, free wills as well! Good luck!'

<h2 style="text-align:center">liii</h2>

Jiban's walking out in the streets all alone in the night in a city very well known, well developed and of course very beautiful! The business part with a female company is left behind for this moment a moment for himself only for him all alone to feel him, to know himself all by one by his own self. Looking around all at the shiny glorious ski touching high rise monuments of the present time and the present civilization made him a little thoughtful also about which he doesn't know how. He took a look at the displaying beautiful female models with all their elegancy and looked inside in search of his wife Shanti sitting or living alone inside the house a home which they both made with their efforts with love and dedications but the love doesn't seem to be giving enough comfort and happiness to his Shanti. She's his love but still got carried away from his heart, his surroundings and his present life. All just happened but how? Who's responsible for the change or the inconvenience in the life of Jiban no Shanti? Is it his ambitions? And why? Did he ever ask for this? A rootless life in no bondage holding Shanti meaning Peace which in their life is only a name for the sake of the name to keep their home calm and quiet physically or a looking good couple in the looking good home they make out of silence while in the hearts of this couple one is with desires, in ambitions and the contradictory one constantly keeping a pain to make it a real home with a soul. Shanty can't really love the house they are possessing in the solitary environment when it doesn't make any content with a feel of home existing life with a soul which might be the word Love only? But why? Thinks Jiban sometimes' I did everything to to make us happy. I worked hard days and nights to make money to make a life together. I brought the materials of modern life in nature to make a home in love to live in love, peace and happiness together to make a life with a soul together. What did I do wrong? Why am I suffering running away from my own life in my own home? My shanty is living alone in alone in my home staying beside me apart from my soul! What took us to depart from each other?

All in sudden he felt himself very lonely all alone in the entire world in the town as far as the eyes roam around to feel a life all night time glories Disco's, bars, music in the streets as well as inside all the fun and glories and charms for night time human night crawlers seeking some reliefs in fun and fantasy to release all the stress they get in achieving all they want for life in pain and regret.

'Hi!' how are yea! All alone? I can give you some company!' the beautiful night girl looked into his eyes all dressed up in tattoos and a two piece a short bosom cover with a bottom cover. Said again 'I' mean--- if you want--?

'No thanks! Jiban pushed himself against his will to get out from there walking faster intending to go to a nearby shop to do some shopping but looked back to the street girl thinking' sometimes people ignore the very reality of the real life while achieved success to live better or even in luxury like him. He didn't know how far he came across the street on feet in search of a store. He couldn't find any shopping place or might have missed already for being so unmindful? At least he can see a souvenir store ahead by the side of the street.

He bought some souvenirs like a significant doll, an umbrella in miniature held by a girl by the traffic post, an expensive sunglasses and finally an elegant poster portraying the main city where is standing now. Bringing the outside world in his pocket doesn't make Shanti happy at all now-a-days. But still the love remains for the loved one doesn't matter as a trash or a treasure.

4

9 pm on the Saturday evening. Shanty's waiting for Jiban to receive him from the airport with a fear inside god knows he might call any time to give the good or bad news saying that this time also he missed the flight! She hopes not! Thought Shanty what she hopes now-a-days she herself doesn't know anymore. She doesn't know her husband's arrival or non-arrival any of these is good news or a bad news any longer. He's unpredictable now. Still at least he gave her a life to keep her alive all these years by breaking her silence in her survival with no warmth at all! But recently nothing can give her those sparks of life she used to get the sudden sparks of life in the boringness, in despair or even in a sad mood. Shanty became all shanty shanties which Jiban doesn't know why and how. He's now all himself only follows his wishes, his instincts, and his plans. He makes big decisions' all by himself. He cares for others more than including his family which is only his wife all by his wills only. He's self-guided, self-planned and very confident to set

his goals he doesn't want to lose his love when he cannot give up a bit of himself for others especially Shanty knowing his other half considering his own self to possess herself within him. He needs full attention from the dear one while he loves more himself than others. Shanty doesn't know whether he's a selfish man or not who moves forward with all the energy gained from others through their supports to gain or achieve whatever usually all the people want to achieve. The same way he possesses Shanty all into himself without giving up a bit of himself for her or for her choices. His love is his full possessions can't really let it go while he also has his full freedom to share the time and passions with another other than Shanty doesn't really want to understand that it hurts in the heart of his beloved who cares about him a lot. Perhaps this is what's called of a particular type of human nature which is very natural, distinct and unchangeable with distinction. But this is love! Shanty has no complaint about having someone considering his or her own is also called a Love. She's happy no complain at all just a bit empty in the enormous emptiness in his absence.

It's very late at night Jiban doesn't even feel like to look at the watch. His spirit's down and all emotions off only know that heading towards home a home which consists of only one family member "Shanti'! Where there is no Shanty in the souls live there containing only a silence of the heart, a dumbness of the feel of peace. The very egocentric Shanty's still might be waiting for him might even doesn't know why, for what reason? Love, devotion or affections? Sometimes, might have been turned to be a very habitual as a duty also to wait for the only family member ceasing the chemistry between a man and a woman? Apart from being a businessman Jiban now-a-days also becoming very thoughtful. He can feel Shanty from the very inside to see her inside to understand to love her with an unexpressed love which can't touch can't tell for some reason in no reason! He feels her pain but can't help her to remove it while doesn't know whether she is built in like that or the circumstances meaning including him as her husband to be very responsible for her situation which basically binds him within too. He might have been running away from the odds of their relationship which can't really keep them then in any kind of a relationship to live in their own home to make it only one home for two? So basically most of the time they are away from each other to live individually minding their own business while staying very close to each other under the same roof.

Its 3.45 am in the morning when Jiban reached home. Coming back home always makes him feel a home from all the businesses out with all the stress associated with them. A tormented or a tired soul to come home to relax, to rest to get itself some relief from all the sufferings, all the hardships from the travelling, from all the making up things to come running for the home sweet home! After all secure and pure! He didn't bother to ring the bell for anybody and took out the key from his pocket to open the door. Shanty might be waiting at the entrance to greet him with a smile a shallow or a single with no beads of life. Doesn't matter he came home. Jiban came back to Jiban to the home he created with his hard work and devotions to make it a real home where there is his Shanty his love still loves him or not he doesn't want to know. He only knows it's his home where there is his Shanty lives forever only for him.

'Shanti-------- where are you? I know you are here---- Jiban started calling his wife his life partner as entering the house. But couldn't see her right in front of him as usual. He got a bit surprised as well as worried 'did she get upset about my late arrival with no phone calls at all?' I know--- she used to do that before hiding herself somewhere else in a corner of the house to let him find her where she could be. 'Great!! At least she came back to herself!' finally!

Jiban put down his suitcase taking the little gift bags brought for her. Looked here looked there entered the bedroom by coming across the living room and dining in search of her. All quiet, all nice and tidy but no sign of Shanti 'where are you? My shanty! Jiban started calling loud now with a fear of losing her doesn't know why. He searched everywhere the porch, the kitchen, the garage, the washrooms, the open roof up, the, the Cori-doors except his bed room their bed room to enter there later with a hope that she might be sleeping there with a hope the last hope not to be failed to his heart for anything bad happened.

Once more Jiban looked around before entering the final chance to find his Shanti tried to see Maria to ask about her Mistress but couldn't see her too. He couldn't waste any more time looking around thought better to see her in her bedroom 'She's there----definitely she's there---- she can't disappeared from my life-------

A big blow of wind in the early morning at the sun rise gave a shake to Jiban as soon as he entered the bed-room door. The door was open the windows are as well as with the open light chiffon curtain blowing with the crazy wind up front to blow his heart and his shirt to shake his heart to squeeze at the very next moment in an unknown fear. He looked around no sign of Shanti his wife his life partner. No sign in the washroom either. The bed is still nice and tidy the entire room including all furniture are very clean and tidy. Shanty's missing only but her picture' together with him are there hanging up on the walls with many other posters and paintings around portraying some unique ever living or long living images of human lives and the beauty of Nature itself. Shanti is only a tiny bit of life on earth but an enormous significance in Jiban's life. A life without her is unbearable.

He sat on the couch losing the color from his face looked out at the day break still a little dark as the Sun rising very slowly by giving his light to the word very slowly from the concealing truth of light and the life all nice and quiet only one thing but the main thing missing from his life. He could make this world he could live his life, could enjoy also but only by holding Shanti into his bosom in his heart. He never realized that he will miss someone some day in his life that much to feel very empty inside. Then why did he running all these years only after the worldly gains? All his efforts seem now has gone in vain when there is no one to appreciate and love all his achievements after all. He feels himself dumb and pointless while suddenly got himself into motionless in the entire room even in the entire town trapped into his own ambitions and emotions making no points at this point while no one basically the loved one is missing might have been already left by ignoring the stupidity of the humans in such a human life where basically nothing makes perfect as while running after money or fortune when lacking in life to enjoy those for life and when the life itself is very young and right to enjoy there is no money or fortunes to spend some on cherishing the beauties of life. He feels like got lost forever by losing Shanti only when Maria showed up by the door looking at the Master the poor Master in the poverty of feel when the entire house is full of treasures and riches to live in luxury and life for living in beauty for which all the efforts and the dedications to be failed in this much emptiness and irony to regret for fooling himself by valuing the world more than himself.

Asked Maria, 'when did you come Sir?'

'Just a little while ago. Where is your mistress? I don't see her.'

'Babi left. I don't know where and when, she was sitting in the living room all evening and was busy packing things all day. But I didn't see her leaving. Madam left without letting me know. Here I found this letter on the table by the kitchen.'

Jiban hurried to get the letter with a shaken hand and the mind said, 'where is it? Give me! Give me!'

MY Jiban my love,

I loved you all my life never thought that I will leave you one day by realizing that my husband do not love me anymore. You don't need me anymore any longer. I'm a also like a piece of furniture in your dear home sweet home and a piece of furniture expensive or non-expensive don't really want to know. You are successful in all the worldly matters and materials and in the contrary I'm good for nothing. Neither can make you happy nor can myself with all of your riches, your luxuries. I'm a failure in this life making no sense to live. In this mobility of life I can't help anyone basically fit for nothing. Demanding life and earning life make sense now-a-days not only making a home nice and lovely full of love and passion as well as devotions. These are all old concepts only money makes a life now and I'm incapable of doing anything in order to provide that. Neither can I make money nor can I make you happy. I feel down and good for nothing actually. I wish you all the happiness of the world and all your wishes to be fulfilled. I know that I'm an inevitable part of your life. You have love for me in the heart but no time and space to express I'm also the same full of love and passion just can't get the beloved one to express. In a way we both are the same living and caring human beings to each other in no touch emotional or physical while even a cat can keep us in touch. A lonely Dove can't make its way to live or to fly. But I made my way by choosing to fly in the open sky. I know I belong to you. We both made for each other but still living with or without you make me nothing but empty only. We're the couple ducks swimming through the water in the lake together searching for the bites all across knowing not hungry or not needing those bites to collect nothing for something or not. We are the hearts of the house with no beads. We are two bodies living together without touching each other's soul. I'm very within you living inside you might be the part of you which you keep within as the other half of you not to feel, not to see, not to touch as your instinct or your senses say that I'm you so not to worry to hold the part which is always with you. But you don't realize that I'm all empty all lonely sitting in a corner of this big house in all the luxuries making no life for us together. You possessed me while consumes me not realizing that we're two different persons supposed to be in a love relationships to make the home a sweet home.

Wish you all the success and all the happiness, health and prosperity and all---all you need to be happy. My dear, I love you forever! You deserve better!

Be well!

Your Shanti

Jiban didn't know what do what to say or what to think just kept looking around the empty room ignoring all in there. Looking at his empty eyes Maria said, 'Madam left all these packets and piled up in the corner there.'

Jiban followed her to look at the spot in a corner of the room to see a pile of boxes small and big look like all his wife's favourites, different boxes of jewelleries for different occasions and all the gifts given by Jiban in their entire conjugal life mainly only on the anniversaries. He lifted his eyes again with a question towards Maria and Maria's answer was 'those are Bhabhi's expensive jewelleries and accessories. She told me to take a good care of them.

Jiban couldn't hold himself within himself anymore to sit on the carpet to cry out to empty his bosom 'O Shanti! I earned everything for you. All I did was for you only! All I made created only all for you. All I achieved only for you I'm nothing without you!

Come back Shanti please! Only once more! I'll never leave you again I promise! Never ever! Let you go! O Maria please find my Shanti. Do something please I can't live without her. Please!

O Maria, Maria!

THE END

STORY 2

A sin city a satanic world
Kamrunnessa/ April 2018

Far and far away a world unknown and never seen before where there'
the lady called Seema's constantly trying to land on the ground as flying
up but very close to the earth. Fiery burning blazes are all around but
only the fear touching her heart not the fire as would be touching her
body. She is flying around with constant pain and fear as losing the
sights around at the same time trying to hold onto the objects flying
shiny, useless or even meaningless with no basic shapes or colors as they
are not familiar looking at all. The land is visible every now and then
to disappear again to catch to land after all. Finally she pulled herself
together to leave the idea of landing. She chose instead the big platform
of water whispering 'that's better! Let's dip me down into the water to
escape the upcoming fire. But Alas! No water! It's a frozen land of ice
to slip around basically!'

'What's going on? No water no land, no green not even some green
signs of Nature at all! I can't even see the big blue sky up there too! It's
all dark! No! It's not. It's a different world of just a different feeling an
unknown world in nowhere might be?

Finally at least she managed to scream out to get rid of the mystery
of the misery 'Abeer------?' her sixteen year old boy came running

towards her to rescue the mother from the mess of her regular bad daylight dream.

'It's morning! Do you have school today?'

'Yes Mom. I have an exam today remember?'

'O, yea! Sorry beta, go get ready. I'm coming in a minute to make you some breakfast. Seema tries to leave the bed for the morning time responsibilities.

'Don't forget your medicine Mom!' Abeer advises his childlike old age Mom now.

'O.K. good to take medicines to wipe out all the hard feeling. God knows when the world will be back again to normal. May be never ever again. In fact there never was any like called 'normal'. The word called 'Normal' doesn't have an explanation for what does it look like and for what kind it stands for, like what things or facts make certain things 'normal'?

'Not again Mom! I have to go now. I'll call you from school. Don't miss breakfast and lunch. Please Mom? We'll have dinner together tonight.'

Abeer left in hurry just like his father. Seema knows he'll be late tonight also. Knows also that doesn't matter anymore to her the mom knows that the son might be going for dinner with his girl friend. Seema doesn't go by the time or keep track of time anymore. She doesn't follow the routine for the medicine or can't maintain her life accordingly on a daily basis to follow the chart for drug intake or the food intakes by following all the meals and breakfast time. She doesn't feel like she has anymore any goals for life. She doesn't care what' life for anymore any longer is as she believes in survival only not living a life with feel and aim and gain to pine.

Too much to think about. They need some time to relax life is hard what can she expect to do or get from the life now the world seems falling apart at least to her. The pain remains inside as abstract things are painful but invisible to catch to dispatch. May be this way now only can transfer to others those who are in close relation to her.

Her morning time has been spent in the garden. Nine o'clock flower have gone fading away so does her spirit. They will bloom again with a new spirit again making a brand new every day time they bloom to die out again just by the time a very short time. She took her medicines not the breakfast to eat. As usual started worrying about her son and the smelling problems around. She is all alone now except her only son Abeer beside her. Seema broke up with second husband who brought her nothing but the heavy rain fall from Mother Nature as Her blessings showered on her to cry out with no fruit of fortune or a favour of any kind except what she begotten from her first marriage. So her life spring got stopped here with no flow but a barren place of earth to be stable for an establishment of a kind which doesn't grow doesn't produce only fades away little by little to the destiny to decay. She is retired from life as well as from work holding onto her only son to beam dim and deep inside.

It's a bright summer morning can't really stay longer in the garden as the sun really is burning up with it 'whole might to produce enough warmth to make a warm day just at the beginning of the day. There' nothing to do inside except some cleaning. Seema didn't feel like cooking as no one else at home to share the food. Turning on the TV gives her nothing but a headache. Movies; Drama serials all seem very monotonous. Music doesn't attract her anymore or even gives her a relief from the same everyday life boring and with no life at all to have some good feel after all. No! No life left for her to cherish with a heart. She looked around her nice and tidy home inside and out. Every single thing including the soap dish in the kitchen sink or the photo frames and other decoration pieces on the TV stand kept very clean and tidy on the wood surface of the stand. She keeps every single thing clean and shine. She wipes off the dirt everyday from all her belongings except the burden of her memories filled with all the hard feeling to get heavy enough to shade some off the heart. The abstracts are nothing but cruel by being untouched to fix or to repair. Working hard all her life gave her achievements in positions as well as in possessions like a house, a car, furniture and many other necessities including money to go on or to carry on the life. Still emptiness tells her all the time that money can buy things but not the soul of a home or of a life. She looked all around again to find a piece of life with a soul to get frustrated once again while standing finally in front of the family photo taken a long time ago. A piece of family picture portrayed very carefully to the value of a family life with her son, signs of love together as a couple twice in her life happy or not smiling though! She stood a longer time in front of that photo includes her only son Abeer doesn't know why. Finally went to take a look at the picture of her mom and dad but still with stone eyes. Looked around once again all around the room as well as the whole house as far as the eyes follow as if in search of a sign of a living thing breathing with life or in life just like her all around in the house. She kept browsing her eyes at the indoor plants living and breathing like her soulless with no real life while living biologically. She started to feel the limited life as an endless phase of time share in pain or no pain in numbness with a dumb feel of enormous tolerance.

She looked back again at her late mom in the glass framed photo with a boundary to find meaning of life kept through generations. At this point she performed her little prayer dedicated to the almighty God Above all. By looking at her watch she took her purse to go out. To go to her office where she's volunteering for the single mom's gives her at least a busy phase of time pass with some dignity and a meaning for being alive.

II

Women's federation for women gives Seema a strange feeling also.
Sometimes she realizes that a part time job like this actually gives her a relief from home where there is basically no family life in the family in real sense according to her sense and sensibility. Today she came to the office to meet the new client she met last time. It's 2 p.m. not many people in the office. Seema entered her chamber and started dusting her desk as usual. Cleaning the environment is like cleaning

her heart full of junks of thoughts to get rid off along with some hard feeling all along her life now to refresh the memory for better work. Atul the new client didn't show up yet. Seema ordered a cup of tea to have in the meantime.

Shikha came in 10 min earlier than her appointment sitting in the lounge already seen by Seema from her chamber. A poor young lady not very pretty but still eye catching for her two deep eyes. She looked calm and very content despite her arrival here for some help. Lot of women come here every day for rehabilitation or a guidance to move on leaving behind the present situations in miseries or misfortune which brought them here for help. Seema took a thoughtful look at the new arrival of a shattered piece of floating life on the waves of life. She doesn't look very sad or worried or even a broken hearted lady after all. 'Very well!' thought Seema even though the look only doesn't always make the sense to read someone's mind or feel the heart. Calm and quiet earth doesn't express always what it contains in her deep bosom.

Shikha showed up as soon as the bell rang from Seema's chamber. She entered the counselor's room with a smile and stood shy behind the chair on the opposite side of the table to sit face to face the counsellor. She took the chair as asked by Seema to sit and kept smiling as if doesn't know for what reason.

'How are you young lady?' asked Seema in a professional manner to continue like 'and what brought you here today?' The upper position lady smiled so did the one who came for help in her bad time. They both smiled together as if they know each other for a long time under all circumstances. They seemed familiar to each other for an unknown reason.

'I'm good.' Shikha's answer and Seema's reply is like

'I know, even if we aren't good still we answer to someone like that. Answering 'good' is as usual as an essential piece of beautiful courtesy to begin with.

Okay-----can we talk in detail now? What brought you here? Asked Seema again by sitting in a position to sit and relax to hear the whole story from her client today which brought Shikha here.

'Okay! Now, how can I help you today? Asked Seema now looking into Shikha's eyes.

Shikha kept quiet for a while didn't know what to say and how to say. Seema made it easier by asking 'what are you doing now? Are you working currently?'

'No.' Shikha answered looking down on the floor.

Okay! So you need a job. Very urgent right?'

'More than that. I need a place to live immediately.

'I see. Sure! We're here to help you. Where are you staying for now?

'Nowhere.'

'Meaning no place to live. Any family so far? Seema's enquiry to her client by now got some confidence to speak up.

'A three year old son.' Shikha bent her head down again while answering the questions asked by the counsellor.

'That's O.K.! It happens. Sighed Seema to ask again 'divorced I guess!'

Shikha didn't answer to that.

Seema asked next 'what's your education so far?

'B.A.' Shikha's answer.

'Good!' how did you hear about 'us?

'My uncle passed away two months now. He paid the house rent till next month after that I don't know where to live and what to do. No job yet.'

'And your husband left you? Seema wants to know the whole story. Shikha kept quiet all the Seema wanted to know about her husband. Finally Seema gave up on that factor to enquiry.

Said 'okay! We help with both a job and residence to provide. Not to worry. We're here only to help even we can rehabilitate your son too. We have a daycare centre here you can leave him there to go for a job training for now. Have confidence and no worries okay? All will be set later on?' So, Seema the counsellor stopped asking anymore questions and proceeded towards the procedure to enroll her in their programs to fit her on a ground to move on in her life with a son for now by handing in a form to fill out for now. Seema cleared the process and the programs as follows a suitable job training first of all with a shelter along with her son partly funded by the Govt. until the client finds a job. In the mean time she will do some volunteer job as much as possible at the centre. Her son will be taken care off before he goes to school. And Shikha will have to find a job and a location to live with her son. After getting a job there will be no help from the centre. And the organization will charge her a fee she can pay whenever she is ready to pay. And that's all. Hearing all this the existing smile from her face disappeared instantly to make her bright face covered by some dark cloud. Looking at her face Seema felt all her pain throughout the ups and downs in her life with two ups beside breaking and making a new life or a home with a hope together with a new spouse to fail again to fall into despair after all. She can see a junior Seema in front of her to help, to pity or might even hate to see the brand new picture of the miseries of life which reflects her present relaxed life in the mirror of the cruel life drama over all. She looked at the girl's pale face to ask 'how about ordering a cup of tea?' The poor girl looked down to say in a very low voice 'o.k.'

'Good! Be brave! Everyone face reality more or less. Never to lose hope.

Come on! Cheer up!' as added next words with full moral support 'your whole life is ahead for being brave and happy at the same time. Look for a better future for you and your child.'

Shikha lifted her face to look into the counsellors face again thinking this must be specially for her an officer in a position talk extra support with someone who touches his or her heart with for some reason. On the other hand Seema lost herself again from the present job handling situation for a client with a solution from the organization when her own life has been wiped off her all enthusiasm to live with a hope and cheer. She lost the presence of the present victim of present situations of life or the very ancient figure of fortune or fate or the society who control people's life like this. Seema lost her own faith in life how can she make another life by providing some hope with some support for the sake of her job. She carries on her job with full heart only as long as she is at work at home she is sleeping in dreams good or bad either of them are fake and living while awake pining and dying for life in life which is either nothing in everything or being dead in living hopeless and aimless. Her lost faith showing her no vision with hope for the new victim in the nature of the life Shikha might already have been started to dream of a life together with her son or of a better future for her son but she believes all in vain. Her negativity might ruin young futures so she keeps quiet but die hard inside. As soon as she started thinking beyond her job she started getting to be numb and stoned eyed again knowing her present and future life again ahead. So very quickly she put an end to the meeting today without even saying a 'Good By' to Shikha her present client to deal with. Said in hurry 'Go to the counter to register your name and your son's as well.

Thinking alone on the way home by driving made Seema think to be born alone to die alone has a truth of the beginning till the end but the truth of being all alone between these two doesn't really make any sense. It can't be! It shouldn't be! And after all it's not fare at all. The more Seema thinks about her life the more she falls into despair to aspire to fall into the ditch of her misfortune at the same time judging herself it's not only her who thinks that he or she is the most unfortunate person in the whole world. Its only life itself to live or to carry on when always things aren't favourable always. Big world and huge populations to find one's own or to make one's own.

Abeer didn't show up tonight at all and the mother also lost her motivations to look for or to check on him. Kids have their own life now. 'O, well people are now only people beyond the family bondage'! Feels like losing her own bondage from the family tie a blood relation or might even from the bondage of life itself. The motive is to live only not to die to live and not be desperate to hold onto life who doesn't seem very favourable to her? Or even to all? Seema cooked a bit to eat a bit after a long day. This little lonely dinner would be her only meal on the entire day. But she drank a lot of cups of tea and coffee while watched T.V news constantly throughout the day especially bad new around the world except the time being at work which makes her deal with all non-favorable situations and stories of the clients. If human life is all about miseries and struggles a whole series of wars, earth quakes, flooding, storms, incidents all mainly bad news make a news rarely some good news. Slowly losing interest in all as before she used to pick up some news to discuss with her son for criticism and for judgement together. Now she doesn't seem very interested as seems these are very normal to happen while the world happens to be collapsed and the earth to expire and die by shading off all her beauty, charms and excitements to its inhabitants to feel. The inhabitants won't feel any pain or pleasure for anything seemed be very charming or painful to feel like an incident. There will be motions not many emotions like sadness, happiness, hatred, pity, sympathy, regrets, anger, agony or anything else to love and hate their world embracing to live with some motivation or enthusiasm. For some reason Seema feels a strange feel of relief by the thought that she is expiring also with the expiring world with its slow decaying beauty or the charms of life. Abeer looks at her sometimes now in a very strange way seems seeing his mom different something is not very likely about her. After finishing the cooking Seema went to take a shower and asked the mirror 'Am I different now? Tell me how? Am I capable of looking into my own son's future? Or I'm giving up all the hopes about me and everything belongs to me? But why?'

She cooled her off into the cold water bath tub to think like 'that's only the body not the soul if I have any.' She came out of the shower to pick up the phone. Its 10 P.M its must be Abeer!

'Hellow?'

'Mom!'

'Yes!'

'How're you Mom? Is it O.K. if I stay out tonight with my friends?'

'No!' she sighed to answer 'take care son!' looking at the mirror again out of the bathroom she thought herself all in a sudden 'Let me have a cup of tea before Sujon comes home we'll have dinner together then' to lift up her eyes to look at the wall on the opposite side to get to be remembered that Abeer's Dad is no more in her life, in nowhere at all!' the gift of life for a short while seemed very cruel to play a role of a hypocrite or a short phase of an illusion of love and hope. A little spark of life which was only from her memory also stayed so little for a sensation to fall back again in her death of the soul. She feels herself a duck as the duckling grows under its bosom of warmth to grow to be gone surviving on its own later on doesn't even know the origin where it came from or who was its mom when it itself becomes a mom. No bondage at all?

Abeer's dad left long ago broke up with his wife but couldn't break up with his son his own child. That's why Seema started to feel like human civilization has come to an end where there is no family bondage the tie is getting loose day by day for the hardships of life. Now both father and the son doesn't care about each other anymore. Abeer even is losing his attachment with his Mom also. He goes to school from there goes to the library in the meantime may spend some with his girlfriend. Study and a company that's all! This generation' learning to mind their own business for survival only. When home sees the mother poor mother to love and care a little when' out forgets home for the sake of the study. And as long have a company doesn't need to think about the mom. Same with the mother she is busy at work and distressed so at home spend the major portion of the time in despair and regrets. Seema feels like she is a living dead an ongoing life in a daily routine with some sleep, with some dreams or no dreams or even with some bad dreams, some work, some care for the body or for the stomach, for the environment to live in and still some worries for her son to live still. At least as a mother if there is nothing but only for the sake of humanity. After all they are still humans in the human society to keep up all the values as humans.

II

Days after a week, weeks after a months, months after an year this way a pair of years have been gone but Abeer did not show up yet to say at least a 'H!' to his Mom since he left for the different city to complete his graduation. His school friend calls sometimes to ask whether he is coming back soon. The mother thinks 'this poor girl loves my son!' thinks Seema always whenever she calls but forgets again very soon to inform about the girl to Abeer. Sometimes she thinks again the girl loves her son but how about her son? Does he look back or think back to recall someone special to him or all the same on the wave of life to forget and to get what's present for what's the next? He sounds very happy, busy, surrounded by a lot of friends and over all doing very well at school. All that matters now people die for progress, for betterment in life by doing well in study or at work to carry on what just like Seema may be they don't know either. Are they all just like some floating fish to swim only? No! They aren't. They have dreams, goals set to set forth for a future to survive and to do well in their carrier in hard competitions. They die hard to get themselves to the goal while in the mean time they fulfill their hunger to fill up the tummy with some food, fulfills their desires to have a company to relax which is only a requirement in the mess of the dying hard struggles of survival for a future otherwise they will be drowned into the ocean to be lost stand on their feet to stay alive with a value at least not just swimming like fish surviving by swimming only. The young generations keep up to keep going and the love thing play no points in their relationships with their boy or girl friends. They make friends with the opposite sex to make a company for each other on a short time basis. They make love making a friendship to break again to make another one, break-ups and make-over's are little than making a new whoever stays and whatever other than love stays in a relationship needed nothing extra to carry on but just to go on. Even a pair of souls is better in love to make and keep. Abeer sounds very busy, happy and surrounded by lots of friends in spare time. And over all doing very well in his studies. All that matters now as people die for progress, work hard to achieve whatever common in life money, positions, carriers to get whatever they need to survive as well as to live as humans in the human society through struggles, hopes and despair at the same time, rise and fall, proceeding back and forth throughout the journey through life in despair and repair, in pain and gain, with good and bad all the way through the rough and tough life after all.

We see the platform plain and simple but to get there it's very hard and troublesome to thrive through. A prairie land looks beautiful but when get there all visible to view make a life there new; on ups and downs through dusk till dawn; walking on the heels kneeling down on knees; passing through the wild; cutting through the tough with a sharp knife; all the obstacles harsh and hard; tough and rough; through the rise reaching ups; sleeping through creepy craps; to make a life building a boundary bound to bind in combine to make it human safe and sound.

Any ways the loveless and soulless Mom Seema cares only about some love and care from her broken family. The only company remaining her son is away for the sake of life to build up after all. The reality beats emotions and the success in a boundary established dies soulless to regret only. So where is life to struggle for? Where is love for each other to care and share? Sharing company sharing hearts to care to make a life better? The betterment bounds only bonuses of bounties to break the body by sickening through the soul to reach no goal only soulless survival through the endless encounter. People die or regret for the breakdown of a structure or a monument of the civilization they built with their own hands. They make relationships for love for heart to lose again to die again to get it back. Competition at every sector makes life going with a speed in the race of a betterment of the civilization. Struggling through competitions makes the heart and soul as well as the body of the civilized thinner and thinner day to day basis while for the civilizations to get more and more attractive or better for better in quality and standard. The phone rang again very loud at Seema's solitary moments. A spark of a sudden joy for Seema again! 'My son! What a telepathy! I just thought about him!' Poor mother ran to pick up the phone but the colors of the spark of her cheeks has gone again when the other side said, 'hallow aunty, how are you?

'Who's calling?'

'It's Deepa'.

Oh!'

'Do you need any help aunty?' answered Deepa very passionately informing that she found some body to do some chores for Seema.

Deepa hesitated to ask about Abeer for who she actually called at Seema's number. Seema smiled at the childish Deepa's act then answered to the girl 'Abeer? He didn't come home yet he has some exams. I'll let you know whenever he comes thank you Deepa! Thanks Hon!' Seema put the phone down and thought a little bit about the generosity of the girl while liking her son a lot to offer a help to the mother of her boyfriend. She thought about the girl for a moment thinking 'poor girl! Piety on the silly girl likes my son a lot whereas he's not paying much attention or missing the girl to call in the meantime since he's gone.

Seema has been all alone all day expected a phone call from her son throughout the day. But No! No respond from her only son and Seema did not eat any meal today just lost her appetite. She let the maid go after finishing some work for her by paying full amount of the money for her help. When people are young and struggling with hard work for money for the very precious life they need to hold on it or to cherish before it fades away but when reach the point of the decaying age the life gets boring or a failure all along and they get old to see charms of life have left for them the final and the last chapters of life. Then they start to realize the meaning and the destiny of the short life to feel others rather than for themselves as they see themselves in the young generation doing the same without knowing what's going to happen or what's going to be left in the long run. So the dedications to humanity make wisdom to hold on for the afterlife or for the sense of the spirituality. Anyways, she keeps herself busy at least while it's easy to fly away on the wings of time by doing something by consuming the time to eat it up by killing it in a meaningful way. Also she doesn't have to bother to know how much time has been gone or spent with no value except fooling around sometimes.

Abeer came home the next month for Christmas vacation by skipping the last one which gave his mom a spark of happiness over her brown face with some extra brown and burned marks of hard reality to put a seal of age on her elderly face for at least some grace for her son for being a mother after all. His arrival this time is a surprise for the mom who pines and dies all the time for the only son the only family left in her life now. He didn't call him, didn't send a message saying he's coming just arrived like that to surprise her to see the spark in her eyes. When the doorbell rang Seema even didn't want to open the door thinking what trouble might be waiting at the door when didn't know the best surprise was waiting for the door to be opened. The mother got stunned at the presence of the son right in front of her eyes which couldn't be believed in the first place. The smiling son said 'surprise! It's me the one and only son of yours!'

By breaking the dead silence the poor mother opened up her voice a--beer! My son!' holding each other makes up the bondage of love as a renewal of the natural bondage of love for each other the mother and the son. Abeer jumped out to say, 'another surprise for your mom! Ta Daa------! 'Seema looked outside the door was opened by Abeer to see a pretty girl not Dipa but another one a brand new one standing with a smile and confused looking at the mom and the son together repeatedly might be afraid to be accepted or not by the mom of her boyfriend. Seema's sudden spark of happiness in her eyes disappeared as well as from her cheeks by the disappearance of the sudden blush of the happiness as just said in a low and dead voice 'h!!' and to her response cold or warm as an welcome the son jumped up again to introduce the girl by holding her in his arm lightly 'mom this is pinky". The poor mom lifted her cold look up to ask 'your girlfriend?'

"Yes!' the son answered promptly while very excited to show his new adventure to his mother. Poor mom thought a bit for the poor Dipa. 'What a day!' asked them to freshen up by whispering that into her own consciences while the world doesn't care about anything anymore. Leaving the boy and the girl to their free time to be together she entered the kitchen to make some snacks with tea. Lunch will be served later.

Shikha spent almost a year to get a job by getting herself trained for the job. She looks great, feels great and brave as well as doesn't look like looking back to regret or to pine for anything better in her life than this. She is wise enough to take things easy rather than being upset and distressful. Life is a precious gift of all as everything around is basically for our life. After all she brought a positive energy to her work place to make Seema enthusiastic as well as energetic. Shikha is bright by carrying the light of hope within her to spread it around her environment. Very often she cheers up Seema to get along who is always basically hard working while very distressed inside to show not much interest in life and its offerings of some good time to cheer to clear the mind to go on with new hopes and goals set to make the life a life not just a survival to carry on as a burden on the shoulder with enough hard feelings. In a few months at the beginning of her carrier Shikha also fell into despair to repair her life by joining the hard space where she lost something with the loss of someone very dear at the same time good enough to make a bruise in the heart but says sometimes to herself only while struggling for a position on the ground to stand 'struggle makes a life while it builds a life. We are strong no point to despair. Seema looks at the junior coliuege seeing as a teacher on the ground the same ground of both of their lives to learn from her strong mentality and in a strong faith. Seema remembered that Dipa came last week in search of her son happened to be her boy friend that is not anymore. Boys and girls meet to say now-a day's 'Good Bye' to make a new relationship one after another as all they need is a company. Poor Dipa still didn't know that her boy friend is not her boyfriend anymore he is now her x but she didn't show any expressions to show herself as angry or upset or hurt or even annoyed by the very loving boyfriend of her own to rely on. She met Abeer as normal as with no hard feeling. She kept spirit to keep her well with all as present there at the moment. Dipa continued to be as social as always with all. Nothing to worry about as she thought as the Mother Nature changes seasons in different colors only the differences is the past season comes back in Nature not the lost love in human life. It was Seema who seemed to be hurt in the real sense when her own son greeted Deepa with a warm welcome to introduce her replacement with Dipa saying, 'Hi! Dipa, meet Pinky a very sweet girl with a cheer as if nothing's wrong to make a new girl friend one after another. On the other hand Dipa got nothing to say but to look silently at Abeer's new girlfriend in her own place which was her own which she never thought to be taken by somebody else. She has no choice but to accept her own misfortune and her broken faith in the person who could have assumed that someday he will be cruel enough to forget the old for the new again! We need a change in life but not like this a broken heart is broken can't be seen to diagnose how much to fix as always as unseen to be touched. But the very next moment she took Abeer on a side to get on her with some fiery words out of anger and frustrations right after saying 'Hi'! to her rival very nicely. The spark of anger and frustrations into the nice ball eyes sparked to vomit out some words from the heart like 'who is she? Is this you do making girlfriends one after another? Nice! Very well behaved son! Keep it up! The more you get the more you benefit yourself. Enjoy! Life is too short. Don't miss it out!' Abeer doesn't seem to have any reactions to what Dipa has been saying to hurt his feeling answered normally 'meet my friend Pinky actually she is my classmate.'

'Then what's she is doing here with you?' Dipa's angry as answered very rude.

'Why she is just with me. You don't like her? Dipa stared at him with a fiery eyes didn't know what to say to her stupid and dumb x boy friend at this moment when he brought another girl with no guilt at all in front of his old one. Is he out of his mind?' Dipa doesn't know the answer to the behaviour of her X boy friend for who she had been waiting with a lot of concerns to share with a desire to die for his company after so long. But look! What's his attitude? No regret no concern and no shame at all!

'O yea? You made another girl friend saying what's wrong with that?'

'Oh! Come on! You are still my friend. My best friend ever!'

Dipa doesn't know what to say next but only starred at Abeer like before to leave the place as early as possible.

Time is passing by. Seema feels like only herself' still alive when no one is around, no one cares, even no one is physically present in the house or in her family to live as a family to make the home a real home. Practically, no one is around to help this poor mom in her need also. Time is flying too fast doesn't really know where it's going to end. Only life has an end but not known when. Seema asks her fate why her life got stuck at this point pointless, loveless, companionless all alone to be mocked by the time itself thinking its movement couldn't carried her away to a better destiny where she can at least live for the time for her time in the time sphere. People say time passes very fast by carrying our lives with its movement on its wings but Seema doesn't think so she feels like life has a time when its' retired from all the work and responsibilities to sit still with pain and pining, with hate and regret, with expiring hopes and desires in despair longing for a company, with a mind full of belongings in the past and a hopeless hope in the present.

Abeer called last night as he decided to go for a new job in another state. Every time he changes his job or gets a promotion he changes his girl friend too. 'May be this is the modern trend?' thinks Seema each time. 'Well time flies and we follow. We don't change time changes itself to change things, to change us too in order to accept the change in time. 'Seema's time is an ending time her life ended two times by the end of her two marriages and now ending the third time by the loosening attachment with her only son. In the meantime she also thought about marrying her son to make a family to value the family value but no! These boys don't listen. They don't believe in marrying a woman to make children to get stuck at one point of life. Feels odd and old. They believe in total freedom while the mom wants to say that humans are free to make their choices or very free think and do things within a limitation which make them just in judgements but the bondages and bindings make them humans as having the senses with sensitivity over all the basics of the conscience. The sky can be the limit but the human qualities which make mankind the very human keep them in limitations as making them humans not animals. Abeer' always as busy as he used to be he doesn't pay heed to what his mom is lecturing. This generation doesn't want to listen to any lectures by anyone other than the contents to learn for study for school. The very normal life is becoming an institution piece by piece for different aspects as created by our needs for the changing social behaviours and aspects to create enough problems to be solved by the institutions as a consequence. We have no choices but to a client full of problems arise for us and by us while constantly struggling to adjust ourselves to the current trend of everything I mean all the aspects of human life. As a consequence personal life is shrinking away while the professional life is getting swollen to cover the major part of our lands to occupy us as well as our life or our existence on the very blessed earth happens to be our world full of natural resources again for us and to make a world of ours. When the money is life and the time is making the money to breath in life then it is only money makes life breathing in the time as carrying away our life breathing in time bought by money forgetting the blessing of the fresh natural air as a blessing from Nature. Just like this we are losing the blessings of Nature boundless boundaries of natural resources to live in to breathe in while making things all artificial.

Anyways I was talking about Seema a mother and a woman and also a professional in an important organization happened to be in an important position? Whose position now has been taken by the bold and the bright Shikha a very sharp and intelligent woman of the present world of humans to survive well to raise her child well to go through all the stress and issues of life with enough courage in her heart and soul to boost up the fallen stamina of the former one who is none but Seema to regain the energy and the courage to finish up the non-finished work for the fallen society where not much values and pure and positive human energy left. Broken hearts and mind giving birth only to the broken societies to live as a group of unhealthy people as a family as well as an unhealthy society to make a world of people in a ruthless Nation among others on the globe to make an imbalanced generation to live with less educations, less moral values, little understanding, ignorance and arrogance very unfortunately.

A flock of unknown birds flew away with a lot of noise in the middle of Seema's thoughts might have given her a shake to shake off her negative thoughts while thinking too much worrying too much to get herself free of worries. Seema looked out of the window again to view the gloomy weather outside. A while ago the flock of the birds gave her a shake to come back to her senses to be in the present now she started to follow only a leaf apparently a dry one flying around detached from its home the big empty tree on the other side of the valley. Seema can see and feel the emptiness around as if the world has shaken all of its treasures and beauty in Nature. So far the eyes gaze around no signs of a living thing. Where is everybody? She asked herself the wind is aggressive while hopeless blowing with a loud hissing sound around as if it's a haunted place where no one's around. Again she started to dream about an end of the world where all the people had gone before to their destiny without a notice to take some time to prepare them to leave the place for better. There is an emptiness all around as if she is roaming around in nothing but in an emptiness where all going to their final destiny by leaving all behind. The rapid decaying world gives her a boost to think about the end only where there is no life only the vast empty prairie land with no sign of a living thing. The sound of the wind over an empty land gives her a feel of a haunted place where all died out of a plague or so. She didn't know that she was dreaming a bad dream of an end to the world with a dead smell in the air with a hooping sound to give her enough feel of horror.

'Mom! Mom? Moooooom!'

'Who! who? Is it you Abeer?

'Yes Mom, don't dream a bad dream again here I'm your son!

Finally Seema sat up to see her son closely after quite a bit of time. Looking at his Mom Abeer felt an enormous pity for his poor Mother living all alone to dream all the bad dreams to worry enough. On the other hand Seema felt a gilt to be ashamed of her foolish dreams out of reality.

"Oh! Bad dream!'

'I know. Its o.k. it's very normal for you to have bad dreams while living all alone.' Then he looked at his mother to think deeply by staring deep into her eyes thought again, 'my poor mom what a pity living all alone away from her only child said, 'mom! I want you to live with me. Can you?'

Seema got very happy as her eyes smiled in silence with the happiness expressed in her face. But she joked to say 'o yea! Only if you marry a girl.'

'I will, only need some more time to get some more establishments in my life. But you find a girl like you I like only your kind of personality. You are the best!

'I know it's all the sons like the mother first then the wife.'

'And between a girlfriend and more to give proxy'.

'Really! How many they need to practice matrimony?'

'Mom!' they both laughed very loud after a long time. A little family of two became live and alive to think and to do things as a family together. Abeer went to his room and the mother went to the kitchen. This time he didn't bring a girl at home looks like already have gotten some maturity as well as some responsibility. Seema started to browse her mind to look for a girl among her friends if any of them has a good girl to marry her son. Shikha comes to see Seema time to time to provide some help to the lonely lady who's now her only family besides her son. These two lonely ladies make good friends together after all. One is retired and a moral support to the other who is still young and strong to carry on whatever comes on the way through the journey of the life in struggles, hardships and all the efforts to make a life in real sense for the mother and the son. Apparently Seema and Shilka are now each other's support. The two non-relative relations are now means a lot to both of the ladies. Two years ago one was another's Boss and now one as an elder sister to the other who is none but Seema the kind, though, and compassionate Seema while Shikha is strong, progressive at the same time very positive to carry on no matter what. She is the bold with beauty. Actually her thriving up nature makes her more strong and attractive to others to follow who once got followed by Seema. Therefore, these two ladies one is another's elder sister making a very strong emotional support for each other. Seema's son is old enough to look after himself and Shikha's still little. So Seema look at Shikha's son Minar as the Abeer's childhood figure to love and care just like her own son. Sometimes this human world seems very strange for human behaviour and attitudes in terms of their emotional attachments. Abeer is Seema's weakness as she miss's him all the time but when he is not around in her need she makes up by holding onto someone else like now relying on Shikha and her son.

Abeer came to say 'hi' to Shikh's son said 'hi aunty!' to Shikha who's more lively now came closer with a 'bye' and 'hi' by holding Abeer into her bosom as her own son or might have been felt like his real aunt. She make jokes also said again, 'so, how's going? How many now?'

'How many what?'

'You don't know what?' Shikha looked into his eyes deeply and directly. Said with a smile 'forget it.

'Any ways sister said that you're going to marry for your Mom?'

'It's Mom wants me to marry a girl for her to take care of her.'

"Hmmm! Nobody cares about nobody that much now. Are you trying to make fool out of her?'

Sunday morning. Shikha made her plans for today at 11 am will go for grocery shopping her special guest is coming to her apartment for a visit a visit to see his fiancé after a six month period of time to know each other after all at home which might be a romantic visit for both of them Shikha and Mishu who is also working with her at the same organization and introduced to her by none but Seema her boss a good friend, as well as a guardian to an orphan Shikha and her little son Masum two orphans in two generations.

Shikha never talked about her husband or about Masum's father even anything about her marriage. Her files with all her information's are locked up in the shelf in the office room. No one really bothers about anyone's background all the office does to help the people especially the women in need come seeking for help. They provide help which only matters now. At least in such a bad days some organizations or the people do not look for an opportunity to pay an attention to help the people in trouble or in need to be helped. It was a year ago when Seema introduced Mishu the co-ordinator in the office happened to see Shikha a lot while working together. They got very friendly to each other to do things together better than ever. Eventually they already made good friends together. They went for lunch together they use see each other on any break at work. But this is for the first time they're going to meet at home Shikha's home to make a family together to make a real family later. Shikha cooked some dishes her favourite hoping Mishu will like them also. Shikha took out a sari from her closet never wore before in Sohans life time to think whether to wear that at this time when going to see another man already chose for her life. But what can she do she doesn't have any good dress or a sari bought by herself only. She never demanded anything for her for luxury a she only cared for love may be which is why life played an irony in her whole life to prove that life is not a bed of roses rather an ocean to float on with all the ups and downs on the waves. She kept starring a pretty long time on the sari bought by Sohan her former lover as well as her life partner very well organized marriage by the families with a lot of blessings to shower on her to bless with all the happiness and success in her life. Again life is so tricky and wicked to play all its life time to test us by setting exams we always assume to be real all good and bad all through our lives one after another. In the childhood Shikha lost her Dad eventually to lose her Mom and the family altogether in all the crisis and miseries to lose the husband also later on and the uncle too to ended up like this now on her feet to take care of herself as well as her only son decided not to depend on him while putting enough effort to raise him very carefully. Shikha is aggressive doesn't want to hold onto something or someone especially her son to be a means of her support in a time when no one is around just like her Boss Seema a mother of a son just like her to hold onto an emotional support for her life a very lonely life. The son showed some changes in his behaviour this time like agreed to move to Seema' city to live if becomes able to manage a job in the city to live with the mother. But Seema can't really hoping to be so lucky to have her so beside her. Life has taught her also a lot to lose as losing hope instead of faith in it again just like Shikha who's now surviving or thriving with all her might to get things right as much as possible. Frustrations and despair pushes her too into the ditch of distress to get lost to lose faith in life but remains enough strong to struggle through a difficulties. She is a survivor now tends to see the positives in life for the good for her only son and for herself too to get along through all the difficulties or all the failures to push forward to success. She got herself well established already to have a life to live normally. She's almost there from where Seema started the respectable job in the same organization but again afraid to be ended up like Seema as well. The missions in life as well as some work keep the mind busy to worry about things or to suffer from uncertainty but still reality teaches or even forces people to thrive for better for survival under circumstances. Seema sees herself as the old Seema in Shikha when they were at their young age while she was also struggling for survival with Abeer while the first husband left her. Sometimes she worries about Shikha more than herself by forgetting her own. Women in situations or in old age when no one's around to care them much lose their own self in caring about others for which there is no answer or any reason. For my opinion, it's the failure in life as when women fails to achieve or to get what they wanted or hoped or even expected to have do not take place. Loss of hope and failures make them got frustrated about their lives to give up their hopes to start to concentrate upon others if that makes the fulfillmets to achieve what they wanted to get for the person. A matter of divinity also grabs their feeling to do good for people. At least this way they can get a meaning for life. To Seema Shikha is like a responsibility. Sometimes she thinks like if she had a sister she would have been as responsible as now for Shikha. Parents in people's life do not exist forever to give shelter to their children all the siblings then look after each other as much as possible. Besides, Shikha came in her life as a blessing to make a company together in her loneliness. Most of the weekend's Shikha comes around to provide some help for Seema. Shikha wanted to invite Seema also today but thought later it should be on her own day as a couple together with Sohan.

By 5 p.m. in the evening Shikha finished all cooking when feels cool and good to entertain her special guest. It's not a repeat of a love scene in people's life she never was in love madly for her former husband. It was an arranged marriage to go straight forward to begin from sleeping together at first night to the kitchen to the rest of the matters in life. She ever didn't have a break to think about loving someone to make a home together while in her life it was her uncle not the father to stay alive to take care of her feeling with the choice of her own to choose someone or to judge someone while already chosen by the guardians. Harsh reality taught her to accept things by compromising. She had been learned some phrases over and over from her well-wishers all throughout her early life like 'life is not a bed of rose' or 'reality is hard to accept but making it a mission to keep going is noble' and she is wise enough to go on with proper balance. She faced a lot as a fatherless child in her very youth to make her stronger to face more and more of a challenge. Shikha found a sharp tiny beam of fire in her hidden to develop for good. She knew this girl will do well in her life.

Almost time for Sohan to arrive. Once again Shikha looked at her items she cooked. She cooked new stuffs for her love or might be only a match to think for her as for liking only.

She cooked all the good dishes she cooks now a day by skipping very carefully only those she used to cook for her former husband and she doesn't know why. She doesn't believe that she loved him very much still to remember his feeling that he liked them a lot to taste. She kept going well in her marriage became a mother in one year carried on all her responsibilities as a wife and as a mother as well. Never demanded much of anything either love or things for life. Always thought of the blessings of life. In her twelve years of marriage she and her X celebrated only the 10th anniversary of their marriage and on that special day Habib bought her a precious gift of life without even expecting at all other than love. Both of them never ever said 'I love you' to each other. Never ever Shika said to Habib as a complaint like 'you don't like me?' or 'you don't love me?' like things to demand love and attention from each other never ever even they got into a fight in demand of any kind of emotional values to be in demand as missing from their life. They lived together in peace and co-operations to carry on well the conjugal life to be happy, healthy, prosperous, and productive and well motivate to raise their son as healthy as possible to do the same. But why she can't forget Habib especially why she can't provide the food to someone else other than only Habib her X. This is definitely the blessings of love shared together without telling or admitting occasionally by treating on all the special days like birthdays, anniversaries, valentine days, etc. in the wave of life when two or more people share together with enough faith and understanding in respect for each other as well as by keeping values by valuing each other. 'Isn't this is love! Yes!' thought Shikha to realize the next moment 'then what is this now? Isn't it love also or just a need to carry on? Why not? This is love too knowing each other by understanding one another for the second time for whatever reason for some sort of emotional or practical support while both of them helping each other in cooperation's at work as well as making a good friends together then this is love also the love again for the second time for life. Of course for life! Life needs a support of all kinds along with a company to go on.

But Shikha doesn't like to share what Habib shared with her she want to keep that separate to keep that respect. A new life is going to start for the second time in matrimony if it happens in real. Till now they have been seeing each other at work and sometimes outside only for lunch and in the office only for the coffee to share a time separate other than work.

Almost about 6 p.m. everything got ready Shikha set the table too only foods are remaining to serve. Very quickly she put on a sari an ordinary sari but still sophisticated. It's with dark chocolate stripes on master looks elegant though. She knows that she looks gorgeous in sari but doesn't really feel very romantic to get excited to show herself to the present would be husband or a life partner to carry on the life which is eventually a second time for a second choice after all. Everything of first time of everything is special of course. As love for the first time, marriage, being stood first in an exam at school, attending the job for the first time, even wearing an adult outfit like sari for the first time also is as special as many other first time achievements or events in life. But still a keen little sense of romance is there in all of her preparation for this evening for an special person invited very eagerly in her home to start a new home all over again from the existing home for a new beginning with a life partner for the second time who knows this second time might bring a brand new beginning of an era a brand new for happiness in her life for the rest. Son Masum is already well acquainted with his would be father while still doesn't know that his mom's planning to marry again and this man named Sohan is going to take his dads place for better or eventually for the worse. On the other hand Shikha's thinking nothing but hoping to see a better life together with someone she can love to make a family once again with a new life partner.

Sohan arrived at around 7 p.m. looked very charming while very bright with a smiling face said, 'sorry a little late went to buy some flowers for you' while handing in some flowers to Shikha with a deep look deep into her eyes as if wants to say, 'I appreciate your arrangements, your time and affords for planning an evening like this.' His look also proving that he liked his finance's looks this evening very much.

Sohan arrived on time, he ate dinner with full taste and with an appreciation for the cook, he chat all about his day in going grocery shopping, paying bills, seeing some fiends in the meantime, and talking on the phone with some of his relatives after a long time. He continued talking for about a 10 minute time period continuously by forgetting about asking his dear finances' wellbeing or so also about his would be son from her would be wife except when interrupted all in a sudden to be asked by Shikha about herself as how is she doing. Sohan got embarrassed nothing more than that as answered 'I always love you you're in my heart. Actually I don't need to remember you while you are actually staying permanently into my very heart.' 'Very funny!' Shikha got cynical. Very normal for her while all day she had been making all the arrangements and preparing all only for him then how can she expect that the man whom she loves now to be married eventually very soon to make the relationship a permanent one for not to be questioned by people. That's not the only reason they need to make a family to live a normal life together again for her it is going to be her second time but for Sohan it's going to be for the first time. Sohan tends to be a normal person grew very normally seems not much critical in thinking as well as in perceptions for life. He's easy going takes everything easily to do with no concerns to be critical to take critically to think that something might be hard later or something is not very just. He is a life flows like a river with no concern whether the flow of the water will be stopped all in sudden to its flow to be stopped. He follows the routine of life knows only the list of to do things if anything happens to be a concern to look at he goes for it to try to fix as much as possible. On the other hand Shikha is always as worried about something even though things are going well but still she has to think that something might go wrong even like losing Sohan at this moment while already lost someone dear in her life it's like the fear of burning the tough for the second time by taking a wrong bite. Sohan is enthusiastic while Shikha is faithless while already lost her faith in life through all the struggles in her life. Once by losing the father next by the loss of her uncle to lose again a support to hold on to get at least to get herself under a roof and her feet to place on a ground on the floor of the house. In the meantime lost her loving husband too and now hoping Sohan as a blessing in her miseries to be a means to live the life with heart and soul once again. She is a survivor tends to stand up again from the fallen to carry on and this time almost solely on her own feet to go on by holding Sohans' loving hands of support which are at the same time her lost love and her support to hold on to go on whatever comes forward to face in the ways of life.

Masum is only a two years old child known as terrible two to be hyperactive all the time to keep the Mom busy enough all day long. He would jump up the bed, drop something into the toilet, would put something unusual into the mouth to make the Moms' day a miserable one. But presently he is very calm and quiet to keep Mom's guest very cool to go on nicely with her would be husband might be! Sohan is really soothing he already read a story from Masum's story book holding nothing but some pictures for children to wonder to make stories out of them in imaginations. Shikha smiled at Sohan's great capacity of making stories out of nothing basically suppose by viewing the picture of a little boy like Masum by the bank of the river shown in the very book linked to the next one where no one is there near the river except a lady appearing a village lady in a sari in the same spot where the little boy was he said 'woops! Where did the boy go?' Masum wondered with fear and wonder both in his eyes to get the impression that the little boy has been missing from the spot while the mother was not there to save the boy. Good enough for a terrible two even though he still doesn't know any language still good enough to warn a little terrible twos and very good enough to be able to make an impression like that from the pictures for a teacher. Said Shikha then to her would be 'why don't you teach in a school? You are good!

The answer from Sohan was 'then who will work with you together to see you while at the same time to help you?'

'I can take care of myself. '

'Yea, I can see that!' to smile. They both know that they need each other to laugh loud enough.

Shohan's day was very nice today in seeing Shikhs's lovely little lodging along with her company in family setting environment other than everyday office where they work together to talk less and to enjoy less by sharing the time together by feeling each other. After having a heavy dinner Sohan felt like having some rest after at this point he took a careful look at her present girl friend to feel her from very close to see her inner beauty when got an opportunity to see her from close to see her beauty through the see through sari as for the first time he realizes how beautiful she is. Masum is out of their sight might be playing somewhere or simply making a mess for the Mom to clean up later. Sohan asked by leaning on the sofa 'How big is your house?' Shikha pretended to be annoyed answered 'say apartment it's not even a house!'

Sohan looked at her eyes carefully to ask next 'You like a house?'

'Why not!'

'A big house?'

'Why?'

'You know! You are the one who is not happy in this little apartment. It's Ok.' said again 'nothing wrong to desire something. We'll make a big house together. I want to see you happy.' Then squeezed her nose saying 'silly girl afraid to dream! Life is all about dreams!'

Already 10 p.m. Sohan seems enjoying the time tonight with Shikha so does Shikha. Good to have someone beside as a life partner expected to be a lover or a friend or combindly in both roles permanently in a husband a life partner in bondage in friendship as well. Shikha got worried and thoughtful for moment thinking, 'will I be able to get what I want at this point?'

At some point both of them realized that Masum already went to bed to fall asleep to give them a scope to have some intimate time together. Tomorrow is still a holiday.

It's been a while that Shikha started thinking about getting married but there is no response from Sohan he's still like that comes to the office does his work with full heart to be enough sincere also, maintains his collaboration with Shikha his co –worker but now -a- days somehow Shikha started feeling like now he is acting only like his colleague to share the work to be done if needed to finish together. Sometimes he goes out for lunch by him doesn't feel like going together with Shikha anymore. Shikha started feeling lonely again still strong enough to go on with her life by taking care of her only child. Sometimes she takes a closer look at the single mothers who happen to go alone for their life. Now - a –days people are getting shorter in a group as a number either single or as couples or even single either as a man or as a woman. When there is some spare time Sohan still likes to talk with her as he also talks with others in a group. He is a man of heart goes by his heart never panic, never restless, never worried nor even upset on something. Taking life easy makes him passionate, calm and quiet to take challenges as well as to be peaceful to have a peace of mind. He does his work without being touched by any stress like a fish swimming into the water doesn't make it feel like swimming with hardship for its life the way the water flows by making some little waves doesn't make the fish like pushing the water hard with hard labor. He goes with the flow of life doing a job maintaining the routine of life doesn't make him feel hard. He doesn't feel the burdens of life. He goes by doing his jobs without thinking that he is pushing himself hard to carry on all the responsibilities as a big burden on his shoulder. He lives a life with full passion without being getting stressed by all its problems or responsibilities or even by feeling the pain on his shoulder to carry on all the aspects of life. He only looks for what's there to do not at the responsibilities to feel pressure on himself. He seems easy going by taking all the challenges at work or in the personal life.

Two years have been passed Shikha still likes to hope that there is something permanent called a feeling between her and Sohan as they always go along to work and share something together. In the meantime Sohan got promoted to a counsellor and Shikha to a co-ordinator basically now they don't share the work between them as the office helper. Very inside Shikha wished to be proposed by Sohan when he got the better job to do as in her imagination or in her delusion what she wished to get a permanent solution for their relationship without noticing the fact that Sohan is a free bird to fly to purposes to purposes or business to business and most importantly to the wishes to wishes to enjoy the life more or less to at least to get some relaxing moments in between the to do lists. None of them fixes their mind on a mission to follow. Shikha's already a broken heart doesn't dream beyond out of the reality only hoped to have the present friend or the co-worker to have him a little bit more in her life for the life's demand or the need on the other hand Sohan is also not a play boy he is sincere too but shortly as soon as an purpose is done or gone he is free of heart to go for the next with full attention while a little intention stays a bit longer or keep that thing he loves for longer or forever as the way Shikha feels for their relationship thinking even a flying bird tends to make a nest while knows that the wind or the storm might blow it away. Sheikh's heart and mind both feel this way now as the life is teaching her hard lessons all the time.

Time and tide wait for none' shikha keeps that in her mind all the time and now it's her boyfriend sohan who basically is staying in her mind to think about after her parents, her uncle after losing her family then Masum's dad and now Sohan another canoe on the floating river of life to hold on with the risk to loss any time. Shikha knows sohan his character his tendencies, his views of life as well as his very nature. She started to believe that the fate chose her to teach her all the negativities of life as by knowing her life now she is realizing the nature of life now too especially her whole life as in a novel whose remaining chapters have been waiting blank to be filled up by the all sad stories about her to make an irony of life itself.

Very slowly and eventually Shikha and Sohan started to be apart from each other to have lunch separately, to go home separately at their time because they both now in different positions. And Sohan is still the same happy, enthusiastic, motivated, ambitious and still very passionate for life except the fact that he doesn't seem like missing something which Shikha has been pining for which is his company. At work place they can't see each other without a reason but after work he doesn't have any intention to look for an opportunity to see her. Sheikh started to believe that he never loved her even as a friend or as a short life partner together while working together. Recently he never showed any interest to drop her off at her place even sometimes they both tend to go home at the same time. Basically they never made a relationship to give it a name in that case Shikha can't really claim anything to possessed by calling it love, friendship, a life partner nothing and most recently about a week ago she went to his office room to see him without any file to be signed he looked into her eyes to say with a nice smile 'is it allowed to see the Boss without any reason?' Shikha didn't know the answer while it is the very truth in a workplace this kind of behavior in the name of extra understanding actually not allowed since Shikha got the job in the organization from being a client to a favour all the people or the colleagues didn't look at the matter as a different case. But now thought Shikha while got ashamed enough 'Oh! Yea! Now he is the big boss!' said politely then 'Sorry Sir! I forgot that now you are a big boss! Alternatively by looking into the boss's eyes to reply for the insult he has just provided her. She hoped that the present Boss understood clearly what she meant to leave the spot with her cheeks burning red with enormous insult.

The flying love bird has gotten another beautiful object by the next desk clerk by Shikha's desk a new female love bird apparently more beautiful than her the Boss Sohan now calls Shikha to send the new clerk with a specific file to take to him and very recently Shikha noticed the new girl's waiting on her Boss after work. So the love bird suddenly found his destination after all a position and some new gateway to the life's fascinations to have some fun to enjoy the life side by side performing its noble missions in work and responsibilities to take as an obligatory.

Shikha's fantasy broke in a systematic way again through the experiences by knowing the world as well as the life itself for all. In the last six months she dreamed all like keeping her boyfriend from her work to keep in her bosom then dreamed about making a relationship by making a home to live together as a family along with her son. Knowing the known unknown world made her an iron woman hopefully not to very rude to people or to be very cynical about life to lose all hope and charms of life. 'Life is life' as she realizes she makes her mind up to be realistic after all. As a tender hearted woman a woman needs to learn the irony of life as well as the tyranny of people. Life is all about good and evil from outside and from inside. We get evil from outside to be attacked and from inside from our very heart to die hard within. Finally she got rid of her thought of marrying someone thinking to acquire some permanent help from a life partner. Now-a-days all kinds of partners are all temporary. People get closer for some purpose to leave after the purpose has been done. In most cases marriages are all temporary while taken for a permanent solution for life. People marry for a purpose divorce for a purpose in most cases just like better opportunities like a better job, in most cases the clash of personal interests make the partners separates from each other and their children remain unattended by the parents while the parents have to look after their own life in the trend of a hard life to live by basically all one way or other. Shikha at her 40 years of age leaned to be thankful to the Above One for blessing her son to be taken care by his Mom who also by the grace of God acquired the capability to take care of her son. No one will be able to know more about life than herself after losing all her supports one by one to provide her support by becoming a support for her son. The time and trends are now showing the paths to become independent eventually leading to the self-conscious people to become selfish in most cases. The judgements between right and wrong needs to be left for the situations created again by none but destiny only.

Finally, Shikha lost her life support while life lives now by only by the support of the bodies two legs and two hands along with brain in the head basically like a robot with an artificial intelligence to keep going as commanded by the folk supremacy to carry on the missions of life a lot more for the society and a little for the self itself. We are basically now biological body machines to carry on what the command says. People don't need to marry to produce younger selves from themselves to support the world. In a society where the foods are made and packed in the factories, education, businesses, entertainments, socializations and contacts, shopping, sightseeing, arranging things like parties, news media's and all are being possible by only technology through easy access to all only on a device like a tablet or a cell phone as a miniature to do our jobs very easy to access from our very hands as well as on our laps the needs of emotional support from the family by its family members don't seem like needed badly anymore as even things are becoming hard to maintain as the family bondage to create complexities only to get separated from each other.

My lonely and lovely lady of the sin city finally became a mere job only for her mission for the life which is her only son Masum to whom she is a support for his life. All her life she hoped and asked for a support normally and naturally and when all of it taken from her to leave her behind with only what she needs for survival along with her son. Lost her family where she was born, lost her son's father whom she did not marry or the other way his father didn't show any interest in her to make his life partner as a wife. He was jobless and lonely at that time when she took him as a mate to make him a life mate to live as a couple for the life. When she was very upset to be in despair the uncle got a candidate suitable to him to get her niece to be married to him for the safety and support for his lovely niece to die himself peacefully eventually to die hard broken hearted when couldn't do that. People still make love here and there while do not mind to make children but to deny to accept them. It's funny while still people have the sense to reject the odds out of social systems then why they make a child out of the same systems? That means people still care about the principles, rules and regulations in a society. People still like to live a normal life guided by some rules as still tend to keep the values to live like humans. Still we are human beings living in a human society to like humans not like animals or like savages in contrary to the civilized people. Then why do we tend to be careless to be inhuman or cunning or hypocrite to deceive our own selves while trying to win over some innocents who happen to rely on the powerful? Human conscience defines very well who's weak and who's in power to empower the other. Now only those are tend to be good or honest or reliable or even polite to the others who are basically weak. They listen, they obey, they respect even it's only them who still care and share for good. We're still not totally ruined. I mean still we have not gone back to barbarism or back to the primitive life again. By restoring the entire human society from barbarism we can't really go back there again. So it's hard when we claim ourselves as civilized to behave like an intelligent savage being unlike a human being living in the very human society doesn't even look like savages at all.

My story almost has come to an end when could not make a happy ending unfortunately. Before I close I better pay a visit to Seema to see her condition in such a situations in a society like this where both Seema and her like Shikha tend to live only to live as in a survival process to keep going.

Seema was at home when Shikha came to visit her. Her front door was all a mess looked no one really takes care of anything anymore. Her garden is full of grass to grab all the nice flower plants into their bush. She could only discover some nine O'clock flowers are still there as closed and faded beauty in color as Shikha doesn't know at what time the 9 0'clock flowers died. It was raining heavy recently and Seema's porch looked full of mud with fallen leaves scattered all around. Poor Seema! An elderly woman lost her love, her husband's one after another to no fatal disaster but to another women each time while where in the society only the fittest can survives in some cases also the youngest and the prettiest doesn't fit for the survival but only but for the better. Those who are left behind as rejected products, objects or obstructions can survive just like the fallen dry leaves on the ground unattended and of course neglected while as humans hit by the waves of life apparently as fast as it could be blowing them out to still remain as fallen as to show the difference between the old and the new, between the fittest and the rejected to make a brand new world of beauty and youth to represent energy? Ironically there's not much rejected are remaining to clean up the mess just like Seema's former nice flower garden. Thought Shikha considering now herself as the junior Seema to acquire the same fate by the grace of the Above Who creates and destroys all. Then why we care? If we create all to get destroyed by His will then why we worry? Of course for the survival, to carry on the very blessing of the noble life we got even without asking!

For a moment Shikha thought Seema might have been known or guessed somehow that she is here as she always do but no! There is no sign of her today. 'Is she alright?' Shikha got worried all in a sudden to knock at her door constantly till it's open. But No! There is no sign of her. Then after an hour she started to regret for the presence of the elder herself who as an elder sister favored her a lot even by being the boss at her work place. Sheikh also started seeing herself her future self in her Boss the elderly Seema. Neither Seema nor Shikha crossed the line for reality, for the survival or even for a little luxury or for some desire for life to desire as a human being after all. Shikha doesn't know how long she has been standing in front of Seema's unattended house thinking about her as a lot to pay as a tribute to the favor provided by the kind lady considered as an elder sister who cared from heart. When the sun started setting by slowly bringing the dark in the darkened heart of her soul she realized that Seema might have left this place to go somewhere or!-------- 'Time and Tide wait for none.'

THE END

STORY 3

'My illusions'
Kamrunessa \ May fist, 2018

How about I imagine myself as a lovely Princess of my heart sleeping a long time in a very dream land and while once all in a sudden I dreamt of a wizard who came in my dream with a gift of a curse. And I got very fascinated and surprised at the same time to ask 'what is this?' then he smiled to leave with a smile saying 'you'll know all along the ways.'

I woke up at the darkness of the dawn and looked for the wizard with full attention. Nope! No one in sight while paid a full attention. I looked everywhere in search of the gift given by the nightmare couldn't find that at all! Then I concentrated on my homework instead and completed with full attention to look out the window don't know in search of what? A dark shadow followed my sight coming out of my note book to disappear in the early sunshine instantly. The Sun said 'good morning' to me. I rise and shine as everyday not like the Sun that much bright with a shine. Outside in the front yard the mango tree is nice and blessed with all nice young green mangoes hanging with full joy downward creating a beauty as well to show the world the blooming fruitful youth to follow. And I'm fresh from a nightmare a refreshed memory in the mind and the soul to go for the day with full heart and energy, with hope and delight to light the world in my day today. Mom called me from the kitchen to take the breakfast knowing like every day that I might not be able to finish eating it or even might not even take a bite at all. Time to run and it's also time for Mom to insert the Tiffin box in my bag.

A few steps more then it's the school my school the sacred destination for all in the childhood as well as in the youth. I'm very enthusiastic today as waiting with full attention with some tensions as well for the third period as got a lesson to prepare the summery of 'The three wise men' with enough excitement also. And I believe that I did a very good job in summing up the story in short and meaningful content ever. Just could not wait to prove my talent.

Finally, it's the third period Mrs. Rebecca will be arriving soon. My heart started pounding as I knew I did a very good job in making the short summery out of a big story. Mrs. Rebecca came 10 min late to the class. I was still worried and waiting for my turn to deliver the work done. As a student I was obsessed with my assignment as proud of the good work of my own while worried at the same time not to be valued or to remain unattended the hard work done by me. And that's what actually happened while as all of the students including me were waiting with worries by thinking of the fate of the finished job was done by me very carefully especially by me. The teacher Mrs. Rebecca really and actually totally was thinking about something else. She started walking in the middle of the rows on the passage of the student sits in two rows by asking us to remind her where she was or we were last time. While got reminded about the homework for today one of the student reminded her and she came back to herself by asking the back bench boy a friend of mine whom I don't like at all. To get disappointed in double disappointment of one for the failure to catch Mrs. Rebecca's attention to my good work, second for my dull friend to be lucky to get the teacher's attention to read the summery to the whole class by ignoring all including me! Yet more disappointments were waiting for me which was my dull and back bench friend stared reading all my words exactly as written in his book as an assignment to be claimed his own. As I questioned Pintu how did he get my notes he got surprised to say 'what do you mean? I didn't even see your notes how would have I known about your thoughts? Right! What am I thinking? Might not even possible. I also got ashamed of my thought to be believed that my thoughts have been taken or stolen by my friend which is absolutely impossible! And till now I couldn't get answers to my miseries all through my life so far. Still I couldn't get the answer to my question or my wonders believed to be being guided by a wizard to be robbed off my thoughts by people everywhere and every time till now. So I despair at the thought of losing my credit on my hard work apparently very special.

The spring of my life came late when I felt fearless to fall in love with someone I liked very much. The thought inside like 'at least no one will come to share my boyfriend! Everything is not for sharing! I used to joke with one of my friend saying 'at least no one will steal my boyfriend!' we got married at the age of 38. Bichat's life was straight unlike mine. We both got success in our own field me by spreading out my thoughts and ideas being permissive and submissive non-professional willingly submitting myself to my fate for good believing in the divine will to submit my noble and valuable thoughts for the humanity in general. In fact very painfully I forced myself to accept the fact that there is nothing I could do to stop this whereas no one believes my stories in the first place to proceed from there to help me out in my miseries. After a while decided to shut my mouth against the forgery before people start to believe that I'm some kind of freak or delusional or even a little psychiatric. I tried hard to make myself very broad minded to sacrifice my own interest for the good for the society. Only that made me to live in peace by forgetting all about forgery or being read my valuable thoughts by people, media's or businesses. I consoled myself so hard by putting the ointments of consolation for soothing the heart burn. Sometimes life makes us helpless to accept such a fact with enough pain to pass something out very private and very dear to sacrifice solely by giving up the soul. My sense of divinity made me to submit myself to the Lord of my Fate. I started coming in the banners in the streets, in the movie stories, in speeches

Dialogues, T.V. Talk shows, in social gatherings as talking on my chosen topics in my private journals or ideas or perceptions as well as my points of views pointed in my studies while I studied for my sake to do something even for the sake of the survival. They argue about my philosophies, my points of views without even knowing that it's me who's pointed out those issues they were talking about. And I had no choice but to participate in the conversations or in the discussions of the issue. Sometimes the criticism of my own work been said by some of my known people somewhere else. God knows for what reason people used to treat me like a queen or the opposite like a slave to their wishes at the same time. When I am nobody but only an object whatever kind doesn't matter a slave to serve people selflessly as well as a queen to be treated Great by the people to serve them as their noble lead while has no personal choice to make without her people's vote. The great servant has a great power to be treated great while all by the people, for the people and by the people. No one never ever said that they heard me or came to know my projects or that particular idea was of mine. I know the readers will think that I am giving them a wearied and extraordinary story which can be only out of my own imagination or my even my madness believing to be really happening in my life. That's true, all my life I wondered about all. I felt like I'm living in a dream land like a fairy apparently very cursed by the wizard by the end of a dark night or at beginning of a brand new day. Still better than no one at least started stealing my husband my life and my love. At least at that time I had a lovely home to live in love peace and harmony after all. The worst part of my miseries is being hated and manipulated by whoever I'm in contact at work or in social relations. I work for my company by helping all others. I got hired by the employers in any company to share my ideas and knowledge. People still copy my work or thought with full privilege and full right on no right at all. I'm not that kind of extra ordinary talent or a computer with full encyclopedia to help people all around with answers to all questions. Time to time I got depressed at the thought of being myself as an intelligent object or a tool to be used for the use for all. The worst part of my miseries is being hated and manipulated by whoever I'm in contact at work, or in social relations. At work by help new people by helping directly or by being helped others as a command from the unknown feels like I'm bound to help others as designated by a divine Lord of the myth or a chosen one by people only while have no foundations of strong wealthy or world platform to keep my own identity not to be taken by others. Feels like I get hired by the people when I get hired by the employer. Sometimes feels like me that I'm a Super woman or a wonder woman in a movie where I'm the one who's dreaming all these with all the wonders of all while living in an unknown world. Best to be defined my position, situations and condition is like a slave for all by the grace of modern technology for the easy access to me. Sometimes I get dragged by the force to be up and down at least I'm not a loaded ship full with the load of books of knowledge to be carried while floating on water only. At least I'm a human being among all human beings get carried and guided while a might with their rights. I'm not boasting to have enough ideas as well knowledge to be considered by the world to use and abuse by different kinds of folks according to their perceptions no wonder!

In four years of our marriage life Bishash had only one job to stick to on the other hand I had to change total three. A consulting firm hired me first as a Direct executive to promote their business by representing myself as an influential. By the grace of the Almighty I prepared an extra-ordinary strategy by making only a creative speech to influence the clients and again by the curse of the wizard as usual got all copied of my creation by all in the company very soon. This way by promoting myself every time in a company by my innovative techniques I gain self-satisfaction with full pleasure for a short time to lose that again to do or to create and invent a new. Especially when people start to think that I'm God gifted have no much credit of my own to create every time something extra-ordinary therefore I do not work hard to put enough effort to be paid enough to be valued as a gifted after all? Since got considered a Gifted Gift by the Lord I'm supposed to be a chosen not as a human to be possessed by people with full right by deleting my own right even my identity while still a Human the other part of the man version of the human One to be copied by all or been chosen to spread out among people. Therefore I never ever understood my position, my existence, my purposes for life the very human life while have all of a human only without possessing a pair of wings or a Super human with no hunger, no other physical instincts, needs or even some usual demands to fulfill for a flesh and blood body after all. Super Humans lived with their wisdoms to get valued and honored later after going through a lot before being recognized but for me even I don't know who am I what am I and for what purpose I'm here in this very world of all people possess and process to cherish to live on or even to enjoy their lives. Don't I even look like a woman after all? If I'm a woman in flesh and blood an object to be followed for different purposes then why not being valued or respected at least as a human only in contrary to a slave of all the ages of human disgrace. If I'm a woman then people have all rights to possess me as their copyright. Who am I what am I and where am I coming from never understood my position. In a social gathering last week all of the guests together started talking together about the latest Titanic movie as someone follows 'what a wreck!'

Another 'what a disaster! Did you see how people were struggling to live while thrown into the water to float only until a very reliable source comes to rescue them from the death pole from where there's no escape basically.

3rd guest said 'o, yea swimming breathless to survive with a hope whereas no hope just to cling onto something.'

4th guest said, 'I like the scene showing how swiftly all the furniture fell off, tables, chairs, and all the dishes with dinners just got swept away very swift in no time at all!'

Then me as I commented 'they portrayed a very good picture of an enormous ship wreck in a storm very huge indeed to sweep away all the lives while they are all alive to live by enjoying a good time on a ship as a voyage through the life. It's a matter of life and death. Life is certain while we born but not the death while we die anytime much unexpected in most cases. It's about all uncertainty along with a painful struggle for the survival and to be rescued while drowning into the sea which can cause life and death at the sometime. And at my comments and realizations of the facts make all throwing a cold look at me all together to say 'we know that' meaning more criticism they were expecting and I felt a little embarrassed to answer very quickly 'but it also presented a love story in classism in the society along the way.' This time while they looked back to me seemed feeling satisfied by a bit more criticism to convey my knowledge to others. I feel myself silly when I see people consider me as a book of knowledge to convey some of it time to time as on demand and besides that have no value of me to them while all of them get along just for friends I make no friend for me only provide some services to people to get along. I always feel very down when I see I have no status in the society to hold a position to make friends with them. I blame my fate for even being their slave to be invited to be read by them as a book of some knowledge with no much knowledge but to share whatever I know as my duty or else I won't be of any use. Therefore, I ask myself every time 'who am I? A chosen object to be there slave? What a misery! Poor me!' when they are done with me they talk, they rejoice among themselves I'm left aloof in a corner avoiding the crowd as its pointless to talk while they are chatting, drinking, taking food, laughing loud while the poor intellectual dog got to watch only. I make no friend of my own as my own family considers me as an especial to keep silent until being asked to talk and when my purpose has been fulfilled I'm done there to sit alone wherever best like in a corner calm and quiet by avoiding talking all nonsense like others or among others. Feels like every move of mine is permissible. Funny is as the youngest in the family I was treated like this everywhere as an non mature while young and later as an extra in my brother's or in my sister's family still for the same reasons immature and an extra to the guests invited. All my early life I felt myself an ugly looking, naïve and of course a stupid who basically didn't know how to talk, what to talk about as a junior of course! Same fortune same situations, same position followed everywhere till now as still immature or doesn't really matter. Sometimes I also feel myself as a fallen angel to deliver knowledge to people as a wise duty to deliver to people on earth. As a mortal on earth being among all mortals I wonder all the time who APPOINTED ME TO A NON-designated position from where. As a wise person it could be a great duty feels very poor and down to my own self. I also hate my life enormously. I hate my life to be cursed by my fate. And I don't know why I'm different than others. Sometimes I feel like I'm a lemon to squeeze out all the juice to throw out the fruit regardless into a bin where all the waste remain to be thrown out to the final burial of no use at all. Sometimes I even think of a banana plant which has been used and eaten by people from top to bottom as we eat the fruit, the flower making the fruits meaning the banana trunk heavy and down with all the bananas to hold the remaining flowers which gave birth to all the fruits to hang finally at the very bottom of all the bananas. We use the plants big leaves as plates for the refugees to be fed on them piece by piece as a plate for the poor and for the elephants to eat by simply chewing them. We eat the flower itself also in some places by boiling it to smash to make a veggie curry out of it. People even eat the trunk in some places as inside it has a soft tender tube of vegetable to cook to be eaten as a veggie dish as well. And finally we burn the remaining of the plant when that's dry as a fuel. I'm an educated woman educated myself successfully but failed to build up a career vey unsuccessfully at any cost labor, enough efforts and dedications to whatever efforts were made by me as a trial training, studies, job search and so on an ongoing process. I'm a bounty of help for people for the bounty of disgrace from people with no gratitude, no regards, no recognitions and no appreciations while taken of my own inventions and thoughts for some respect in some sectors to be valued with full attention to be attended by the proper places and sectors to utilized for good in the proper place for productivity of course. I'm deprived of to be considered as a part of the common people as well as a part of the non-commoners to be considered as valuable as any of the valuable part of the new generations to be considered in contrary to my thoughts, ideas, regular activities considered as the inevitable right of the Nation or the society to be taken regardless as if I'm appointed as an individual to serve for the people or the nation with no pay at all as got appointed as a selfless self to dedicated for some sort of divine mission or as a slave sold by none but by myself for no reason but to be sold foolishly my stupid illusions or some sort of devotion to be considered for what which I don't know yet. May be it's my helplessness by coming in a foreign land without any relatives or some of my own people to be considered as a noble generation not to be used as a slave or a refugee. I speak three languages as in two of them very fluent in reading and writing both and in one only to speak.

People here look like don't want to study themselves instead to learn from me by considering me as a role model and I still don't know for what reason as they all are pretty educated. Might be they want to save their time or don't want to learn more. Learning at least might have been saving their time to do well and work more by doing good for them as well as for the society they all live in. So I'm at a job to make their jobs easy or to be more productive. I don't think I'm all knowledgeable to help the society by giving the light of knowledge by saving their time for study. Considering myself as a boundless feed to people gives me nothing but misery only while I get robbed off my own self. Sometimes even to feel that while I do or say or perform they copy makes me feel like I win and they gain also. In that case while I'm not myself then what's the point doing things or saying things thinking might be a good one a simple comment, an ordinary idea, some words derived from my origin to be taken as new for ornaments in some writing on a banner for advertising or for something else. I even get copied by my style as considered sill to me but I see later people liked that thinking might be a good one. These observations make me feel nothing but only delusional to see a psychiatrist. So basically miseries after miseries, feeling myself being copied for my attitudes, ideas, thoughts, concepts, my made up phrases as well as my style. It's very funny while I like to dress up like them as living in their culture to be considered a good or better or even more cultured or stylish in contrary to something like to take my style That's not unusual people always like to take something new from each other.

There is no doubt that I'm basically an insignificant individual to be taken as a subject to be taken to know my culture by knowing the ways of our life style, ethnicity, culture to facilitate in most cases especially when we go for study. Knowing people by knowing their culture is nothing new. We like to know each other also to take some of it. This way people around the world get mingled to derive some of others culture into them while not much concern about them. It bothers me while I'm considered someone to be taken as a role model to be valued while at the same time to be considered as a slave to be bound to give up myself to the superior. Making a V.I.P. makes instantly a slave or a thing insignificant for no use sometimes makes me nothing but a trash to throw into the bin or to be taken off the pearl from the shell to leave it as a trash again. Am I making you all laugh here? No wonder! It's not a tragedy as the sole misery in someone's life who really doesn't know who she really is. I know you are going to put mercy on me. I'm the relying misery on your mercy. It's better to be pointless point rather than to be a valueless value. Sometimes I'm even a malice while try to merry. My fun turns back to me as someone else's fury while not even allowed to have some fun which make no sense to people who actually incapable to understand or don't allow that fun. My hard work becomes horrible, my fate turns furious, my desires and my ambitions become theirs as if I'm the one something or someone to show the ways to follow by giving away some visibility out of the foggy ways ahead to remain myself into the fog. And why I'm getting this much negative while I'm very blessed with a loving husband who takes me in all he loves in his life as his registered wife to live in nonregistered hatred of people. Am I not very blessed with two lovely children to be taken cared by me as a mother while considered as a Nanny in the role of a blessed mom? Am I not that kind of a quality and a value to lose them to others for being considered to be a selfless and valueless value of the very noble considerations? Blessed me! Good to be possessed by the holy matrimony while the matrimony itself is possessed by friends, by

the society as a whole society to consume me and all? I'm the doll here a female one in the house the male one dancing by the tuned played by all one party over another the lowers to the uppers with powers shared by all except me who even don't have any power even over her own Children. In a family children get loved as a lovely doll in a family by their parents elder siblings but don't get treated as a doll while being treated by the whole society including the ones' in the family into its tummy is not very nice at all. It's more like a sober way to keep someone educated and valuable to be used as basically a subject common for all without any recognitions or considerations to be remained just like that with no identifications on peoples' mercy and their wishes but into a loose grip after all.

Any ways looks like I'm writhing a terrible story if pain to present to the readers to make them sad or even to be amused in some ways. It shouldn't be this way to describe my position or my situation. Actually after all I take things easy and positively to go on with life like anyone else. Different people face different reality nothing we can do about it. The great technique is to take things easy as is to bring the changes later eventually happen in our life when we comply with things non favorable to us. We make things favorable from the no favorable, impossible to possible. But in this case of mine please do not think that I'm making or imagining impossible to be possible. As I agree if this is so I should be able to make things right while they seem not to be right.

Let's see this way in our life we get heard time, we fail to avail something sometimes in most cases. For instance, we went for a high paid vacation once full family to make us change the rooms we booked in the nice hotel total 4 times, we visited the historic place in Cancun going totally without water the question of food intake doesn't really bother when there was even no water around with or without money in full heat for all the bright and the Mighty Sun to walk all day on feet as a holy pilgrimage for all including our children whereas others stayed at the same place got themselves packed with food and water for the day as picked up from the resort while got informed or instructed earlier.

Our fate didn't forget to give us enough hardship on our vacation too as well as on the hajj. After all of her jobs to play with some people in their lives blessed in miseries as well as miserable in its mercy. It has to play with people while given with the creations side by side on a mission after all. So we tried to enjoy things while site seeing with full might as being given a valuable gift of all time to be seen with full attention and evaluations to value the gift only by ignoring the jiggles and juggles of gain with the pain. Finally at night all quiet and cool to see and enjoy a night time show near of the horse riding performances of the riders on the horses with songs to make us forget all in a cool breeze of the evening. After all gain after pain is noble and nice but losing for gaining isn't always pleasing or giving us any value while lose more to recover by the gain.

So, in short this is all about the wisdoms of the gift of life we get which neither can we give away nor can we keep with full heart to live comfortably or happily as we always expect to happy in our lives after and over all. We still dream along the ways we live along the ways no matter what. Life is consistent along the ways in hope and faith and at the same time inconsistent in failure and the in the lack of faith all the way till the end. This is me a total failure in all my life. The most terrible reality is my tormented thoughts which I don't know whether to deliver to someone or not. When I keep them within me or very secretly within myself I see or feel the worst part of my tormented, confused and deprived soul. All my life I'm big dreamer to dream about my goal set. I work hard whether putting my feet on the ground or flying on my wings of dreams and wish to make my dreams come true my growth is a flow of my spirit to gain the success in getting whatever I intended to gain and always failed to finish a project, a job or failed to accomplish or to determine. So this is me a failure in my whole life. The most terrible reality is my tormented thoughts which I don't know whether to deliver to somebody or not. When I keep them within myself very secretly I see or feel the worst part of me, of my inner self tormented, confused and complex fighting within its own state of the heart and mind when I see them written somewhere on the banners by the main streets, on

T.V. shows, in the movies, dramas, on the talk shows being discussed by the participants with their points of views. I'm horribly upset for being cursed by the almighty to be sucked off my own self to become public while my points of views have been discussed by them to be watched by me? What an irony in the world!

Ii

The psychiatrist noted all I said with no comments, no conclusions, and no suggestions at all except by prescribing a medicine to be taken on a regular basis. And there are more weaknesses as well as the problems disclosed by me to be repeated by the people known in our society repeatedly might have been considered as a treatment for me known as resistance which I tend to realize later in my life might have been to console myself after getting so much humiliations by the people known in the society in the circle of the relatives as well as my family members. All behaved the same to treat a member in the family very globally to make more naïve and mental and unsocial to live like a tool to be treated like a puppet to be robbed of her own identity in her own capacities, capability to live like a real person on the very blessed earth given and created by the Almighty God to be shared equally by all? May be I'm also the one in the form of a female part of the human to be used for some good reasons at the same time to be humiliated by the male and female both equally as dominated by the male while humiliated by the female simply by their silly little jealousy which can be consider as a silly little agony in their very heart which is not really necessary in fact very silly to get rid of! All hard feeling had gone away while the dose of dreams started to affect me with high doses. By the very grace of mighty medicine I got relaxed flying on the wings of dreams as if got the very charms of the charming world around felt like no worries, no responsibilities, no hard feel on some decision making as felt like got carried on the charming chariot held by the people who make a world of our own in which I'm the Queen in the middle of a charming chariot to go along to make a world made by them and enlighten by me the imaginary Mighty Queen of the fairy Land. This way I didn't also have the hard feeling to work more for less to treat myself with a little cheap thing for a big wish of my mighty soul after all as a queen! Friends and people around got real things to do like a proper course or a job training programme to do a real job or to build up a career. I used to be very proud of me whenever I could deliver some knowledge by the end of any conversation they were making thinking to be the good one even then as to be considered to be the final solution to the problem. Being fooled by my own illusions or delusions as they considered my disease considered to be a mental disease made my family, my surrounding people, the society, my country people even my family members to take me as the youngest child in the family to be taken care of by diversions, delusion's, as well as by talking down or even worse by talking my valuable thoughts delivered sometimes by me to be taken with hatred and negligence as I did not come from a noble family so it is allowed to take valuable thoughts from someone insignificant who doesn't have the confidence to value herself. So basically I was sold by my own wish made to be fooled for fancies or by the fouls or even the hypocrisy very common and conventional since the beginning of the human civilizations to civilize people with self-deprivations for the better for the society? Where we all live with equal rights to be shared? I even started imagining myself as a Queen wherever I went to be followed by people. Sometimes I found my favourite T-Shirt or a pant or a dress I intended to buy by the very entrance as if got displayed there in the shop only for me even in my size! What a grace! People like me! They love me! I am someone I'm something! What a grace in a big country! But when I see people in the social gatherings with my own community people I can't really point out what's my job, what do I do? 1rst few years I delivered my educational qualities, what are the degrees I achieved in my life, time to time tried to prove myself as well –knowing or enough knowledgeable to hold a respectable position in the gathering. Later started to feel ashamed of my incapability to even find a job for survival the excuses made by me for staying home for the sake of little kids, or for sickness I got rid of that too. Also stopped being fooled by the people who used to encourage me for tutoring hourly at different schools or interpreting or teaching privately at people's house at night. Tried real hard to get into a real job when realized later that it was my job to help and to guide people or even to give them business ideas by sitting at home while talking about different concerns or doing thing things derived from my culture to make them learn the best from my own life as followed. So basically all the degrees I achieved with all hardships in my life had no value what I know what I do what life I live are important as an example from my community as the best one might be to be followed to improve the society and the business by getting treatment to leave the weaknesses I have to get rid of? Only the pain for me is that my life or my non-paid subtle job in my ongoing personal activities made their life with dignity along with an identity and I live still like an underdog without any recognitions even worse that I'm basically living in a darkness of the whole mystery to point out who am I? A Groundless feet on no ground makes no reality in real life only a heart full of dreams even that also as groundless emptiness in no figure to make or to create. A nameless life and a mission less mission has no success no failure to give basically nothing. Finally pain and gain lost their purpose in my life after all through the struggles made in my life by me by the grace of the divine destiny only that's pending to reach out of no reach. It's a blessed life from the blessing form Above I guess with no blessing on earth especially for me so much gifted to shower the entire world where there is no room for me to keep my share of the blessings. In fact might be I'm the one who's the total blessing not to expect any from me as the cow don't drink its own milk?

Getting a pass to pass the life or earning some pennies to carry on is good enough to live such a life while am bound to keep going with some pennies to pick up some food and drink to fuel the life to keep going with no mission no ambition or even with no discussion to make at this point when all efforts have been made to be gone in vain. And when I'm now very desperate or upset with my life as it gets more strict asking to leave the shelter I have to find my own way by leaving my life partner who's at least kind enough still to take care of me doesn't matter with dignity or with humility. Now I see myself as a fallen angel again on the groundless ground with no family, no parents, no siblings to support at this point and moreover if I let the people know my conditions only those come forward by stretching a helping hand to take the advantage of the situation to make business out of me as a Gifted again to make business together with me with the blessings of the gifts. And of course you all know very well what happens when an fallen angel loses her wings to fly can't really make its feet fit on the ground either.

So, now the purposes of the gifted doll has been fulfilled in most part as used as a role model in many sectors and factors to be done finally. But still while man opposes the Devine proposes still has something to do to keep going with a full might and the right to live like a man (woman) which now you can see what I'm doing now? Writing! All stories of the modern folk. People shut the doors on my face meaning slamming the door at me and I opened another door of my own to survive with full right and might. The gifted guts were cut off when not need no more while the gift of the divine stretched a bit more with new hope. I started to feel like where I descend now from the dream land to the reality or to the bad dreams from reality. Of course from the fake dreams of the fake reality to the reality in real sense hoping the life begins here. Sometimes still I get confused with the question why I get so much hatred, humiliations, and negligence while I carry a lot to give to people my thoughts, my ideas, my creativity, my knowledge still to live in a hell. Being a good person with some wisdom really is not for this world anymore. Only one question buzz in my head like a bug who brings the world to the end it's us or the one who created the world to end? What cause the fruit to be rotten the decaying nature or the pollution caused by humans to raise a fruit tree on the very soil with the much needed fertilizer to be mixed with some chemicals? What bring the nature to decay in the Nature itself naturally in the system of the life till the system of dying process by the Nature? Is it us who ruin ourselves by polluting our body and soul in the same ways to be ruined like this physically and spiritually or its' just the ways to be ended up like this to be dead or destroyed all at once on the specific day of the day of judgement? If the present polluted human mind and soul caused very naturally through decades or even by centuries caused by the over usage of all the resources we got once to share by the whole humanity till now the we're not much to be blamed. Things get over used to be abused, to be polluted as well as similarly our souls when day by day things get harder and harder we find ways to avail things when they don't get to be done in normal or legal ways to make our spirit polluted to make the whole as polluted as needed to end? Holding onto the principles makes good people die too. When good people die they get the same dead end all rotten-polluted dead bodies on the same fate. But only our hopes, humanity, honesty, chastity, decency, ability and quality can conquer the world to be believed I guess only for those who still hold onto the strong ethical senses to be valued divinely. I know these are all my wearied feelings and understanding hoping not to be blamed for judging so much.

iii

Saturday morning. Kids got me to stay home for the birthday party preparations. The little one's Birthday. She is celebrating only with some friends. A Birthday! A Big celebration is being celebrated only with some friends? It's Time to move on as our kids are growing with some friends only no problem with that! Moms always there for your help basically Mom's like to celebrate children's birthday more than her own. That's Mother Nature. So very quickly I left to buy some necessary little items like disposables, cutleries, soft drinks, napkins etc. as also looking for the finest Birthday cake was the real hard for the glory of the party. My 14 years old little Princess occupied me for two hours to find a good one finally. A busy working day at home was waiting for me to make the great party great after all. Bishash is still in bed sleeping while snoring with full mouth open and loud. Both I and Bishash planned a dinner outside in the evening while kids will enjoy at home. Nira started bugging again for a nicer party dress for her a new one as the old one's are old. A fashionable brand new would be nicer this time and I denied to go for the second time said, 'go you two sisters go together to buy another party dress and remember at the same age of yours now the mom had no party at all to celebrate the birthday on any birthdays every year except only a home-made cake baked into the kitchen oven to celebrate the mighty birthday of an ordinary candidate of the century to remember who took birth on the mighty date to celebrate as a lovely kin to all others to live on the earth after all?

'How old are you mom?' asked Nira and Mira scolded her saying 'don't you know? Why bug so much?'

Nira started to cry to defend herself 'No, I'm just trying to make Mom to be happy. I like to have my Birthday party nicer this year all arrangned nicely by the help of Mom.'

'You mean with the smiling Mom?' all laughed together to make Bishash wake-up and cheer up on the very day of one of his daughter's birthday"! All started to scream in cheers together. 'Good to have a family after all!' thought me, 'life is precious as a gift together as a happy family.' The emptiness in my heart is the emptiness of my soul an unaccomplished success in enough progressing and processing process. Does career mean everything in our life? May be not with that much desperations while has another parent in the family to take care. This kind of mentality is permissible in our culture only on the other hand it's hard to run a family by counting every penny al through the months counted one by one to reach a minimum goal to fulfill some needs every month in twelve months. Still better living in peace pushing away some need.

Suddenly, after a long time I felt very blessed by discovering the love by remembering each of our kids birthday. The first child Mira's day was the most exciting and loving for us to have the 1st baby born in our love for each other. That spring a long time ago sixteen years ago in the early morning of that spring made me and Bishash's love and bondage in marriage very special still to remember. First day at school, first exam in the life,1st love, 1st marriage or only marriage, first job interview in life, first progress report in the first school all 1st days are remarkable in life. Some of them were with enormous anxieties like the first exam in school, so do the 1st job interview or getting the first report card from the school. The rest most others carry happiness, love and sweet memories for ever. Life is precious with both excitements and anxieties together side by side as happiness and sorrows as universal as forever. So why don't we celebrate our love in giving birth to a new generation by making our two daughters? 1st we fall in love with someone then we make love to that person and then in the third stage we make a new born baby to give birth to a new love dedicated to the family by making a family in the bondage of nothing but love. So, Love Love & Love! It's very justified to go out tonight for me and my husband together on a dinner while two daughters enjoy the party at home with friends.

Finally, the expected romantic evening! My fascinations about the discovered old love in a new bottle carried my busy day on the swift wings of the long hours to be felt shorter. After finishing up all the work for the preparations for the Birthday party I took a fresh breath in relaxation to feel it was only a glimpse spent in a breath by accomplishing all the work in no time at all! I felt like I should buy a dress for me too on the special day. But no! It will look odd at this age after all it's not my birthday!

Nice evening out! I and Bishash chose roadside restaurant to sit outside in the cool breeze of the nice summer evenings. I don't wear a heavy dress to feel heavier on the cool evening. It's good to be in a nice light green top over the jeans to look younger looking and attractive at the same time. My husband is also very happy, calm and quiet as well as content as always as a successful man ever! Never get over re-acted or over excited over anything good or bad. As a man he is always very clear headed, cool and calm to handle things in reality to be practical on the other hand I'm all illusive, delusional, a dreamer while a looser to fall for despair while aspire at the same time to live to die, to hope to distress at the same time as always as the life of mine keep playing with me by giving hope to take away my wishes to return it back again to make my gains as my dreams, an illusions to swim in to get rid of it by all my efforts to fail again to reach it back again. I guess it' only the hope after all I hold on to live the life or to guide me and to keep me in myself to carry on at least.

Whatever! It's a nice summer evening which only matters at this moment. Life is good with its all necessities and more sometimes as in some gifted good time, with some romantic moments like this walking and spending time together with my love in a cool summer evening. We don't realize that somewhere in some places some people are endangered, living in a crisis of some sort while we are blessed to a good life after all. Looking at the empty space makes no life by ignoring the filled up half or more of the bottle. Life is good when we feel good.

Sitting by the shallow stream makes the evening very romantic for me at least while got out of home after a long time. I guess my life partner feels the same said by facing to me,' you look beautiful this evening. What makes you happy? What's going on! You look very romantic today?'

'I shouldn't be?' I'm naughty too!

'No—I thought you fell in love again!'

'Is it wrong to fall in love again with my dear old lover again?' I continued in the save joking mood.

'No--- just thinking what makes you comes here looking very special!' Bishash still murmurs with joke.

'Why? We're not very old yet! Or you want to see someone younger?"

Bishash got up now by saying, 'not again!'

I looked at my husband this time to ask significantly 'why you don't feel good when we come out? I'm feeling romantic! It's spring! I want to remember our days in our springtime. Don't you feel something? Why don't you recall our days?'

Bishash looked at me to say 'come on silly! Let's enjoy the time only you and me!' we walked a bit forward to sit on a nicer spot by the shallow spring looking beyond at the lake with floating boats with passengers for roaming only I guess! If there's any destination might only be the other side from this side just for fun by boat riding. For some reason I got excited again in expressing my joy in a song as started singing in a low voice not to be heard by people and again asked by my husband, my former lover to be loved again as asked again to Bishash 'Come on! Cheer up! Don't you remember anything? Come on! Feel something, remember something!'

'all I remember we were sitting in a coffee house to chat and chat most of the time tweeting like love birds while most of the time very argumentative about love whether we were really loved by each other or not!'

Said my dear husband after a pause. And I answered instantly with a sigh 'yes it was a time when we were very young to expect only love from life just like me as an emotional fool by ignoring the very reality.'

'I know, you were a silly!' Bishash squeezed my nose.

'And that's why you're in a better position as a career and I'm not!'

I added again by asking for a cup of coffee as said, 'I was so much in the craving for a cup of coffee.'

'Not for me?' Bishas reacted as he was always a teaser in our early life. Good to look back to the back sometimes.

'You are not a food! 'My answer to him now!

'If I were then what would you have been doing?'

'Eating you up!'

'I know what you girls do.'

'A woman now!' my answer next.

'Oh! Yeah! Now you can swallow me up as a whole because you are big now.' Bishash started laughing to say again 'I was big then to have a crave for a cup of coffee to keep me awake to maintain the everyday routine to think ahead rather than to dream.' My dear husband started lecturing again as a boss as always blaming me all my life for my dreaming tendencies. I don't mind anymore but today at this nice evening in the nice weather after a long time it did not make me feel good at all. And I got sentimental as before said 'you mean I'm not practical to become as successful as you are!'

Bishash got worried for hurting my feeling on my day said 'no. no, Shapna don't take that way. You have done enough! Let's choose a menu. Nice evening nice weather after all!'

Meant to be romantic in the late spring made me feel stupid especially with the person who's very in contrary to my characteristics. He can make business out of life while I can make life out of harsh reality. Two different personalities never contradict each other to live together but only thing is both of them make a pair to live together with compromise only! No problem! life is all about 'making a life out of no life or out of less life like putting some tunes into the verses of words to make a song to be taken as a piece of music to turn the harsh reality in a rhythm to carry on with some charms in the life. Time flies back not flows forward. Whatever is gone is gone, the lost youth, the charms of life with some enthusiasms don't come back like before. Trying to be romantic at this age made me feel insane by forgetting reality once again, again and again. Birthdays come back again and again so do the anniversaries but not the time which performed the first love, the marriage ceremony when the real wedding took place but not the celebrations of each of them every year. Each of the year is a year unique and distinct separable time phase at the time when it is. Celebrations are only the memories in performing the same in duplications. Memories remain in the negatives while the performances in the past can't be the same in the present as time takes away the charms with its decay. So both of us came back to life in reality in the present time to enjoy food and drink with full heart and soul by ordering our favourite dishes in the present desires. Taking a sip of my coffee helped me to get rid of my fake romantic mood which actually only a fake trial to be young again to act like a young couple in the old. Thought me! 'Let's get rid of the burden of the silly emotions after all to enjoy the day as well as the very nice summer weather here.' We talked about our two beautiful daughters while having dinner. They are big now it's a pride to feel now as parents to raise them up so nice!

I pointed out first 'do you think they are enjoying the day very much?'

'Don't worry they are o.k. you are still the same worrying about them all the time!' said Bishash.

'No, just thought about them."

'Don't think too much. It's not going to give you much.' 'Bishash is always Bishash always between the judgement of paying and gaining, to pay how much to get what?' 'Good! Two different personalities make a balanced life with perfect fulfillments after all!'

MY DEAR HUSBAND STARTED reading the newspaper was placed on the table and I looked around to take the beauty the place, of the people around walking on the street or sitting quiet. Groups are in excitement with laughter, cheers, and loud talk while the couples are boring and quiet neither into conversation nor in the mood of love or romance to feel for each other. What a day! Has all the charms from earth has been shifted some other place like filmed only in some movies for business only? That makes sense while life is now for business and work for better for better than the so called charms, love and romances should be used only in the film industries to make business out of that for people to buy some time in love and romance filmed by the film makers to enjoy that part of life in the films to see and feel better in colors, glamour's, and costumes with also in the good performance in dance and songs to view the better versions on the screen as dreaming of the feels with charms in real life while there is no time or opportunities to have the real life. Performances look better sometimes even feel better that's why it is called 'sweet dreams!'

Bishash still is very much concentrated on reading the newspaper while I was still watching people couples young or older either sitting quiet or into serious talk just like us which is very normal. Young folks go somewhere else to tweet or to kiss or even more as love birds, older people like us like to sit and relax in a place like this surrounded by big big trees some of them are trying to reach the peak of the sky if not at least already touched the peaks of the high rise trees to compete with the man made creations or inventions. The ways human civilizations reaching up and up leaving the life and love behind for ambitions only is nothing wrong with that as life goes on and the civilizations move forward or reaching up with the developments. The problems remain only for those who pine and die for the lost heart just like me to be known as nostalgic. They are right in the heart of such a big city with the very speed of progress in a satellite based civilizations with great evolutions of technologies with a fast moving modern generations with the speed of life in the speed of cars with lost values, the value of life and it's all the charms, beauty of its heart and the beauty of its thoughts where everything and all efforts of human abilities are only to thrive for survivals only where we can't open the book of romance or some emotions too only for life.

Still can't resist to try to bring the lost time in youth in love and passion. I tried a bit by saying, "nice weather! Very gentle breeze! Have you seen those trees very beautiful some of them look like umbrella's giving shade to the public in the very sun?' Bishash lifted his eyes up to say,' Sun is almost gone they are waving nice wind to people.' 'Yes, it is nice!' I got very excited to see him awaken 'really? You like it? I like this way, sometimes the time and the weather in such a place!' Bishash smiled said, 'I don't know whether out of criticism or romanticism said,' especially at the time when we relax in hard work by filling up the stomach by swallowing food in vigorous hunger and die hard to get all the materials and things to keep ourselves fit in the speed of the competitive society. Are we living Shapna?' These last words spoken by my very practical husband ever made me wonder at his feeling to feel the same way I do feel. People have some general understanding, feeling as well as the views to see life in their thoughts and understandings. So we all live on the same boat. We are the emotional beasts in general. But any ways, I fell in sadness by feeling Bishash's emotions as always tend to take him as an iron man. My wonder at his insight made me feel bad for him 'a man is a man after all!' a dreamer lives his life in dreams by feeling less good and bad both and the others I mean the regular people with not much thinking or dreaming live the life on the ground sometimes smooth sometimes very harsh. None of them escape to feel flying as an escapist in the sky or living on earth to be in a world of delusions. When after a long time when my heart touched my life partner's heart to be the same I felt like an enormous burdens of my despair removed from my heart to feel myself a lot lighter. So I made a joke to make the air lighter saying 'I didn't know that you think that way now-a-days?'

'learned from you and still learning.' Bishash smiled.

'Making fun of me?'

'Why you think I'm all materialistic? Don't forget that a body has a soul inside too'.

"I wish!' said me again in a joking mood (thought inside I asked for rain tears came down) what a blessing! All at once! Bishash hold my hands felt warm said 'let's go for a walk around. Very nice out! We walked down the streets the shops of trades stood aside. I took a look at the glorious things kept in show cases. On the shelves in the stores while passing by as much as possible. All the delighted things in the road side stores, the green on by the road sides, and the beautiful high rise buildings in the urban setting made a nice look with Nature in the nurtured present societies of us. Walking on feet with full feeling in the midst of crossing high speed vehicles was useless at all. We sat on the side of the shallow lake water at night a nice view to watch and feel in a mood no less romantic in the break of everyday life with work, home with household matters, children and so on. The crowd around us and we are in the midst of all, the reflections of light on the lake water, the nice cool breeze with all the beautiful views around together with all the people as a part of human society in the very civilized human society in both Nature and nurture made me feel great together with my dear husband after so long in a good mood just like me! The cool breeze at night in the lighted city made us feel each other somehow whether is not like a honeymoon or not it is definitely something good to remember as a good memory for me at least especially when I started feeling myself a trash in the treasure well now I'm a treasure in the treasure of the present civilizations after all.

The evening was nicely spent after all kids were all happy in the Birthday celebrations I guess as they did not call to complain about anything. We as parents think kids are always kids we fail to realize that they are growing too by learning all. When we are out of home they can manage things sometimes even better than us. We took very long in the streets down town. A lively evening after! It was dark after midnight none of us willing to go home. We were ourselves after a very long time in the very refreshed hearts and souls as if we came back to our youth from the future to the past with more feeling of youth when it was gone with less to feel more later by capturing it from the time machine. Standing under the lamp post made us close to each other heart to heart. No, we don't kiss like teenage lovers on the streets after all we are adults now but somewhat wish to do so at this point we couldn't bring us back to very past by the grace of the time machine. We felt each other after a long time spending in the real life which is nothing but all reality made Bishash busy with business while made me hopeless, selfless, domestic, self-dedicated dumb to think all gone all done after all the phase of life has been closed to start the new chapter with only the kids to be dedicated while lost rights to live. Thought raising a family means to sacrifice for all for the good for all to accept the fact that I'm not included in that "all". A mother needs to be considered to be a dedicated mind for some sort if divine feel of serenity or the serenity of the divine devotion to feel Great or to be considered great by the people as a Mother by remembering 'Give me a good mother I shall give you a good nation' by Napoleon Bonaparte. And this kind of considerations my the people or by the self-dedicated self-made me in most of the Mothers faithless, lost self-confidence and low spirit aimless, hopeless and down feeling to be negative about everything. For a long time the way Bishash kept him out of recreations the same way both of us lived a life biologically by fulfilling the demands of the body by depriving the feel of the heart and the soul. Keeping away the soul from the body doesn't really make a life to live properly.

The shiny moon up over the lamp post smiled very nice with boundless glory that the dark shadow of my own self looked and stood up to me to disappear in the dark again by saying 'Good Buy" to me. That's the same shadow with a smile this time looked wishing to me. My illusion may be! It's only a good time today. No missing not recovering from them which never existed. It's just my feel to differentiate life and dream from only the life itself. One is tragedy happy beginning with a tragic end and the other is tragic story with a happy ending. Happiness is illusion and tragic hardship is as similar as delusion to turn it to reality to solve.

I think the Goddess of misery put a bit mercy on me. I started hoping to the series of my miseries be gone away. The shadow under the lamp post might be the wizard who gifted me with a curse instead of a gift. I saw him smiling nice and encouraging with a blessing or it might be my desperate wishes to get rid of all of the miseries to see the sun shine with a bliss of a smile. It's me not and only me with a smiling heart to feel and to forget.

Talking myself thinking myself a lot enough. We came back very late that night. two daughters were already in bed. All tidy no mess at all! Good! I looked outside the sliding door the moon is still up with its full round face with a smile, a reflection of my inner happiness in the smile of the fake and borrowed light of the concrete moon is my happiness tonight is also as fake as the light of the lamp? Can't I be happy after all over all the concretes the reality and the burden of all of my failures? Again, no! Only a successful mind and soul can tolerate and shake off the little blows of the wind of distress of unfulfilment. An unsuccessful mind or a soul of a life can be very easily get shaken by any kind of bad feel with or without a reason.

Well, again! So much talks and thinking. My guide my wizard should bring me my dreams not failure!

Late night! Need to go to sleep. Next day should be a day of gift without a curse. Took shower, went to bed. No worries, no bad feeling at all it's my life. So, tonight is only a sound sleep. The sun will rise with a new hope with a new beginning! The Big Boss at my new work will smile wont imposed all unfinished files of theirs on me to check on me to check my wit and to get the work done quickly without dealing with all of them who can at least relax because of me. As I have the gift of grace by the Divine to do the chosen job. Bless me!

'Shapna! Wake up! I'm late you going to be late too! Wake up now! Bishash is Bishoy after all at the very day break to shake me off by my shoulder to wake me up from the dream in a nice dream land cool and nice to wake up and rise and die to work.

'It's morning already?'

No, it's noon time! Bishash is a bit upset by finishing up all his duties to pay all the bills, mortgage, checking today's appointment as usual; after all he is practical and I'm the one who's still the contradictory a daytime dreamer after facing enough of the reality' eye dazzling realm of the heat from the sun fails to comply with the real life. I know my dear husband even though is not a dreamer like me but like to relax after work as usual after all as a human being. So, I try to cheer him up! 'Good morning! Nice day!'

'It's raining outside. It's not even a day break! It's dark down. Look outside looks like sunset time. We had bad storm last night.' I don't know why my life partner never realize that answering very promptly to my stupid question can hurt my feeling a little to piece me off in the middle of a mood I got even to cheer him up? God! Why practical husbands are all so practical when the wives come to volunteer for their better feeling? Only that might be the only reason makes the difference between a man and a woman. But I still remain as normal as in behaviour to answer,

'How did you know?'

'Because I don't sleep like you.'

'Mad at me?' I asked with open eyes.

'No, just upset a bit.' My husband replied also said 'sick and tired!'

I know deep down he is not happy also because of his wife's failures. He knows me also understands me but what can I do with reality? So I try to keep my spirit up said, 'come on! Cheer up! Quickly get ready. I'm going to the kitchen to make us some breakfast. Last night was dark now it's raining as a blessing.'

'Again! Said Bishash, 'poetry can't make a life.'

'I know money can!' my quick answer hurt my husband I can tell looking at him. Bishash is Bishoy again and I'm the survivor this morning cheerful and enthusiastic after all along with a fear to lose something again like a loss of a faith again and again. But again with a hope which gave me a hope lately for a new day. Let's see! The company is booming so does her hope from a little to a big one a tiny bit of a hope with a fear to be a big aspiration.

Bishash dropped me at my work as usual. And I entered the big gate of my office to see at the very entrance to greet me or need me by saying,' here she is! 'What took so long? We were waiting for you. Some would say,' don't you know we are incomplete without you?' Raka always hugs me to say, 'my love, and my help.' But no! The ground floor this morning is all empty. No one is there to see me or to welcome me. I felt empty inside with an unknown fear. What happened to everyone? Inside in the rooms everyone is on their desk busy and serious at work. All of them lifted up their eyes to look at me all at the same time and I got the panic inside again like ever '0 no! no! Not again! I tried to pull myself together but couldn't. How can hoping the very thing and the only thing we hold onto snicks out again and again of a grip so tightly gripped? I took my sit among all facing anyone or seeing anyone beside me whom I don't know any more yesterday's friend turned today all to some aliens once again and this time for forever by wiping out my Hope once and for all.

At 11.00 p.m. I tried to do this morning's work with all the associates actually all of them unlike me. They live a real life and I live a life of a fairy in fake dreams and which never lands on a land to make a life ground for me. If I think I'm really a fairy sent on a divine mission by the Fate to face the hardship to accomplishing something some sort of a divine mission for the good for people through me an Angel in the skin of a human to be failed again and again in the trial to accomplish something very worldly as a matter which is because I possess a human heart to pine and die to get what humans wish to get? The Fate determines to do whatever divine is through me and I fail for my foolish worldly reasons as the body and the soul aches with foolish reasons and childish attitudes toward life. I suffer the same ways the humans suffer while happens to be believed by the people of my surroundings as possessing some very non-humanistic qualities or behaviour like extra-ordinary in beliefs and behaviour to wish, pine and die for the same.

At 11.00 a.m. I am here in the Big Boss's room to do something very great and noble to do from my perspectives after so long dreaming of all along doing a little bit better jobs at the big office means a lot to me by hoping to have a position in my life to feel myself 'Great!' after all the follow ups of the dreams. It's done! I'm done! No more funny me, no more fooling me! I go get my 'good bye' from my last job ever! So I got up and walked towards Mrs. Robinson's room without looking at anyone else here. I know they aren't also looking at me the noble job is accomplished, all of my colleagues are happy, successful and proud of the big project we finished all together. My feet on the high heels started aching as tired and stubborn to walk forward and also I started feeling dizzy by figuring out the scene in the big Boss's chamber as entered. 'Hi! Mr. Robinson! How are you? Asked me.

'I'm good thanks, how about you?'

'I'm good too.'

'Good! cheer up! We've accomplished a big job together. You did great! Aren't you happy to lead the whole group including me? That's a big achievement what you say? Isn't it?'

'Yes sir but---

'Oh! Don't worry about the promotion. You are special we can't go without you. You are still an associate what you think? Isn't it great?'

'But Sir, ----

'I know. Here is your bonus. Meet all of them they are all very excited also very grateful to you. Only your patterns and plans brought us success. Aren't you very proud of yourself?'

Streets are a bit quiet lunch hour is not here yet. I walked out of my office building walking in the street feeling like a fallen angel who lost her wings to fly fast and easy beyond the reality. Am I or was I dreaming all my life? Did I forget about the real life? But just at this moment can't really remember whether I said 'good buy' to my Boss before walking out that building. But if I look back to my very childhood until now. All hard works dedications for my studies to all the training I got in my whole life to do well at work various work. Some well-wishers said all my chronic failures all through my life to 'set a goal, mix your mind and work hard to accomplish the job'. Some of them preached with very wisdoms 'giving is taking in a way not to be distressed and so as saying also like, 'You won't have to ask success will come by itself. What did I feel at this moment is to see myself through insight to see myself as an Angel walked out of her path of wisdom on the concrete ground which doesn't give a way to an establishment in life to live with dignity or with an identity. Now-a-days wisdom is a fake reality in fact it's a dream which led me here that after so long of so much failures and after so much determination and dedications couldn't get a position after so long and at this age.

Just like my school life or the entire student life while I couldn't answer to the expectations of my family and my parents. This time also I won't be able to stand properly on my feet for my hope's of all the achievements in disappointments to my husband Bishash is actually should have been named as Bishoy my love my life my company all my life who was there always for my pain and my suffering struggling through the harsh reality to hold my hands to stand up again and again.

The sun is up shining and heating up the world very bright but I'm very tired of walking don't know myself to where or for what. Recalled myself by looking at my tiny little watch to add the time. It's 1p.m. and have to go back to the parking lot don't know walking for how long in the street to bring myself where. Felt for a moment that just recalled myself to look at the watch to see the time. It's 1 pm and I have to go back to the parking lot to get my car from underground parking of the office where I work just left behind is apparently very back to walk back to never come back again. No more miss trial for a carrier, no more cheating myself with fake dreams which don't come true.

It's a long way to go back to get the car to get back home. My legs got froze with pain for the first time. I walked a lot on streets before to catch a bus to get to the subway train station to catch a class on time, to get my daily work on time but never felt this much distress out of the tiredness of my soul to move forward or backward on the way of life. I looked up at the Sun, felt my feet to decide to stand under the traffic light post and this time my shadow did not get a space to show him up. The feel of my illusions or delusions did not make me to have a feel of having a gift with the blessing or the curse of the wizard.

STORY 4

Illiusion Again!
Love Love Love\ kamrunnessa

Bubbly has to go to school very early this morning. She finished writing her essays by 11. P.m. last night and declared to her loving husband Rana that 'tonight no hunky punky I have to wake up early morning tomorrow.' She says that most of the time so Rana ridicules fake as always 'no, baby don't sleep yet, if you sleep earlier how I can I sleep by holding you? You are my sleeping beauty and the charm to make me sleep a sound sleep after all'. Bubbly broke into laughter as happy as always says very gladly 'no baby not tonight. Tomorrow O.K.?' she came down putting her mosquito net on to say 'good night!'

This is our Bubbly an early married young lady apparently to an older man. She couldn't finish her degrees before marrying Rana is considered enough to let the wife go back to school again for her future? What kind of a future is my husband expecting? Am I not good with having a life partner along with a family with two happy members in the family now? This is Bubbly now a young woman an innocent lady happens to believe in conventional society in a country like ours? She goes to school as it's a system or a habit of the society to go to the school with all heart and efforts. And we believed in men's indecency not women's. They should be a loving wife, a mother and a household keeper to make the family happy for the good for all. How about her future? This might be my thought and her husband's not they just do things to their women without thinking the women's future while the future making no future for them while they dedicate their life for the children, for the family and in some cases actually in most cases for the love for the husband as well as for the family the entire family later to be considered to a huge burden to throw out respectfully with some modest bullies or some tortures very moderate to tolerate to die nice inside unlikely as dying hard to death. And never got into this kind of

Thoughts before as when she was young, beautiful and very enthusiastic in all the meanings, all the fascinations of life a lovely young ladies life. We always try to live the life being in the present by forgetting about the future as when we are very young life is very good with all the fantasies we tend to feel by forgetting or by thinking the fact what will the tomorrow bring for us even when we see an old person in front of us or a sick person similar way to figure out the sufferings of life in bad time when no health, no wealth, no support, nobody around. We live in the present with pleasure we live in the past with pleasure again in the pleasant memories again the present but by ignoring the future which might bring the fury of the fate to take revenge on us for enjoying the life by ignoring the suffering of the old by being so bold. Time place and fate always wait for the revenge to take on the innocents who willingly or unwillingly get carried by their emotions or by their innocence to ignore what might be the consequences of life for flying in ignorance which is no essence to keep the presence of the innocence. Babbly's innocence keeps her happy as she only dies for love, pines for attention, and goes shopping with her girlfriends to hang out at the same time and also make over for a party and dies hard to throw a party for all. In our words she's a babe for her darling, for a party, for all the fascinations for all the womanly desire. But one thing is good she doesn't go astray. She is serious about her education still without an aim and her Prince Charming is her little elderly husband to take care of her well. She fell in love with him just at the very first night and still keeping the madness in her love. No child yet though. Rana is serious no children before finishing the university successfully with a good result.

II

A summer day very nice and charming with a clear blue sky but it might not be in the sky of the heart and soul also. Bubbly doesn't know why now-a-days she becomes a little nostalgia to think a bit more than the regular routine of a daily life. She took her shower got dressed up to set out for her parent's. They wanted to see her. It's been a long while they didn't see their lovely still girly girl Bubbly. On the other hand Bubbly had been very busy with her studies to finish up the M.A as well as Rana with his business. He wasn't home last night went on a tour abroad for business purpose of course. This is happening frequently now-a-days. Her days go busy but the night lonely pining for some love far reaching for a sound sleep to dream at least for all good wanted all the life as perceived to be good in real sense in this one life. But the still innocent girl make her sleep by dipping her heart into the memories of the past in all the lovely moments to make the present pleasant. She is a dreamer after all as well as a lover in her life with all the positive energies. But now somewhere somehow in her heart she sees to recognize the infidelity of life a life which was always very tricky to her as she saw the blooming of the flower by ignoring the stings around, saw the nice flow of the river or of an ocean not the storms to make the nice flow of the water turned to a foe in making it a flood or turning badly in a huge tsunami. She has started to lose all the fascinations for all the charms made her to live in charms only as the charms of Nature as well as the charms of childhood and the youth to see and feel things all as charming as facilitated while an innocent immature mind sees good only by ignoring all the evil or by judging things only positively. Thinking positive made her life in most part but now it's hard to accept the facts over the fantasies. She felt all love in her marriage now can see life, the hard reality which makes the room for love getting shrink a little day by day. People go for needs work hard to kill the time in their life to keep a space for love and romance or even for some good time with friends and family to cherish the life in charms. 'Living' has become 'Making a life', 'Love' has been turned to 'Love making', Institutions make no careers to give us a life as life itself is now the career depot to make the life back from the institutions to the personal life, from peoples life to the institutions. life is all institutional where we don't make our life the life institutions makes us life as the childcare or I can say day cares making children, schools make students, universities the universe, family's making human workers or the man power to support the systems not planned but built in or within to make the whole universe all within.

Finally, Bubbly reached home 'a sweet home' after all most of the conventions still preserved to follow, to feel, to greet from the heart, to cherish and to forget the harsh and hard reality in all good or even better from before still not that bad as humans are making robots not the robots making humans. She brought her new dog to show to her Mom and Dad as always. She likes to see them happy very happy by her new excitements every time. So they picked up the little doggy with not much hair on it to cheer at her new pet in excitement or as an adventure to show to her parents to make them excited by her latest excitements or an adventure to be appreciated. Both of the parents showed enough excitement to her like a show and tell excitement only the mother faked her excitement by concealing her disliking for the ugly dog to herself only just like her dog long time ago in her childhood when their dear dolly daughter brought an poor orphan from the street to give him a shower by taking him to the bathroom and started ordering the care taker to go shopping instantly to buy a bunch of cloth. The father kept quiet not known whether to appreciate the little girl's attitude and the activities or not but the mother was very much shrieked with all her fear and hatred for the very ugly and dirty conduct of her daughter her own dear daughter her lovely Bubbly.

Any ways, as Bubbly or their only child had all her advantage to take on her only parents by inheriting their only soul only for her they could not say anything but to obey her wishes and orders to follow only. Bubbly became very happy finally by seeing her new dog taken care of and loved and patted after all by her dear parents. She felt relieved and secure for her very lovely Tom. But as usual started feeling for Rana. He didn't show up yet! It was almost the dinner time but her husband didn't show up yet. How about her parents stop worrying about him? That makes her more worried about him. At her old house by that time she enjoyed her evenings in the garden again with no flower yet. What a day! Why things are not going normal? It rains when it's not supposed to, chills when even it is not the winter time, humid when it is not cloudy at all in an ongoing nice breeze after all. All the systems of Nature are now in no systems. Bubbly got worried about the climate also that's also very unusual for her nature.

Rana showed up at 9.00 p.m. just before the dinner was served at the table by guessing he might be? Coming by then as the flight supposed to land earlier before the dinner time if doesn't delay. What a co-incident! Bubbly ran towards the door with all her passions and emotions just like the way she ran towards Mr. and Mrs. Abbas earlier. The earlier woman and always a woman were hungry and pining for love as always. Before our Bubbly started bugging her husband with a bunch of questions all in a short breath like a little girl again as 'why didn't you call me? 'What took so long? 'What time you got on the plane? 'Exactly what time you arrived? Mr. Abbas stopped her before she asks the last question as he knows what's going to happen next as if trying to stop the fight or the breakage of things in his house. He doesn't want to face an ongoing argument this time when his little coming late after a long time to see them. Then Mr. Abbas asked the 1st question to his son-in-law 'how are you Baba? Long-time no see! Long day right?'

Rana admitted 'yes very tiring! A long journey. Can't sit like that all day long.'

'Things are not good now-a-days. Lots of plane accidents. Be careful. Try not to fly very frequently.' Mr. Abbas suggested as an elder as always.

'Its job Dad! We can't do anything about it.'

'Yes you're right!' the father-in-law's answer' by the way, where you have been this time? I didn't even ask Bubbly!' asked Mr. Abbas again.

'O, yes, it's nowhere but Singapore for business only.'

'I know, I know what else it could be!' Mr. Abbas nodded his head. Bubbly kept quiet and set the dinner with no talk God knows how. She helped her Mom to serve, to organize the kitchen, to put away the left over after serving and watching her husband with a fully fledged silence no one would know how and why. One thing for sure she was waiting to see Rana in the bed room to tell all her stories as well as to hear all the stories from the listener in private. She left earlier to the bedroom not very sleepy but dreamy. Dreaming of her love to be served after a short gap of the absence of her husband in her melancholy she felt in the absence of Rana of something she desires the most. She looked around the bedroom to find out if there is anything missing to make the room nice. No! Nothing! All neat and clean. A room, a bed to desire to fall into sleep after a long day waits for Rana only of course. A long pining and wait time a moment to desire a lot to love, to cherish the nice moments, to romance in the presence of her dear husband Rana who's here now after an absence shorter or longer she doesn't care its always the same the time without her husband always the same in feeling shot time is never short while a long time period is not in count to her absence is the absence of something dear is missing for decades. She put a flower bouquet on the table for decoration, to give it a charming look to desire, to feel and to love to make a night special to meet her excitement inside. She put on the new short midi to be comfortable but started getting sleepy to fall off into sleep a very tired soul in longing while waiting and imagining things possible impossible at the same time in expectations of lovely moments of all in the Prince charming's arrival at the same time in the fear to lose him in an unknown evil of a bad time or so. She started trying to keep her eyes open as well as to feel the moment as a special after all in the trial to meet and feel that as a lot more excitements waiting for her to hear from Rana from his trip to share a series of all adventures by forgetting the fact that her husband actually went on a business trip.

She couldn't realize that it's been an hour that she has been waiting for her husband who actually was still at the dining table in conversations with her dad may be! What a misery! She felt herself as a fool for the first time. It was all her obsessions couldn't make her realize that life is not all a romance. She found Rana and her dad at the dining area chatting or discussing about things. She couldn't resist herself at this point to go straight to the dining area in search of her husband who actually was with her Mom and Dad as they were carefully listening to Rana about all his stories on the trip as well as looking at the pictures taken on the trip. If Rana's companions were not her parents she would have been very mad to be angry even to cry out in pain. So she joined the little party of three to make the number four and finally fell into sleep didn't know when. She found herself in the same bed together with her husband in her parents' house in the morning and couldn't remember how did that happen when did she fall in sleep and who and how brought her there. She couldn't remember even where she is and when did Rana come back from his tour in the first place but the very next moments she managed to recall all to her senses. At the same time got upset to fall into despair by the thought that her dear husband didn't get a chance or make a chance to his wife in private to have some moments in love as a couple or even in some talk about anything! She doesn't like to think that he lost his interest as a man to get her in love or love making. She hates to see herself distressed or that much weak to pine for someone's love that doesn't even remember her anymore. But again she knows that's not true deep down they both love each other very passionately it's just the reality which makes people hard and harsh to live only in such a time when everything is shrinking time, energy, feelings, passions and emotions all at the same time. Rana says, 'it's even humanity people losing every day for the sake of reality. All its matter is only the survival. All of us just struggling for survival as we share and care only when we need each other emotionally, practically, in a bondage, in a relationship, in a business to make together and at work while honestly everything is now actually working out for the sake of survival better or regular doesn't really matter anymore everywhere its only the survival techniques. She got up and went to the wardrobe to look herself in the mirror judging herself still beautiful or not. She is! She is still beautiful thought Bubbly. Then why her husband doesn't want *her* anymore? Doesn't matter what she thinks and what she expect from her husband it's the attraction which make their love into a relationship to keep a bondage after all! She wonders why he is not mad for her anymore. He loved her so much after their marriage. He praised her for her beauty, he praised her childlike attitudes and activities, her innocence, her love, her madness for him, appreciated all her talk, moods, her laughter,, her sweet smile, her dress ups, valued her happiness, fulfilled her desires along with all her demands. She felt herself as lucky as the luckiest person in the whole world. She was loved, she was fulfilled enough actually a lot to fear to lose what she got by the grace of the luck or divinity.

There was a time when Rana looked for opportunities to be with her all alone to touch her to hold her or to kiss her. Now the entire world is important to him except her. He goes to sleep without even noticing that she was waiting for him and in the morning makes jokes about her for being so silly for some instances, makes fun of her by nodding her a bit by appreciating how she is looking in the morning in the night gown she was wearing last night till this morning. Actually she opened the wardrobe drawer to look for something like inner wear with some inner desires to find if Rana would have bought something to bring for her to hide into the drawer. No! Nothing! He even didn't say Hi to her by seeing her alone in bed before going to bed after a break to at least to long her for a passionate touch. Well! Whatever! Bubbly got herself back into reality to look at the photos taken by Rana at his business trip for fun but not exciting at all because she wasn't there to share those moments to capture in memory to remember later. She was still trying to figure out the places behind the photos all around Rana. She thinks making a tour all around is a tom boy like attitude especially all around the world. All she cares about going to a place very nice and romantic by Nature or the historic places to thrill or to feel romantic by the sight of beautiful places in a natural setting. She values historic values to think of old places, old people, ancient life ancient aristocracy, adventures, stories of their life made by ancient time to thrill to wonder, to become very curious to become romantic or to regret not to be seen the past. God knows how much wonders or wonders of the world untold and unknown stories were made by the ancient times through all the evolutions. Bubbly likes to read stories, novels and historic events to wonder, to think of and to dip into her imaginations to make her own movies only in her mind. She loves tragedies to be fearful about losing her love to someone else.

Browsing through all the pictures taken by Rana kept her busy for some time along with her imaginations according to the stories in the books she read earlier. She got confused about a photo of her husband seeing him very happy all alone in a very nice place thinking 'why he's very happy without me? Or 'he likes the world not me!' he enjoys his time alone. That means I'm not in his heart anymore or even in his mind as well as into his world"! etc. and right after the very common suspicions especially belongs to the women' mind very mindfully to think 'how about he's in love with someone else?' here she might start crying or going to grab her dear husband to bring the daring questions to the darling of how he dared to do this kind of nonsense?' and to his astonishment when the husband questions like a stupid 'what? What nonsense?' to answer like, 'You don't know? How dare to lie when it's all very obvious?' the poor victim would only like to know what exactly made her mad and by knowing the reason not even a reason just an assumption a very wrong assumption the silly Bubbly will fall into an enormous shame to regret, making her environment very cloudy with no reason at all and for doing that regrets to start her misery once again in the guilty feel to kill her valuable time with her husband after all.

After some more thoughts she tends to decide in her mind or to feel in her heart that she doesn't exist in Rana's world anymore. Why me always in almost all cases get fade up with the woman in their life even taken to be their 1st love or the very married wife to live the life together. That's it! This is it! He's enjoying his life well alone doesn't even care about me anymore! And that makes her to find a clue for his affair with some other woman or a girl friend to find a clue of a girlfriend with him in the pictures taken on the trip. She got desperate to find at least only one photo with a woman on the trip 'come on! Only one photo with a woman or a girl to prove! And very fortunately finally after so many efforts she got one to find the clue to prove her husband's infidelity to herself only? Silly poor girls and women depending so much on a man for love and life, care and share, for stabilities for reality and over all for the society to give up their own self in someone else' their choices, their destiny, their goals in the life, their freedom, their careers, their honors all and all as an inevitable part of the Man or the mankind.

She found the picture she was looking for as a document of her pain to see her husband in the middle of a bunch of stuffs from his work place where there is a woman also fortunately to be very fair and standing just next to him also with a smile to be very happy to be in her husband's company? That's it! Her fears and her imaginations according to the stories read by her or the movies viewed by her matching exactly the same so nicely! And all in a sudden she looked up by putting down the photo's still keep gazing at Rana with full big eyes with enormous wonder rolling up and down with the ups and downs of her mind. Not only that she woke up her dear husband from sleep when he needed more sleep usually as a wife she always knows right after an exhausted overseas trip for work.

She didn't even think about the fact that he might have been very tired to be shaken by the sudden wake-up call early in the morning comparing to other mornings as usual as on regular time for wake up for work. And just like Bubbly this time Rana woke up to roll his eyes with wonder not knowing what happened and where he is asked, 'what happened? Are you o.k.?' Bubbly looked into his eyes thought for a moment to make an answer definitely very pleased but instead she kept looking the same way at him to say very slowly in a very low voice 'nothing!' a whispering as the anger went down to turning into compassion. That's very womanly to suffer inside to get tortured by their own inability to speak out about how they feel about certain things when not right to them especially an emotional issue which most of the time basically no concern to men as they don't see those as a problem to think about. This is called a woman after all loving, caring for all and passionate all at a time in the inevitable part of humans known as woman. Bubbly even didn't ask a question about the trip as already questioned and quenched her curiosity to extinguish her anger out of a silly suspicion. So the 'Good morning' to the arrival of her husband, her beloved lover after so long as stretched and magnified by her own worries and pining heart for love always a hidden emotion which can't be expressed that much in a world now when people are basically fighting in reality only for survival, thriving for better for better as some people also thrive for the existence only either in the remaining aristocracy or in the harsh reality only to make a place to live. Rana opened up his eyes again as was almost gone back to be closing for the demand of the eyes to get the human into the world of sleep saying' come Babe come by my side, my sweet heart! I can't sleep without you!' again opened his eyes from the very fallen soul and mind dipped deep into the lap of the sleep fairy to wake up for a moment in sub conscience to express his love for his Babe his lovely wife after all whispering again 'don't worry I'm not in love with anyone. Trust me! I love you.'

Days come after a day, day by day. Time is passing very swiftly by carrying Bubly's day to day feel, her compassions, her analysis of her own soul how it feels time to time love, care, passions, expectations, suspicions, doubts and desires, anger and emotions, hope and distress, all the demands of the soul and the dedications to lose all together time to time in her life which sees the world with all the human feels mostly pining and dying every time when fails to feel the same as expected. Still life! She realizes as always to live and cherish after understanding or realizing a little the reality which makes a life with all opposites to meet the goal somewhat in between or in reconciliations after all for all to live with understanding or accepting positively when everything felt harsh or hard. She is now almost at the end of her university degree to be finished she took finance as a subject against her very emotional and imaginative mind and feel. She took that to challenge herself which is also a fascination too for her adventure. Her academic achievements are all very marginal but she is very creative in thinking and making issues or in her creative thoughts after all. She is happy overall only the future will tell what she is capable of doing. Her home, her families, her life, her mind are all very clean and tidy except her mind which can't be as clear as the blue sky and the heart which can't be as happy as to feel good and fulfilled. She is also empty without a child; she is empty without the frequency or the consistency of Rana's company. She is healthy and happy looking but inside deep down the sea what floats around with the water up and down with the waves or without can't really be explained. Most of the time she pulls herself back together from falling for so much demands of the heart, from sadness and pain for the failure of all the disappointments.

It's a good day today Bubbly is free to do whatever as the exams were just finished yesterday and they also made love after so long. She was busy so did Rana. Life is neat and clean with no trouble or concerns at this point. The sky is clean and all blue got no clouds, no colors, and no clue for rain or storm or even for the thunder to blow the mind. A neat and clean and very tidy phase of time so far. Their talk, their having dinner together, going out together sometimes for different purposes were all okay. They had been living together in peace and harmony. Normally when they talk about themselves along with others; we see the peace and harmony they kept in their life while the harmony in the heart remains empty we only feel and pine very secretly which is why bubbly is very happy today the morning' looking very sunny or bright to brighten up her day. She's bright inside that's enough. Bubbly started feeling good about her achievement at last. Getting graduated is a big thing after all! People like to succeed and be happy at the same time very unfortunately it doesn't happen most of the time in most people's life. There's always a discrepancy in between. A success or achievements is an honor and happiness is all about feeling good in one's life as well as in the very heart which is very necessary for people's well being. When a big achievement makes people happy other things in life can't make them happy in most cases as being honored or being successful in some achievements with honor cannot make a person happy when he or she is not happy in the family life even in luxuries when the most desired Love is missing from the luxurious living just like the body and soul a healthy man is not happy inside for some reason or some concerns. Also most of the time when health is not good wealth can't make the person feel good. A soul dies in the sick body as the matters make a man miserable good enough to cause the heart to fail to function. Bubbly can't match these two in her life to be fulfilled after all. Most of the time she tends to be or meant to be happy and to feel the fulfillment in her life still can't accept the fact that life' not about all good. Good is there but we only needs to understand the limitations to compromise to be happy with whatever we are getting by seeing and thinking positively. Over all she is alive she is lively by conquering her distress to live without stress. Most of the time she tends to be happy or meant to be happy by having both success and happiness together in her concern to feel to live happily over all. She pines and thinks a lot but manages to live fully fledged in between two.

Another day in her life to expect to be happy and lovely in love and passion. This time on the graduations day to celebrate with all the heart to succeed and progress to move forward. This evening seems to be very gloomy while she expected herself to cheer up with all her friends she invited to her place to join a little party. Shiela showed up on high heels and high up hair all bundled up on her head. Mina came forward gliding through the doors dancing and singing 'here I'm------going to make a great party la—la----'.' She's always like that said Shiela by watching the last couple entering the party room forward as sincere and happy always joining the group with some modesty as well as with some courtesy to talk about later all the recent happenings in the country. And Bubbly definitely will go with the first two delighted friends Sheila and Mina and the 3rd couple will remain for Rana to chat and spend time in the party instead of his lovely dolly darling Bubbly as ever.

What happens next eventually Sheila, Meena, and Bubbly will be roaming around the house at the living, dining, kitchen and the pond along with the garden beside. They are all cheerful, laughing loud eager and dear to everyone and everything. Mina and Shiela started to show their interest and love for almost all of the things in the house. They question about the rare decorations, decorative pieces in the living room, new look of the kitchen and the new furniture the host bought. And bubbly got very proud of her belongings associated with her love for her home to make a home with love and prosperity as keeping love for the home for home making while the prosperities is expected as always for anyone on earth to move forward to make a life always better ahead with some expectations to bring more or add more from the phase of the time in prosperity as awaited as always in human expectations through the evolutions of the civilizations. Moving forward is always with the expectations in the ongoing process to progress. Bubbly is cheerful in her expressions as happy as ever in showing all with a lot of enthusiasm. All the guests loved to sit by the pond in the garden and didn't forget to do the mistake to pick some flowers or tear out some leaves without a reason.

Shila's always naughty she is the one who tore the leaves and picked some flowers. Not only that, when Bubbly looked at that she said to hurt her in fake looking into her eyes 'does that hurt you? How about I pick Rana tonight for some fun? Bubbly's naughty too said in answer 'nope! Try that! Pointing at the statue very favourite to her as got from France!' all cheered 'Oooooo! No love for man! Only for money!'

'How about we make a statue of Rana? Asked Mina still smiling.'

'I know what you mean! I love the matter and the man both meaning man matters and things are needed some of them are favourite unlike the favorite Man!

'I know, come on! Just joking!' said Shiela and answered Bubbly again

'I know! Didn't get serious. Loving things and loving a man or any person is not the same'.

Tina's still very naughty said 'how about I judge the status first and marry the man later?' all cheered to break into laughter.

'How about love? Do you marry someone without loving the man? Tina again.

'I do! My love comes from the gain as in the childhood I tend to love my dad only when he brought me a doll. All broke into laughter again to make the party an enough worthy.

Bina was quiet all the while commented now 'yea! take the thing and let your love go! Hand over your husband to me how about that?'

'Are you serious?' screamed Tine in excitement 'I didn't know you that you have gone that far with my husband?'

'Come on! Choose one take the love in exchange with all the things you love or take things instead of the love your husband I guess!'

'What you mean? Come on!'

'Now you upset! Can't chose between two rights?'

Bubbly came in-between after so long to say 'money doesn't come alone but the things they are basically the needs loving things or the passion for things can be eliminated but love is an essential as emotions for devotion for both who need and pine and for the one who provides or loves the person similarly in love with the lover who's seeking.'

'So they both are the same in love basically to love each other. Again Bina the wisest friend after Tina. Boring Benu left alone as a lady out of the circle the friend circle. Again its Shiela the tall and bold lady of the party to make the party hot by bringing up some issues to make fun to catch an attention from all said now,' why all women and no men in the whole party?'

'This is home only hosting a party not the entire state to celebrate.' Once again Bina to bang the party in to roll in. Then she looked at Benu to say only 'how about you? You still look very serious and silly to be in a bachelor's party?' Benu looked bit thinking in silence. So all broke into howling, shouting, cheering ups, talking loud, dancing a little now and then with the loud music and the poor Benu left alone again to keep silence. Bubbly got up to go to the kitchen to serve dinner. While all were enjoying the party with full heart and cheers while Bubbly started to serve the dinner Benu appeared leaving her chair to say, 'Hey Bubbly! And all! Bina, Tina, Shiela and the silent Rana, Benu what are the items in the menu?' all looked back by the shout to break into laughter again. Finally! She is alive!' tends all to think.

All five ladies got together to make a real chamber of ladies in matters of all kitchen matters near the kitchen in the very lovely and luscious discussions of food fares, cooking cutleries and dishes and decorations for the best for the belly. They started talking endless thoughts of one food item or a dish and the discussions in various ways of cooking and making that one. Time is running out for dinner. Bubbly knows her girlfriends found the real place to have real fun in real discussions including Benu so better be hurry to help preparing the dinner.

Party's over. Dinner, drink, chat all over to wrap up a night on the week-end for the next week-end for the next day of work. Rana went to his office room from there and Bubly went to the kitchen to wrap up all the materials all the arrangements in the kitchen, outside of the kitchen, all over the house. Two hours ago Rana said 'Good Buy' to the guests now said 'good bye to his wife to go to bed. And the present mature Bubbly will still be in the kitchen to put away things to make the place tidy once again especially the kitchen for the next day. And once again like many other times in her marriage life she had her tired & sleepy husband as if he has gone out for a long time from the present life from the family together to rest in peace or to relief in escape? A busy childless and lifeless life makes her depressed now-a-days. Sometimes she feels like she is just opening a page in her day break every day to close again to open again a new one not to read but to perform her story as already written by the Divine. Why this life is like a set up series of duties to perform like it or not every day on each next page next day. Passing a big period of life time with hope only to go and to break at the end. After all of the guests have been gone Rana was asking about everyone in details their names, professions, and where do they live etc. especially about Sheila seemed very curious about her.

Most of the time he gets curious about others especially about ladies and also likes to spend time outside more than at home. Time and maturity made Bubbly a lady from a baby to a lady. Time changes people while the tide carries them away. Some people believe in fate some people believe in the nature of life. May be the wind and rain made the soft sand turned into hard rocks. Rana is busy so does Bubbly. But still there is a "But" about her. She seems O.K. looks O.K. by herself but the failures in her emotional expectations might have been making a deep dent in her heart a dent in emptiness or has been made slowly day by day to make a seal of pain by every day resistance. She accepts the fact that life doesn't go by the expectations or the dreams people dream about besides, emotional things are might only an weakness to make people or a girl the present woman like her a hard rock inside and a friendly person outside to get along with friends, family the very dear darling husband to carry on the life in full-fledged expectations to expect as is to be accordingly. So the present Bubbly try not to expect more even less in just expecting something very little and insignificant while valuable to her only to be disappointed in getting that. She tries herself not to hurt herself. The beginning of a marriage of a man and a woman is romantic in most of the cases, with some couples the romance still appears in time to time as the situations allowing them to feel. Bubbly realizes now to understand the nature of all things in our life anything new is nicer as old is gold a value to hold. Good times and lovely memories make again a time to time as a peep into the reality. We get carried away by all the duties in our lives but love prevails, romance to comeback, sorrow and sadness die to make the room for the happiness again and again time to time. It's all about I guess refreshments of life a life we live in reality as it decides to be carried out in hardships, in work and duties, in pain and gain, in hope and despair time to time, cherishing life also in the mean time to time to live, to refresh, to enjoy, to feel and to rest.

She's working she's busy carries on life, love and all the care for her husband and keeps her share only in the heart which never ever expires where there is a secret chamber still passionate still very romantic, hungry for love with only a difference doesn't expect much, doesn't dream about the things pining for, doesn't die, doesn't regret for all she desires very desirable from the heart. Sometimes she thinks that a child or two might make a difference in the love to make a real bondage in bringing them together in a refreshment of the desires shared equally by both. Work gave herself respect, a maturity keeping her mind and soul a maturity, keeping them also busy to keep her up not in regret for the things not achieved or not been felt when wanted to be felt. Rana makes her depressed sometimes at his too much materialistic concerns. She makes herself valuable now over all of her childlike behaviours and activities in reality. He makes her concerned about his too much care for the worldly matters, money, luxuries, luxury cars, about tending to get a big house for only a pair of people to make all in care of social status.

She looks at the orphan boy on TV who feels himself so happy fulfilled and grateful by getting himself a thing only out of necessity as getting himself to be fed by only a bowl of rice. While she thinks like why can't we be happy by getting ourselves only the most necessary thing we need at the time? Not possible life moves on for all with time needs as well as demands increase very slowly. Living makes necessities also necessity makes life. We can't stop life from moving on it needs to grow, needs to move on with a growth for more for maturities not only for demands as it expands, need to expand for the life cycles by Nature. We humans are the inevitable part of Nature actually the main reason in Nature for whom all the creations are we born, we live, we use all to live, we keep all for ourselves, we take of all again for us and for the Nature with all of its resources by fulfilling us by all the resources' given for us to use, to take care, to make more or to keep for the growth, to take care for the same reason. We are the centre of all the creations, all the resources' to be cherished and to be used at the same time to reproduce. On the other hand we are the consumers of the natural resources' at same time we are the distributors as well as the producers and keepers of all in Nature. All together humans, animals, birds, rocks, vegetables or all in the growth of the jungle including all five elements of the earth are actually using, making and keeping each other for the work of the world or for the care for the earth in keeping, valuing, expanding, in the betterment of the world and for beyond for a part of the universe.

Anyways, I was talking about the relationship between Rana and Babbly as a match good or not happy or not honestly never ever that was a concern to think about in a marriage parents look at the fact that if there is any problem or not if not to be seen then don't worry. They are happy life is not all about happiness only. Rana likes to fulfill all his ambitions and dreams but to Bubly life is all about pain and dreams. The pain is real to feel deeply in touch of the nerve. Feeling pain can be an urge to look for a job to do on daily basis. The dream is fake and deceitful desires in giving us hopes to fall into despair when not achieved and couldn't be reached or even got misled and hurt by running after the fake fairy of our misfortunes. In general people know how to keep the status of their present achievements or the social status whatever they achieved for their dreams and hunger like Rana the difference is they still hope to get more to hurt someone's feelings then love or whoever then loves or the person who love them. Something with Bubbly she knows the word now 'love and passions' are only a matter people need to live like healthy human beings but still can't get rid of the pain she got for being a human to add more time more attentions to their love. Rana quits the spot very quickly the spot of their private time for some togetherness in love and passion in feel of the good time or good environments for some 'to do things' and opportunities to such a moment of desire. She keeps those 'to do' things for later to do by valuing emotions and the heart over all.

Rana is busy now-a-days so does bubbly as both of them are working. They are not unhappy but they have become feeling like boring. Rana is progressive and Bubbly is just alive tends to be alive which is why she gets herself into despair sometimes when life doesn't give her much life to live with full heart. Rana and Bubbly are not unhappy in the conjugal life only the life itself got boring to them. The husband is progressive and Bubbly is alive as always tends to be alive in life to feel and to cherish which makes her fall in despair as well as for her emotional needs, when the present life doesn't give her enough life actually enough love she desires over all from the person she loves very much to get the return or the attentions she pines for from the dear one or the one as selected for her to be loved and to be taken care of with enough love and care for the rest of the life as a partner to share all and care for each other in a bondage basically nothing but in love and commitment for each other. She dies hard with boundless love for less. They are opposite personalities basically what makes a woman a passionate woman and what makes a man a man unfortunately. While Bubbly's love dies deep inside Rana's ambition rules his life similarly from the very deep down of his heart to the very top as if aspiring to get himself on the pick of the mountain of the ambitions as to aspire. They are like two opposite river flows falling down into the same existing ocean ever and ever.

They both feel the need some of children in their life for the fulfillment of a marriage as always for all to make another bondage in life in the family life. When the life got boring without some excitements as for the aspiring man to get something new and bigger every time on the way always one after another for the ever aspiring heart for more and more when the achievements get familiar to desire a new one eventually a better one in a society where basically all are doing the same in the very competitive tendencies with one another in the name of progress or the very developments by losing their time and energies in making the life and running only for getting the success in whatever they believe in the trend while in the contrary to Bubbly only passions and emotions in life are important as the life is getting lifeless in the lack of life in plenty of time to sit and relax to feel and think, to love and live. As every moment our hearts die when the emotions and passion get pale to make the flow of life to flow in different needs by making a new direction to flow up forward. This is life is like a flow river to flow forward only. Better not to look back what are the things got lost, what couldn't have achieved, what got missed or gone unnoticed. Life' a phase of time line which is fixed for each of us without our acknowledgments for how long and to what destiny to end up as it is destined by the destiny already.

So they both decided to have a baby or two in a couple of years. Kids will be running around playing while demanding love and attention from the parents to make them provide love for their little kids not to demand themselves some time to provide love to each other especially for Bubbly a living soul for love only? When it's time to provide what she desires all her life to be an asset to provide to others with full pleasure. Good to think that kids could bring some joy and excitements in their life to make a new life. She is working for two years now. So they decided to have a baby and Bubbly prefers a baby girl cute and naughty playing, talking, and running around the house to make the home a soul and a life. They have been trying for a year but nothing yet! She didn't conceive yet. Rana is very busy now-a-days. Most of the time staying out of town. The days when he's home when at night time he's free of any phone calls, at the computer work or doing some paper work or even if he is suffering from some tensions out of his businesses for the cause of some delays, some un-signed contracts and so on then he's not in the mood for anything. Some of the nights he's just tired to look at his wife a wonderful woman to love dressed up nice for the night in a short lace night gown, a laougndray or might be in a nice Sari. He's never rude to her still cares for his wife. He doesn't hesitate to buy things for her in care of her comfort or in care of the value of life to provide her luxury or luxurious items. But just forgets her Birthdays to buy her a gift secretly to surprise her with a wish out of love and remembrance but still remembers the Anniversaries for social status to socializations in a Grand Party thrown by his initiative mainly all after all.

All's well except some love in the relationship to put a soul into the body of the bondage of the marriage which carries the whole big luggage of all necessities of life in the items, in all the goods, furniture and all and all things they need like all other people in their life just kept very nicely in the house as a house keeper compared to a suitcase to bundle up for all the useful for the body without a soul or the combination of two souls into one to make some love between the people into the house of things for the desires mainly material not that matters out of emotions, devotions and passion for pining of the souls living in the house to make it a home in love and care for each other. Home's are now look like all as a Home Depot storing all well into the storage of the life a conjugal life living as a family together in love and blood relations but in no relations at all! like a couple like Rana and Bubbly a married couple in a marriage making their home a business or a Home Depot in storing all the desires as well as all the ambitions in shoring all the goods for the good for the comfort of their eyes to see new desires are all there to comfort them in achieving them at least after so much dedications to work and business in devotions to have a good time in relaxing in a reclining chair to view and renew the souls by viewing all the man made materialistic monuments mighty in elegancy and aristocracy to beat the competitors of their circle by being a successor all ahead in achieving all those materialistic goods and things very luxurious! Human ambitions ambitious mind only can perceive life with two eyes only to see the life successful in materialistic achievements. While metals can't make a metallic mind then why to choose only the materialistic world to make us happy when we can't really feel the life only can't be free of our bindings in the boundaries to feel us free? If this is life we are living all of us on the blessed earth then why we are to live with a heart and a soul possessing all the emotions and passions? Perhaps to eliminate the complexities arise out of human emotions as well as all the conflicts? So it's better to be Robots to live this mechanical and the materialistic world we possess now by our will power or powers only. How about modern half robot half humans turn to the total robotic beast then what would be the world look like? Perhaps we all have some ideas from watching movies on this image of life. Mix and match of the living and the objects can't make a life can definitely make a living thing in the shape of a human body if there are two one possess a heart another merely a machine can they make a life? If not then why still we try to perceive or pursue life when there is no life basically? Hard question!

Let's forget about that! We are still humans only hard part of the ongoing life making people hard to make things hard when they things hard they are still very human but only in the form of the evil ones only by forgetting the other part of the human soul which tends to be good to others as well as their own soul to live still as a human. There's no difference between the passengers on a flying up aeroplane and the vehicles on earth on the roads they all are still equally the same people with heart and soul as humans. So the progress of the civilizations doesn't have to be living only in the bodies by forgetting what we feel while we possess a soul inside.

Anyways, going back to the life of the Rana and Bubbly couple. As a consequence of the nature of their ongoing present life or of the husbands that much busy life motivated or urged Bubbly to go in the same way. She is working, she is busy. She doesn't have time for love making or to regret for what's missing from their marriage. She's kind of given up on her desires most probably by putting a Vail on the flow of the heart or just lost interest in the aspect of the life which was once considered as an essential or important part in life has become an aspect or material from love making to child making to regenerations only. Emotional things have been considered as a material very necessary for the ongoing life which shouldn't be stopped for any reason. Precious life is no more precious but has to be carrying on. As life is life an urge to live after all and over all that's how is the living.

Bubbly's moving on with her busy life a daily life busy and fussy, sleeps beside husband as tired as her husband by the end of a long day. Only on the week-end Rana is not home most of the time to put her in distress to think like 'why do we make money by working so hard for life when there is no life? What for? In answer to that sometimes Rana says 'life is hard needs to urges people to thrive not emotionally as depending on love, emotions and passions as the fancy veils on the soul I and body starves for food. No money no food, no shelter or anything that's the reality. Bubbly wonders when her very husband talks that rude. How men from an enough rich family can see life from that perspective only. Do they try to avoid the old wives considering as a cup of cold coffee? Is this all just an excuse? Might be! That's what it is! That makes her to fall into despair again. She blames herself for being hungry for love. Why some people especially women from cultures like theirs are bound to love only considering their spouses or a lover only a special one to them and no other choices from inside the heart or even form the society? This might be a matter of discrimination which made a women subordinate to a man to lose their freedom of choice, freedom of their speech, freedom of their thinking while think by restricting the thoughts according to their Boss's choice and that Boss is either the beloved father next to him is the Husband, father in law, even before the loving elder brothers to be abide by to restrict themselves from all their choices to avoid troubles tend to arise from the society not still very favorable to women especially. They need to be great to the family, to the society by sacrificing themselves by sacrificing their choices, wishes, and their freedom. They need to make images about themselves as in a nursing role of humanity to present them to be considered respectfully by the society to live with dignity and to that all they need to sacrifice themselves for all at every chapter of their life in all the various roles they play as in the very incredible shape of a Goddess starting with the role of a Mother once a daughter, then a sister next a wife need to be called simply only a woman. They are the one needed to be judged all the time.

She talk to herself sometimes like 'why is I so much in love with someone who doesn't even understand my love or me? Why people pine for a special kind of love from a special person in their life? Why they die an emotional death for an emotional thing which is nothing but the silly "love'? Is this an instinct to love and to be loved? Does Rana love his wife? Did he ever love anyone? Did he even feel empty without someone special in his busy life specially now when he is also a successful man? It doesn't look like that he might still be the Mama's boy very o.k. in his daily life with all the to do things from brushing teeth in the morning to the bed without the lullaby only and Bubbly thinks she couldn't replace herself for the Mom's lullaby's by making him affectionate for her company or with a touch of love in bed. She thinks that after all he's happy unlike her as they both are different in character. She wishes, she could be like him. Living like an animal with fewer attachments is better than suffering in love to slow down the progress of human civilization. He's good, he's fit for the current time trends. Bubbly thinks she is not. She is emotional she wishes if she could be like him living like an animal with less attachments to anything considered human emotions better than suffering in love to slow down the progress of human civilizations. She thinks like 'he is good very fit for the time now not me. I'm emotional not very practical, I love to suffer, and I waste time in vain. He's strong, he's fit, he's happy and over all he's progressive. I live with pain in no gain while in no need at all. He's alive, he lives, he cherishes, he thinks, he looks up and go forward without looking back and he takes all whatever it takes to live and enjoy.

Last year Bubbly and Rana went out to the sea beach on a very nice trip. She was very excited and in love with Nature, the Sea and her husband together were very special for the first time in her life. She gladly considered that as their honeymoon as they never got it after their marriage. He left her right after their marriage for his family while it was time for their own honeymoon as they never got it in their married life. Bubbly was all alone as she is now. The melancholy mood of her still haunting her mind, the soul and the life of course. She thinks too much now. She is still melancholic and pining for love all the time. She had a good time in the latter half of the holidays. They enjoyed the sea, the sea beach and the nice weather at the beach. Bubbly started feeling that she was very emotional always pining and dying for love. She feels like she is also very melancholic at the same time. What goes wrong if her husband never ever said that he loves her? She is the one who is very much a love seeking child. She is so much in love with Rana and she blames herself for that she is a love seeking very week low grade creature asking for love as she cannot live without a love while Rana never ever said that he loves her never showed any madness for her. His madness for his newly wedded wife was. He loves proportionately, he lives carefully, and he makes plans very carefully for the proportionate time periods for each activity or for the responsibilities to carry on. He's money making man not a machine to live a life also which enjoys, fulfills desires without dying for that. He works to take

A break in the meantime to feed the soul some enjoyment as well as some rest by not being so rude to the life to live with some passions an emotions after all! He's alive. He looks, he cherishes, he thinks, he looks up and down and forward not down; he looks up and forward and not back, takes all whatever it takes to live and enjoy. Last year they both went out of town to the sea beach was a very nice trip. Bubbly was very excited and in love with Nature, the sea and her husband very special for the first time in her life. She gladly considered that as their Honeymoon as they have gotten after marriage. He left her right after their marriage. He left her right after their marriage for his family somewhere close to the Beach somewhere close to the beach and where they were on their pending Honeymoon. They had a good time in later half of the trip as in the first half he was away with the company people working on their project. Basically she was all alone to be melancholic again as she has been considered by her dear husband as second concern besides some important others or his work or any sorts of business. 'Well'! She thinks sometime this is fine as a life partner to be shared by all other concerns why you think Bubbly?' she was all alone to be melancholic as she is now as always. Bubbly have been thinking too much now-a-days as now she's thinking why she can't think of any other things beside Rana who never ever even said that he loves her, never ever showed his madness for her even proportionately for her love for him. And now after a long time of their marriage she's thinking about herself. She is thinking why she's so much in love with Rana who she never saw before marriage. if this is called falling in love at the first time instead of falling love at the first night then in her case like many others might be this is the trap set by the divine power to make people suffer from inside severely as a heart disease to suffer eternally? Mainly for women as their small world consists of the home only make family with some expectations consisting into the spouse and some children to make a small world of their own. And if this is selfishness or mean to feel and see the world through personal matters and the desires for the heart then again they are not to be blamed as they are not allowed or considered in general as someone free and dignified by the society to be out going or to be the part of the broader world in the major part of the human world where women are still considered as the subordinate portion of the other half of the humans to be their partners, supporting energy or help as an inevitable other part or humans. Funny is if man consumes man then women are in some points of view are being consumed by men who are the superior in general. And unfortunately still are being abused and amused as well as in the most degraded scenario still are being abused and finally still are being sold directly or by wrapped up in modesty in nice costumes when the Nature makes the natural objects to be consumed by the others.

Somehow Bubbly also believes that Rana is a good husband as he is very responsible and duteous as cares for her and for the family of two for now as a couple as both making the life partner for each other. Bubbly realizes now that he is not much available now for her. Her dutiful husband always maintains a routine to make the home and the day flawless without missing anything for comfort. He brings everything for her except himself with a heart to make a time good to spend in good time for sometimes together in talk, in making some fun, sitting together to watch TV. Mostly romantic moments to have in their love relation if they would have any. Rana tends to take care of the life without missing anything for its comfort except a heart which desires some more for the soul to love movements together in the garden with a cup of tea, sitting together outside into the moonlight out in the garden to love Nature to love each other leading to love making in bed. But her partner is the love which makes a life for the living as being alive in keeping someone alive also in some respect also in the inner unspoken love for the partner, the life partner. It might be very secretly as if the soul of her says that she always have had a life to keep her alive but the dreams she dreamed of some love, romanticism, togetherness and along with some dreams in some special moments of life. She knows she is not a dreamer only her dreams are live in reality if the body is necessity the soul is the spirit to feel to be alive in good and bad both. She is not a teenage anymore she realizes her madness in love especially in the marriage which is very life to make a family life by nourishing and nurturing the essential urge to stay alive.

Bubbly regrets sometimes for being so much in love for pining and dying for love only. That's because her husband whom she loves only was less seen, less felt in the lack of his appearance in the daily life as well as in her dreams of life and love a lack of passions to make the bondage passionate and strong in a bondage which makes a life in love. Sometimes she feels like she is a sensitive alien on the contradictory contemporary world of concretes only therefore, she is an illusion on the earth to be considerate as an alien where there are human beasts are making while keeping life by making life with goods to live biologically as well as in concretes in keeping the life in making the life. Will she be wiser now? Practically, I guess since she thinks all of the time she should be a lot more the Beast of the human kind or an ideal person like Rana to run, to move, with less sensitivity and more livelihoods. Bubbly gets suspicious now-a-days too by thinking like 'does he loves someone else? Or did he ever love his very wife? Didn't he ever had a family to love or to establish what is called 'love' and 'regret' rather than to be in love of luxury and comfort only?

All she knows now he has an uncle only who showed up at the wedding with full family to marry him all she knows that he lost his parents in the childhood.

One more year has been passed bubbly managed to find her own life all alone on her own journey through the life. She goes shopping, sees her girlfriends, by throwing a party sometimes quiet often besides her commitment to the job she also started loving the money she earns it feels good that she can make a savings of her own when she doesn't have to spend the money for the household which has been taken care of her husband who basically very gladly takes care to fulfill his blessed job after all. She started to love her hard earn money too at some point also to worship money only which at least keeps her alive urging to stay alive. Desperate money lovers are might have been the same kind as deprived of life as her? Recently despite Rana's being out of town quiet often they made love very often as it's a part of life to live healthy. None of them now talk out of emotions or thinks of love basically no time to think only moving on with work and performing duties for the life they set as a life, a home neat and clean as clean as their heart and soul with no steins of hatred or regret, hope and the pain in failures, love or passion, sense or sensibilities. The home is beautiful and sophisticated in designs and decorations, with all eyes catching modern furniture in decorations a home beautiful, very nice and clean with a look very excellent in exteriors and empty in souls like a candle lighting no light to light.

They live, they melt, they spend time together at home and outside they talk with less arguments, they see people to socialize, they talk with less arguments, they work together to buy stuffs or make their home by beautifying the concretes while souls of it remain inactive no love, no passions with devotions to one another, no mistakes in the relationships to make a relationship reaping everyday a little to make the bondage strong. They are happy or they look happy, they are normal as normal human beings in the very normal civilized world needed to be. They are perfect after and overall only they could not make a child which could be the soul to tie them in a strong bondage of love. As a woman Bubbly's empty bosom makes her whole world an empty place. And she questions herself most of the time when her husband is out of town at some nights for business she gets worried by the thoughts if he loves her or not whether he loved anyone in her life at all. Most dangerously when she asks her 'what if he loves someone else out of the town where he goes for business?' over all she cannot think of a life without love a real and passionate love which she thinks she doesn't care anymore but she does still. A love people pine for can't be fulfilled by the touch of a soft tissue baby. She is standing in between her "love' and her life which is basically her husband Rana between life and luxury, or between life and status? To Bubbly it seems now-a-days that Rana only is running without a destination also to reach and fooling her or even himself by living a life which he usually doesn't want. Then what does he want? It's only Bubbly who's making a home with all her efforts with heart and soul. Its only her who wants a child badly he just tries to help. Why he is so much into business bubbly doesn't understand. He doesn't look like very ambitious or luxurious in making a life with all luxury items but runs out of home quiet often. Are these all about the matter of business? Or something else and someone else left behind to urge him to run, run, and run! Or might have been someone left somewhere behind for whom he's back and forth from home in haste all the time. Bubbly wonders to think who and what is pulling him back or somewhere to someone to go back leaving his wife behind out of their marriage? All he does is living a soulless life in all things and luxury without even a child to have for his own soul or for the home to make a sweet home after all? It's all about for more progress for less life in no love for life. But the progress in life for what when there is no life? People like Rana runs after the development or for the progress materialistic and practically for the worldly matters and materials. For Bubbly trying to move on or proceeding in life in developments should be for the betterment of life for each of the family members. Passions and emotions make us human in more attachments in the family bondages and love relations again to make people human. For bubbly betterments should be for the betterment in living a life with better education; better living; better outlook; better thinking; living with love ;respect for each other in a family; and in humanity for being a human in the human society. From Rana's efforts given to his busy life to improve or to earn love and thinking are missing. But he' living as a man a straight thinking man perhaps making the life easy busy with no complexities by thinking too much or expecting too much especially in the matters of emotions. May be the male spouse here out of the Bubbly couple is winning from the contemporary perspective of life but which one is perfect or right we won't be able to know.

The core of the complexities out of Bubbly is to have some love in a relationship to make a life as well as bondage between her and her husband which is basically missing. Even though she's enough mature now still it' a concern whether he has love all for someone especially for his wife who's not only home maker but his life partner. A Heart to heart relationship required for that. She started to think whether he ever loved someone or he loves only matters and materials out of the body only for the body not the soul? He works, he thrives, and he sets a mission or a goal to fulfill the life, he sets forth to establish for whatever establishment needed for life especially for the better family future. He's good here. But again the wife thinks since he's not robotic or a robot he should have some emotions to hold the life partner with some emotional touch or with love. Sometimes men think this is love for the spouse and for the family with children while they work hard with devotions for the sake of the family. That makes sense too living together, making a family, making a home a physical home dedicating constantly the physical work. He's never rude, never soft, never angry,, never shows extreme happiness in laughter or in extreme feel to hold with a tight grip. He's just like get going with a flow expecting better neither up nor down. He maintains the routine of life by doing all the to do things as perfectly as possible as if thinking too much or pining for something new or not possessing to have that like his wife to have love in the life which itself a love to hold in having the aspects of life even the materials of life meaning fulfilling all the necessities in life. He's a shallow river flow flowing regular with not much ups and downs of the waves or the flow. Therefore, he seems to be right to the world while Bubbly might have been already considered as an emotional silly beast pining for something in extreme or not to be considered not very necessary to pine and die while life is still good without and in inconsistencies to worry about. The river which is spontaneous with a spirit very content to be guided to a direction in the same speed doesn't need to be regretful. On the other hand his wife is still a bit childlike to be very emotional and excited at new events in gain or in loss. She gets excited, she cheers, she's joyful, she's sad, she's mad, as enthusiastic at the same time, to be upset and frustrated at some matters to even fall for despair. On the other hand her husband always is calm and content as Bubbly never can't read his mind or feel and see the inside of his heart. She doesn't want to know all of his heart. She only wants to know if there is love for her which she always pines for.

Finally, after thinking a lot Bubbly went to bed by closing the book of her heart ever written with a lot of questions and confusions. This is the difference men do and women die for nothing most of the time when there is everything. I know no one agree with this even me. Women do contribute to the family, to the society as well as in a life she cares about especially when she is in love with that person. Thinking about abstracts is no useless moreover very useful women do make a home and a family with love, affections and dedications. They provide the glue of love to make the constructions strong men build to live in as a family, a couple or even alone. When men are the body women are the souls to be alive the way as they should be. If a woman like Bubbly wishes more, fails to match the dream with the reality, expect more and hope if do not fall in despair and when fails then it is not harmful at all after the entire world has been made with and by a man and woman both together in deficiencies in all that matters.

Finally, Rana and Bubbly managed a long vacation after a long time. They both seem very happy and excited about long holidays together to enjoy doing whatever. They sat together to enjoy to decide what to do, where to go in a lovely evening in an special autumn with tea and to Bubbly's surprise Rana made the tea for his lovely wife to say, 'here is my autumn gift, a cup of tea only for you! It's for you! You love tea a lot so I made the tea this evening only for you and me together to make us happy? My princess!

'O, wow did we see the sun this morning? Where did he show up? In the east or in the west? Bubbly laughed loud to see this new Rana.

'You don't believe! You don't know how much I love you. You think I don't know what you like and what you don't? It's all about our present life Baby, and this business. The half of me is you and the other is your choices. I like to enjoy and to feel the way you feel and this vacation is a gift to you from my love for you.

---- Really? I think I finish the tea first and then try to understand what's really going on!

-----why you think I worked so hard to take some time to take off? I'm spending money and losing money from the profit to be made by now!'

----looks like you're regretting more for the money. So it's the calculations between loss and gain? How much money we lose to gain some time in life to live for some good time? Is being around together you and me means a fooling around to you by losing money while the time is money now-a-days?

-----don't be so sarcastic dear! You think I don't like to live? Making money only also is not a life.

------then what you are enjoying in life? How? Do you enjoy when you go out for a business? But how? Do you love me or you love someone else or just a rational.

Rana took a closer look at his new wife in the old one to say, 'you are not in a good mood now. What's bothering you didn't you also wanted to go for a vacation? You complain all the time! Come on! Let's celebrate our chances to take for some fun all alone you and me! You want to go for shopping this evening? What do you like to buy? I'll buy you anything you want!' Rana looked again to say with a smile, 'we'll buy love too from the market if you think that's also being sold in the market to buy and sell with money?'

Bubbly's still upset, Rana came closer to his wife to hug her and said very passionately which his wife never experience before. Said Rana, 'come! Come my love! come on! My Aunonto, my love! I know I couldn't give you much time for us together but only for the business or you can say for money. One day you'll realize the need of money. Only life can't make life its only money which makes life to buy time and life together and if you die for love that's next. Bubbly smiled looked happy and released herself out of her all complexities or the lack of happiness. Still the question remains whether she is still free of her thoughts of being neglected or cheated by her husband. Too much expectation finally makes emptiness in the heart of desires to fail to achieve all we want more than what we're being expected to have. She still thinks cynically like in the whispering mind of hers '' yea! For you! All efforts and hard work for you only! I'm for you, all the time you make, all businesses, all your efforts you make for you, all your choices you make including me, you chose me long time ago considering me a possessions to you! You live by grabbing me! I'm in you I'm your life which you deny in your conscience while I'm living in your sub- conscience who you can't neglect finally after all!'

Bubbly got along finally laughing, smiling, also cheering up time to time to have a good evening at tea time and at the shopping might be in the clear sky with a tiny bit of shadow of a tiny piece of cloud. All will be well when the cloud will melt. After getting so many excitements Bubbly still didn't know why she re-acted like that at the happy moments this evening. She consumed a lot of bitter feeling in her betterment to be melt like this in such a moments in her marriage which was actually unexpected when day by day the hard feel made her to lose all her dreams, changed her from a silly and innocent young girl to an woman almost like a widow who doesn't hope, doesn't dream, doesn't feel much but lives only to finish the pilgrimage. She's back now again with Rana with her husband and her love her Prince Charming doesn't matter whether for only a month or less doesn't really a matter' she thought vacations come back again and again so does happiness after pain.

It's a rainy day. Bubbly packed up every single thing they both needed. Clothes for her as well as for Rana, make ups, jewelleries, tooth brushes and so on. She is very enthusiastic today so does Rana. They spent a whole week in love and happiness in togetherness to live a life about a whole century to count in length as it was after a long longing especially for Bubbly so she felt each moment as a decade of life in death a death of the heart and mind along with the very soul to feel. It felt like all the fulfillments of all the desires been achieved in only a week as sometimes not only the hard times feels longer than normal but the moments of happiness too when its achieved after a long wait in struggle. She came back to her childlike activities with all her excitements by flying from here to there. She felt like her old self when she was with her parents to see the Cox's bazaar but Rana said these beaches are better here while we are abroad by being lived in abroad. She wanted to fly to the old sea beach of her own while it' quite impossible she knows that too but asking for something not possible at that time is only a demand to establish herself into her husband's heart. Mom called while she was packing 'yes Mom!'

'Did you take some warm clothes? Sometimes it's cold by the beaches' 'I know, don't worry I'm mature enough now!'

'I can see that. Still don't go swim deep into the sea. Be careful about the big waves. Be alert all the time. There are big waves very dangerous! And so on. On the other hand the dad called Rana to give him some advice like, don't leave my child alone at the beach be together, enjoy together.

'Don't worry dad! I always do! We shall be fine.'

'You can go to the city for shopping at night my daughter likes shopping a lot.'

'I know. I'll take a good care of her. When the time arrived Bubbly got very restless for no reason and hugged her parents tight also for reason again. Mr. and Mrs. Abbas looked at each other looked suspicious and tough at the sometimes asking 'is she all right?

Rana and Bubbly said 'good bye' to them she hugged them again by coming out of the car for the last time like a baby girl of them used to step out of the car to hug Mom and dad in her childhood. Rana smiled and hold her hands very passionately to leave to catch the flight on time.

A very short trip on the plane from Dhaka to Chittagong. They sat together side by side and Rana doesn't let her hand go always tending to hold her tight as if he's going to leave. Bubbly thought 'what's that! He never does that! Is he in love? Or falling in love now for the first time with the old one?' still me! Smiled bubbly again to her foolishness.

While they reached the Hotel in Cox' bazaar it was evening time and Bubbly got very tired and exhausted. All the time from Dhaka to Chittagong Rana was helping her at every turn on the plane, on the bus, in making tea or coffee for her, in choosing food, helping with fastening the seat belt and all. Bubbly's very happy and blessed to be felt for having so much attention from her spouse for the first time.

The hotel room here is nice and tidy. Rana got her a special room by the sea side to view the huge sound from the sea sight with extra money to pay.

Bubbly' still very excited by the sight of the huge water into the huge and huge waves up and down providing a cool warm wind through the window. She ran to the window as soon as she got there Rana got very happy by seeing her happiness a lot of excitements after so long. He doesn't know why after so long at this very moment he feels like he's in love. Thinks where was this me in me? He thought only a bit to leave in hurry to check on the arrangements here by telling to change. Bubbly didn't look back to see him leaving. After getting herself so much into the beauty of the sea suddenly she felt herself as got lost into the sudden emotions with such an excitement with all the passions in nowhere when she looked back Rana was already gone instead of Rana the care taker responded instead to ask, 'Sir asked you to change and relax he'll be back by taking caring of everything if all' O.K including Dinner. By the way, I can bring some coffee or a cup of tea while Mam, you take some rest or anything else? Bubbly's mind got lost for a bit to bring it back to sense said 'yes bring me a cup of tea after 15 min. I'm going to take a shower. If your Sir comes back tell him not to leave again I'll go with him to the shore.' The helping hand nodded his head assertive.

Bubbly started getting romantic by the thought to shower in the luxurious bath tub to be in the luxurious well embroidered robe in white to look at her wet and set for a mood especially if her desired man would have been there. Rana likes her in robes after shower whenever she takes a shower. She knows there's a slim chance for that today. As she started humming a song felt like she got lost into the sound of the sea. Always a hoping mind put itself in sleep to give it a rest to be free of all the pining and dying wises and desires of the ever silly and knaggy heart of her own where the pain and pine go together. Easy to get excited but hard to feel to be failed. The blowing splash of the sea waves started touching her heart even though she is not actually there while as she is singing nice and the sea' roaring loud which one is the most sweeter no question about that! The heart couldn't sing the melody of her heart but there's something which has a different charm in the big loud waves of the sea as in the roaring of the heart of the big sea very melodiously existing in her song as if very sharp and keen and silent at the same time a voice in an unknown melody to be known as very common into the hearts of humans still to be known. The huge big oceans can roar loud to make their waves loud, huge and scary as they pour their inside out but a human like Bubbly or anyone can sing only very sweet and sound from the heart where there is no oceans big all open in expressions can only make a language of the heart to pour out a little in words as sung in melodies very sweet and sound. The rhythms of the heart beats can make a song only no slogan but can have the motions nice to make someone dance very nice with the beats to be beaded nice! The melodies breath from the very slow to continue to breath and feel only. A melody of the heart can breathe and feel only to make another feel the same way if only when can feel the same ways as it flows from the heart. She's happy out in a new place but where is Rana? She thought he might not have gone too far? She asked him in her mind 'come on! Where are you? We need to have a cup of tea together in such a nice day!' The Beyara entered again with a tea pot full of tea along with cream and sugar. But Rana haven't showed up yet. She asked the man, 'Did your Sir said anything about him like what time he'll be back or how far was he going?

'Sir just went to look around for your convenience for later for dinner with you Mam!

'O.k. you can leave now.' By letting the man go she felt suddenly that she's very tired to call Rana again as she called a several times to be tired by now to check on him again as he didn't pick up her call. Now she got anxious! Where did he go? He doesn't have any business of him here? Strange! why did he left me alone? If he's around he should have been here by now?' thinking all these didn't bring her husband back to her very soon. He called her at 9.P.M. while she already had enough traumas in all the tensions. When he came back to the hotel room door to knock he guessed knocking her heart hard to scare her while she must have all the worries about his arrival as felt guilty also very inside of his heart. He was right Bubbly was tense almost got mad in search of him. Her voice and her hands started trembling to ask 'where you have been?' I was so worried you only went out to check things for us you didn't tell me that you'll be that late by going somewhere else! The last words buzzed in Rana's heart as some loud hard beads to be scared by his wife's true guess. Yes, he's guilty. But to answer her questions he promptly answered very eagerly 'that's right! I picked the place for dinner to have tonight together. It's a nice place you'll like it.'

Bubbly kept gazing at his face quiet long to read his mind and didn't know what he's up to said in a very low voice 'I thought we'll enjoy the time together but you left all alone leaving me behind. You disappointed me you even have no business here!'

'Sorry babe! Didn't realize that! It won't happen again. Let's go now!'

'But where did you go? It's been a long time!

'Doesn't worry just walked around to locate good spot for you my love? It's a huge area takes time to come back.'

'Hmm! Bubbly kept quiet all along the way to the sea side restaurant. And they had a good lobster dinner with less talk and excitements. Lot of time she got suspicious about her husband doesn't know why. Why he came back here to spend his vacation time is it to make over their lost honeymoon or something else she doesn't know? Thought Bubbly 'she forgets to walk forward holding Rana's hands. It's dark all along the sea shore but nice! Lights are all around to give them a nice look at the beach area. All the big hotels were lined up on one side on the edge and on the opposite were the sea the big container to hold the huge water a cooling, soothing sight of the beauty and the feel of the heart on the opposite edge of the beach area.

Bubbly's mind has been gone far away in nowhere no home, no feel, no pain, no pining for anything. She looked forward sees nothing; she looked back from insight still sees nothing. Looking forward for nothing, looking back leaving nothing back. A state of the heart and the mind where there is no hope, no regret, no desire, nothing to ask for nothing to desire, nothing to hold from the past or from the present only a numbness in pain captured her heart and the soul to feel nothing but only a huge gap of emptiness. It's only water, the water and huge water it's a big sound of water in huge roaring in the huge waves up and down in a sequence of the rise and fall with a big sound loud enough to occupy the heart very hard. It's only a romanticism of a strange feel. Rana came closer to her put a hand on her shoulder very passionately but when she looked back to him his eyes seemed written with the same language in the letters of the same feel. As if they both formed a new form of humanity together one half to be the men everything else's left behind they love and lived, they hated and struggled for gain to put themselves together to be in happiness, in sorrows, in frustrations, in disappointments, and in fear and distress sometimes. At this spot by the cool sea they met as a couple with the same feel looking at each other into the eyes to see the same picture, same phenomenon of the feel in the in each other's eyes. They hold each other's hand and walked slowly hand in hand very far knowing no destinations in the darkness in the nice cool weather. The sound of the sea and the cool breeze was the only company.

For a little while they got lost into one another without knowing for what. All in sudden it's Rana who spoke out in the middle of all the nice and cool and the wearied sense to feel all around 'here! Here is the restaurant we came for! Dinner time' running out let's go to the other side.'

Looking into her husband's eyes bubbly answered 'yes, let's go'. But the very next moment couldn't resist her to ask 'do you come here very often?'

'No, why?' 'It seems you know all of these places. You look very familiar with this place.' Again by looking into his eyes.

'What makes you feel or think like that?' Rana is doubtful.

Bubbly looked at him with no sign of a doubt or suspicions but only wanted to know to say nothing in answer. Rana started to walk faster by holding her hand as a very hungry man for food by making her hungry too. They came back to life in hunger an urge to move forward. As they took a table in the sea side restaurant a beyara came forward to ask, 'how're you Sir? Have you just come today?

'Yes!' how are you?'

'Good Sir!' it's been too hot here! Now good. What should I bring for you tonight?'

'My entire favourites.'

'Yes of course! Does Apa moni have something to ask?'

'no. no. she's fine. Bring the drink now while we wait for food.'

Both of them kept quiet to drink the Fanta and the coke to look out the sea. Each of them definitely has his and hers own feel. They didn't appreciate anything here together since they landed. Bubbly doesn't know what her husband's thinking by looking out with or without feeling his present company his wife his life partner or an Apumoni like many others? The waiter definitely knows about all the "Apumoni's Rana brings here very often the ways he knows her husband. There is no doubt about that Rana comes here often when he is not available for her at the same time no doubt about that that her husband is cheating on her regardless. The way he behaves as she is a possession to him not his love or someone he cares about or even someone for whom he has at least a little respect or he cares about. Does the waiter know only Apumoni come here with her very husband or more or even a new one every time? And me?' thought bubbly 'am I the licensed one?' this kind of life women usually live to live or to survive only? Can a man survive like this? Food's served on the table lots of food items Rana started eating like a very hungry Lion doesn't even look like seeing

Or hearing anything. May be even having forgotten about her that tonight's company is his wife unlike his regular company's. Well, there may not even a difference between a girl friend or a regular company and the wife considered to be the life partner. Then why marriage? Does it means to be bondage a sacred bondage to keep in love and faith and dedications?

Civilizations and the civilized people are taking different new turns to change the society in order to make a new world of humans with different perspectives to bring a change. Ironically they are bringing the destructions to the society by allowing all bad and odds to let the goods or the values out of the human civilizations which make people or humans to live organized, disciplined, educated and valuable humans in human societies to live like humans in humanity and with human values. Loosing human values make us ugly in the soul, selfish robots taking every turn by commands on the pay. When humans lose humanity they turn either to monsters or to the manmade robots to ruin the natural phenomenon or the Nature and the natural qualities in human behavior while in the loss of educations in discipline. We thrive every day for new inventions, technologies, for better products, and fast mobility. In order to do that we consume artificial foods to become less capable for better living or more productivity. Now we are less energetic, less healthy, short living and less motivate. When the fuel is less the lamp burns to lit a light big in size and more in power to make more light to lit and diminish all almost at once in no much lasting. Love is diminishing so does friendships, marriages are hanging far to reach far for a person or for an individual in demands of the capabilities to run the family, that's how the marriages are breaking, societies loosing time to get and set together in friendships, peace and harmony to still keep the Humanity? A robotic man or woman developed by the artificial intelligence can thrive for a little to do as its job to make a less lives or basically can take care of an individual only as being commanded. No sharing no caring make no man, no family, no society, therefore no normal nationality, no balanced world for humanity in life as it should be in Nature with nurture, natural in nature, spontaneous, balanced with education, energetic fed by resources all natural, wishing normal in the capacity, achieving goals in set, producing products by utilizing resources natural, keeping and valuing nature and resources with educations in an environment where laws and restrictions make rules for oppressions making no monsters no robots mechanical. Of COURSE IF POSSIBLE FOR NOW! Coming so far in civilizing the civilizations. Civilized people and the civilizations are taking new turns to change the societies. A wife can stay home to share the responsibilities of the household to make a family doesn't really make any differences anymore. People move on with new outlooks, new perspectives, new concepts, and new points of views tends to make a difference, a change while at the same time losing the values, loosening the bondages and restrictions. People like to see the life the the way each person wants to see in leading it, in facilitating their choices and wishes. Time and the vast mobility changing people's outlook and the society loosing values every day on the happiness family members bring home by sharing and providing. That' how the heart broken women tend to leave all their expectations, desires of the heart while suffered so long to take a new turn by getting rid of all the distress and emotional weaknesses to move forward and by giving up what they used to expect as the other silly half of men the emotional women as depending nature and a home making tendencies for love and affections to move on with all that only provides for them to stay alive only!

Slowly Bubly started eating not like Rana but as slow as always. She doesn't care about being loved by someone anymore because that's not going to happen. It is hard to be loved or loving someone. It is unlikely now. By finishing up the food she asked right way by grabbing the drink 'is we going shopping now?

'Now? Rana fell from the sky said,' are you nuts? Its late night! We'll go tomorrow.' Rana's rude and bubbly' sarcastic said 'I thought you will buy me anything as you promised earlier?' Rana tried to be a little gentle now said, 'we can't always make things as we plan.'

'Yes, hard to rely on people now-a-days you won't know who's telling the truth who's not. Who's making promises to break up who's not? It's even more challenging to keep a relationship in a marriage. After pausing a bit Bubbly whispered,

'Rana!'

'What?'

'Are we happy? Bubbly looked him into the eyes to say with a deep sigh, 'you really don't know? May be you even don't care! Time and ambitions carried you away. I'm not the only woman in your life. Right?' Rana got silent very silent and wondered what to say in answer. Bubly proceeded again saying, 'I know you have no answer and nothing to say that's the truth. Some people marry for the money and the Princess is the bonus. Who won't love that it's all reality. Money makes people happy.' Rana got stunned and looked down to say, that's not true I love you now more than ever. Don't misjudge me darling! I really love you.'

'Then you don't have time for me in between your girl friends?' Bubbly continued 'you don't know whether you will carry on like this. Sometimes you pretend and you cheat on your own self! Your own feeling! That's why no baby yet because you don't know whether you will make a family with me or not. Your mind never was settled. You always had girls or girlfriends but you married me because of a reason.'

'Look honey! I really fell in love with you now I want a baby seriously to make us a family together. I was just wandering all these years. I am stable now. And I want you now. I love you it's you only now. I know I want you now. I love you! It's only your face deep inside portraying in depth to remain forever. No eraser can wipe it out.

'Yea, but still you can't get rid of your old life and habits, can't really get rid of old friends or the girl friends?

Rana saw tears in his wife's eyes which made him more emotional. He came back to her very passionately touched her by the shoulder to hold her by the other hand to say how much he loves her. Said,

'May be I needed riches but I loved the Princess.

I take your father as mine. A grace and bless when you are mine.'

Bubbly couldn't hold her laughter in the tears while Rana asked, 'how's the rhyme?

Bubbly's husband laughed loud to keep the environment cool and warm by making his wife to smile. Finally they loved each other truly and fully. Didn't even realize that they spent the whole night at the Beach the Sea shore with its cool to see the sun rise from the water up and up slowly to smile fully in the sky to make the world rise and shine while the couple here on the beach already raised from a nightmare to rise and shine in happiness with the beauty of the rising sun for a new beginning of their life.

THE END

STORY 5

Kamrunnessa/ 2018, march

Baby! How much I love you!

Shawpon has to hurry to get ready to go out for a walk on such a lovely day when everything is OK. He started to dress up really nice and Mom's has gone out too to see her Aunt. Dad's not home as usual like almost on all holidays. What a day for everyone every day! A family together with all the individuals together. Life's moving on with business, society and with the so called family which is no more a family. Rebecca brought the tea when he is already ready. Finally got a date with the girl he always dreamed of. He met her in so many events so many times to make the unknown to be known. First in an elevator when she got her attention by saying, 'I like the speed' as he entered with a full speed to catch the elevator. 2nd time she threw a smile a very nice smile towards him to say 'there is nothing wrong to talk' apparently in a cafeteria where they both sat together each at a different table for a cup of coffee but closer enough to see and talk a little with each other. Third time she handed in her mobile number to call saying 'nothing wrong to call.' Shawpon took a look at the piece of paper to figure out the phone no to call. Then again thought 'why would I call? Who the hell is she? But never saw her again anywhere anymore for a long time until finally the day he discovered her contact again on the little piece of paper to dial the number to find out at least who 'number is it. 'Hallo------?'

'Who's calling?'

'That's my question who are you?'

'Meaning how did this number in a circuit came in my pocket?'

'You mean someone gave you my number?'

'I recall your voice? Who are you?'

'The person you called that's who I'm.'

'Your name?'

How about you tell me your name first?

'I'm Shawpon?'

'That means dream. I'm not dreaming! Any ways why did you call?'

'Just to confirm the person who I thought could be you?'

'Do you know my name?'

'No! But I know a face very pretty sounds like you. Only a special face can possess a voice like that!'

'Hum----sounds like a lover have just fallen in love with an unknown! Any ways, how did I know you?

'We met several times first time in an elevator last time in a coffee shop where you left your phone no with me?

That' how I got it finding a circuit in my pocket with a no on it thought could be yours? Very nice of you! Otherwise how could I have your contact?

Hm……! Missed me right? Anamika twisted her eye brows with a question. She thought a little then to say again, 'yea…..! You had a long hair up to the shoulder right?'

Anamika thought a little then said, 'yea----- you have a long hair up to the shoulder right?'

'Really? You don't know me yet? Can't really recall? Let's meet again then. I'm free now -a –days just give me a date. When we can talk?' Shawpon joked a little. Anamika wonders said, 'So your business is to meet people?'

'What you mean?' Anamika sounds sweet and bitter at the same time.

"You sound angry. Sorry I didn't know that now-a –days girls offer to meet a man as a date?'

"What you thought? I'm on man power business? Was that was your expectations? Ok fine! Where you want to go? Which country?'

'Sorry lady! Never mind. I like to see you sound like there's a connection something got missed by mistake. Let's see if we know each other very well or no.'

'There you go!'Anamika hung up with no greetings at all.

The day they fixed to meet was a Friday again in a coffee shop very little and cosy with not many people. And the sweet chilly fall evening started to fall with the falling sun into the darkness of the night but no Anamika yet for Shawpon to give him at least a break in his boring days. So he started getting very curious about the phone number along with the girl sounds very mysterious as well. Sitting in a fast food restaurant waiting for someone doesn't give him anything to enjoy while on a mission to date a girl. He got bored enough to regret for his boring and charmless life. No life no excitements, no time spending with a girl friend no quality time to share with the family then either! Then what is the life for? Especially when you are young. Finished school going now for a job training programme really! Life' nothing but a burden to cut out to get through to get the other side whatever is the destiny waiting there. Dad says, life is not only a spending time. We need to have wisdoms and values to make our lives valuable to get valued by others as well as by the Divine above. Shawpon smiles some time by the thoughts and innocence of Mom and Dad had by thinking how they were fooling themselves all their lives.

Half an hour has been passed Shawpon started looking at people in the restaurant basically and naturally beautiful girls caught his attention. He keeps his wishes or buries his intentions to see and feel beautiful girls by browsing his eyes on all the pretty young girls under his eye sight to have one of them in his dreams at night. The dream girls are all actually his sweet nightmares to be dreamt of. He wondered at the blond young girl in the restaurant a little far from his table with a sexy blink of her beautiful eyes wearing blue mascara over the black eye shadow. She keeps talking with some other girls of her age most likely. None of those girls happens to cast an eye at him. 'That's ok! I am fine! I don't mind I don't die for a girl! Waiting for one only if doesn't' show up still its fine! I will dream of you hey! the blond girl! Tonight! Good to have you to view!

People came in people left still no sign of any girl happens to be looking for someone waiting for her. Nope! One or two single girls came in but didn't look like looking for anyone as Anamika for Shawpon. Shwapon's dream remains only a dream only if the mysterious girl Anamika doesn't show up. Thought Shawpon what if she came in and left when couldn't find him as not known by face? His face got covered by the thought to wonder at his own weakness for an unknown girl just known by the sweet voice? Sometimes a sweet voice attracts a person for an unknown sweetness of a voice sounds very familiar. It can happen only the mysterious divine defines to make a significant pair of love.

Anamika showed up just when I decided to leave and about to leave by the doors to leave which made an entrance for my date just on time to meet each other. What a co-incidence! Is this called love knowing someone without knowing? While we looked at each other in the eyes we felt like both made ourselves to recognize the soul mate of both of us. May be this is called destiny? Let's see where this love scene created or made coincidentally to be felt to take us to what destiny. As she arrived to say her common spoken words I guess this time with a naughty smile 'nothing wrong to go for a walk after'. And I looked at her to ask to make sure it's her. The ways she always utters those words says it's her own though 'who? You! Anamika! Finally!'

'What, you thought I won't come?

'I knew but was confused by the thought that you might not be able to recognize which one of all the girls you would be. That's all. My answer

'So now you know and what made you think that it's me? If you thought that you won't recognize my face?'

'May be my heart says?' I joked.

'O, yea? You mean to say you're in love with me? How about all those girls you were watching by now did you like any of them? Looked like you were done to leave?

'Come on, you sound good to say that means you like me.' Joking me again.

'O, yea! Love at first sight?' Anamika again, as taunting as always.

'No, love at those words 'nothing wrong to love someone.' We both laughed loud to clear the air to make us a friend together very well-known with no confusions no more. We asked each other the questions like 'how're you?', 'How's everything?' and the answers like 'Good! But very busy etc. after all after a long time of knowing and not knowing each other.

'I asked her again, 'are you always like that????

And it's her again answering by dancing her upper lids of the dark deep eyes to say only 'like what'?

I looked at her lovely ordinary face knows no bound of beauty naturally as if derived from the Nature each time differently as many time as we met with those words 'nothing wrong to -----'. But said me only 'never mind! To her question for now but continued in mind thinking like who are you? A ghost? A stranger? Might be! but not ordinary at least to me. And asked her instead 'where do you live?'

She answered 'in a strange world to wonder!' she started laughing loud again and I said 'you're a ghost may be? Where do you live?'

She said, 'let's see'! You and me together as I said before 'nothing wrong to go out for a walk.' This episode of a love and lovers prelude in a rubbish teenage talk ended up here to start again while on a walk.

Hot summer evening very close to the sunset time. Anamika is on a pair of leather sandals with a pair of blue jeans and a sky blue cotton kurti apparently good for summer time. Shawpon looked at her short straight cut silky hair looking very nice. He is not very much in love with her to watch all her beauty at her face, in her eyes, on the cheeks or lips. He's only feeling good in a company together with her. They both din not talk ever before with each other even at least to know each other. Looks like none of them cares for each other. For Shawpon only the curiosity brought him here to see the unknown from a close look as she always appears all in a sudden very randomly to throw a few words repeatedly the same as touching the heart with no touch Shawpon still is not in love or a relationship seeking young man perhaps neither does Anamika. Shawpon follows a day to day routine and gets bored most of the time gets upset with his parents or with the only sister who doesn't bother to talk a little or to share a little bit of time together with the only brother. 'What a misery! What a life!' Anamika appeared time to time to give him a knock after all. Now either he is looking for a company with her or hoping to live a life with some company. His boy friends are not happy with him at all because he's considered to be an egocentric. He goes by the routine and beyond with a heart and mind to regret for something or pining for something missing. Anamika fulfilled his missing spot with a hope a hope of getting a company when he is empty or upset to regret at least by hearing the odds in their lives.

They walked quite a bit with no words at all. Shawpon got lost in his own thoughts and doesn't what was his female company up to. All in a sudden it's her said again to break the silence by saying 'how are you doing today?'

'I'm good! Very glad to see you again I hope this time I'll get some more to know about you.' Shawpon got surprised to answer at the same time while all in a sudden the same way she always surprises him by asking a simple question like that then smiled to say, 'I hope we'll be fine when we get there. I mean your home. I hope you're not a fairy.'

'So you know how to make jokes?' saying this Anamika smiled too.

'May be!' his cold answer doesn't show any enthusiasm to feel the time they are sharing together. Anamika looked back at his face to see more to say like strange world! Strange things! And people! And all the events all around!

'Now, what you think?' asked Anamika finally

'I think it's true we both are seeking something which is missing in our world now. Right?'

'How do you know? Asked Anamika and answered as well 'the way you know?'

They both looked at each other in the eyes stopped for a sec might be to look into one another's eyes to read some thoughts very common? Anamika hurried suddenly by saying 'I have to go.' And hurried to disappear very quickly for her home or no home.' thought Shawpon with no curiosity or questions to lose company so suddenly without any sign or preparation to take a leave with at least a tiny bit of courtesy as two social animals always do after all. But he did not miss to say 'good by' to his company along the way when all in a sudden when the female partner just left him by taking another way for her destiny on the narrow paths of the regular neibourhood as she changed the direction to another narrower one by leaving a very shallow hope for him to make a company out of her in the desire of his heart. He took a rickshaw then without knowing that Anamika headed towards her home on her feet only. Such is life different paths for different people so does the destiny.

Shawpon reached home by 8.00 pm while expecting no one at home. He also finished his dinner on the way home. Mom talked to him at noon time over the phone said will be home late at night as always. He didn't see dad for more than a week was told that going overseas on a business trip. The only sister showed up at the door to open for him. By seeing her Shawpon felt himself a little at home. Sister Minu went straight back to her seat to watch the movie right after opening the door for him by making a face like did a big favour for her brother at this time. No one expressed a word to each other. When we see or feel a place crowded or chaotic we expect some peace and tranquility but if the tranquility takes back the life in a family in silence or in an environment with no soul at all in the name of peace then what to expect from each other in the family to make a family together? Thought Shawpon looking at the only sister in his life and most of the time only one member in the house to talk in the soulless family where everyone is busy and mind their own business as if getting involved in sharing time and the life with the family members will make the life more lifeless. So it's better to be busy in business meaning own business by forgetting about all of the life or the current world where sharing and caring make nothing but all chaos; debates; conflicts of interest and choices; ideas to hamper the peace of mind as well as the peace in life. So in order to keep the peace in life we have to go speechless by taking away the soul from our life which is in a way sacrificing something valuable to restore the life itself. Sacrificing the soul from the self by keeping the mind only for good for the survival can be the life for now.

Moving forward that's only matter's for survival but how about very soon when the life cries out in demand of its inevitable other part which is none but the soul itself then the survival of the life might get shorter as heart and soul go together for living in the body. The way the whole universe is coming into a device called a little cell phone our whole world is also being captured in our head parallel to hold a lot into the head to forget the heart to feel. Feeless and the soulless lives together paving the ways to make us robotic to get us to the destructions may be to make a shorter existing human world as we believed to be making life by wishing, feeling and longing.

Shawpon asks his sister sometimes 'don't you get suffocated sometimes living like this?' while his sister asks only 'like what?' Shawpon gets confused to answer Minu's question with a question 'can you divide your days in the consisting items of to do things in comparison to feel things or to enjoy things?'

'I don't care!' Minu answers like a teenage damn care girl as always to leave the sight of his stupid brother neither does want to talk even.

Shawpon knows what to do now. Definitely will browse the face book account to comment and recommend with a great passion after all! At least some life after all! People are coming in contact through face book. The small world making the life smaller as well as easy to access all together on one small device. What's wrong about it! He pays thanks to God for having at least some life from face booking after all. Still his peace loving mind doesn't allow much from the face booking like commenting recommending as the basic comments make him mad sometimes. No life from live lives around at all! What a life after all! In a minute he felt himself very hungry and when opened the refrigerator he could find nothing but breads and butter along with some donuts, left over some cake pieces, cheese, jam and jelly and all the beverages. God! When will the weekend come to have a real dinner on the table? Busy life busy mind, with some cold hearts into the ticking clocks. By slamming the doors of the refrigerator he picked up some fruits from the dining table to go to his bed room just like his sister as rude as a while ago. At least no more school to study at night. Good to get a break between the study period and the working life. A sound sleep is more than all the valuable things to get at night after all frustrations, failures and boring activities throughout the day. He laid his head on the pillow and the feet on the bed to be rested after a long day of frustration only. All day to learn things for a client catching company makes him very tired and down spirited fearing how to convince a client with some good impressive words with some lies among them very carefully to make him more tired in the business after all. Constant talking with constant repetitions makes feel like a broken record to play repeatedly.

No money yet! Spent a lot of money for getting the bachelor degree and now for the job training programmes makes him putting even a bigger burden on his parent's shoulder unfortunately still working to rule the family for reality. He feels like people work more study more all the life for earning for living by working more for less and by studying more than enough by spending money. In both cases time and energy get spent more for less in life to make a real life in enough space of life. Means pain is more than gain. Having life is less spending life in time and energy spent is more. Again this way also life is always less and short in comparison to all our efforts with hope.

After taking a shower Shawpon threw himself in bed to have a sound sleep for the rest of the night at least to have a good time in sleep when no feel in sleep a senseless sense dumped deep into a good night long sleep can be considered a silence in an unknown world where the life sometimes prevails in dreams once again. Waking up in the day light brings back all the realities crystal clear hard and harsh with an open eye. Dreaming in dark is a sweet reflection of the life we face in the day time while we forget about all the realities we face day to day basis. Good to forget all of the realities by dumping ourselves into a deep dark period of time with closed eyes in an unknown passion with no emotions sometimes only a fear when it's a bad dream knowing not that it's not real. Therefore, he looked set the time on the front wall setting the alarm, took the blanket spreading all over him to make himself cosy and comfortable to remember his early ages in the sweet and passionate care of the mother. There is nothing much to feel now other than feeling himself worthless, empty or might even be a pain on the parents. Still one thing for sure to remember to worry 'is mom home yet?' But very slowly he's is getting rid of worrying about his mom when she is late for home. At least he has gotten the faith in time and place along with the destiny which can't be that much cruel to take away all from his life. Early in the morning he would see his mom sleeping in her bed in her room sometimes on the couch outside the room to get assured with some enthusiasm to set forth for work only an irony of life now as only work makes life now- a- days to feed the body to work again to continue the living not the life as the souls die very time every moment in everyday life. He thinks like we are now only working machines to work out our own life which no longer a life making process by some work needed for it. Sometimes in the morning he thinks about his early age when used to fight with the little sister when Mom was getting them ready for school while making breakfast for them, finding clothes and shoes for them, watching them for brushing their teeth properly. When he was in high school most of the morning he couldn't find his socks or his pants as Minu put them in the laundry machine to be washed with her clothes and that led the two to fight and shouts to wake up Dad to join the chorus of the chaos. Now he regrets for the chorus of the chaos as the warmth of life in a foolish fight in the family. The sharing along with the caring for each other along with all the madness in the warmth of some emotions bitter for better associated with some togetherness to make a family. They are still together but feel like someone or something stole the charm of life in passions and emotions by wiping off the sentiments in senses. They are still living together but individually minding his or hers own business. Living together like this in a family while each one's mind always occupied with one's own business can't really make a family where there is not much bondage left for them with each other. Shawpon thinks like very soon caring in the family will be only on sharing like expenses with exchanges.

It's been a long time since Shawpon saw Anamika anywhere anymore at all! What happened? She lost her magic or what? He started worried and wonder at the same time wondered by thinking how soon she lost her interest in him worried because he got afraid that his dream girl decided not to see him anymore. But why? Doesn't she find the same reason to find him? Or it was her only an intention to surprise some one by saying something little but a more to the person whom she likes to be enchanted by saying a few words of fun by showing from nowhere all in a sudden. Has she forgotten him totally or she's just like that a spark to sparkle all in a sudden to disappear by enlighten the heart of the man she wished to win for a moment to forget in the next moment. Still Shawpon hoped to see her again. Deep down in his heart the magic words of her charm portrait a wish to see her again after each meeting. And it happened she did appear from anywhere to charm him again and again a few times. Shawpon started feeling empty by the thought that he might not see her again. Has she forgotten her? Thought Shawpon again thought the very next time 'it can't be!' She's a fairy to him she will come to wish him some good time in no time in the long space of frozen time with frozen hearts. Last time he met her at the fast food restaurant where he is sitting now as awaited for a long time. Last time she appeared and disappeared without showing him her home. He started thinking about her like 'who is she? Where is she from? Where she comes from to surprise her all the time? And why she disappeared last time before her home comes by? Who is she and why appears and disappears all in a sudden and why is he recalling her so badly? What's the connection here? He's thinking about her recalling her presence while she's not around, no phone call, no dates at all?

When he met Anamika Shawpon was floating around with no job a mission for life but now he really needs a company to share a quality time together sometimes. He asks himself sometimes 'does the egocentric Shawpon needs a company a female mate or so called soul mate for the soul?' 'Does he really want a female friend like Anamika whereas he never could maintain his friendship with all his school friends for some reasons same thing with the college friends and the university friends. He always kept himself away from all his friends which made him aloof all his student life. For being a good boy kept him away from all and made him aloof from the society. He doesn't smoke, he doesn't go to a club with friends on Friday nights and he can't pick a girl for the night. He is non-social, he's lonely and he is also uncultured within himself with his own thoughts and beliefs apparently are wearied to all. He hardly keeps his soul at work while works just wishing to leave the work behind at the work place where it belongs and only there he shakes all the work done for the day by shaking them off hard enough so that they don't bother him again when he is out of work. He leaves his work every weekday evening at the work place by cutting off the soul from the work he was given to finish to set forth rapidly for home to rest his soul in peace to be alive in life with some pleasure of the heart with the family. His passions make emotions at home finally. Minu's busy working 9 to 5, chatting with the boyfriend on the phone all evening and night before going to bed and very soon going to marry the rubbish robotic Robin. Finally Shawpon going to see his parents finally on the week-ends to consume his entire Dad's lectures with constipating hard to consume or to let it out. And it's only the Mom finally on the week-ends for her baby boy with some motherly love. The only entertainment he gets is going for playing soccer. Some weekends are lucky to go out for watching a movie. At least these ways he can be in touch with his friends the same friends forever who never will leave him considering an insane or boyish or foolish after all.

Finally, now after all Shawpon can see himself as an adult who has a job to do who can marry a girl to love and to raise a family but can't get rid of all of her complexities. He likes to live in a family but gets himself dipped into his isolated world of imaginations where there exists nothing but an emptiness of a world where he can't land with a hope to accomplish something he doesn't know what love or family or a good career. Actually he's a good young man capable of avoiding indecent conducts or desires, foul social competitions, conflicts of interests with an open mind, as well as superstitions and greed. He is neither stubborn nor overflowing feeling to achieve desperately or to destroy in anger or frustrations. Therefore he doesn't fight for his interests to distress himself along with all his surrounding people. While all his good characteristics make him a wise young man his friend circles consider him to be foolish or a fool instead of making their senses to make him a matured man. Basically he is an easy going kind of man floating on his own wings of time to do things easily only with his instincts in her daily life or at work. He pines but doesn't die for wishes or achievements. He's easy and nice never to hurt anyone's feelings also try not to his own to regret for hurting someone's feelings or his own again by insisting to get something out of reach or far reaching.

Still a man after all in this nice evening after work didn't know why he's started to see Anamika and why she appeared in his life and has she started to appear in Shawpon view, why he has started to miss her recently it might be because of her long absence and also he's free of worries now while working and longing for a company after work to share and care the time and the company of a lovely friend or a girlfriend after all! Will she show up again to surprise him to enter his little life again to be permanent? Will she read his mind with the surprise of his wish or his feeling? Does she feels the same he feels? No chance! Let's see!

'How are you man?' there she goes! All in a sudden she really showed up to surprise Shawpon exactly on the same spot on the road where Shawpon was expecting her. She shook him off with her sudden appearance and her loud regular vocal surprise. Oops! Almost was going to be hit by the rickshaw! O, Lord! What an absent mind! The rickshaw driver reminded loud to be careful on the roads while walking or passing said 'it's a very busy street in the city. Be careful! Sir!' Shawpon got very surprised by looking around it looks like the place when Anamika brought him walking with him last time. Why she left all in a sudden without even showing her place. He kept standing in a corner of the island from where she left last time to see him again next time. Shawpon wondered at this kind of co-in-incidence every time she shows up just right at the moment he recalls her or feels for her or even expects to see her badly even wonders why he keeps thinking about her all the time to miss her a lot. No one can answer to this kind of madness people sometimes keep inside something for someone called love? Shawpon started to wonder at his feeling for her considered to

'Love' for someone. He loves his home with his mom and Dan and a little sister happens to be wearied only to him. His heart and soul is his home together with his family. His own place own family he grew within into the heart and soul of it. It's his old place with all love and passions. Loving someone as a life partner later in life is called love or pining for something new and different to progress for the rest of the life or to continue in regenerations is making a family with children after out of love. His delusional mind or his dreams giving him the visions of someone who can be his future love for life. But the Corner room in his house is still the same. All remains the same as always the house, the furniture, people, or the whole family remain the same as long they are not departed or moved away. A family breaks apart or the members move away but the ties remain still the same but with the absence of the loving people the home remains empty of a soul sometimes pining, dying sometimes or feels empty to be fulfilled. Shawpon doesn't know why he wonders without an aim or keeping no memories of anyone in his life to love that person beside his family. He stopped at the same spot in the neighbourhood from where Anamika departed to locate her residence nearby but left very mysteriously without pointing it out. Might have been to remember her in curiosity or in doubt. Why almighty God created the creature called human with clay to breath in the air as the soul to wander around to and fro to no destination at all? Of course to the unknown the final destination and hereafter to wonder or to live an eternal life? At this point he remained standing still quite a bit to feel, to find the girl called Anamika as if only Anamika feels his presence to his pining soul from wondering to find the truth as he felt like he needs her to go along the way of life and beyond.

The spot where he is standing now is an island a triangle on two opposite corners pointing two ways of the neighbourhood by the lined up series of houses facing one another the small side corner also faced some houses as well. Shawpon looked all around where there's no clue which house on which side or in which corner can be his dream girl residing by landing from her own world of wonder? Houses are all around lining up with each other shoulder to shoulder all together as brothers or soldiers of residential monuments to hold people in their wombs to shelter them with love and care once and for all. The pointing corner of the island pointing an unit very inviting with a nice and little garden of flowers but in some different big flower pots and with three palm trees in three different big flower pots.

For some reason Shawpon got stuck at the same spot to move out of the place while unable to step out from the pointy point in the corner of the island as if feels like his obscure beloved lives in that house particularly. He already intended to knock at the door by going near to the house to only her who is named with a name or no name at all. It took a long time to think with hesitations and confusions to knock at the door and while all in a sudden he gathered the courage to knock finally to knock no matter what, the door opened by itself with a lovely surprise in the same lovely voice saying very mysteriously as always 'hello! Is it me you looking for? I can see in your eyes, I can see in your smile!' and our hero turned around to his wonder to wonder at the girl he has been dreaming of to laugh loud at the same time both together to their joy. Without a date a destiny made them see each other on a day with no time fixed no preparations and for Shawpon with no clue of the place where his girl could be when his heart badly looking for her to see his wonder girl in its time and space for what reason not known yet. Anamika got very loud said, 'Hei! You handsome! What made you come here? How did you even know that I live here?'

Shawpon joked now saying 'I can tell where you can be. You can hide you can run but I still know where to find.

'Finding love or just a company? Anamika knows how to make fun too!

'Both make the same meaning which one you prefer?' Shawpon twisted his eyes might be for the first time with a girl other than his sister by answering the same way Anamika asked.

'M—m—moo ho! I separate them for now I choose only the company but can't confirm yet! Suppose like this way if destiny makes us to see each other again?'

'You mean mysteriously? As always as you are! Um---Hm! ----! Now you know my address though?'

'You're clever and playful. Are you always like this?' asked Ameer.

Life itself is a mystery why don't we play a bit? Anamika got naughty again.

'To beat life or us meaning ourselves'? Shawpon's no less tricky now.

They both decided to go for a walk. All the way Anamica talked was about her school, her mom, her brother and her sister explaining how boring the life is and how irritable her brother and her sister. She kept going like this 'I hate when sis takes all the advantages. She takes mom's car everywhere, she gets the entire good boyfriend's, she goes party's throws parties at home, she goes shopping, money and mom all on demand for her whenever she wants. She is the one doing well in school while enjoying the life at the same time. She doesn't care much about anyone else. You know what? She is the survivor in this world now being selfish minding her own business. It's good to be bold and happy I wish!'

I asked 'and what do you do? What kind of time you spend for life for what?'

Anamika put up her lower lip to answer with a deep sigh 'I'm all dumb! And stupid to care all about the family, my mom and my sister whereas only mom cares about me no one else!'

As Anamica kept complaining about her life in no life by blaming all her family members by being forgotten about my presence or even my existence to be passionate about the moment when I'm here her boyfriend or just only a friend to give at least a thought on going for a cup of tea or coffee by stopping at a coffee shop! So he thought to stop her going that much upset especially when his friend is here for her after a longing to see her only? But he is not that much boring to make his girl to forget totally about her at least He put some mercy on both of them while none of them much happy in their family life as right at the right moment. Anamica stopped to ask about the same by pulling herself together to say' let's go for a cup of coffee!' by putting her loud voice down to walk forward with an spirit at least to cool her down after all by seeing herself in a mood definitely foolish to say, 'sorry!' Shawpon looked into her eyes to console said 'it's ok! I don't mind. Life is more or less the same for all.' And thought at the same time with a sigh inside Anamika is irritated and upset while at the same time I'm empty. Both of us are upset about the family. We can make a good couple together at least by giving some company to each other.' They walked towards the main street. For a moment Shawpon got very absent minded thinking by holding her hand very passionately to reach half way on the road towards the main street thinking, 'what a co-incident! No wonder he got someone unexpectedly while he is so lonely to make a couple just like that?' Anamika still is very quiet might have lost her voice to the complaints very irritably! After all finally made a friend at least coincidentally to cool her down after all hoping to be a new beginning of a new life by making a friend at least! How about Shawpon? Does he have a feeling for me?' thought Anamika thoughtfully as life makes no easy solutions? 'How about his family is it also like mine or even worse? Are we going to walk the roads of life together like this?'

They took tea together with some snacks. Anamika opened her mouth first 'what do you do in your spare time?'

'Wonder around to look for a company just like this?'

'Come on be serious!'

'I'm serious right now as my intention got fulfilled by your company. Lucky me!' looking at her again said Ameer passionately 'really I like you. You could be my best friend and a very good company in my loneliness!'

'Why don't people like you buy some company from the friendly company shop?'

"Really?' they sale companionships? Are you sure?' Shawpon started joking the same way Anamika did.

'Yes! There are stores like 'Female company', 'male company', Dog company shop', 'Cats company shop" etc.

How about named like, 'Looking for a company? We sell all male, female, boys and girls and all including cats and dogs'

Very funny! They both started to laugh loud to empty their bosoms of the soul. But Shawpon got serious again said,' I'm serious now. Right now my intention got fulfilled by getting you as my dear friend so no regret for getting a company. Looking at Anamika into her eyes said again 'really, I like you. You could be my best friend, a good company in my loneliness.'

'Lonely? Are you lonely? Anamika exclaimed to her astonishment' you want me to believe that you are all alone in these days when the world has gotten the internet, Facebook as a social media and--- also live girls around as visual as real behind the screen only can be felt even though just can't be touched. Doesn't matter while you are not ready yet to make real relationships with responsibilities.'

'Yes I don't like fake relationships and face booking. I don't believe in making and breaking relationships at the same times hundred times. 'I'm a good boy don't you want to believe my words?

'O well!' Anamika made her face by showing up her lower lip.

'Seriously! I go to work and come back home on time liking my family over everything else. If my sister is busy I watch T.V. a bit then go to bed like a good mama boy. I miss my Mom and Dad. Only they can make my time some times on week-ends. What a life! He sighed a bit which miraculously also touched Anamika's heart with some inside to share with right person.

'Me too! I'm not happy also I don't like my Mom work that hard day and night. We need her and she needs some rest. Do you know why the life is so hard? Little sister gets all advantages of Mom's company. She goes shopping on week-ends with Mom and buy things for her. On the other hand I stay at home very willingly to finish all the unfinished jobs usually done by Mom. I know all Mothers love their children equally!

Shawpon hesitated a bit to ask 'where is your Dad?' Anamika kept quiet didn't answer at all moreover the question made her mood down to keep quiet. That night Shawpon came home with enormous guilt for hurting Anamika's feeling but inside felt a little bit of relaxation by sharing his feelings with someone like Anamika he believes and feels the same way as both of their lives are empty one way or other.

Minu's matrimony got fixed and she is very busy shopping for her own wedding. Sometimes she let Shawpon to buy things also for her wedding parties. Sometimes Anamika helps Shawpon also to buy things for Minu. Shawpon thinks sometimes this way he's practicing shopping for his own wedding in near future sooner or later. What a day everyone is minding fulfilling their own business only!

Long time! Ameer didn't see Anamika. He doesn't know why she dips into water sometimes or hide herself behind an invisible veil not to be seen when she doesn't intend to. Again suddenly she showed up but this time after almost three months after joining Minu's wedding party with full heart. She is as strange as always said at the door as always' nothing wrong to pay a visit!' of course with a nice smile this time also. And Shawpon counted this is for the fifth time. She keeps quiet for a long time to talk then to talk to make a joke only once or more suddenly. Sometimes unhappy and lost people remain quiet to dip into their mind which apparently empty to roam around in emptiness to find something which could be a spark of some life to diminish their pain in pain or no pain to deliver a joke to the folk to be socialized or to refresh the air. Shawpon thought a lot about her. She is thoughtful, she is funny, she is friendly and also helpful to people. Both Shawpon and Anamika are seeing each other quite often without realizing that they both started feeling for each other. Now Shawpon realizes why he thinks about her when she is not around and why he counts each time she shows up for a good number. He called her many times during the last three months. She is here now in his house smiling, laughing, joking, talking loud with him and nobody else because nobody's here today. Mom and dad both are busy at work. So she's a delicious glass of water in the desert. They both fulfilled each other's company with a passion without realizing that they are coming closer to one another without noticing or realizing that they are falling in love with each other. There was no notifications for love for them, no preparations and no dreams. It's all reality not a fiction. They don't know that they miss each other they don't realize that they both stay in each other's hearts without a remembrance which remains seeing each other or not seeing.

Anamika's getting more and more calm and quiet every day after starting a job. Both sisters are very concerned about their family and the mom. The poor mom has been all alone in the struggle of life with two daughters since they were born. Anamika

And Anushka both are similarly concerned about the mom for the sake of their family and life and reality only Anushka a difference. She works hard cares much but still likes to enjoy the life with passion and devotions. She goes shopping buys her favourite things by saving some money from the household expenses kept in mothers care. On the other hand Aanamika is mainly concerned about their future, their mom and all together their life. Life is her realizations of reality, her sacrifice for the family and her devotion to the mom and the whole family. Anamika breathes in life in love only in Shawpon's Company. She puts all her funny and serious concerns gathered from the news, from a movie or from other shows on TV or from real jokes in reality while in touch of human conducts. She enjoys a free time together with Ameer in talking, sharing, laughing or even by pinching each other. Both of them are working and remaining busy more than earlier. In Anamika's home all three are gone for work every day. And in Shawpon's since the evening till the bed time at night. Mom and dad meet each other sometimes at a place after work like a market place or a plaza or in a restaurant to relax before going home. Minu is better off with her new life at home with her husband Rafa. They look happy so do the parents. Now their only worries are Shawpon. If he gets married to settle down then the parents get a relief. They both need some time to relax after all. At least at last in the closing chapters of their married life with two children by raising them up with full devotions and concentration with a lot of sacrifices as the parents do. Life seems nothing but struggles all the ways down till the end. At the same time the completive Shawpon neither rely on destiny nor on the life itself and who doesn't even look for finding the true meaning of life. He even sometimes drives Anamika mad by asking such questions like 'why is life? Why we live and why we die? First of all why even we're on earth which is not a damn fun to have or to have some meaning to live. Did we even ask for a place to live? Why it is life and our existence to struggle for a living?'

Anamika on the contrary would say 'then would you be happy to sit still and relax watching T.V all day long?'

'What do you mean?'

'Wisdom Man! Its wisdom we try to carry on all through the life experiences. We are Humans not animals but still in contrary they show us humanity or decency in contrary to barbarism without an education.' Anamika's answer.

'Why there are contrary situations and contradictions in behaviours in Nature as well as within us? Why making the fire and the water at the same time to put out the other? Why good and evil existing side by side all the time. Why making life hard to make it easy at the same time?' Shawpon gets irritated.

'O.k. Boss not much thinking relax! We still live still make a life within all among all as life prevails. Bringing a new born on earth is precious while death is painful but when we believe arrivals and the departure' are from and to the same destiny then we consider ourselves nothing but all temporary guests on the earth from the Devine source. So we don't make life hard by thinking too much. We carry on relying on the divine as blessed as we can be.' Wise Anamika again.

'Aright! Now who's the Boss here?' both Shawpon and Anamika laughed loud to set forth for a walk as Shawpon mentioned that they met each other after a long time and also it is nice very outside. At this point Shawpon also whispered into Anamika's ears saying, 'we need to live together forever!'

'You mean to marry?' asked Anamika very hasty.

'Why not? Don't you like me?'

'It's not that!'

'Then what?' Shawpon insisting.

'I thought you don't love me.' Anamika got naughty again.

'Come on! I'll talk to my parent's tonight.'

Anamika just said "OK!" in answer. Only destiny knows the destiny of love.

Two years later

A summer night. Shawpon is waiting on the neighbourhood it's like taking a walk in the nice summer breeze. He's not alone his wife is with him too holding his hands very tight in love. They look a very happy couple together in love. It's good to see couples in the city in love with each other while not in love with disco, clubs, or theatres all around. Definitely they make an example for a lot in this time of fast moving human activities or the daily life to carry on all the duties to be done very fast on the fast moving life vehicle by leaving the life itself behind or even sometimes by losing it at every turn to take for duties and on the platforms of the daily performances to perform only to carry on the life with no feel, no regrets, burying the love deep down or even with no love at all! Of course the time is of the progress of the human civilizations. They took a small table to sit to have some food at least for dinner. The young lady looks pretty most likely newly married still very romantic looking as a couple. Shawpon ordered some food a bowl of chicken mushroom soup and his wife ordered a piece of salmon. The couple looks happy as continuing some conversations at ease with a nice smile on each. The lady asked all in a sudden 'do I look beautiful?' and her husband got very surprised to ask 'Yea! Why? You're always beautiful."

'But you didn't say anything!' the lovely young lady replied like a complain to be ignored.

'I always do darling! You're always beautiful!'

'Really?

'Really now take your food. I'm going to the restroom. He left her for the restroom.

It's a bit long way to the restroom as people were making quite a bit long line up waiting for the restroom. Shawpon got upset still five people ahead! Oh! God! Suddenly at his whispering the very front lady looked back to comment on his concern to add some of her own. But alas! What a co-incidence! It was no one but Anamika same way she exclaimed too 'You? How come?'

'Global world!' Shawpon didn't show his surprise remained as normal as always. It's Anamika's question first 'where you have been? Did you just disappear without a notice?'

'No'! I was just--------there. You go it's your turn. Shawpon pointed her to the washroom.

'What took so long? Asked his wife when came back.

"Big line up what else?

Answered Shawpon while taking his sit back.

'I see! Thank God! At least you didn't sleep after all! They both looked onto each other's eyes to laugh a loud. A friendly behaviour in a relationship. Shawpon thought about Anamika instantly thinking how these two ladies possess same kind of personalities! Anamika used to joke like that sometimes. Are all the women like that? Definitely not.

Dipika's talking nonstop all about her former life, her school friends, family and schools and school life. Her nice tales tell a lot stories from the school life which are more or less the same for almost all the people. Childhood or the young age memories are always all the sweet memories of life. Recalling the old memories is valuing life. Dipika did not forget the teacher the English teacher used to recite poetry very nicely from the heart. She didn't forget the math teacher used to say, 'solve this math or I'll pull your ears to smile with a mild threat after all! She recalled her friend in grade five used to boast about her possession of a big showcase full of chocolates her dad used to buy to fill that big furniture for her pleasure. She loves to make fun of her childhood classmates dreaming of a showcase full of chocolates. Dipika is nice Shawpon likes her attitudes she is funny and childlike and less thoughtful while Anamika was more interesting by putting her funny stories along with some thoughtful concerns time to time. They both are live, both like to make fun and telling jokes. They are good companies for anyone. They both share their taunting talk talky tendency. But now Shawpon is thinking why both ladies in his life resemble one another a lot? Is this destiny which is pointing at him to remember someone whom he left behind without a thought? Or even denied his own self by denying what he actually desired to have? Life is full of irony. While people like him very tiny at heart to hold onto something very small like a flake of life like only a company from the opposite sex to have some love and concerns to live a big life in the boundless bounty of thoughts and imaginations in the mind associated with heart which is actually as the sky. But being practical and limited is controlling a self-getting lost. Mind-set is important to live a normal life as a normal person in the human society as an inevitable human after all.

Dipika still was talking while Shawpon left the sit in search of Aanamika to come back in a very short time and didn't talk for a long time to say anything at his arrival again. 'Why he's so restless?' thought Dipika 'O, Well! Might have gone to the restroom again!' Azmol finished eating his food very quick, talked nice and loved his wife all in a hurry to leave as early as possible. Said to Dipika 'Let's go! We're getting late. Let's get up and set up for home.' At the same time looked around to find his former love in present sitting at any of the tables.

Finally got out of the place by pushing the heavy front doors for the way out. And Anamika was there outside stopping or waiting for who l didn't know. They looked at each as a much known person after all. Before Shawpon said something Dipika asked with curiosity 'did you know each other before?'

'Yea we were neighbours for quiet long a time.' Shawpon answered pretending very normal with some fear inside to be caught as the lady's appearance happens to be his finance. Before he says anything anymore Anamika said very promptly 'we were good know neighbours to each other living in the houses face to face but didn't get much to talk.'

'I see!' Dipika's short and normal answer.

'Here, my husband Rakib. We just got married not long ago.'

Shawpon shakes hands with Rakib saying, 'what a pleasant surprise two birds in one kill!' all laughed together.

No one seemed care much about their past. Time passes for people to move on with the new whatever comes or whoever suits for the life as a life partner or as companions in different sectors of life personal, family life, work places or anywhere else's. It's all situations time place or destiny may be? Time also changes and covers all the tensions, failures in life, all the discrepancies like a cliff with all the ups and downs in the heart ever healing when it is hurt.

Four people in two different couples no one could tell who took for who in the chain of a holy matrimony. Among both sets of the married couple's two persons form each couple named with the starting letter a not happy totally the ways they look? It's my understanding that Shawpon and Anamika could have been better off by marrying each other. Dipika looks very happy too by the side of Shawpon the person who loved the lady now happens to be Rakib's wife! The old love secret is not known to the present partners of both of the couples. They all look happy that should matter only now in the present without looking for a clue to find out are all of them are happy or not. Happiness is one's own perception and when it is mutual it's a touch of heaven on earth I believe.

All four of them were standing there at the same spot for near about 20 min finding one another's identity. Who's from which part of the city or the town, got education from which university, schools or colleges, are they working and where etc. Dipika noticed that her husband and Anamika talking very passionately as they both found their old friends looking very close to each other even after a long time. At some point Shawpon asked Anamika, 'how's Mom and the sister? And where are they? Is she still the same or got married also just like you?'

'She's matured enough now got two children one boy and one girl.'

'Happy?' asked Shawpon again.

'O yea!'

Anamika also asked about Shapon' sister Sohani if she is good. Happy with her husband or not etc.

Answering to Rakibs wife looks making him very happy while in a joking mood as if they know each other for a long time. The color of happiness made Dipika's cheeks has gone bright at once. She kept looking at Anamika's happy face as talking very happily with her husband as if opening up her whole heart to a very well-known friend even more than that. She kept starring at Anamika looking as happy as talking like opening up her whole heart to a very well-known old friend. Shawpon 'always in hurry at home and outside never like that to talk and sit to relax by pouring out the heart to her. Always busy doing this doing that as something will be missing from home if he doesn't do that little job on the other hand Dipika fears to lose the value of the emotions in a relationship. She tends to believe that a little or a little longer time together as a husband and wife or as a couple they need to spend some time in love and romance. Well! This is reality what can you do? Being in love before marriage is different without the harsh reality of all the work and responsibilities after marriage when making a family by doing all. If Anamika would have been married to Shawpon they both would have been in the situation like this. Any ways, still Dipika can't resist her jealous mind seeing them so happy, spontaneous and full of heart whereas very dutiful to the wife to take a good care of her. Is it only making a family together? Only maintaining a relationship for being a couple as a husband and wife? Is there any love in her husband's heart to talk like that with me?' Dipika felt that she is more like a responsibility than a relation heart to heart. Dipika started feeling sick to hurry for home. She doesn't know for how long she was watching her husband by starring in a motion. Finally spoke out 'Let's go I'm tired!' But alas! The answer from Shawpon is very negative for her in her this kind of realizations as to be answered by Shawpon 'little bit, lets finish up the conversation here------. The way Shawpon stopped Dipika hurt her a lot because she couldn't finish what she wanted to say. Now Dipika herself stopped him what he wanted to finish. She got emotional at once to ask him with her red cheeks said 'conversation about what?' Shawpon got surprised and ashamed at the same time in front of Anamika at her sudden change of the mood he looked back to see his newlywed wife's angry eyes with a blush on the cheeks. He never saw his wife in such an appearance as rude as ever. He started to hesitated to hurry to leave to keep Dipika's concern said 'O, sure, it's late let's go! Sorry Babe, we just met after a long time as the old neighbours! Sorry to keep you wait! How are doing? Didn't you enjoy the time tonight?' Dipika came down realizing her sudden irritating and odd looking behaviour in front of all said quietly with a courtesy 'sorry we have to go it's getting late. Nice meting you all it's a pleasure! See you again come to our place sometimes Etc. Shawpon looked back to Anamika very passionately for not to take off his eyes from his former love might be the only love? Dipika noticed the thing in his eyes with a pain in her very heart through her dark eyes holding the pain of a dark cloud in the look expressing while trying hard not to express at all.

After shaking hands with each other Anamika addressed Dipika 'come to my parents place one day.' And Shawpon got surprised knowing that Anamika had a father too! Anamika asked Shawpon very happily with a lot of self-confidence 'did you ever meet my dad?' but very carefully restrain herself from expressing any wonder or asking anything about her father. Long time ago only this fact stopped his parents to marry her. They both broke into loud laughter might be both have had the same thought of the reason for their break up by concealing the pain inside. Anamika looked back again to say 'nothing wrong to pay a visit to my home.' They both broke into laughter once again but this time with a pain in the eyes before saying the final 'Good by' by taking the opposite directions each couple for their home while the hearts especially Anamika and Shawpon left wandering in the memories behind where they met tonight to confirm different destinations for each as failed to make a relation to make the same.

Shawpon kept trying not to get rid of Anamika's thoughts from his mind by telling him that Anamika means nothing to him. The word meaning of her name is 'no name'. Therefore she means nothing to him. She didn't have a name as her dad was missing long time. Basically she had no name by a visible male parent which prevented them to marry socially and from family values. Even though she has a name a maiden name but still the absence of the father for a long time for any reason prevented her and her sister to have a social value for the so called honor for no honor for women ironically. They had their Dad no doubt about that but still the absence of the father caused a lot of problems and dishonor in the society to Telerate with enough patience after all! They have their identity they always had but still its society in any culture looking for a clue may be to differentiate people from people? Shawpon and Anamika could have been a nice couple if they could only marry each other. The pure and neutral destiny can provide Love in a boy and a girl to fall in love to be happy divinely in a relationship whereas the human society makes things complicated to stop the passionate Love to bind them in the a holy relationship which could simply make them happy in their lives. So instead of the happy ending of their love they ended up in happy binding of the holy matrimony only for the sake of life only?

Shawpon and Anamika departed with proper courtesy to leave each other's company and special company after so long by chance to meet again after so long! As Shawpon took off his eyes form his love which is Anamika ironically sitting beside his wife in the car made his heart only wandering back around his love he left behind for 'Home sweet Home' looking back to whisper in his soul saying 'I love you babe! I still Love you! You don't know how much I love you!'

THE END

STORY 6

Our World
Love Love Love/ Kamrunnessa

Frank is still in bed lying upside down while the Sun out is very shiny and nice and bright. Mom got stunned at his bed room door nothing to say nothing to do but to keep gazing at her son a very adult and pretty grown up matured man. Mom always sees this way. Her son her little babe still a little child to her still doesn't know how to sleep. She feels in the very morning to fix his blanket spreading all over his body with love, care and affection as always as a mother. Every time every day she forgets that her little boy is now a grown up man to take care of him. he's no more a little child but a matured man a married man and leaves his bed room when realizes the distance between her and her son. Now there is a second woman in his life to take care of her son, to take care of him and give him a good company beyond love. But this morning Mrs. Edward realizes way more than that every other days. Cynthia her daughter-in-law is no more to there in his sons room might have been gone leaving her son. Realizing that, very quickly the Mom senses to take care of her son right away together with the mess in the room made by him.

His bed is a mess. Pillows are misplaced, scattered here and there underneath the bed or on the carpet or on the floor. The open window is cruel enough to bring the bright heat of the sun inside to interfere with her little babe's sound sleep. But Alas! He's no more in happy and drowsy mood shown up in his face rather upside down in bed by letting his back heated up by the Sun with no concern at all! Mrs. Edward called upon him to wake him up saying. 'Rise and shine my boy! Wake up my Boy? ------'but no answer nor a movement looking like rising to shine by the wakeup call from the bright morning sun with His very bright and heated light whispering into his ears to say 'time to leave the sleep!' but no signs yet for a movement to consider his concern to get up by opening up his eyes to hear, bear and cheer. Poor Mom looked around to pick up all hidden CD's, books, Magazines, underwear's, trousers, from the floor with a lot of motherly love to organize all and to clear the mess. The open can perfume bottles on the side bed tables, keys, cell-phone needed to charge and the most alarming alarm clock after all! The Mom needed to stop the alarm first to let her son sleep more. 'Poor Lad!' thinks Mrs. Edward at his sight. She managed to finish up all the tidy-ups of his mess in the room but trembled very inside with the thought that would she be able to tidy up his life again?' for now she's just gathering all of her daughter-in-law's stuffs from here and there in the room to put them away in the closet, in the cabinet drawers and so on. Then she looked at their wedding picture. A lovely couple once fell in love with each other to get married to live together as a man and a woman as 'happily married ever after----- perhaps to fall apart again by the cruel destiny forever?

It's only a week that they lost Cynthia but how? How Mrs. Edward could forget that she is no more. She has been coming to this room ever since then when her son's wife disappeared. She doesn't realize that something and some body is missing from the house or even or even from the very bed room of her son and his wife. She can see only her son embraced into her bosom very close to the heart. Every morning she comes to see her son to wake him up like her old lost child in his youth or in the adulthood. Right now she got shivered at the sight of the son's way of sleeping upside down motion. 'Is he alright? Oh! My! My! My poor little child! We lost Cynthia!

Frank got up right from his upside down posture to straight sit up in bed with his two wondering eyes at his Mom, 'Mom! What happened?' Emily cried out to run close to Frank to hug him as if just woke up from a bad dream to realize where he is? He rubbed his two eyes as usual to ask with another kind of wonder in a wandering mood of a mysterious mind 'what happened Mom? Why are you crying?' Emily wondered at his wonder now with a full suspicions to think like' is he alright? Now frank got worried about his mom to ask with a fear inside 'what happened Mom? Why are you crying? The mom got surprised again at his mood to say very silently 'nothing! Everything is alright. Don't you think that you have to go to work?' Frank looked around and asked with his still sleepy head 'What time is it? Where is Cynthia?'

'She's not around. You set up and get ready. Breakfast is ready. I'm going to make a cup of tea for you.'

'No! I want to see her. 'Why did she leave without telling me?' 'I want to know where she is.'

'She's coming. She's coming! I'm going to call her. Don't worry she'll be back!' frank looked around to look back at his mom with a stone eye 'where is she?' very rude in voice.

'Did she take all her belongings?', 'where are all the photos of her?" I can't see her around me anymore! 'Tell me what did you do with her photos?' 'She ran away! 'Didn't she?' did she ran away with her new company?'

'Come down what are you talking about?' Mom got a bit worried. 'I'm talking about Mathew! Where's he?'

'What's wrong with you? Who's Mathew? I don't know any Mathew.

'I know very well what's I'm talking about!' this time the poor Mom couldn't say anything but left him all alone to himself to realize all about his missing love.

Emily started doing her morning duties as putting dishes in the dish washer, making tea and breakfast for both the Mom and the son. Most probably only the mother will have the breakfast which has been happening for the last seven days since Cynthia disappeared to leave them all alone. Frank's not feeling well at all. Emily shivered again with a chill inside by the thought 'Is my son going crazy?' what if he never ever come back to himself all again?' she prepared her breakfast took a sit at the kitchen table to have her morning meal before being left for work to leave without putting anything into her mouth. And for the rest of the day the 1ˢᵗ domestic chapter of her life would have been spent totally at work with an occupied mind and the heart as well. A busy mind which knows nothing but work and a heart which eventually forgets a home with a child also containing a heart just like hers a very sensitive piece of a human body part set inside by the Divine to function as a piece of the body machine part known as an organ to generate the very human feelings humans feel and learned by heart as if when it fails the entire body functions fails too? The heart generates all the human emotions to be felt by the people individually each as a human body each containing a heart as an organ to feel love, hatred, pain, happiness, anger, despair and all other human emotions usually felt by people as for being humans also get heart broken by the non breakable emotion called Love!

Emily took the lunch break today not to have lunch but to spend the time alone in tranquility to have a time to think. There's nothing left in her life to think about. She doesn't look back to regret by wandering in the past. She doesn't think ahead to plan ahead or worries to wrong the future in the dark to fear about. She's moving on as she did move on in the past with hope and fear, with fear, happiness and sorrow, with success and in failure, with desire and submitting herself in destiny, in hardship and at ease with help and in no help, with ups and downs being rich or poor. She came all along the way down here at this present point once holding the hands of her only son her only support to get him on her side.

Seeing her son as a broken spirit lying upside down in bed breaks her heart to fear to fall apart with thoughts like 'am I going to lose him?'

'O God! What did I do wrong? Tell me please, please!'

'Are you O'K Mrs. Emily?'

'OH! Yea! I'm O.K.' answered her to her colleague Rebecca who happens to arrive sometimes to have her lunch at the same place.

'You don't look good though! Is everything alright? Asked Rebecca again.

'No, no I'm Okay! I'm fine don't worry.'

Sure? How's your son? Is he going back to work?

'No, I think he needs some more time alone."

Emily ate a little and worried a lot to sit there in the lunch room to take an hour in nothing but to worry and sitting there quiet shivering inside all alone after Rebecca's departure terribly which no one can notice nor can guess even taking a look at her. She's still very calm and focused at work. The only son of her she rose all alone with enough hardship is going through a terrible mess in his life never been expected by a mother. Still she doesn't know how that happened. Why her daughter like daughter-in-law died so early without even a notice which none of her son and herself could realize? Emily remembered Cynthia's face an innocent face with pain non –reflected in the beautiful face. Poor Mom thought she would have been free of that girl. Poor girl! Poor Me! All we wanted to share the same person with the same feel and the demand of the heart and soul. She remembered her innocent face with a pain inside in her chest which didn't take place in the last seven days after the poor girl Cynthia's disappearance. Poor mom thought she would have been free of her daughter-in-law but Alas! Out of sight didn't cause the out of mind! All the last previous days all seven days she pretended to be free of her worries to be all alone with her only son her only company in her life. But the cruel destiny mocks different ways telling can't get rid of me so easily!' people buries their miseries very inside to run away without looking or knowing it or ignoring it. It was Emily who chose Cynthia for her son three years ago ironically later to turn against her for nothing but only for her son's sole company. The mother wanted to bring a real bride for her son three years ago by throwing all his toys dolls; he used to play with in his room in loneliness since the very childhood. The mother didn't realize that a chosen friendship for her son can be o.k. to the Mom but not the unwanted love he started getting for her she didn't realize that Frank's emotional attachments to his wife could bring an unwanted misery in her life to make herself jealous at the same time to be destructive without knowing. The emotional crisis became intolerable for the mother-in law and the chaos in the family and in the relationships caused enough stress on the daughter as could be taken the daughter-in-law as her own daughter or accepted by the grooms Mom to avoid all the problems, mental sufferings and the break ups in a family. We plan nice and straight but re-act insane to make crises in our life in the family, in the society as well as in the Nations to break into a war? Mom feels very awful at her conducts in the last three years. She felt empty and lonely inside when her son and his wife started getting along by sharing a lot of time with each other in love and company when Emily found herself lonely. They wanted to go for a honeymoon while she rejected to accompany them logically thinking like 'they should be alone in such an opportunity to make the holy matrimony happy and meaningful'. Time to time they went out for shopping, movies, or any other relaxing places she rejected to go with them again as didn't feel like going with them when felt like tired and exhausted. And she thought after 'they are young and energetic I'm not'. She wished them all the happiness from the very heart while again couldn't resist herself her very inner self which couldn't take her son loving the spouse very dearly just like another female competitor means to be another woman in her son's life. It's nothing but the deadly human emotion called jealousy unfortunately which prevails over all sometimes even very pathetically in the very heart of a mother depending on the only son for the same reason for which an woman depend emotionally on the husband as their support mental as well as practical. The mom is enough out going and open minded still can't really resist her demands as the other half of the son's life partner. Mom and wife are not comparable but still both comes insane for some instance. The possessive human beings unfortunately are always happen to be very sensitive and touchy.

At some point after one year of Frank's marriage Emily's nephew Jimmy started visiting her very normally being a friend to Frank and Cynthia to get a new job with more responsibilities to become a responsible one in the family after all. He started to feel himself the only family buddy in the family over his Mom's head. Cynthia started a training course. Life got busier as they all got busier. Tom eventually after couples of month started staying late after work on the other hand mom and Cynthia came home early in the evening to sit together with tea and talk. If Frank came home early in the evening to sit together with tea and talk then Jim also sometimes came home earlier to share the family time together by paying a visit to the aunt as well as to see his secret darling Cynthia (without Cynthia's knowledge). Lot of time he went for shopping together with Cynthia by taking permission from his aunt but first from Cynthia's mother-in-law lawfully! On a Friday early last year Frank came home early while Mom informed that informed that Cynthia went shopping and Jimmy accompanied her. Tom got upset but didn't show his anger or any concern about their going along most of the time instead chose to sit together with his mom to watch T.V. after a long time as if the Mom-Son relationship got restored. The destiny didn't know about Frank how he was feeling inside but definitely Emily was very happy. Poor Mom! Wants to be happy in her Childs Company also while the son wants the same in his wife's company. It's hard when happiness is so rare in humans life from the same perspective for two people as for both the Mom and the Wife wish or desire or even need the same together with the same beloved person in two role's one as a son to the mother another as a husband an inevitable life partner for life.. Life seems to be a crisis in most of the cases always in indescripency always there are two for one precious or the most loved one to share and care from the very core of the heart. Sometimes feels like the life has to be this way a heard one while it could be an easy solution? But always we fight and fight at every sector of life seems sometimes to me that it has to be this way! Competitions make better but fighting for something emotional to achieve between two sometimes becomes deadly and definitely creating a non-peaceful situation to make people miserable with enough pain as if living in Hell. Fighting for Love and eventually is basically aspiring for the most precious and rare thing to get to make enough unhappiness and eventually enough fight also.

The work place started to be empty very slowly all the employees are about to leave one by one in the evening. Emily left her chair with a very slow motion in a little enthusiasm. Now-a-days home makes no home to her. Even three days ago Emily was jealous but alive to feel life in the lacking emotions of her son towards her. Frank and Cynthia used to make life together in happiness, in jealousy, in needs emotional or regular worldly matters. They made a team of thee in love, crisis and emotions in both good and bad feels. Today she' the last one to leave the office building leaving the door behind her back for home.

Driving in the streets in down town is a bit tricky and tiring in the mess of the traffic mainly sitting in the car a long time in a traffic jam moving very slowly which makes her mood different to ignore all the mess in her life. She becomes absent minded in the slow moving traffic with a tiring spirit in a tired mind makes her feeling numbness in the light headed situation, a sense with less sensitivity to love or to hold onto the precious life. She doesn't know what surprise she'll get while entering the home expecting seeing her son after a long day after all.

6.00 p.m. in the evening she opened the gate through the garden to unlock the door to the entrance of the house porch. Frank's not around doesn't look like went out. Must be in his room all alone thought Emily but got afraid too to see him or to stand in front of his room all alone in nothing but melancholy! 'Poor Lad! Why we raise them? Thought Emily again in a deep sigh from the core of her oppressed heart. Cooking dinner didn't give any relaxation to the working woman at this age now. She was dying to see her son only after for a long time pining for seeing her son better! But doesn't know dying to see him well after all the mess what surprise will the destiny offer to her through the mess in her son's life! The poor Lad definitely going through a lot inside through the sufferings of this mess of the time!

A mother always a worried woman of a son got worried very quickly again to look for her son just at once thinking is he alright? Did he eat all day? Or even leave the bed at all? Very slowly Emily entered his room to see to her astonishment that her son was still like that as in the morning time in the mess with the posters lying upside down flat on his bed with pillows scattered all around on the floor. Emily's lips trembled a little with the fear of losing her son thought again 'is he alive?' just like in the morning she called upon him to wake him up to sit up.

She stepped in to get surprise once more at the sight of his mess definitely was looking for something. Emily didn't have to wake him up the son pulled himself up to sit up only to ask only one question looking straight into her eyes,' where is all her photos?' the Mom got confused 'M---------here—here, look! You both look so beautiful together? Look!' Frank still is nude as in the morning said, 'where are all the photos? don't see her. That's the only one I can't see her anymore!'

'I'll find her! I'll find the photo's for you. Now come for dinner. Did you eat all day at all?'

'I'm not hungry. I lost all the photos can't see her anymore!'

'She's in your heart son!'

'I don't care! Who came to my room? Who took all of them? Did Jim take all of them? I'll kill him if I see him again in the house!'

Emily hugged her son to say' it was you! You got rid of them. I don't know where you threw them.' Frank stood still took the shape of a angry roaring beast very loud looked like a helpless looser who just lost a battle to someone who he doesn't know looked very deep into the Mom's eyes to say very confused, empty and bitter said, 'I see all ours you, me and Dad.' Then the very next moment cried like a child' what did you do to her Mom? Where's she? Did she eloped with Jim? Tell me Mom! Please tell me the truth! Please! Please! I love her. It wasn't me who hurt her feelings. I never wanted to lose her. It wasn't me who hurt her feelings. I never wanted to lose her Mom? Why did you do that Mom?'

Emily felt herself like a stone statue with her stone eyes casted at her dear son. The child her only child of hers didn't know what to say at all except to fix her eye sight only on him as if to find out who is he in front of her! The room of frank seemed shaking side to side in her obscure views from where she was standing at the very entrance. Thought a moment ago to hug her shattered child of hers but couldn't move at all! Her view around her son seemed shaking as in a movie scene of the final destruction after all the mess and the miseries of the characters in the movie. Everything began to fall apart. The shaking bed, the tilting window, the blowing curtains on the windows, the shelves, the chest of all the drawers and all! All the photo's in Franks room started blowing around up and down all over. She couldn't find her instead Frank is in there came in a vision of her drowsy eyes as a little toddler holding her husband's hand with a little smile very dear to her as always as in the happy movie scene. She started seeing frank's father just beside her all together as a family way far back a long time ago not present in the present lost world of hers.

STORY 7

Live for love/Kamrunnessa, 2018

'Love Love Love!' Ashik' excitement to draw everyone's attention
'What's up? Asks Mohan.

'Just wanted to see the love birds this evening!' I knew you two would be sitting here this afternoon! How is my Mohona? Very soon would be your girlfriend?'

'Shut up! Find your own! Says Mohan.

'That's why I'm here what you say Mohona?'

'O, yea, yea, yea, nodded her.

Honestly, looking for someone like you Mohona! Do you have a little sister like you?

'Get lost! Yes I have! A tiny one!

'Then you are the perfect one!'

'Get lost! No one will like you man!' Mohona smiled.

Anyway, both of yours names sound the same as pronouncing with the same letter Mohona & Mo-----han! Ashik likes to be cheerful all the time.

These three friends are 3rd year university students sometimes go together all three of them sometimes as a pair of Mohan and Mohona together and the single love seeking young boy Ashik with them in the number of three. It's just a month he broke up with Hashi after having a whole year of an affair between them to break up with no reason at all! Both of them said that they got bored of each other. They don't like each other anymore! If someone ask them why they say they don't know they just need a new friendship with someone new. Among all of them Mohini is the most matured one says at their respect 'if this happens between two lovers then imagine the future of our so called marriage?

Ashik' always naughty says, 'no long term relationships, no bondage to make the life a big luggage, no kids, and no pampers no bottles. Don't worry there's going to be some factory to make babies all independent no trouble, no bottle, be carefree, be happy!'

'Very funny!' Mohona's anger again.

'Need a change man! Grow up!' Mohan can't stop making a comment after all said very seriously into Mohona's ears' 'didn't work! She got her way and I got mine! The love bird doesn't stay in one place! We can't force each other to love one another by force.'

Mohona smiled to say.' Yea, I know! But Hasi said the opposite.

'What? What did she say?' Mohan looked anxious.

'Forget it! I it's the love it's you and your love which flies away from wishes to wishes doesn't really know what does the heart want in real sense!'!

"Mohona! How could be so rude to me?'

'Never mind! Carry on! At least in your journey through the life all through the motive of love and fun in search of the fun enjoying the life going from love to love?'

Ashik never minds Mohona moreover seems to be fond of her as accepting both her friendship and hatred or I would say her leadership role in most of the matters while both Ashik and Mohan prove themselves to be immature and fun loving. But the difference between Mohan and Ashik prove themselves as Ashik doesn't stay still on anything on the other hand even though Mohan goes like Ashik in his company for different fun achieving activities but can't really cheat on Mohona or is really in a serious relationship with her.

While all three of them represent the modern trend of the young generations along with their love and friendships in relationships they also represent the nature of life in aiming, living with or without some passions in friendships and love. While life and living include love and friendships do the values remain aloof? Time goes by in its own way so does the life itself. Mohan, Mohona and Ashik all finished their studies to achieve all their degrees successfully. Now appears the work life to begin. Mohan already managed a high position in a non-Govt organization Ashik's still flying from branches to branches as still a love bird while keeping his feet on the same branch of an organization and Mohona started to teach in a girls college without pay for now as if the educational institutions like to take women to provide knowledge and care for humanity for free for quiet sometime to be established once again on the mercy of people to be considered well devoted or enough devoted for humanity from home to the institutions to prove themselves the conventions of the part of the human race to share and care by giving up all their aims and wishes to prove again that they are still the same women to sacrifice themselves for humanity after all. None of them got married yet as they still meet each other quiet often. Today they are going to meet at Ashik's place after about a three month period of time.

Hot summer evening time its 7 p.m. in the evening. Mohan and Mohini appeared together as a couple in Ashiks' apartment. A two bed apartment in a congested apartment building in a very congested neighbourhood in the old city where the heat and the humidity took place with full might and right to compress the cool and the nice breeze to stay inside the little compartments on the high rise monuments of current civilization where only the air conditioning cools the air to keep the little insects known as humans to breath in life after all!

Knock! Knock! Mohan and Mohona stormed his door buzzed to give him a shock. Ashik hurried from the kitchen with a smell and smoke from the cooking activities but remained very silent by holding the door while opened with full excitements to say,' hi!' only as if no one invited them.

'Can we come in? Mohan opened his mouth first.

'Do I know you all?' Ashik's still serious to be pretended.

'Back off man!' Mohan came in followed by his life partner Mohona and still in no named relationship and Ashik took Mohona's hand to show her his kitchen to tell her to finish cooking he started while Mohan took a seat in the room by the entrance.

Mohan objects 'whose wife is she your or mine?

'None's yet! If she marries me today she's mine and you back off!'

'Mind your language enough jokes! Go back to the kitchen I'm really really hungry!' for the first time Ashik take a look at both of them with a real courtesy to remain modest and said to take a seat to both of them.

Mohan looked and said to his partner, 'nice! But very little as an apartment. How big will be our apartment?' 'We'll see. Let's get married first! Mohan's answer.

'Not to hurry let's save some money to start a new life new but well prepared.'

'That's true!'

Mohini said, 'how about me? You guys are making plans all alone without me what kind of a friendship is this?'

'Yea! Stay away from us to keep the friendship only!'

Mohan's kind of enjoying taking her back to Ashik after so long in their friendship can't really make a time very often to meet together. Ashik's responding to his friendship in a different way by concealing his joy in silence by talking without a cheer used to do in the university life that might be for the presence always has been aside as in one is to two relationship of the three who already left them alone as they are the same gender to make herself aloof on the balcony right behind the kitchen from where she can see the neibourhood at least to think ahead of the conjugal life in a little apartment in another neibourhood like that.

Finally Ashik finished his job at the kitchen to sit and talk with his friends cum guests to his apartment.

Mohan opens his mouth first 'So? How is life?'

'Just like as is but one thing for sure we are growing up. What you think Mohan?' Ashik looked at Mohons's sari said again, 'I like your sari.' In return Mohona asked 'and me? Ashik looked back very critically to examine to comment carefully pretending to be very wise at the same time 'I like your hair!' Mohan interrupted this time 'don't look at my fiancé like that! God knows what will you say next!'

'Don't worry just joking! You know I'm no serious about girls!'

'How many so far?' Mohan's question

'Don't know though! 'Ashik pretends to be damn caring.

That's true we are growing up not you!'

'What makes a man grow up? Bank balance? Marriage? Status? Name, fame? Happily established in the society? What? What makes a man happy? What makes people happy?' Mohan now!

'You know better what makes you happy till now. I try to be a man a true man! In all you just mentioned now!'

Mohan put himself in a serious mood so does Ashik also today. He asked Mohan this time 'So? Have you fixed the date of your marriage yet? I know you guys are very seriously in love. So when you going to marry very soon or need some more time?'

'Still need some time' Mohan smiled said, 'let's play cards a bit before dinner.'

Mohan and Mohona left two friends alone and started looking around. She entered Ashiks bed-room which's actually a mess, there's not much to notice a double bed with a head-board behind the wall and on the wall there's a poster hanging sticking itself on the wall portraying a big busy city in a developed country unlike here's a night time vision with lights, cars, sky touching high rise towers, buildings trying to reach the sky, big, big monuments, statues, people basically some or few on the side walk standing in a group most probably street girls or night time traffic, all the Cd's are scattered all over the floor, the bed's in a mess with the bed sheets and pillows and CD cases as well.

No curtain on the window beside his bed and the table on the other side is a mess also with some books, note-books, pen and papers as well as the 30 inch T.V. on the middle definitely a room of a messy boy in the mess of his unplanned and non-organized life. Of all of the three friends none of them have a family in the town. Mohona visits her family by going out sometimes, Mohan calls his parents and all family members time to time rather than visiting them and Ashik never talks about his family at all. He likes to fly as a bird or fly away from the reality of his own family in bondage as if no bindings, no regrets, and no concerns at all! All he cares is trying to enjoy the life as much as possible as if life is running away from him on the wings which never were favorable to him to give him some real life in a real sense! He still tries to keep all the values of the life bird which itself likes to flies away from them. By keeping its meanings, values, or destinies all in his heart without sharing with anybody even without letting his instincts know about them. He seems to be ignoring all of the real life by overlooking all of its hardships, by floating on the surface of the flow of the river only. Swimming deep isn't going to help his motive or in the other sense the escapist mind of his own from his own self? Looking for the deep meaning of life is only a burden of the severity of thoughts only which might be right from my view but to some extent we are neither a love bird nor an escapist living a life by ignoring all the responsibilities or the values to be abide by. But he's not what friends think he is. He goes cheerful from his thoughtfulness, from a little seriousness about matters to meanings to mind his business and the basics of all the fun and cheers from the bounties in boundaries providing from the fund to offer. Friends knows him as an irresponsible young student. They don't think of his seriousness from where his silly fun making attitude comes out. They still don't think of his pining for someone from his deep love for that person. Friends can't think of his seriousness in any matter. He's also a lover likes to share and care with someone mutually with someone when also loves to expect love in exchange. But this kind of fun loving or making fun kind of person can really love someone in the fear of losing it if tries to get it or touch it might be gone like the morning dew on the grass in the early morning sun. Being afraid of losing the love refrains a man like Ashik from his desperate pain in love

Mohona started looking for something in his room. She searched in his books and papers, in his drawers but couldn't find. What that could be? Might be the same thing as all of them always wondered' where is he from?' only a picture or an album might answer all that!

She took some time to sit on his bed at the edge to think about. This careless friend fun loving but still inside very empty looking for something couldn't find it. Mohona looked outside the window all is visible is the vast clear blue sky getting narrow sometimes by the high-rise buildings just the ways the hardships of our lives cover the freedom of the life or our dreams is always a barrier in our life in our hearts as well as in the relationships.

'Here you are! Dinner's served. Tonight you sit and enjoy and me a male as a female going to serve you!' Mohona looked back to the friends arrived in the room and answered at least to think a bit about a matter like this!'

'I do that also while I cook!'

'yes!, that's why I always tell you that you are running from reality or actually trying to by ignoring it while basically living within it.'

'Like?' Asked Ashik again by joking.

'Look at the mess in your room! You keep good books to read and CD's to listen to music, a T, V. to watch the world and to entertain at the same time an open window and the one and only poster of a hard city life? All in a mess only!'

'That's why I like you! You are my true friend.' Ashik cheered again by coming closer to her as always to give a five. And Mohona shook herself off to approach towards the dining table for dinner saying,' I'm hungry! Let's eat!'

iii

It's Mohan and Mohona's marriage ceremony today. Ashik is very busy all morning through the afternoon searching for a perfect gift for them especially for Mohona. Whatever he chooses to buy rejects the next moments thinking she might not like that. Definitely he chooses Mohona over Mohan to please her with an extra ordinary gift. He has gone to three different market places so far by this afternoon and finally settled down on a big and very expensive painting of the top most artists in the country. It's elegant, outstanding while at the same time eye catching in water paint. The colorful painting doesn't express anything particular only the obscure patterns of the shapes of the multicolor mind diverting different directions pointing at nothing but directing the mind to different directions in the all natural phenomenon to meet the different states of mind. The barren light blue canvas making a little show of the blue sky while the clouds making a back of a showering down rain in the shape of a cloud as a giant pony tail of the lady's hair at the same time from another view looks like the rain-shower is showering down by covering the Sun as it's little orange flame of the Mighty Sun as it's all little orange flame is peeping out from the face of the fiery sun in the sky. The whole canvas is displaying the colors blue, orange, and ash from different dimensions for different patterns. Overall it's a piece of art which is very beautiful and eye catching.

Ashik knows her as the best friend who would definitely like it very much.

iv

Snigdha rushed through the gate to get to the car waiting for her to take her wherever she wants to go. By taking her seat very quickly she also put on her lipstick very quickly, fixed her hair and looked into the front mirror to a beautiful lady very appealing even to herself. Do people love them the most? Thought Snigdha instantly to be lost into other thoughts associated with the one called **self-esteem!** God knows how she will do in today's job interview! She is not worried to get a job desperately but wants to impress a place in a business to drive herself somewhat a bit valuable as a woman who can possess a place in business too! Dipok is very busy now-a-days she has to make her own time too at least needs to keep herself busy in something to do which is very productive. Time is changing human life is now mostly like a fast driven car to merge with the other human traffics. Whoever left behind can't really catch up to the speed very easily? Snigdha holds onto the traditions and the conventional trends in the culture to go like a real woman with womanly behaviour mostly and the culture.

By the way, she reached the office on time got herself to sit and wait for her turn for the interview. However, her file has been sent already to the interview Board with the offering of a cup of coffee to sit and relax till then. Eventually it might take the next 25 min to wait for her turn in tensions instead of some patience to relax with the offered coffee. The wait time definitely produce enough palpitations to sit there in an enough long wait to die hard for an ordinary job as a receptionist. She took a sip to look around; all the candidates sitting there with a mouth shut as if forever to sit still and straight on the same ground for a job! They all looked very tense except herself who really doesn't need a job very desperately at this moment. She doesn't need to die for anything. When she was sitting very comfortably by gazing at all others around at the employees on the other side she got capable to view all the ladies nicely dressed up as the employees of the company all sitting on the computer with a headphone no doubt about that they are the commercials communicating outside for business. They don't look up neither they move only the visitors can see them they can't. Their eyes and the minds are all set for their business or at the work set for them. They don't bother who's coming, who's leaving, who's even sitting on the other side waiting for a job interview or not. They mind their own duties in categories in a group or individually. They don't have to look up to see what's going on around who's coming, which one's leaving, who's arriving, who's even looking at them. They are set to mind their own duty to perform while others on theirs as the watchmen or some monitors or a manager coming time to time to see how's going everything? Snigdha got tired at some point to look only at the door waiting for her to be open which is opening and closing by someone time to time for the candidates time to time one after another. Among all for how many will the door be open again after closing this morning behind him or her/ when it was a matter of pass and fail it was really a serious matter to be worried in the University or in the college when she faced the interviews to pass the exam with distinction but today it doesn't matter anymore. She felt like she won't be hurt if she doesn't get the job.

Snigdha got lost a bit in her own thoughts while banged by another opening of the door awaited by her to enter but when she looked up she saw a big fat man came out the door instead of a candidate and just walked away by passing her looking at the same time. 'This one must be the chief one of the institution!' thought her.

Finally she entered the special room should have been called a gate between Hell and Heaven and our lady entered the chamber with the usual tick-tocks in her very naive heart! She started whispering to herself also like 'I don't care! I don't care at all!' thinking of a table surrounded by multiple officers eventually to judge her but to her surprise she viewed only one man at only one singular while regular a table as only one singular Boss who was none but the fat big man she viewed by the banned door at her sight a little while ago. When he came back to sit at his place she couldn't feel or notice anything bother her significantly or to frighten her especially. Snigdha kept standing with a confused mind in front of the Big Fat Boss couldn't really figure out what's she going to face to face in an important event in a person's life. The Fat Boss opened his mouth first to say, 'I have gone through your file to see all academic achievements very impressive but how you can impress me?' Snigdha trembled a little inside to put her eyes down as got confused again. The Big Boss of the Business looked at her examining her very tiny bit with a very keen and short look into her eyes thought a bit by examining her face actually to say by putting the ash in the ash tray from his smoky cigarette 'sorry!, take your sit.' Snigdha didn't mind or trembled inside to take the sit in front of the Monster Man of the Business to favor the fairy out of the reality. While she got to be sitted in front of the man she still didn't know the man. She just lifted her eyes up again to impress her question about the question just has been asked and the smart Boss read her mind at once to answer without even being asked the question again said, 'yes, I was wondering how you can impress me if you get the job today?' the poor candidate wondered again to impress her confusion into her eyes by lifting them up and again to put them down. The ugly fat man smiled again by smoking some smoke in a little circular or a spiral shape to create by the smoke of the smoked cigarette to say,' Good!' The ugly man said next, 'I mean what you know about us and how can you impress us by putting your contributions to the running business of communications.

'Sir, what will be my responsibilities?'

'Good question! If you know what to do you will know how to do also. We're a telecommunication centre but your job is lighter. We can hire you as a receptionist only. Very easy! It's Just a natural skill by being talkative, appealing, making you inviting, by being smart and beautiful at the same time. You're all of that 'Good luck! Close the door behind your back. See you again.'

'See you again!' That means I'm hired?' Snigdha wanted to bid a 'thank you 'or a "Good Bye Sir' or saying only 'See you again!' but couldn't get a chance again as the Big Boss didn't even look back again at her or waited a bit to hear her last words to express her gratitude or loyalty to the man who just gave her a chance to work at his organization. The same way she walked out also without any curiosity or more interest in the company where she just got a job. She even doesn't know whether she would take the job or will have the same spirit like the way she came forth to the office for an interview. She took a look at the time it's not the lunch time yet! She can see Sweety on the way home as she thought for no reason. When she reached her friends place she wasn't there gone for some business. Snigdha felt like she's loosing herself by trying constantly to co-op with the present busy life. Sometimes she gets tired, she gets bored, sometimes even depressed to sit and look from inside out to figure out what's going on. While empty having almost everything in life. Basically no need for anything as food is ready on time for every meal throughout the day, home is neat and clean, furniture and all the needed accessories or things in life are there, money's in the purse to purchase life in love and luxury, plenty of time to spend at ease to sit and relax, to enjoy, to cherish by any resources', except for only one thing a 'company!' good that this evening she's busy with some old friends. Won't get bored again! On the other hand Mohona's also busy with party preparations in her house that evening she invited a lot of people from her and Mohan's as well. It's the end of the week to have some fun after work after all.

For Snigdha life is just a flow of time to be carried on its wave to let the self-go. She doesn't bother any kind of extremity in anything in having or in the sufferings in the life. She likes to be carried on time's wings as floating in bids, in the wide open sky with no pain, no gain, no regret, no being upset on anything. She feels herself neither blessed nor cursed on the God gifted platform of life to hold onto something desperately to be upset on any failure or any kinds of desires to be gone unachieved. Therefore, she supposed to be an aimless, hopeless, dreamless holding onto the short existing desires to be fulfilled on an ever exploring mind which roams around on no expectations. At least an expectation to have a good time with something or with someone who shouldn't be an oppressor after all!

By 6 P.M. Mohona finished cleaning her apartment, did some decorations by collecting and recollecting the flower vases, by cleaning the bed skirts, by organizing some furniture by putting them aligned or re-organized. She put on a cotton sari to keep herself easy to do things around. She looked tired but still beautiful with a spirit to cherish a time with friends after a long time felt like didn't see them a long time. She didn't even see their friend the best friend Ashik didn't even get a phone call from him. All the arrangements have been done! Food is ready actually ordered to arrive on time. No one's here yet! Only Mohan showed up by 6.30 P.M from work looked tired and exhausted as asked for nothing said nothing but asked for a glass of cold water. Easy busy life is nothing but to live in work, on an aim, with anxieties a life to build with hope while with a little of happiness to gain as constant struggle into a slim beam of light through darkness meaning hopeless in uncertainty. It's a kind of running not actually racing by chasing the life of a commoner to gain some hard earned currency to carry on. For a middle class couple like Mohona and Mohan it's like a mild challenge to take on everything on daily basis with some struggles to keep them up or to be alive by establishing themselves on the platform of the middle class category of life. Survival and establishments in the society with some dignity and identity means a lot to keep going with extra some strength to carry on the hard boating in the floating river of life.

Ashik showed up first out of all the guests invited tonight by Mohona and her husband. They kept both of their guests busy in accompanying.

Dressing himself up didn't take long at all after coming back from work. Careless boy has become more careless and messy. He changed his shirt and pants to feel relaxed by taking off the ties and dress shirt-pants after work. Didn't feel like to take a shower but sprayed some perfume instead 'what a mess!' thought Ashik' if that unknown green lady shows up there then what? How will I look to her? Would I be able to introduce myself to her in such a mess?' thought again 'who cares! I'm what I'm for now just tired and exhausted. Girls die for me not me for the girls!' he tries but can't get the green out of his mind he never ever thought that someday he'll be haunted by a lady ghost as appearing like his dream girl after dumping so many real girls! What a mess! He shook his head by blowing his hair to bring it to a style named' a careless careful after all to impress some people in a different way. At least he's alive to care about how he looks or about a style but to who? All the guests and all the green girls are even greener in his dreams. After thinking a lot about the Green whom he can't really pull out from his thought but deep down to take it as his 'Love' a word which he never really wanted to embrace in his heart never even let it grow to be planted deep into the heart to grow. He hung out with girls, made love to them, had fun with them in spending time together with one each time but never the 'falling in love thing really happened in his life yet which actually takes place by itself allow it or not.

Any ways three friend got together after a long time and started having fun before anyone else showed up. Mohona made tea for all broke into loud talkies about politics, jobs market, movies and the ridiculous city they are living in!

'Did you like my gift I bought for you on your wedding? I bought it especially for you.'

I know because you like me a lot'.

'As a friend only. Mohan interrupted. 'Come on! Don't be silly! Mohona's answer. All laughed loud with a cheer. The party already started by these three friends before anyone else showed up. They already got a bite of the fun in the evening. They took three chairs on the balcony to enjoy the weather not very nice but a bit chilly. It's a mild cold in the dry season. They don't see nice around but only surrounded by the buildings all around. Some greens peep with some flowers of different kinds as if sneaking from the gaps or the cracks on the concrete buildings to say at least a "Hellow!' to the strangers also sneaking in the busy life of their own all humans and plants mainly all humans and a little plants most probably to remind the civilization not to forget about them. People of the city now make their gardens on the roofs as no choice at all! The city has to accommodate all the residences and the commercials by constructing multiple buildings mostly developing high and high up at each step more for the civilization to live civilized after all. So the constructions need to wear the hats of greens and colors of the flowers to remain still with a sign of the mighty Nature who's actually the provider of all. It's not nice to suffocate the people over all! Some big trees are still high up the high rises to show that the Nature prevails while nurtured now-a-days. Still all these friends can have the taste of a cool breeze from nowhere but generating from the gaps, cracks, of the buildings and from the gaps between the constructions. The way we all are living and breathing in the shortness of breath in pollutions and destructions as well as all the frustrations plants and trees are also still being planted or growing in the wild nature to keep the Nature for the sake of the survival at least for the remaining breath of the human civilizations.

All three friends got a little time together to sit and relax looking down on the road at the city especially in a criticism which never ends. What can the people of the country do to fix people' things while the populations are overwhelming and overloading the city's getting polluted day by day.

A little breeze of fresh air touched Ashik very softly. He felt a bit relaxed in the midst of his old friends to say, 'Nice breeze! Still the air breathes in all the mess!'

'Yes, as we feel suddenly that we're still alive in all in a congested busy city with a busy life. Sometimes I feel like I'm not even breathing or steaming out myself from the hyper active boiling machine!' Mohona started laughing loud while all others joined at the same time. Mohona got up and went inside to receive her guests as all started coming by now. Ashik made a comment by saying 'at least we got a little time together after a long time!' the host left by leaving the two close friends together. The party was not really a social gathering as got loaded with enough guests in the limited space in Mohan's house to make the apartment hot, loud, and congested with people and by the end of the daily life struggle. Two bed rooms held enough people to accommodate at least to facilitate them to see each other on a week end for a break at least!

Mohan and Ashik were still on the balcony out of the crowd inside till the dinner to be served. They came in to pick up some food also. Ashik got his food to sit somewhere to eat. All the rooms were occupied. He found an empty place in front of the kitchen to sit. The table got empty everybody might have taken his or hers food for dinner. Ashik was sitting there alone to have the dinner while a young lady most probably left behind appeared at the table to take her share. As Ashik lifted his eyes to his surprise he saw the same beautiful face he always thinks of in a different appearance and Ashik got surprised to see his dream girl in real. He knows her by the identity of green sari now. He couldn't make a mistake to recognize her in black and white. He barely was eating but constantly looking at her beauty a face with a sharp little nose, two beautiful bright eyes, and a shiny forehead holding the beautiful burden of a thick hair hanging at the back in a long hanging down bread. She's skinny, a medium height young lady but still attractive overall but he still doesn't know for what for the beauty or for the personality.

She's all alone today also to be calm and quiet like most of the time. She carries her culture and conventions in her look and attitude. It seems she likes being in people but kept herself distinct or aloof from the environment. By taking her sit she also looked for a spot to be shifted didn't even care that Ashik was sitting near too. She took a chair near him and started eating independently without any hesitations and on the other hand sitting beside the dream girl Ashik fearfully started to have a chat. But his heart pounding didn't know how to approach. But Snigdha was concentrating on the intake looked unmindful though as she's always looks like to roam around in a different world of her own. Looks like she is always concerned about herself and the surroundings to float around in a different world neither dreaming nor much into the event or the environment or even the place visiting or being invited to consists of people same kind with the same kind of manners and nature but still not the same to her. She doesn't talk much her existence only make her social as seemed to be concerned about the existence of people all around whom she values by keeping herself a bit aloof. This the third time that Ashik met her. The more he sees her therefore he gets attracted to her doesn't really know for what reason. She's beautiful and keeps a serene beauty in a modern stylish look.

All this time Ashik was watching her putting away his plate from his disappearing appetite by still holding it. Finally the fairy looked back to see Ashik sitting near her wondered a bit with her two deep eyes with a floating look innocent but concealing or keeping a lot deep inside. As Snigdha fixed her eyes at him Ashik dared to say,' Hi!' only and in return she said,' Assa-lamu-alaikum!' Ashik got embarrassed a bit said, 'I saw you before two times'. She answered' really? Where? Without any excitements and with keeping the food into her mouth machine for better processing.

'On the wedding" got interrupted by the question instantly' which one? Mohini's?'

'Yes, you are right!'

'And next? Asked as very much like an interview.

'On the road side by side in the car.

'So you noticed me before I got surprised to see again. Am I right?'

Ashik got embarrassed again for being very silly said, no, nothing just a co-incidence!"

'I know! Snigdha's answer. Didn't want to embarrass him anymore.

The very next moment she started talking a lot by saying, 'I'm Snigdha Mohan's school friend met her again after a long time.'

'I'm Ashik also her friend. I guess a friendship later than a year but very deep as much as years I guess! We're there Me, Mohan and Mohini all present at the same time. We can make a new team with four of us together'. Ashik showed a lot more interest and excitements with no bounty doesn't know yet for what. Snigdha looked into his eyes smiled a bit nicely by concealing the difference in the smile at the boyish attitude of this present newly met man said in answer 'I know I'll see can't really make a commitment right now and left by saying, 'I go see Mohini. Nice meeting you.'

Ashik and Mohan got back together again on the balcony nowhere else to have a privacy to talk. Two friends feel better off the crowd. Snigdha is still wandering and alone watching the guests sitting a bit in one room to share their conversations to make comment or not basically played a silent role to see and hear more and talk less. She has been accepted by all doesn't matter talking or no. She portrayed herself a silent and significant role of a lady in the land of a humming crowd. She looked reserved, lonely, lively, sound and silent at the same time. She also got admired by the ladies for her beauty and her style. She didn't show up, didn't talk, loud to put her opinion up. She's a role model of a silence, smile, sense and the sensibility.

All the sensitive's' words touched Ashik's heart deeply. He didn't know what's happening inside him, why he's thinking about her a lot. A lot more girls or women came in his life. They came and left as leaving no signs behind to hold onto their memory or the existence in their absence on in the disappearance. Meeting Snigdha only three times made his connection to her existence made her known for three decades in his attention to the talk they were talking as two friends.

By 11.00 p.m. Mohini entered the balcony by holding Snigdha's hands to introduce her to her two boyfriends. By seeing her both of them screamed' hey! Mohini what's up?'

Answered Mohini, 'meet Snigdha my school friend'. Both of her boyfriend's said together again 'we know her already.'

'Really? How did Ashik know her?'

'I told you before about her that I saw a green girl on your wedding remember?'

Snigdha addressing Ashik. 'Yes! Ha! You were talking about Snigdha? I can't believe! He got very surprised said again,' do you know that she's my school friend? Addressing Ashik.

'O! I see! This much already?' both Snigdha and Ashik looked at each other felt a little more familiar to one another. Said Ashik again indicating Snigdha as followed by his former concept' how about Snigdha makes us a group of friends in four two by two?'

Mohini got surprised again to scream loud this time said,' what do you mean? Do you know? Got interrupted again by the new subject as she spoke' wait a minute! My husband just called. He's on the way just ten min away to pick me up.' Snigdha doesn't know why she took a critical look into Ashiks' eyes and the pale face for a moment as if they both understood the language of their look.

Our girl Snigdha kept a little silence to say 'Good Bye' bid instead 'Ok, Good night friends! Hope to see you again!' she just left by casting a look again at all three of them for the last time. But Ashik kept looking at her departure as she was walking away to get the door to walk away for home with her life partner. Mohini joined with her friend Ashik to console him said, 'sorry I didn't tell you before that my friend is married. I couldn't figure out that this is the girl you were talking about. I'm so sorry friend! No hard feeling! But Ashik kept looking even though she walked away out of his sight might not be out of her mind! Mohini felt a little pain inside for her friend realizing this one might be his real and first love after all the girl friends he had before 'poor Lad!!' thought her. Looked like only Snigdha's departure left a mark on his heart as he was standing there by gazing at her departure even though there was no more of her signs at all.

'Wow! Sounds like a poem might have been named like 'departing hearts'?

Don't try to fool me you like her don't you?" 'What's the point? She's married!'

My fault! I should have told you before that day if I knew who your Green girl was.'

It's okay the heart is known as a bird flies around to come back again.'

'To the cage? All three started laughing at Mohona's comment.

But still the question remained. Will Ashik be able to forget the 'green girl' with whom he might have fallen in love after playing with different girls in different colors, shapes, and beauty.

All three friends Ashik, Mohan and Mohini didn't show any tiredness or any impressions of sleepy eyes at all. They were sitting there on the balcony as in friendship as ever. It's an opportunity they got after a long time to get together. They were talking, feeling the tranquillity of the night out after a long time out and beyond in a bondage of friendship which never gets fade away. But still there's something which has been absent is Ashik's liveliness. He remains a little absent minded and calm against all their excitement tonight.

Heading home for Ashik at 3.00 a.m. in the morning driven in a taxi in the city street didn't make him sleepy, tired, or exhausted but very escapist beyond the surroundings. The tranquillity, the calm and quiet late night time didn't make him a poet or romantic but a lost lover failed to achieve or feel the real love built in him very silently in the past few months even without his realizations or recognitions. He can remember all of his past relations by recalling all the different girls in his past life without an image of each of them in his mind. But the green girl showed up in his life as a green forever in his heart. If he could have achieved Snigdha will she be his real love forever? He doesn't know may be maybe not as he feels in his aching heart now in emptiness. An emptiness for loosing something which she never actually got in real sense. Then why he's still looking for Snigdha on the road side beyond anything else in the street?

Finally, he realizes to console himself only that' maybe it's love! A real love! Which I was looking for all my life. Then why I got myself cheated like this by fooling myself and dumping all those girls to play?

The taxi got a little bump all in a sudden to stop him thinking that much on a regret and with the bump he's thought got a new way of thinking 'is Snighda happy in her marriage? Whenever she showed up in his life incidentally or by the co-incident she appeared lonely and detached from the surroundings. Why never showed up together with her husband is she as empty as him deep inside? Is she looking for a love real love or a company in her life to be settle down? May be not. Life doesn't offer any kind of settlement for any kinds of desires of the heart of the humankind. People talk about justice sometimes poetic justice! Is this a poetic justice for Ashik? He asked himself finally, 'how about I go for Snigdha? Will she be mine? No way! How about I see her again will I be able to make a connection with her? May be not! She's might be only a floating 'green'! Grass? Never really settle down or even wants to.'

The night approaching to dawn. He's two more blocks away from his home while started feeling a pain a little sharp pain in his heart of vast emptiness.

THE END

STORY 8

Born Free
Nov 06/19

This is all about me my life, my fate, my future, my feelings and over all my choices 20 years living in a different state other than mine which made me feeling myself an alien from totally a different planet always being concerned by contradictory thoughts and believes to understand to keep some of my own with modesty and to adjust to keep some of my own with modesty and to take some extra's or alternatives to mix and match. For instance, about the matters clothing's and costumes, the food, the life style, the routine and over all the conflicts of beliefs and cultures. The constant fights with all the differences in life, in the environment or in the society made myself like anyone else very confused, all the time disturbed and in most cases very isolated. If you go out with some friends from different cultures to hang out with some of your own some of you would like to order a glass of wine while socializing by sitting together in a restaurant, some of you would like to order another kind of meat which you can't share even might have been allergenic to it by custom or for the sake of your ethnicity same way the matter of the ways of dressing up. The fact is we like to enjoy some of other' activities but the problem is while the heart desires to go with the flow as easier as without any bindings or barriers the body rejects to shed off all the clothing in layers of cultures and beliefs and prejudices to let it go with the flow to be the same to take freely in full heart pure and secure as a born free to feel only by heart whatever it desired to enjoy with all others despite the differences cultures the cultures make. You need a swimming suit to swim in the ocean water but your culture barrier doesn't allow that from full heart of your own. If a huge ocean in a huge boundary wishes all in a sudden to raise itself so up and out revolting with full might and right pouring all the water out raising up the consequences would be nothing but only ruing the world by causing death and destructions only. For humans like us coming from a different culture and habits can go swimming with compromise in shorts and in a tee which definitely will make him or her a jerk to the rest of the people definitely won't be very comfortable or enjoyable for the poor wishing awkward aliens in the wonders of the Great lands. The fact is some people like me can't change them totally by putting on shorts or Bikini's at the Beach neither can drink the wine. In a way, people like me cant change themselves totally for the need of the society to get along to be the same in heart and soul. People like me just like the snow to view as the white snow but can't take the same cold or the hardships of the cleaning of the bounty of the cold beautiful burden of the snow white snow in the daily routine in winter time. Handsome young men of our culture can enjoy the beauty of the beautiful ladies but can't just touch them to embrace them into their bosom to feel and hear the same language of the heart. So basically, seeing and feeling doesn't make a real relationship after all. But the point is living in a multicultural country we get and variations to verify a lot of the odds along with the goods. Living together even only seeing each other make ourselves better in nature, behaviour as well as having a outlook, looking at things and differences in matters make us somewhat a better understanding, welcoming and open minded to make a new world in varieties to find the beauty in the difference of colors, shapes, sizes, nature and beauties in having or feeling different aroma's, colors and beauties in the differences to have all or at least a bit of all.

Sometimes I myself feel like a poor me and poor us! Why do we suffer in the middle or hung us up in the blowing wind when can never be settled on one. My best friend is very wrong. He fell in love with a charming classmate of him very long time ago eventually got married also to live happily ever after to come back to me after 15 years to tell me to look for a place to live alone all by himself also said, 'dost I'm broke! Nancy left me all alone she took my kids also with her said, 'I'm not worthy of taking care of my children. What happened with Masum is as after having a very life together with Nancy in very love and harmony in fun and fancy, with the honey and the honeymoon even after having two children lost all the charms of life in the over flow of the charms! They both got fade up and bored with little money for schooling for children, for the stress for work for both of them and overall in the discrepancy between costs and capacities for both of them. The very love for each other turned to a liability to each other. My friend started seeing his lost old friend to talk, to spend time in talking and sharing pain in lost old friend started seeing a girl also from his community.

So recently after going through a cold relationship between both the wife and the husband the loving wife got rid of the loving lover from inside to declare a war upon my friend. Very suddenly she became a responsible mother good enough to kick him out of her life. Poor Anise! As a single father can't see his children by visiting Nancy's place very often nor can he bring them to him to live together. Missing the x-wife or not definitely the poor desi Anise isn't feeling well at all! Came a few days ago to visit me to talk to me to empty the bosom of sorrows by vomiting out at me and didn't know to be sympathizing or to provide some kinds of help in his bad time. Definitely can't fill up his empty bosom with anything like having a break in relief of what has been going on lately, no joy, no sign of any kinds of a relief in any kind of some better feeling in the peep of a shallow sunshine through the cloudy sky at the time of his miseries like this. The time of happiness, joy or even recoveries from this time of misfortune seems far reaching. Still at least tried to listen to his miseries or miserable stories made up by destiny, or by the society or by the ongoing systems from the very roots to be performed in his real life to make him enough miserable after all.

I tried my best to build myself a man in a good career or would like to call it a position to be in for the good for life ever in the land of opportunities well developed, well founded, well established over all a land which believed to be the landing on the land meaning a landing on the land of all the dreams also landing from the Mother land considered as the Heaven of our hearts to land on the land of reality to face a real life living in reality by leaving behind the land of our hearts. Developing me or developing my career ended up in reality to find a place by affording with my own money to live first of all after landing. Aspiring from a distant land by counting on another's sky touching civilization in the constructions of their sky touching high rises can't make a real life down on the land where its people actually need to land and live on their own feet. Social barriers, culture' in differences in understanding each other's as well as the language barrier' make a life not very much in dreams in the dramas' on the real life stage performing everyday every morning till night. The comfort we bring home founded on discomfort to have enough pain in the afforded comfort we finally achieved. All kinds 0f ironies in all kinds of discrepancies while makes the life a liability in the expectations of the hard earn luxury. Life is good life is bad it's all true despite where we live a place better or worse. But still some places suit better for some people according to their need and life style as well as their capacities mental, physical with the affordability of all others. There are factors not the same everywhere all I wanted to point out is thinking a place better than our own can't always make a better as we thought. People need to move or move on with their life from place to place as it is as universal as real. I tried my best to build up my career and to make a life better in the foreign country eventually my whole family left behind for the sake of dignity or for the very attachment to the dear own land. Sometimes people do not like to move from the place where they belong or feel comfort habitually or for the sake of the love for the Mother land after all. Most of the time memories pull people back to the attractions of the love, affections, the invisible attachments of the heart to the very love one' can't break the ties of all affection's. Reality makes you feel and face things different. I found myself learning, educating, training, and adjusting constantly to the differences to live in different ways of living, surviving, and most of all and most importantly to establish myself with full heart to develop to say as a citizen of this country while being an alien. I did everything from the very beginning taking courses, trainings, educations and also finding a job also for the sake of the very survival as well as to determine the life itself. But the fish from a small pond got lost swimming into the ocean to get a lot of lost and found for it while also failed to make a way to live properly with full spirit and comfort. So, finally now I have decided to move back or going back at least to try to stay back again if not permanently but for quite some time to live there with full heart and the with the real feel of the heart which still remains the same as a Bangladeshi one with love in hatred, or with hatred in love for the Motherland definitely not so favorable to live permanently for sure. Basically, going back to the same birth land as enough unfavorable to live in comfort and ease where basically the comfort is the comfort of the heart believing like 'this is my place where I was born if not still the mother who gave birth or the father descending from a root generated the family with so much of love, passion, a sense of togetherness being in a family as a generation with at least some of the distinctions in identity or in some kind of nature and feel believing to be in our own as in a family as well as in the greater sense to be in the same motherland in a home-made big home made by the mother together as a parents with our father and all other siblings. The blood is human running the same in all the same humankind which is the same by the grace of the Lord still when we picture a family tree it makes us think as running in a distinct blood so we make the differences to point out like 'a blood relation'. It's actually all about our emotions and passions for our things felt to be our very own to hold into our bosoms to feel and cherish in the very close relations like our parents, brothers, sisters and beyond all others ascending from the same tree consists of all the branches and the fruits it' holding. We are all the same as humans the visible distinction is only in the different colors but still some relations like blood relations and love relations make togetherness in distinction. Again it's all about human passions and emotions which I believe and beyond the mystery for why a brother or a sister or the mother or the father still recognize the child didn't even raised by him or a sister can tell that this is her brother who she never saw in her life after she was born for some reason but feels things the same ways. There are mysteries beyond our understanding we can't define. Any ways, I was at the topic of my going back not really actually visiting the every land of my own to give my heart some comfort it needs to be in its own where it used to flow like a river very natural as only a part of the Nature. Being nurtured makes us better, gives comfort to our souls and better living to the heart and the body but again the Nature remains silent in the silent language of the hear besides life is hard doesn't matter where we live where we born physically and biologically.

In this book of mine actually I started to focus my stories on the 'Love' thing in our lives and I think I found my way to love again the love for my country, the love for my siblings, my family and the love for my lost world which pulled me back here into this country a place of love and hatred from the very heart.

It's march 2nd 2025 when I reached Dhaka airport landing from a far and far land where the Nature is half frozen and the people are already half robotic. 6 years ago when I came to visit some young boys offered me some help for the luggage I had to lift and carry but this time the whole air-port area seemed like a busy and speedy motivations of people as running fast by carrying the burdens of their own on their own shoulders as at the same time minding their own businesses only and each passenger is his or hers own responsibilities with no help offered by anyone in need in the entire place where everyone on the same mission to mind only their? No help was offered from any kind of services with or without payment which made me disappointed but at the same time the self got very tired too. After all still a human.

So after taking a long time by looking around for a sign of some sort of help offered for the buggies finally, I gathered enough stamina to pull all the suitcases and started pushing the cart very slowly with no spirit at all. One thing seemed very good though which is there's no rush no crowd people seem very organized and well behaved. The checkout was neat and systematic. The counter called upon names serially with the information's for materials to be needed at the checkout without checking the passports instead with the display of the documents behind with the picture of the passengers'. It made the checkout time shorter than before. And I got failed to get the lost emotions of the heart as actually came in search of that missing thing from the other world.

Everything is fine I took all my luggages on the hook to get going. Now, don't know the way out so looked around to ask somebody. People are all around but no one's really paying attention to anybody else. I stopped to my wonder to realize again 'is this my city of Dhaka?' 'Are all these my people usually compassionate to each other like them or not, at least do they care to know each other with a smile by offering at least a fake courtesy to help as I expected from somebody in that spot to say, 'can I help you?' 'Nope!' no one's paying any attention to anyone else no matter how a person trying to get out with all the burdens of needs carried on the trolley.

Miserable I an alien in my own land stopped by the exit looking out for some help. My shoulders started to ache as I have some problem and already took a look at myself in the washroom mirror to wonder at myself 'm I not a beautiful woman?'' am I too old or too young to get some men's help or some attention at least?' the helpless wondering woman which is me in a land very known to be totally unknown at this moment. So I looked out through the exit to view some vehicles were stopped and picking up people's suitcases and bags to take the passengers' to their destinations. How about me? Why no one even trying to catch my attention to get a ride in favor of me? 'What's going on here?' All in a sudden I just realized 'Global world!' And I went back to the counters again asking for help. The check out people knew my condition and one of them happened to be an old lady answered in my language 'did you come after a long time?'

'O, yea! A lot of changes!' no one even paid attention to my questions just guided me to the counter in a corner in order to pick up some packages of help with paying. I took the package two for the major services as follows

1. Picking up my luggages.
2. Getting a taxi or any other kind of a vehicle to drive me to my destination or the address I am heading for with an enormous wonder and discomfort inside by looking at the bill I had to pay.

The car started with full speed in energy driving like a speedy modern machine slave to run for the modern or the past's present and the future's super speedy time to adjust to its super speedy life to serve better. Wasting no time means respecting time in submission to the time and the trends with no complain at all. Accepting all the changes in the time is a positivity as a result of people's obedience to the life trend either man made or the Nature's selection to be abide by with no complain or any sort of negative thoughts coming out of the very positive human mind of ours own. We run the cars run in speed full speed by keeping us in comfort by letting us sit on its seats to still run in discomfort of the hearts with worries given by the time again the ever changing time which' constantly changing with the ever changing human minds for the demands of the present time's requirements for the believing good for us or for better for better in the change to accept the facts not like before to manage our time and our life in changes in better or worth to be worthy in time which offers you better or worse for the good for the brought up time which is by the time itself not the motives or the intentions of humans to carry on the life looking ahead in positive look, outlook, and overlook when there' basically no choice to cut down some of our favorites or normal' to carry on the life by moderating, eliminating, by some remaking and overall by making the time running fast with speed of our work as if carrying on the life in all the speedy vehicles' to make our life go fast while can't avoid the furious' are being made by the same time in the same process in the name of better for better in life.

Since the time we're now in the time making money making life so the driver doesn't intend to waste any time. The more rides the more money makes the survival better and easier. Me, the restless soul finally took a break to look out. Streets are better looking in fewer crowds. I don't know whether the pollution or the chaos and stress in life killed half the people already. Selfish and cruel I thought for a moment 'wherever happened happened for good. Less people are good for the living for the remaining people. Large populated countries wish to have less population for the betterment for the country. People die of diseases, accidents, wars as in the city streets by accidents at this point I got a jerk to look out stopping me from thinking instead to ask the driver 'what happened?' the driver's answer is normal said 'nothing! just a bump on the road. I looked ahead to realize that we're on a shallow road from the street to wonder still places like ours keep narrow roads side by side with highways and paved streets. Well! Life is all about big and small shallow and narrow side by side with large and small, broad and narrow, big and small, wide and narrow, high and low, tiny and humongous as the discrepancy in nature as well as in Nature. Life is always a mixture of good and bad, life and dreams, frustrations and ambitions, hopes and despair after all and over all. Anyways, thinking about the population sometimes makes us to consider the lessening of the human population as a natural selection if it caused by Nature and natural disasters and deaths as well. The pollutions we need to use natural recourses and in order to do that we also abuse the recourses to cause death, destructions, and pollutions of course and over all. Well, Nature balances things naturally anyways, sometimes natural disasters, sometimes natural death by diseases, sickness, aging, some incidents and accidents and of course by wars. Nature balances naturally that's why there are lives and deaths side by side generations after regenerations and all the contradictions in everything for survival and revivals. Life is all about a complex pattern for survival for all complex creations all together humans, animals, birds, lizards, fish, trees of flowers, fruits, plants for vegetables, insects in and with the materials and of five elements of water, fire, earth, air and sky. While we as humankind as well as animals are made of and contain as well those elements we also become very competitive and complex at the same time in nature while the fire, water, air, earth and sky make all the emotions we get to make us also very sensitive while very emotional to cause enough chaos in our environments together with all others out of our own kind to make wars among us by possessing ego's individually or nationally or even as a group in distinctions with our own beliefs, cultures, tastes, understanding and educations holding onto our own ego's. Different understandings, nature of things and beliefs we create make us aloof from each other. Humankind always fights for power, possessions and pride. Well we also fight for the establishments for our own identities as a family, as a society, as a country, or as a Nation or even as followers of some distinct beliefs to carry on our life separately in distinctions. We are somewhat also kind of an animal natured to fight for survival only meaning the ways animal fight with each other for food and shelter only. The differences is we fight for all for the survival basically like animals as we are the cultured animals with some conscience to fight for more for our pride, prejudices, shame, prestige, passions, emotions, love and hatred to make us humans after all. Heart and mind make a big difference in the matter of keeping peace in human society while our other selves make us animals only by instincts under cover. We make us human in making civilizations in concrete constructions together with the refinement of the heart and soul and emotions. Fighting for basic instincts is brutal but less complex while fighting for all as being animals in humans makes more complex situations and environments in the society physically, socially, in a family life, politically and morally to make a complex world of our own. We believe to be living only or would say surviving only to allow us or make us to create enough problems simply by living our lives in a daily routine working, sleeping, eating, and going out for fun or for reasons make us commit mistakes in our simple life style knowingly or unknowingly. The gaps between understanding and educations create problems among us while we need to and like to go together for reason or for friendships.

Anyways, I got lost again in my own thoughts to make myself enough Socrates to become a cast away better be come back to life the present life which is I am now in the city of Dhaka my city a very tiny one non –considered in an unknown world of a country of a kind firstly an under developed small country right beside the great India. Where I was? Yes! I was looking through the car window by casting my views at the new city of the old Dhaka. First thing I noticed is the big achievements in making fewer crowds. May be I'm wrong this is not a god time to watch the chaotic crowd after all the crowds make the country. Over all here's the reality as 'no people no populations in contrary to that more people to make the pollutions!' any ways here I am back again to the old memories in the refreshments of the memory to see the little non-cultured or still under-developed small county of our own in some developments over all! The coming back of the Old memories in a little change make me feel like losing some of my own in the past, some precious memories of some favorites gets a shock to accepts the new and the changed in things and in nature of things or the positions and places for not being the same. It feels like changing the soul for the new into the hardships of the acceptance. The more I'm looking around the more to watch things out the more my heart and soul starts to ache in a strange pain in emptiness. I recalled the time when we had to live here even after coming back from another country which was the other half of our own. The city was crowded, dirty with cheers and fears, with love and hatred, with sense and sensibilities, with sorrow by borrowing the hope for tomorrow in pain and gain after all with hearts and mind. We lived in life in good over bad, in bad on the hope of the good ahead. And this is the time of hope. The accomplishment of our better future where our all hard work, all our struggle and thriving for a better future got an accomplishment on the establishment of a clear crystal platform in the present future of our hope to stand with a stone heart on the very neat and clean platform apparently hard enough to go on with a balance. The car is proceeding through some big high ways nice and clean in high speed up more to merge with other speedy vehicles. Roadside views do not hold any kind of mess of the crowd or open market in the streets or roads. Big buildings grew bigger merging high up by keeping a balance with each other. We passed some big shopping Malls very high rises. In a small city can't have many bangle type constructions for business? That's overlooking the life underneath between buildings might not be very nice to see or observe.

We drove almost 15 min the driver or me none of us asked a questioned to each other yet. Usually the drivers ask the passengers especially from an airport 'where did you come from Sir?' to continue the conversations from there like 'how's life over there? 'How's the country abroad? Or 'do you have a family there?' and 'who you came to see here?' what do you do over there, how long you have been living there. After how long you came to see your own place? Etc. On the other hand from the passenger the concerns are usually like, 'a lot of change! Ha! Long time! How's everything here?' then they exchange some views sometimes about the current economy, politics and political issues, social problems, compassions to the advanced countries and so on.

The time I took in the past time spent in wondering at the change of the city by giving the driver the address of my sister's house which I didn't know where at all! And after 20 min when I opened my mouth to ask something to the driver he spoke out like a changed robot or a doll we played in the childhood 'we're here Sir!' again the same problem 'will he help me or not with the luggage's? Or I have to wait for my relatives by knocking at their door first and also I have to make sure also that this is the place where I should come to look for my sister?'

The driver did volunteer a bit he got out, looked at me, picked up my suitcases and all my bags to drop regardless rude just in front of the three story building and took his driver' seat back in the vehicle just like that. Didn't even give me a moment to think if this is not the place then how am I going for the next wonder in search of my siblings? I looked at the address again in the little piece of paper. Yes! Everything looks the same I didn't know how to take all the suitcases upstairs as I lost my mind for a moment then realised to call Sis to send some help. Sister Sohani came down with a smile with no change at all after so many years as the smile remains the same as always when it comes from the very heart of a close relation or a loved one's. Happiness smiles through the smiles of humans so does the sadness through the tears to melt it down while a smile is always a smile in happiness or in sadness with a tiny bit of distinctions in the look! Sis hugged me with a lot of excitements by seeing her sister after so long. The nephews took all the suitcases upstairs on command of their Mom very obediently. Good to see the family culture still remains the same. After finishing up the hard job by bringing up the entire luggage upstairs finally I took a long breath to relax after a long day of tensions. Hasna has only one son named Arif. He's a college going young man fulfilled all the courtesies by saying, 'Hi!' and "Hello" at the very greetings to ask also very politely 'do I call you my aunt?'

'Yes, of course!' how sweet! You possess a very sweet voice after all my boy!' 'How about you call me Khala means aunty?'

My niece looked down after taking off his eyes from my sight to say in a low but in a very sweet voice 'khala, how's America? Are they already going with artificial intelligence?'

'How do you know? I jumped up with enormous interest and wonder in his interest in the world.

'Global world!' we do what you do we use what you use very simple!'

Then sister came in between with a fresh towel in her hand said, 'here, first thing first! Apu freshen up now. There are towels in the washroom I'm finishing up the cooking in the kitchen. Its Ruhi your favorite fish remember? Very expensive now but I got it only for you!'

My sister looked at me very proudly but I am boring finally after a long time being here. But my sister said in basic courtesy 'Good! Long time didn't get to eat fish in country style. I'll try to come back here very often!

As I walked towards the bathroom I took a look at my sister's small kitchen next to it. This is for the first time I looked at her apartment apparently very small in size from the entrance where I was sitting all this while which' the living room of the apartment. A little cori-door from the entrance on the left where there is some sitting area very shallow to fit two sofa's one big and the other small. The small one' covering the window next to the door on the left and the big one sitting by the wall opposite to the sitting area with a double bed attached to the wall and two sofa-chairs on the both side of the bed's two opposite heads. One's under the right hand window from the entrance door and the other to the half wall against the kitchen. The kitchen or the little dining table is sitting in the middle of the bathroom area and the kitchen or the little dining. It's a very small apartment but very nice and clean as also very tidy. The nice tiles floor and the bottoms of the walls made the look very nice and cosy. They tried hard to accommodate small families into a small apartment with a beauty with a good look to overlook the shortage of space for accommodations for still the vast populations in a small country like ours. With the speed of the modernism and the mechanism along with the rapid progress of the techniques making our life feeling falling apart from the harmony we hold onto which keeps us together as a family or as a society in unity after all in disharmony in the environment, chaotic social behaviour, pollutions followed by the degradations in Nature and natural resources in growth and progress. The Mother Nature goes furious to take revenge on humans where there is the humanity got lost as a consequence of human behaviour to nature and the exploitations of Nature as well as in Nature. People are becoming short living while trying to keep up the life naturally lived and getting long living while applying all the modern techniques with artificial ingredients and materials to the body consuming in medicines as food intake' to be healthy as expecting to be living or long living in unhealthy physical conditions actually to have the opposite consequences as in suffering more in the hope of getting better for worse. So, basically breaking the laws of Nature or in Nature breaking us off to get the consequences not naturally built or made or to grow in disharmony and abnormal in nature.

Anyways, why do I care to give myself to allow me to bring forth such a long lecture on my own when no one's here to listen? Is it to secure, to comfort, or even to assure me? Life is short getting more and more short by the shortage of the breath or longer by breaking up the breath into many parts to keep them longer? If this is life then why we always wished for happiness in our lives or for a happy and healthy life over all? Just like shaping or reshaping the living by making a nice and small accommodating for each and every small family? can we take an account of the whole populations for each and everyone's or for the entire human populations of the entire world divided by families and their sizes or taking an account of the whole human population by counting each one of the human race against the time left for us to live to limit to live equally each and every one? Then of course we have to count on to the recourses we have in total quantity and equity each and everyone then of course we have to count onto the recourses we have, will be or already left for us till the end of the world? Ironically sounds right but I know sounds crazy.

Sohani served dinner already. When I finished taking bath to come out of the bathroom she was at the table with all the delicious dishes she cooked once I use to love a long time ago. Big pieces of Ruhi fish in thick and shallow gravy, plain white rice with some desi veggie dishes, lentils and some spicy chicken with potatoes in spicy liquid gravy. Food is delicious to remember my mom as the best cook in the whole world who used to cook all those dishes and more I can still remember. By finishing up almost a full plate I asked my sister suddenly, 'Sohani! Where's Meher? He's not eating? My sister dear sister looked up to me by lifting her eyes to say, 'he doesn't live with me anymore.' To my surprise I ask by lifting up my two eye brows up as an expression of enormous astonishment asked again 'What? What do you mean? He doesn't live with you anymore?' a piece of cloud very black spread over her face which makes her a sad lady which I didn't expect to see. She is on her own I just can't believe. She mentioned next, I'm on my own he doesn't live with me but I'm good not to worry much!' The smile from my face was already gone by seeing her pale and mild hidden sadness in her sad face. What's going on in the whole world? OH! Whatever! Global world! After all everything either good or bad spreading with the wind or by the grace of the net!

Another shock! My wonder this time knows no bound to say again 'what you mean by 'on your own? He's not your husband anymore?'

'He's but he just likes to live alone. He just wants to be alone with his work with his freedom that's all.' I still couldn't believe what I was hearing. What's going on here? What's wrong with the people now-a-days? Am I still in the west?'

'The entire same sister of mine! Doesn't matter anymore on the globe where are we living on the globe. People are obsessed while stressed. We're living in our dreams of future which is the present fear now. In a way, we're conquering the fear once we feared to face. Each and every one of us is on his or hers own. Why do you think it's horrifying? I'm fine, Arif will be fine too! Don't worry! Life always teaches us how to survive in no matter what!' said my very sister the same one used ask for every single thing to go out to buy for her! I don't know what to say but only to say to my wonder 'I can't believe it!' Sohani looked into my eyes to read my heart and mind also to guess how bad I'm feeling at the present about the social structures which are almost the same more or less everywhere. Having a very strong faith in one's own self to value only him or her brings each and everyone to better productivity to use the better and the huge productions in varieties to get lost in the lack of inhumanity, being spoiled and selfish in the lack of responsibilities. Their freedom and wishes and desires destroy them in the long run to be dumped into the drainage of human values to be considered as an enormous wastage of no use no more for the civilization at some point for a fresh start once again.

Sometimes I think to myself who brings all the changes in human world is it us or the society or the people who rule the world or it's just the Nature itself in time who lives into our hearts as well as in all the running desires of our own as our basic instincts of the body or for the pain in our souls by providing everything in difficulties to gain, to produce, to keep, to refine, to preserve, having while sharing and to distributing in peace and harmony for the sake of Nature again. We humans as a whole are Nature to keep us up by protecting us by utilizing us with proper use of ourselves. We make the world together things which are important, less important, significant, less significant, majors and minors, big and small, soft and hard as metallic- non metallic, liquid solid, air and soil, values and abstracts which make us human and which comes next after the development to keep that up to make us humans as valuable as to survive properly.

When I got quiet and thoughtful Sohani started to be joking by looking at my worries and asked by twisting her eyes brows 'what happened? You are not eating? Don't worry the scenarios are normal here we don't mind at all anymore. Emotions don't stay longer we've got used to it. Do you think I regret for my husband? Nope! People share together now don't live together. I'm happy as going to work, keeping me up! Staying with Arif to raise him up is all about living only now! as how to provide for the life itself work, home, some entertainments, some rest relationships come next as an extra like you and me now as brother and a sister together once again after a long time to have some time together once again into the bondage of a blood connections together into the blood relationship which matters. Arif is my responsibility before the relationship as the mother and the son together in bondage. Might be one day he will be living away just like you for purpose. He's my responsibility on my part. When people think enough no more productions for populations the------- you know what right?'

Arif went upstairs to his room as he has some studies to do before going to sleep. Me and Sohani remained sitting there talking the past our sweet memories of the past. Sohani is my younger sister always looked after her the way she is looking after her son. I decided not to marry after our parents past away. I was at the end of my education when decided to take care of the family as much as possible. We're only two sisters from our parents grew up well in love and affections together. Looking at the little sister now a loving, caring and responsible mother with no sign of a melancholy or any kind sad or bad feel about her husband Meher who could have been a support for her in bad time whom I chose for her as her loving and caring husband to care of my sister along with the family they make together with a child in peace, love and harmony in a bondage very sacred as a family together. What people expect what do they get by the unknown destiny looking at my dear little sister made me nothing but only sad to see my little sister carrying a huge burden on her life definitely a hard one with no showing off her miseries even to her dear brother out of responsibilities, love and care for all. I started to wonder how Nature makes a woman that much responsible to carry in a real life in the very open and exposed day time reality. I tried hard to conceal my tear drops pulling them back into my eye balls by looking at her speechless and tearless suffering of her heart in the speechless expressions apparently very brave and realistic happens to be very mature over all! Well, this is a woman! Can take all the hardships silently unlikely as a man where the contributions of the womankind towards the human societies are always in most part get ignored in most part because in most part of the society they are not the major earning member of the family. When women get the responsibilities of the entire household in an absence of the man of the house they get to manage the entire home in and out still get enough courage to carry on in silence and with enough patience. So the entire bondage of the holy matrimony has fallen on my poor sister who has basically no choice but to carry on in a spirit very positive with enough patience to prove her a woman as the better half of the very mankind. I questioned myself is this only the spirit for the survival or she is enjoying some kind of freedom to live independently? Can't be! She has gotten tough time and the situations made her tough to forget herself, her choices, her frequent smiles and loud laughter's in the family to laugh at things always not that funny. She's not talking much now time and hardship changed her the ways they change people. I still remember her smiling happy face at her wedding when long time ago I came to marry her at her wedding. Mom and dad were not there but the uncle and the aunt were. All the relations were there to bless her at her marriage it was a happy week to spend in happiness and joy for a week to spend at the special time of Sohani's marriage.

Looking at my present little sister one on her wedding dressed as a bride in red sari and all the jewelleries to look so beautiful as a bride as great as a queen on the stage of the holy matrimony to perform for the rest of her life happens to be failed to be as a wife and a love for someone called husband to lose to the reality of oneness of a self to be alone as a lady once a loving sister of mine happens to be facing the harsh reality like this. What is she doing now? Just trying to survive after all the expectations in her life all the dedication made by her towards the family they made together in the bondage of the holy matrimony? I know it's all about the irony of life dragging some unfortunate people to the basics to accept the bottom-line of the human life after all. We grow up with dreams at the beginning the dreams do you some favor to start with a hope in delight when the plant grows a bit on its own on the land in the soil by spreading its baby roots under to make a light foundations of their stability to grow further in time further when it becomes at least as a grown up mid way student in the long run series of its educational foundations to grow up as an adult fully fledged finally. After reaching the goal to set forth with a job for carriers for the survival of life then the instability of the fate starts to play with its destiny. Being testified all through the life above the adolescences' the charms of the innocence disappears to put people into situations to fight all through the life above all. Still we move on with some dreams in the darkness of the closed eyes in sleep guiding us refreshing sub- conscience to wake up refreshed in the day time dreams to make them real with enough courage making the burdens of responsibilities lighter in some sorts of delusions in dreams to make them easier and acceptable to carry on the same life seemed unbearable without some dreams? Life is all about expectations in dreams between our expectations and achievements between these two what we get is achievements piece by piece broken into pieces to put them together not known when. Life is a life time un-achievements into portions to carry on the constant struggle to put all together into the success not knowing when and how. Sometimes we even don't know what brings the fulfilments in our life or what success makes us feel successful. So basically in between our goal sets and the fulfilments of them there is nothing but the irony of life in failure, in success of a kind in the long run makes no sense after all a person went through life struggle, late success or achievements desired in the failure feeling for life in wishes and desires while already achieved the final or the real maturity in life being old enough to see life from a different perspectives instead of enjoying the success once expected to see and feel and enjoy with full spirit or even some enjoyments and a feel of fulfillment. Life takes all we possess for our trial to achieve whatever in failure, In emptiness, in desires, in hope' and wishes, in ambitions, in devotions through all the hard work to take all together all our energy, stamina and our spirit to either in late success or in failure or even in success with the loss of something which could make us take or accept with happiness to feel and cherish to be happy in the late achieved success.

Looking at my sister thoughtless, dreamless makes me feel that she has become a robot not like manmade like in the world where I live but here in my Bangladesh by the situations no less than the western world or the worlds the as in vast progress in technology and mechanism and the trend of life now in a speed with a stone heart inside and an active brain knows the GPS only to follow the destinies one after another to pick up the materials for life for the family or for the time for work to be there in the work place to earn the currencies for life to go on as an ongoing life machine no less than a car. Sohani's very tough now as the time and events made her like that as if it's the nature of Nature the ways it makes the soft rocks into a hard stone through the constant blow of the wind and the rain from the two opposite sides. Thinking about the family and the family life I looked back to our past together with our parents and all the siblings having a good time in happiness, in fighting with each other, in a togetherness as a family in love and passions without thinking about the separations in making multiple families out of one just like Sohani's and me as a single living a single life. Sohani's wedding was the last memory of the family together with all parents, uncle and aunt, all the siblings together to have a good time in an event making another family tie separately to go on in the same trend to keep the very universal trend of a family making as a generation continuing through generations since the civilizations got evolved. Those excitements, that togetherness even in Sohany's wedding party makes a lot difference in today's present time. It was an excitement to have in all about the wedding a long time ago which have gotten pale and colorless like the pale beige Sari worn by my sister this day today. She didn't care about me as sitting all alone in her home sweet home or about what I was thinking nor even asking a question about my foreign life. As she came back to my side by finishing up her cleaning at the kitchen and the dining area to ask only, 'should I turn on the TV? I'm tired going to bed have to go to work in the morning.' As I looked at her don't really want to put some pity on her instead took the remote from her to turn on the T.V by myself to watch the same shows at least the latest news to know more about the current events in our dear motherland of our own! When woke up in the morning it was not morning but the very noon time 1p.m in the afternoon to see myself still holding the T.V. remote in my grip lying on the sofa. The T.V. was off probably but I didn't know where my mind was wondering in a dream or still sleeping by closing the eyes windows to view the dreams in abstracts away and hidden to see the secrets of the other side of the world or would like to say what's behind the scene in reality. Sohani didn't show me the washrooms last night also forgot to show me a bedroom upstairs to sleep in at the same time thinking all these tried to put my half fallen head out of the pillow to place it back on the pillow as a whole. Then, as I looked up through the open window the bright sun greeted me with some rays to say 'welcome' to my Bangladesh with a note in my left side earlier by my sister to have breakfast by making my own coffee as she left a note saying I'll be back in the evening. Thought me, 'still home of our kind!' which reminded me the student life in the university campus living in the residence with roommates as one goes out another stays and who ever stays for later to leave keeps the key sometimes with a note like this 'I am gone will be come back 2 pm. If you leave for campus before I come back leave the key with the next door girl etc. Making a cup of tea is nothing new for me as I did that in the student life as well as in the foreign life. Sohani prepared my breakfast which is now should be considered as my cold and old lunch happens to be non-eatable for being tasteless while as cold and expired by the expiration of the breakfast time in the morning..

As I looked at the backside of the building through the back window by the dining I saw nothing but all the roofs of the buildings high and low rise with a little green grown in the little gardens on the roofs. I couldn't recall the timing of the season to assume whether it is the spring time or summer time in both seasons we see the green everywhere which apparently very little now as scattered all over in little and little unfortunately. It's a city unfortunately to prove it's incapacity to still keep the signs of Nature into the boundaries of nurturing Nature for the good or for the growth or even for the place to take into the competitions of the fast growing modernizations of the civilizations around the world to make the little space in the town already congested with people, different kinds of vehicles, the crowd of people and the vehicles in the streets down underneath the high rises from above the whole scenarios of the little city looks like the marching high rise constructions for businesses standing side by side all as the soldiers of the solid monuments of the sign of the hard human civilizations as lifeless, ruthless, soulless into the shortage of the green as an inevitable sign for human civilization definitely built and being developing for the sake of humans and humankind out of the very Nature where the Nature itself is being wiped off very ironically for the sake of mechanism for the sake of industrializations, commercials, business in developments in the pattern of all commercials with concretes only where only the flesh and blood humans are the beneficiaries and the users as well as the survivors for whom the change, the modifications, the developments and the growth in civilisations by losing the part of Nature the green from trees, the breathe from the from the Nature to keep alive the main part of the very Nature none but one and only humans and all the animals and insects as well together for the environments and the balance to keep and to maintain to benefit the environment or even the survival of the main part of the natural Nature which is basically providing all for all.

While business is making our life a business then we humans are also the part of the business who's basic or any of their needs basically generating all the business. Life is now all about business to live in environments to go on under the shade of the high rise roofs over our head at day time and at night by the lights making a city all shinny and stunning to make people's lives gorgeously lived in the neon lights where all are basically based on business to make people electricity generated God gifted and created to be reorganized or re-moderated by the humans in the robotic notions to make a new world while don't know be good or bad and while at this point basically have not much choice to make rather than make ourselves also a robot to go on with the robotic ongoing and the day to day developing the robotic world.

Any ways, I didn't notice any rickshaws carrying passengers in its non-stable stable seats neither did I notice ferrywala's selling goods on their heads or on their vehicles on the narrow roads between buildings where people always make a crowd. So the streets and the narrow roads are less crowded and busier with larger crowd than before looking like all busy working colonies of ants going forward up and down down the roads for work and business for the vital survival of the time while side by side all the vehicles and bicycles are merging too in making two opposite rows up and down again the vehicles are also like alive populations carrying people back and forth to the opposite directions as life as always just like us coming to the world by birth and going back in death? In the process of ongoing life and death we along with time of change bring a lot changes in the society. I see now the city is a lot quieter than before with a less honks, less big shouts in the crowds, less chaotic in human businesses, less crowd of small roadside businesses in small road side stores. Higher status people are less visible as riding in expensive rare rides do not add themselves to the regular crowd of people the middle class people along with the lower class people mainly make the crowd by joining all wonders to their wonder only! A little city has not much to show to people and the people also don't really much to worry about or to get excited on anything. In the regular streets or on the regular narrow roads it's only the crowd of people and the cars and other vehicles. The street pictures show only the ongoing regular life in general as travelling up and down for purposes like schools, work, shopping, and all other daily routine for businesses in the daily life all together.

The roof where I'm standing now as shifted from inside the home to the very roof in the elevation makes me see better to have a better view of the current time city view in the capital city of Dhaka. This one is a regular residential three story apartment building belongs to my sister who's renting an apartment on the building. I wished to get myself on the top of those high rise buildings apparently some residential building like Sohany's. They are higher up from where I could see the whole scenario of the city with some green, some water far down and the sky beyond all the crowds of the city specially cars on the high ways running the highways to make the feel of the running city with the speed of the modern city life in a small country in the central city definitely not with enough space but very warm with emotions in the cosy and congested intimacy in life with other lives with still life in passions and devotions into the very culture of its own in nature while got enough nurtured for the Nation to stand in recognitions and with the identifications as a Nation noticeable even though not in much distinctions to recognize as a bad or as a good one to be distinguished as a whatever kind of distinguishing in nature to stand for.

I wished to get myself on the top of those high-rise building apparently some residential buildings like Sohany's. They are high up from where I could see the total scenario of the modified old and the small city of Dhaka still chaotic, crowded in honks and rushes busy or not but definitely hasty to reach the destinations for each and one of the travellers on foot or on vehicles for all purposes. I can see some green just like the small scattered greens everywhere between the gaps of the buildings, on the footpath as the little little water scattered all round the city some of them are little ponds, some of them might be a lake and most of them are just little rain water gathered occasionally here and there everywhere in the rainy season. I can see some green houses on some of the high rises covered by the glasses as covering the planted greens on the roofs of the concretes to hold the non-concrete natural elements like the green plants as sealing the fresh breath of Nature under cover of the glass barriers on top of the human civilizations to keep the value of the greens of Nature by holding it up on the head of the monuments of human civilizations or the concretes high enough to be compared to the tall trees on earth holding the green head on their heads. To my imagination also feels like the suffocating and decaying human creations is trying to hold the breath of the civilization in the green of the green houses under covered by the glass holding some on top of the high rise constructions to keep it up in the decaying Nature in the current time.

Finally around 3 pm. I left my wish to see all from the high up the roofs where my sister along with her son the only son left this time might be for me for the last time to welcome only me. Sohani didn't tell what time she'll be back. The late breakfast making me sleepy again might have not got rid of the jet leg. So I decided to go upstairs to the only six steps up from where I could see Sohani and her family pictures along with her husband and the only son. I could see Sohani and her husband together in the pictures hanging on the wall. She's living alone now but these pictures showing them very present together with her life partner whom I married with full efforts and all the arrangements to go in vain like this? The pictures of her marriage are still on the walls just like a memory of life while the life has become empty of a company to live a life with full spirit together with a passionate and compassionate life partner basically a true lover to live in love, with sharing and caring to go along the ways of life together in togetherness making the life much easier on the carrier on the wings of life. People are very slowly proceeding from the bondage of the matrimony by breaking the bondages out of the created situations or choices of the each individual to get along all alone being a single for the good of whatever kind for peace or comfort or a wellbeing's or for the betterment of the each individual or for the family by cutting of the spouse from the family. While the heart of the human body machines happen to be turning to an engine inside the flesh and blood body by the constant changing life style in the pattern of the daily routine which is very busy to keep up only in speed as well as the changing attitudes of the living people around are not as favorable as before then very normally people change to become a stone heart monster or a machine to keep up the robotic life in proper respect to the ongoing speed of life to become a living machine to carry on the businesses to keep going on command. But now the question is by who or which's? The Almighty God the creator the sustainer or the time itself to go on by maintaining time only not even knowing for what? But still we like to live in love and family bondages to live like the real people but it just don't happen in reality for multiple reasons again made by the time the very changing life pattern and its nature in nurture. Dreams die after a life set ups in hopes after a very short time like having a vacation or a honeymoon right after a marriage in love and hope to proceed very rapidly towards the process of departing notions from each other while failed to keep up the real love in bondage. All happens very quickly like having some happiness which is naturally very short existing for its own nature or for ours to be bored living in the same pattern of life with the same love or the person. In that case people will forget about marriage or even bondage of any kind to live like a free man or a woman to work and to take a break in love to relax only to keep going in work by gaining some energy or stamina to keep up the very busy ways of life? Again it's like fueling the life machine to go on its wheels with perfect speed. People tend to be free thinking as born free while coming from the womb of the mother conceived by the father. It's a system a chain system for creations in bondage in love, care, passions and emotions along with responsibilities for each other as the mother can't just deliver the child to leave minding her own life business while the father also need to take care of the life partner as well as the offspring's by living together in a family. The life cycle is same for all either man or animals. Animal bondages are short existing while many long existing in living together as a family. When there is a time when we start thinking about ourselves only with no care, in no bondage of a relationship the society will turn to an animal kingdom instead of a Human society where we keep each other into a bondage in love, pity, care, responsibilities, sharing along in making a life normal caring and chaste, kind and educated along the ways of life after and over all to be a Human by being a humankind in humanity maintaining a system.

I knew long time ago that money is the patrol of life and for earning this fuel we run in speed by making ourselves a running machine to keep running. Actually, long time ago money was considered as the fuel of our life as for our survival as we can't buy anything without money as the values of life in goods turned into a currency to count for exchange as the media of the value. Once the currencies needed for the life only to keep it up through the survival buying goods needed for life while now the speed of life making us to be really some vehicles running in time with the fast running phase of time. We're fuelling ourselves constantly to keep us running in order to keep us up but we don't know to keep us up in what? In the competing world for the survival or for the betterment of life itself while losing behind all the values with the black smoke behind by polluting the environment like a speedy car while proceeding very fast forward the fast running or fast moving life vehicle for the present developing society getting away in the speed leaving all the pure behind to go forward in what or for what? We don't know that we only know how to move forward for good purchasing the necessary goods for life, running in the competitions for better, for making things better than others in look, in dignity, in values in money only while losing the real values of life even for ourselves to live in peace, in comfort, in love, in understandings, in togetherness with each other, in spending some time by taking some time off from the time machine very speedy and non stopping to relax to think, to see, to feel, to understand, and to enjoy even what we make and create on our own from the resources getting from Natural in a leisure to love all together with us and the Nature itself. We're running constantly by fueling us up by creating or making things for life but we don't have time or even to think about making a time even at least to enjoy what we make with our hard work.

I used to think that the only already developed countries are becoming robotic mainly by performances of ever expanding technologies Nope! Life is all the same everywhere as a global world through the internet. Our people are also very busy and speedy in money making as well as very commercial even to make money in friendships or in relationships in matters friendly in exchanges in the money exchange. We're selling time and life too as time makes money and money makes life? The boundless bindings making our life in two categories one's we are adopting animal instincts exposing them out from the very inside out of the harsh reality to snatch things we need or the cruelty we keep inside to harm to take and snatch from others hands when unable to earn or make by our own efforts in the society where no one care for no one else. A boundless binding of a life is like the life as a chainless train running forward out of the very natural basic instinct for the survival to stop any time to hit itself to the end with no goal no destination only into the darkness of mere death. Another category is the category of people the time is making now is the people in robotic behaviour with no conscience, no regret, selfish sometimes even as selfless as not knowing surviving for what reason by being only an artificial intelligence. We care for the body needs only now for the comfort, for the hungers of the body. We produce things only for the sake of the body it's comfort, its hunger, its desires only coming from the instincts while being selfish we look for only what we need by means of things, if even we do get some recreations that's also short lived for the body only in rest, in comfort and in fulfilling the body needs through the basic human instincts very necessary while work so hard for the fuel to live not for the feel of the life itself in passions, emotions and devotions as real as human beings over all. But if we all totally turn to metallic robots then what fuel we'll need to keep us keep going on our missions which is basically all our business. Materialistic people still do care about others which the robots can't while running after materialistic matters or things in life makes us rude, emotionless motions but going as an iron heart into the iron bodies can't make the robots to roll in spirit to still make a life for life while the iron itself can only work from human brains deriving some from them as made of human brains by deriving some humanistic characteristics to help the real people as made for people. The very futuristic ideas make the future consists of robots only. They exists they live they do all the things on their own as the metallic humanistic bodies with still possessing the iron heart in the iron body. Man can make machines also machines can make man by using the natural ingredients from human bodies as some sort of supplies like flesh and blood, head and the heart. We don't know through the scientific inventions to what extensions man can go to create humanistic robotic humans. Till now, only man can make robots as a machine generated computer in the shape of a man or a woman. The machines can make man also but only the kind of robotics. The Nature consists of a bit of metals as an ingredients but the flesh and blood is only natural to prevent man making man by generating a human heart implanting in the very human body. Nature produce natural resources including metals and hard rock's while man make robots by the help of the technologies which is manmade or their inventions. If our imaginations make a world of robots all in robotic movements and activities without the basic soul which is only natural to prove Nature and its flexibility and natural capacities to prove natural creations of God possessing the very supernatural power to produce and reproduce through the very natural systems as ongoing as ever till the end. People are turning somewhat a kind of robotic nature through the time in hard reality and the robotic inventions by people proceeding towards the developments to ease the life of people in the very competitive and speedy situations to keep going with the very modern trends to tolerate and to achieve techniques while possess talent by birth naturally. For now the main concern is to protect the world from the destructions specially this time when the Nature seems like not much happy to co-operate with the human sufferings caused by them as well as by Natural disasters also caused by people while abuse the recourses when needed to use.

Loveless, passion and devotion less societies only can bring death and destructions by causing wars, natural disasters through inhumanity while ignorant of the very consequences to realize what causes what or what brings the humans, Nature, all the animals to death and diseases as well as the natural disasters to destroy the human world in a large devastations in the lack of preventions of some causes of pollutions, deformations, to the breaking of the laws of Nature to urge it to the devastations by the big natural disasters as a whole all together to destroy the world rapidly or even slowly when we as the very wise humans do not keep the laws, do not respect and protect the natural resources and above all do not make the judgement between abuse and use of the recourses has been given to take care of while at the time to reproduce while using the produced. It's all our imagination that we are preceding towards a robotic world scenario. Therefore, to my concern the end of the present human world which is loveless bondage free half robotic human or half animal half human living in pollutions to get destroyed slowly or very rapidly together with wars and in hunger and destructions.

I stood for a longer time in front of my sisters photo' taken at their wedding where there was me too! We were all in love and happiness especially when I can still see the love and passion in Sohani' eyes for her husband who' no more by her side. Since I started about love stories I failed again and again to find a true love to make a love story of mine. Here I started to write all love stories to get lost in the real life which is even ruder as I see here life is even lifeless now doesn't matter where we live on the globe or where to go for a fresh air to refresh us our souls to breath in and out to live with an healthy and active heart we possess to simply live. A few decades ago when we felt like we were missing something valuable from our lives called 'Love' we started to hold on to life itself to live somehow with getting some fun from somewhere to keep us alive with other concerns of our instincts as the hunger of the heart and the soul as well as the hunger of the body the basic instincts to fill up the tummy with food and for the hunger of the soul we replaced laughter for love, fun and fancy to divert the soul to the fascinations in life, for passions and devotions or dedications to some creativity we replaced addictions like wine, gamblihigs, games even mind games to play people's heart and mind and in the worse scenario we put drugs to divert people from the reality and from the very character of the people to drive them to fall into the ditch of the illusions with the addictions to replace regenerating life for generating death and destructions in diversions.

Fun loving people love to take their part by buying tickets for all the attractions to have fun nothing bad about it. Building up a hobby is not only fun it's also in some kind of a knowledge seeking addiction towards something good. Movies, theatres, circus, vacations, sightseeing etc. all together is life in fun, fascinations, attractions, curiosity as well as a break from the monotonous daily routine of life. All is life to have except those destructive addictions but together with a soul mate is valuable and with meaningful in love and affections to share with someone we love as sharing and caring make a life together with love.

I kept thinking about the past when we had friends to talk to have a chat in a group to roam around something attracts us or by having a friend or a group of friends to have some time together or to go for a vacation finally to have a partner at least to have a life together or to go for a vacation finally to have a partner at least to have a life together by sharing each other' life and recourses' in one of a kind relationship. Finally when we lost that too we had no choice but to live alone by holding a piece of electronic device in our hands as a companion or as a social media or an entertainment and information's. We started working with some fun to make the work place our home after all. So we worked for living and lived with passion at work with some company. Sometimes real sometimes not just like some replacements for the real entertainments as contradictory or as less of the real.

Sohani came home at 5 p.m. she looked good to me not tired at all. Still there are thoughts in my mind the thoughts of missing love and emotional attachments in the family as well as in the society were roaming into my head. Seeing Sohani I pointed out her in the wedding pictures with Mehel. She looked back and smiled as if she 'still likes that person in her life as a dear one. I asked her directly expecting not to hurt her but to ask her, 'Do you still love your x-husband? Do you miss him?' Sohani avoided the actual question said, 'he was a nice person we were happy!'

'Then why you couldn't save your marriage?'

'I wanted him to be my love not only my life. He started to focus on the progress of his profession only. He aspired to be a big Boss in a big position what is he now when at the same time we started to lose our love, our relationship as I started to lose him by losing him in love and company altogether-------- Sohani paused here to make over her hard feeling over a loss. Then I asked again with curiosity or with some sympathy for her or for the loss of the total humanity which is progressing everyday towards a life not going to be human at all! I asked again, 'what happened then? Seeing her quiet I asked again with an emphasis 'what happened later so that you two broke up?'

'I lost him forever------- my sister started to cry as couldn't resist her tears to drop shamelessly.

As I questioned again she cried loud to say, 'he's no more Sis! He's nothing but dead to me! I gave him life for the development of our life---------we're lost sister we are totally lost!' I got very surprised at her lies but kept quiet for sometimes then asked again very slowly in a soft and low voice 'but you said he's living somewhere else?'

My poor sister wiped her nose first then the eyes to say with a pause 'I say what I like to say and that's what I like to believe!'

I kept staring at her for a moment to my astonishments to answer nothing but to sigh very deep from the core of the heart breathing heavy in pronouncing only 'OH!'

Both of us kept quiet for sometime as none of us wanted to talk. Sohani took her time to cry to empty her bosom in pain then started releasing all information's in nothing but all negativity around her said again, 'we're falling apart sister! Most of my friends are single now. As while ago we were also afraid to have a child to rise. The chosen life partner into the bondage of marriage has become a Honey in the every after wedding honeymoon to be apart from being a short time life partner. A bondage between a man and a woman meaning slavery to some people while the cost of relationships makes no meaning in love and passion in bondage either in holy matrimony or named only a relationship to live together for good for each other. While crying made my sister lighter she paused a bit from her melancholy mood to smile while all this while I was starring very closely at her to mean to observing her mood and the state of her mind and the broken heart.

Then I said nothing but 'Good!' in a bit loud to make shy this time. She really got ashamed of her silly behavior which was a meaning just a little while ago in a maturity from the very infinity? Sohani left by saying, 'you are bad! I go make the dinner. In the meantime, I called to inform her Mom that he's not coming home at night. I got only surprised then where he'll be? Sohani's normal reaction said, 'might be in a friends' to finish the home work then after to go to play video games'. I asked again out of my curiosity, 'do they go to movies or hang out with girls?' At my a single question out of my curiosity my sister started to give me a long lecture on the current time strategies said 'No, no movies they make now-a-days only but we make real movies out of our true stories. Our life is a real movie no needs to watch the copies only! Shakespeare is back again on the 'Life is a stage' philosophy! Where no one cries anymore, no one is over passionate, no one sheds some tears on the scenes performing human emotions on the very stages of the Life itself the ongoing human lives making a real drama out of harsh realities not to watch to cry or to laugh, to regret, to feel a pain inside over the loss of a loved one while no love left here anymore to love anyone or anything anymore while nothing makes us a real happy or sad on the gain as well as on the loss. Movie makers are out going to be out of business now! People work hard for the survival only in having mere fun only by spending time after work having two 'W's in words which are the very old and conventional means for entertainments through ages from the uncivilized and the very civilized worlds of ours by going back to the very primitive from the very Prime time. Musicians tends to play or make songs out of the old by selling into the old bottles by filling with the new as when the hearts are no more hearts to flow in making music in the expressions of the tones to tune in an expression of the feel of the heart which is basically a flow less flow of the dead hearts to make nothing but cry outs in bids to urging people to overflow in emotionless motions to dance in the rhythms of expressions of a kind of coming out pain in the time costing the time of their lives in the lack of relaxation, a little leisure, a bit of heart to cherish life and love in the things or with the things people love if still some love peeps through the hard and harsh time to spend in no soul but by get going with work in the speed of the speedy cars to run from here to there for business only. Similarly, not many musicians to play, to sing and to compose some music from the heart when the heart is heartless and the souls are soul soulless. Only some magicians can make a life with some charms or some tricks to play some tunes one of a kind through technology to turn the stones to play but I still don't know what those tunes would be! The dreamless and the soulless cities are now sleeping. You can hear their hearts after work at the bars dancing with the bids while playing hard rocks or heavy metal kind of music after hard work to turn their hard bodies holding frozen hearts to get some movements to flow at least with the bids of music before turning total metallic. After all the flesh and blood humans are now neither human nor robots. They are now in between to decide which part to take to reform themselves to keep themselves as a relique of human spices or to reform themselves as total robotic.

After Sohani finishes her speech with a great concern I tried to make it still human by hurting all her feelings said 'I like robotic reformations! No feel therefore no pain, no regrets, no bad feeling! Why do we have to be humans to hurt ourselves by the very feel of pain, no pining for gaining, no ambitions, no aspiring to fail, to die hard in working hard to reach a goal while most of the time to a be a fool as being a gullible. Why do we have to human to live to die in pain, we only try to smile and fail to cry. Therefore souls have no goal, no guilt no feel, no reason no results, no success no failure. All in all it is only to be alive just for being alive through the survivals only.'

Sohani didn't talk to me anymore just looked into my eyes with an anger which I didn't know for hating me or to accept me. I stood again in front of Mehel' smiling face in the pictures hanging on the wall just beside Sohani standing side by side as love to love captured in the photo frame as a monument of love and relationships. The photo's into the solid metal frames with the memories of a beautiful couples love into a bondage printed on the papers capturing live smiles as forever as a memory to keep while these pictures of love, relationships and bondage might have been extinct to keep the memories as souvenirs' of the old in the coming near future. The departure of the partner from the life of Sohani causes a deep negative impact on someone's life while a deep feel of pain very deep into the heart causes someone like my sister an enormous sorrow to bear like this in hardships of life, in struggles, in pain, in insecurities, in responsibilities with some fear to perform all duties all alone when no one is by the side for a little support. A big sacrifice in love and life or thriving for life in the present living takes life now-a-days. Trying hard for a real life for all children and herself is a real challenge. I looked back to my sister again a piece of modern living death struggling every moment to hold onto life in real sense by holding her present love in both her children very close to her bosom to embrace in love and affections. Even a little older people are now trying hard to keep up the natural bondages against the progress of the very artificialities in the contemporary life into the progress of its development

The very progress in the developments of the artificial intelligence without a real human feel the real and deep thoughts or even true to be one's own self to get at least a quarter or even less portion of a real life lived or felt to the very present generations by looking or feeling back what they had even in just a few years back. This is how we are actually thriving to move forward with no hope actually by losing ourselves in the loss of the life itself in a real sense. I started gazing at Sohani my younger sister still looking at the poster may be at her lost love' lost memories might have been taken her into the world of an imagination to still be thinking of Mehel wondering or living somewhere else not with her but only left to live separately.

THE END

STORY 9

Live Love

I jiggled I juggled all my life making all my quick stories made by those three L words to make only one true story about a true love in life hoping to be my own or someone else's to make the confusing love thing for life to be very true to be sincere in life to make a life for lovers in making a true couple in general by making the ***Love*** word true to be truthfull in each couple'life as general as to be universal as in the communities of the very love birds. But no! we're humankind the very critical at the same time to be very complex in nature to make our life very complex and difficult for any issue while the love birds fly on its own wish as we can't make and match our time with the wishes of our own to imprison the bird in cages of our heart and soul in desires to cherish love on time by keeping it into the bosom at the same time generating by piercing through the heart or for some people through the various hearts of desires in his or hers. We pine for love while we were born in love. We live by fulfilling our hearts and the body at the same time when the body needs food and drink the soul or the heart needs love. We can cultivate food or buy food but we can't cultivate love or buy the souls full of love in exchange of a value even most of the time our efforts fail to achieve love in exchange of love. Anyways, I try not to be very specific or long in making up some love stories again out of different stories made by the love around me including me with some concerns or the happenings very quickly almost all together.

Living a long life in the land of opportunities I gave up my faith and trust in my friendships, my future and my present life to buy a ticket to my home land in a quick decisions by giving up my job last week for being deprived of the position by promotion after my dedications for that in the last eight years while pushed forward to take the next one by giving up mine to a new candidate aspiring and wishing to get the promotional meaning of the higher position actually got taken by the candidate considering more competent and expert to push me down to nowhere.

This last love story is about my friend living in Bangladesh this love is no love but only a pure friendship between two of us and the friend is the friend who got left alone with his two children while the wife kicked him out of her life by leaving the home for him to live in with the children while still considering him worthless as a man as well as a father. So the two loveless individuals a man and a woman are now not only single but also loveless to live all alone by himself and separately by herself. The she individual is considered to be better all by herself and the he is the miserable one taking the responsibilities of the children on his shoulders all alone. So the desire of love dragged them down to live in no love on top of that put then into miseries with a huge burden of the care for the children on the male lover now and most probably will be on the shoulder of the female one. The desiring and the aspiring love and love making did them a favor by imposing the very love Childs as the love fruits from the manmade paradise to get the consequences of the fall! Is that so? I think not! Life is still love with some loss.

Now! About me and my love I die for all my life? Love Love Love! Is this all women? May be! Looks like so! Especially me and my life not as a love bird but as a lover very romantic in search of another as a partner but don't get me wrong of course a male lover only lives for love as die for love? Nope! My fate is also just like my friend the very male friend meant to be in search of a beautiful woman to be in love to love cherishing the life in full. But in my case reality thaught me a very heard lesson to run away from the love thing to make a life in a career to survive to maintain a life lived with bread and butter, bed and bath, and of course in a house for hibernating to work better and live better at the time when the sun shines with enough heat in the brightness to see the world crystal clear in the sun and rain, in the beauty of Nature and it's nurtured, love and luxuries, in vacations and in camping, in enjoying the weather in the exposer of the beauty of the mother Nature to relax, to feel life in all the beauty of life very open in the season favorable to treat ourselves better in summer or in autumn. All the items I mentioned in pairs the most hard one is the rare 'Love" thing. If the weather is nice the mood is off for some reasons in the matters bothers in the real life and the reality. Availing all from the market or by the grace of the present commercials or by the great efforts of the businesses can be availed by the hard earn money as well as the beauty of the Nature when also availabe i n seasons to view and to feel with love for the Nature or for the life and the love partner even if a little hard by making a time from work to breath to relax also not very hard to avail but the very abstract Love is a real hard to avail when the life and the socities are going basically loveless while life less in the pattern of present modern commercial or the very modern life where people are turning to be a robot day by day every moments making things through hard work for the survivals. Ever thriving, ever striving not knowing for what even didnt know whether it's a stupidity or just a careless individual who never actually care about herself or actually a person aimless, goalless, a gullible regardless to pay her all regards to the surrounding people who she care about for not to care about love or to fall in love with anyone any kind of a living person around just like me to live with in the whole process or for the survival for the survival only. My foreign girl friend Sheilla got engaged with someone she loved and lived together for a long time by having a boy and a girl together by not being that parental at all and very recently when all these happened in a very short time all together Sheila got separation from his boy friend too because only she has to take care of the children and her partner remains untouched by the reality and the responsibilities to fly around as a butterfly in search of the bushes or the flowers taking a sip of honey from the core of the heart of a flower to fly back again to another or to set himself free of any kind of a bondage in life requiring some stability into some responsibilities as making a family together with some members by making some children from the couple of their love in love only? He tends to be free of any kind of a tie to tie himsef tight with the knot of someone else'tie to go together with no choice until someone or something set him free or let go off the bindings bounded towards home in the home maker's business.

So, desperate me for a fresh air remaining now on the plane flying back to my place where still I beleive myself to be belong from the very heart and the soul in the real sense from the real sense of the sensibility. It's a long journey nothing to do but sitting constantly on the fixed seat looking out the window through the sky seeing the clouds down covering the cities sometimes exposing at the very beginning right after taking off if someone is lucky to get the window side seat, sometimes nothing to see after a high level in the sky all looking nothing but foggy to keep the windows closed by closing the views to the sky high might be the very sky zone from where only the space ships can start their jouney by piercing through the streight high up the sky. Any ways already spoke a lot about the boring plane journey taking about a two and a half days with some flight change as well. The young man beside me already started to snore putting the head down on the back of the front seat. For the first time I looked at the passanger beside me basically nobody to me but blocking me now to go to the restroom. I looked at the young man about at least 10 years younger than me to wonder with enough pain in my lower abdomen. So, what can I do but to look outside the window to nowhere but the at the sky. Not bad! At least sometimes we get an opportunities to touch the sky. I can see now the clouds the whole soft wool platform of the white sky and the black clouds the whole soft wool of the platform of the white ash and black clouds down there and we are up in the sky above what is beauty with an opportunity to see looked back again at the next passanger to me thinking to knock him to ask how to make a way to the washroom. I have to make his way!no choice! But still don't know how to do that by calling up a sleeping man? I stood up by taking off my seat belt still wondering at the sleeping co-passanger. Luckily an air-hostess came by to listen to me said nothing to me but looked into my eyes to figure out what kind of an alien I am from what planet and just knocked him by calling loud enough 'can you hear me gentle man?' still no no move no reponse and then the air hostess thought to knock him gently. So she called him again by bending down very close to his eyes to wave her hand to call out 'Hellow! Can you hear me?' the young man might have been in a sweet dream viewing an Angel calling him out to make him out to shook his head off the front seats back to look up to check who's calling and very quickly stood up by taking off the seat belt as fast as possible to move out the way to let his next seated passanger with enough repect with the red swollen eyes from the sudden break up of the sweet or the fatigued sleep on a tiresome long plane journeyday. The individuals on the aeroplane knows no one sitting near or far and flying on an airplane is never a fun by sitting a long time on the same seat by economically measured to fix only one person and by consuming the tiny bowls of the meals once or twice on the whole journey as a miniature of a short living life on the space ship to fly far and far away across the vast sky sphere from a long distance in a short time just like the ways the life is getting shorter and shorter everyday in our feel or our expectations from life to achieve whatever an individual desires or even plan to get. One meal a day is shorter in well pached portions to have anywhere any time to make the life easy in busy so does our clothings shorter and shorter to make our life easy while very busy. Day time is becoming shorter while running fast in fast movements and more activities and work and mobility to forget that we're living and half of the night we're spending in shopping or in all the preparations for the next day to make the night time sleep shorter and shorter to make the night time also a shorter in a dreamless fast sleep for the night. It is good for the time while our life is really hard and stressful to keep our heart and mind fast forward forwarding the life fast where 'there's no aim no hope for any good but to survive only while going fast moving in neither a time wasting nor a life cheating life but in less productivity where the machines are the means of productions we just carry out the systems making a system for not to let things go wrong. It's also a process to make progress in life by making our day time shorter with busier movements in work and mobility to forget that we're living in the day time and half on the night when we are in shopping or to make the night time sleep shorter and shorter in dreamless, with a pining free heart fast asleep as tired and snoring like a pig to dip into a sleep time to wake up again in a short feel of life to start another long day in a short feel in a fast moving long working day by making it a short time single day to pass easily in a short breath by making the long day a short time working hours in the existing a long day. This way we're heading fast forward in the short existence of the life painful or stressfull in the numbness of the feel by taking the hard working or fast moving lifeless life to make a new life eternal which makes no life but produce the products of the lifeless life. Time makes now no time to sit and relax or to think and enjoy the life for who the life is. The subjectless substances therefore makes no meaning for life but to run only for the sake of the survivals only with no meaning basically if we still consider us as the great human beings in humanity while possessing a heart and a soul into the body as a running body machine runs naturally on it's own. Our time now is not worthless but definitely breathless in thoughtlessness in a breathless work time to cross over for the next. In a way we're almost like on the board like this now on the aeroplnane sleepless, speechless as well as lifeless sitting objects in no motion at all for the sake of the transfer from a take off to the destination. Basically life is short there is no doubt about that. Living a life brings us to various ironies to experience while now as we crossing the time sphere of our lives we are going fast or flying fast on the wings of the time which' no time machine yet but we are fast moving modern humans making our life shorter in the fast moving activities like an on going vehicle. Basically, loveless and lifeless life heading towards what' not known even not possible to know for you and me.

Finally, the flying flight has been landed on the land by crossing two more destinations on the long way a long way to my native land far far away from where I live now. The check out was quick and easy with some quick questions about my nationality, my home land and about the status I got to live on the land of opportunities. Waited for a long time almost half an hour at the pick ups of the luggages to get informed finally that the missing luggages of mine will arrive the next day. I got it! It got stuck for it's size somewhere. Thought me 'Alas! While we are reputed as copycators of different ways of passing from different cultures especially from the westerner' then why don't we copy those means good for the good for people as well for the welfare of our very systems all over in our country for the same good also? Any way, I was quick in signing up the forms at the final counter by putting the lists of things. I brought in that list of the things I brought in the missing suitcase and I was not all though! Finally at another counter now I got stuck again to clear what's my occupassion is and again thought me in an enormous anger to think 'wont my own people let me in by stepping in the very entrance by proving me by showing all the documents of my identity as a Bangladeshi to enter the very Bangladesh the very Motherland of our own? While showing the identifications of my occupation to the counter to the people looked and felt like all foreighners in a different Land as making me feel like an stranger in the very land of my own made me very sercastic for all through the generations to think what makes us distinct from one another as a distinct nationality while going all around the world?? What caused the partitions between deviding nations with a particual identity in name by what different distictions in chacteristics of humans as a whole? It's all History consequently will take a long discussions as a consequence will go on forever or never ending but definitely whats happening here at the checkout at the airport is all about a system. After all we humans finally set some systems to go systamatically managing the whole human race as a big one to manage in partitions in categories. it's all very simple to take all the tentions and the crysis all through the evolutions of the vast human populations as a whole by deviding into countries and into different districts or so in each country. But all happened through the history which wasn't ever very happy in the happening of wars, battles all together through the history of the human evolutions through a lot of the revolutions in blood shed as well as in all the tentions and the all crysis. Making a life similarly making a world in being in love with the life and with dedications and devotions is as hard as to be proven all it takes through a lot as I mentioned is not as easy as we faced through the evolutions of human existence as well as for the reconstructions of the human history by making a land of their own to live in distinctions.

Any ways, thought me again, 'what a world! What a day! An stranger in her own land?' finally, looking around observing people at least to say a Hi! to get their attention as the welcoming return of their kin citizen. Nope! Surprised again, no one even cares about an handsome young lady like me passing by after all!thought me again 'am I too old? Oh! God!' this place seems more strange to an stranger like me. People looked all like duty bound modern monuments of humans all lined up looking emotionless motions at the counters holding the documents to hand in by passing one by one with still holding in some expiring phases of human emotions in their hearts if still the hearts existing into the pumping pusle's in their bosoms. Have they lost all their concerns don't they feel any pain anymore? Again thought, to my concern 'coming out of an high technique world to the world of our own thought to be back dated a little or more but in real it' even post dated in well consumed technologies and mechanism or the effect of our world look like the world I have left for my own was actually my own not this present one which I entered with great hope and heart to have the lost life back in the lost heart and soul. In reality which is actually the opposite by selling our own for the new which makes neither a soul nor a heart of my own in a lost world out of our ambitions or of the foul of our ambitions and aspirations leaving me no where but into a misery created by us as if the Mother land took a new form in between an wireless soul of our own out of the very soil we are proud of and the very running wires throughout Her body making a new formation by driving the people half robotic. My heart ached a little for something I lost not knowing what. The life which accepted me and all of my life with the considerations as a mixture of all goods and bads towards me, my own judgements in acceptance by the heart by compromising to make me feel now that the life and the world I left behind now is the accepted world of mine to feel myself an stanger here in the very land of my birth to be considered as the Mother Land for all. For a few moments my moods got fused thinking 'where do I belong? What did I lose in order to gain what? Are all of us in the right directions living in a place anywhere in the world by taking off the one we possess with full heart considering our own as our birth land or our Mother land? But what makes us think the things of our own own? What do we do? Or what do we achieve by losing what values of our own or not? Or doesn't really a matter anymore. I looked around once more to think, 'am I really a stranger to these people now?' as I looked around for 10 min to get a cart. At the counter the checker looked once at me to say, 'Go to the counter number 6 for a help means someone who can help a single person like me. I stood outside the airport might have been for at least 15 min to get a taxi. The taxi driver opened the door and picked up the luggages with no greetings at all and drove the car in full speed on the highway and radically took his turn to enter a road ways through some shallow roads between some open market places with crowds. People around there looked rugged folk could be aggressive to rob or steal or even to hurt by stopping the vehicle. As I got scared the driver said, 'Don't worry'! and got up the high ways again from where the sky looks big, buildings down on alignments the monuments of the civilization a vast moving walking people in the streets of all kinds rich and poor as the appearances show. It's day time to view all pictures of a city a small city. The high rises and commercials up and down streets along with the rug roads inside with the rug stores or I would say small small stores selling Daily nesseceties of life. These places mainly remain very crowded and dirty I believe with frequently happened criminal actvities too. I got concerned about me with my appearance with all the luggages in a fear about the possibilities of being robbed off those inevitable burdens of life or even in the fear of being Hijacked or even being ket killed by some strangers possibly some robbers. The little fear inside made me fear the whole city might be for nothing. The driver tends to stop at some point at some snack bars or at a coffe house by saing 'no change at all!' while I said 'a little stoppage may cost a life! for the next 20 min.' So he stopped the engine as the chaos around some girls tends to make some business out of theselves probably? He started driving again without wasting anymore time for delay to reach home for me by taking another right turn in the same area where we got stuck for the next 20 min. The crowd was still behind around the beauty and the body selling business by women in the open market at the very dawn before the sun shows it's bright face for the beginning of the brand new day in rising while shinning. The night time live shows of life with women and wine in open street at the late night streets will be over soon. People buy and sale life to one anther by selling themselves in no concience when the darkness engulf them into it's womb to give birth to the very daily morning, morning time birth of the rising and the shining sun for the bright brand new day in daylight out of a night time darkness again for another night. The darkness has to disappeare at the appearance of the brightness of the sun. The darkness of our lives brings our days from the other view or by the opposite view the days end up in the darknes of the nights simultineously making the meaning of the very life of our own as an alternative phases of the time if we consider them as good and bad coming one after another similarly but whatever it is, is it the law or the system of Nature for our life? Then why we worry? Whatever it is, as the darkness falls after day light while day light comes back right after darkness when it disappeares? However! The darkness always makes a dark sign or a dark mark of a bad of whatever kind on our body or the on the soul. The city police appeare at this hour sometimes to witness the business in the dark which brings out the light a little later at the same spot as inevitable as the duties of the darkness. This part of the night life is as inevitable as the part of human life for the sake of the basic instincts as a part of the entertainment of a kind through the civilizations from its very beginning. We always blame the contemporary time but everything was there from the very beginning of the human civilizations. People remain the same in body and the soul the costumes change only to make differences between times.

The taxi driver seems to a very nice person he asked me at some point to stop at any shop I like to relax as he won't charge me money for his extra time and again to my surprise I thought again 'is this kind of curtesies still available in this time at this era?' anyways I bought some souveniers as gifts for my sister's children and a T-shirt for me as always. The police men appeared again in front of me to remove some drunks from the street never happened befor when I used to live here before leaving the country of my own. The driver apologized again to me saying, 'I'm taking another turn again at some dirty streets like these to watch some bad scenes----- he didn't even finished his words when we both had to watch the chasing police man after a running away theif or some other sorts of criminals definitely minor nor major. I got to learn from the driver that sometimes some people runaway like this by only stealing a bottle of wine from a bar or even some food from a restaurant. As he regtrets like, most of the people are rich now while a little create some scenes like these to make us ashamed!'

I understood his pain inside and the shame causing it just like me. But I only answered to him 'it's life Bhai! Everything and all can't be right or just after all! Sooner we'll get much better.' He knodded his head looking down to take his turn back to the highway from the low level to the high on the high ways from where you can see only the high rises and the walking Liliputians down on the streets side by sides with the speediy small cars looking like some toys to play with like a little child once more by imagining myself as a Giant very tall and up to look down at the buildings way up over the heads of the people. I can see the Talls and the Bigs of the civilization like my Bangladesh as standing high up by ignoring the reality down on the streets at the footage of the highways or on the narrow roads where lies the reality with people in poverty, in decripancies of status, in discriminating humanity downwards in crisis, crimes and the cry of the hearts in poverty and in need, in frustrations, despair, arrogance and protests by raising the banners up or in silence without knowing to stand up against who and what? The modern trends or the trades of goods including people who sale theselves in labour to live only? Deaths and destructions are all very common turns to be taken as a part of the developments by shedding the odds out of the civilizations constantly evolving in some change in developments.

Finally, after almost an hour when I reached home my sisters home actually where I was heading to. She lives with her two children a boy and a girl old enough by now I guess! The taxi driver dropped me in front of their building and just by pulling down all my luggages. So the journey for the arrival by the help of the taxi driver ended here with "Hi's in the beginning as a greeting and Bye's at the end. Simi and two of her children Bulbuli and Bushar all came down very cheerfully to cheer me up at the very welcome to their place. 40 years old Simi my little sister came running to hug me said 'Hi'! with cheers with these very exciting and fascinating reactions like 'have you already seen the beauty of our city of Dhaka?' Before I say anything she said, 'welcome bro! long time! Long time!' Bulbuly and Bashar both are college students said nothing but smiled to say, 'welcome' only. Altogether we reached the 3rd floor with all the luggage brought by me only of course, from the land far far away definitely not from a fairy land to surprise them with some wonders or beauties never seen before. People can reach the outer world from home now only a mobile or the T.V. can bring the whole world to the people where ever they live I mean 'we!' wherever we live as it has become a small world now by the Mercy of the who? The technology? The very human inventions as well as the creations? Its our world improved, evolved, developed and recreated by us only.

It's a holiday today so all of my blood relations are home now. They are excited especially the neice and the nephew. Bashar took a chair to sit on the back side by holding onto the back seat facing to me said, 'how's America Uncle? Have you already got engaged or planning someone to marry very soon or otherwise?' before I said something Bulbuly started to laugh but which I don't know why. They look very naughty as started questioning, 'do you do dishes there?'

I got surprised first not knowing what kind of a question is that but quickly, I pulled myself together to answer promptly, 'you mean cleaning my own after dinner?' they looked at each other to laugh only by answering 'never mind!'

Bubly's question next, 'you sleep at night or during day time?'

Or like 'did they ever take you on a space ship to figure out the possibilities of the future life of our own over there through your very noesy nature?'

The next question was from Bubly again asking 'why do you come to the old and the rotten planet of ours quiet often because you cant get shutki (dryfish) or the very favorite the Puti mach? (another fish) If I answer to that I get every single thing over there they both still will kept laughing even more loud than before as they have been doing since my great arrival as been announced enough earlier to surprise them with a reckoning! Then they said smiling and laughing as they have been doing since my arrival, 'OH! Then you must have been seeking a bride into a'bride in pride in you, this time I didn't intend to answer to these two silly young man and a woman instead called upon my sister loud enough to help me out of these two naughty evils' sight. But still Bashar doesn't want to let me go just like that! Said again, 'oH! Then you must have a handsome boy friend! Right?'I looked at him through a false look of an anger making anger into my eyes to leave that spot in the little apartment saying, 'enough! I need to go to the washroom!' to hear them both still laughing at by back to have the old uncle in their silly and common jokes of their own which don't let them know that I like that too!' but they know! That's why every time I come back they re-act the same for being the same aged. Started thinking again as forwarding myself towards the washroom to get washed up by taking a bath. This homely and family oriented environment made me leave all my thoughts behind out of the worries and negativities in life ongoing or possible in the near future to wash them off under the hot shower in the bathroom where there is cold water and warm feeling into a small concrete chamber under the many story constructions of modern lives to live under and in some concrete constructions for human lodgings for life living still in life with smiling and laughing children of the generations at least they are happy like the little birds in the nests just hatched under the mom's warm womb. Modern life has gone too far with all kinds of progress through the evolutions; evolutions of the tecknology; evolutions of the of the mechanism; evolutions of the science and the scientific explorations in a world now where we are going on on our own feet and thinking in our biological brains half human and half robotic. We smile in progress a little in the corner of our lips or in medium open teeth or a wide open mouth showing all the alighnments; or making the smile sweeter than honey; sometimes loud as a cheers or howling incidentally. We need to measure all our emotional activities or expressions according to the need and with the proper ways to do the business or the socializations in accordance with some matters from where the personal and private matters are totally going to be wiped out. We're sharing personal life, our personal time with a necessary business matter and the business with some personal feelings true or false but needed to be alive or active or even beneficial for business after all. And in this process or the pattern of life we are as human beings in this progress or the pattern of life we as the humans are turning to a creature basically half human and half machines.

Simi cooked various dishes at the dinner all deshi might have been thinking that the brother is deprived of all these in the land far away by living on cookies, crackers and milk to get more opportunities by utilizining the time for more in aceivements of goods by depriving the heart. Bulbuly still is restless in comments and taunting the foreign resident uncle in many ways as possible and her brother keeps smiling by the corners of his two lips as always as noticed by me since I arrived. Basher kept supporting his sister remaing silent with a closed smiles between two closed lips to remain silent with his support to what's his sister is upto. She asked,'uncle, how many hours you sleep over there?' and Bashar answred on behalf of his partner,

'or don't even sleep at all! Bulbuly,'may be only a nap a day right Uncle?'

I already dipped my heart and the soul into the taste of the dishes desi didn't even care what these silly and evil kids are asking to humiliate me. Simi asked instead for more English saying in full pride 'very tasty can't cook like this!''Great!' both the little brother and the sister never stop laughing or smiling looking into each other's eyes to ridicule as asked again one of them 'how many shifts you work ancle?' Finally, I lifted my eyes to these two cute kids of my very sister to say finally in a mood very moody saying, 'I don't work like that anymore. Anymore questions?' they took out all the gifts I brought for them with their own hands from the very luggage of mine and left without eating dinner. I got surprised and amused at the same time seeing their funny behaviors as natural as it is with no courtesies, no formalities even in no concern of their very uncle an unreachable land!! All's nothing but mere fun together with one another as a brother and a sister to each other. I kind of liked that! I looked at Simi now with a full attention my sister! The lovely and the naughty just like her two despicable and the evil children like Bulbuly and Bashar to ask, 'where's Dipok?' by forgetting the fact that he's no more. The sooner I realized the sooner I put my eyes down to apologize by saying' 'Sorry!' to ask again,' how's everything?' She smiled and looked very strong this time to watch how the time and tide make the rocks as stronger as Simi who used to be cry baby till the age of 18? Look at her now! A mother, a service holder to run the family of her own with two children to carry on the life with responsibilities living as a family together with the two children. What a change! Coming for a change from the different world where all these are already very common now a very common things and very usual everywhere as espected by me to be a different than the westerner'.The Global world now making the round globe running as a whole together with all different societies into one society to be the same in nature by the grace of the mighty internate where all of us meaning the very entire human race has been turning to a 'One' global by the collaborating faces on the face book, by the exchange of one another'local behavior', goods, foods, language alongn with the culture' in manners in order to get us all in a change in the mix and the match' of all in give and take, in trades, in the learnings. In order to that to be happening we mostly as an an educated human generations into the give and take or into the process of learning through the regular life in all the differences in all the mix and matches exchanging all our good' and bad' at the same time to make a socity like ours which represents the mess along the way while driving ahead towards home my sister' home after a long time to view all the changes to see mostly people adopted a lot of odd'of other'from all of the as most of the time we as human beings still tend to be get lost into the ditch of the sense of proportions in the mixed up culture's and manners in understading while also very likely to take the bads in exchange of the good' of our own. The suffering structures of the modern human societies breaking up into pieces in small units each as a couple then by breaking up further into an individual to make the each break as strong as possible for better for better? What a world! poor me! Poor my sister Simy! And most of all the very deprived children of our own genarations each centuries created a new new era' through a huge change into human society and now the little little individual socities are also making an individual new modern human world of it's own with enough distinctions in change to change the whole world as a whole in making an ever changing and constructing new world of our own not knowing to what directions they heading forth for good or bad? If for good then what kind? If bad then the question is to what extent? Already we are facing the sufferings of all the children from all the broken families, of the single parents as suffer from the social, physical and mental crisis and sickness as not much care has been given to them. The parent or the parents are busy in making or eaning money for the survival by depriving them as well as their children out of the shortage of time to provide care and share the time they all save apart from all the hard work as well as from the time they share a little for some recreations. All the helping hands are now only the electronic devices to keep us busy staring at the computer or at the screen of the tablets or the cell phones to fasscilitate our bodies from the harm from the modern grace of the modern man made devices which are the only means now to co-op with the modern trend to treat and live the life. The social status is now the suffering bodies in almost each home in our societies almost everywhere desciding the envronment and the surounding to determine the fate of people living in the entire physical phenomenon of our created world causing sickness or any other kinds of consequences to determine the nature of the existing life as well as the health to determine the life time shorter or a longer one to do things by determining the life long living for how long not knowing actually actually. Young people are now old enough in understanding things. We born we get life with things we hold onto one or more choices and things we don't want to loose and when life becomes too cruel to snatch away the thing we love the most or rely on we cry first then get frustrated when can't actually bring it back finally to get depressed, to act beyond normal. Whenever we laugh at the odds of the time or the fortune or the fate we laugh we laugh out the thing to leave forever.

Dinner time was over Simi made my bed upstairs a very small single room beside bulbuly's on the opposite to the co-ri-door as same sized like Simi'. It's a small place for three. Altogether three rooms on both sides by the small co-ri-door whose end corner holding the only bathroom with the shower place. There's another downtaires beside the small dining place between the dining and the kitchen. The small apartment aparantly cosy, clean and tidy good enough to live on a regular life. Life' regular for all the children of the house maintaining a routine for school, for home, for study, for sleep, to relax a bit, to share a time together with the family in watching TV, having Dinner together, chatting a bit while having their meals altogether. Beyond that some love, some passions, some sharing and caring in love in a bondage all together as a relations to each other in the blood connections as Nature commands or demands for the welfare of the humans binding them in a bondage for generations.

It took a long time to fall in sleep at night. I heard Simi's snoring and Bulbuly's loud reading. Might have been memorizing something from the book as we used to do long time ago in school in here.

I opened my window to the night view of the city, the enlighted city of Dhaka at night time only gorgeous looking at this time with lights in the darkness nothing is visible except high and low rise'all around shinning as lighted as well as the narrow looking streets down the streets between buildings with the cars with head lights on the back and the front looking running into the glimpses of light shines like the lightening bugs called Jonaki in the darkness of the night in the bushes in the darkness to make the dark night more enlighted. I was standing by holding the rails on the window to look down at the moving lights on the cars as well as the standings while the vehicle's stopping and the standing lights into the holes on the big big huge and tall buildings holding all the small and small units of lights lighted by the bulbs as all inserted as snicking into the concrete bodies by making them all shinny looking like some shining objects are only standing as the monuments of the contemporary concretes. The wind is cool and soothing and it's still the spring of the year. Not bad! visiting the city my own city somehow makes me feel home when can't just judge the differences between west and the east. The heart flows and feel the same don't really know what in the new form of the old city of my own might be the memories of the old still holding things the same ways to make me feel myself in reviving myself only doesn't matter where it belongs and where it lives at the present time. Strange people in strange nature as Nature created naturally. Anyways, I shut off the views to my eyes to close them for the night to rest in dreams if the dreams let me sleep by letting the eyes shut down for some time for rest while ever roaming in visions possible and impossible. When woke up in the morning it was afternoon actually 4 o'clock in the evening. Simi already left a message saying she'll be back by 5 pm in the evening. So, its another evening since I arrived by overlaping another? But mainly passing through only one good night sleep to wake up basically to the day in the very evening to get another sleep time! Small world in a short time! Sometimes a jet leg feels very romantic in a deep and a long time sleep while no feel ironically in a sound sleep? What an irony! Does the senses sense anything in the sleep when it is basically a sleep in an unconsience or half conscience state of mind in the very conscience soul? What an irony! Irony! I know when we take a long sleep or even a short one during some stressful work we do feeling it's a relief of a feel like we enjoy the time in sleep. But how? How do we enjoy the sleep when we're basically sleeping? Might be our mind tells us to take a break from the very activities in which it's engaged to take a break as assuming to be enjoying the time in sleep while no work no stress for the hard feeling. If I say that's only an escape from the reality but it's still more than that because when the heart and soul and the mind are totally absent while asleep then no sence of us tells us that, 'you are enjoying the time' while our total self was in sleep only as when we wake up to see and feel ourself to be better off in the past few hours in sleep we feel better ourself as if a good time had been passed not lived in all the stress while not awaken to be off work in sleep The present awaken self of our's tells us or finds a consolation that our over worked or the over stressed self has been in a short or loger break from the tormented sensitivity in no sensitivity in sleep while the face tells us by showing it's freshness in the face to feel the good feel in rest which makes no feel basically while were asleep. It's the work of the body system which refresh our body in rest meaning in sleep to make us feel better through the body by the heart. Closing widows of our two eyes to the harsh and naked daytime realities feels good with no feel in unknown satisfactions of the mind in it's disappearance. In another words being dumb and insensitive is better than in being reasons?

Any ways, I needed a cup of tea or coffee but don't know how to make it while don't feel like entering the kitchen actually! Feeling lazy to do anything as felling like being home is being care free for some reason. I stood against the window by the dining to see outside. Down on the roads there are school buses mainly up and down to drop off the school going children in the quiet neighbourhood at this hour. All the buildings shoulder to shoulder containing little flower gardens on the roofs. Some ladies of the buildings coming to the roof to take a walk may be! Or leaning on the balcoly to look out. They're either house wives or or ladies already back from work. There's no doubt that the city got much more conjested than before. I notice one thing which'pretty clear that there's no more of a single house in the neighbourhood all mid-rise buildings with at least 5-10 story residential buildings. People live like bunch of bee's into the little holes of the high or low rises considered as the little little apartments from where people peep out with two eyes of their own to see the world or the sky far up out. Day after tomorrow is the Eid day. I am afraid that it might not be as same as an exciting Grand day like before. Still one more hour for Simi's arrival. I needed to go out for a walk so started looking for the keys to open the doors and found them by the door itself hanging on the wall above beside a hanging photo frame with Simi and Abeer's photo as live as before as smiling both together in love and joy. Might be announcing the lodge is their own which's no more but only in the memories as their very existence even presently in the very picture of their selves in the picture at where they play a great role in preserving old images and memories of the gone, of the old and of the moments non- forgettable. Very slowly the real love in real life becoming only a memory but still while the subjects of love are no more then their memories captured in the moments in love and smile then the memories are forever and I don't know whether they really extict or totally wiped off by lthe loss of the papers capturing the memories of love and passion while the hearts never die as it's always a feel in pain, in passion, in love and rergret, sorrows as well as in happiness, in dying while pining, in ever attempting to hold tight onto smething while losing and ever afraid of loosing something or someone in the tendencies to hold onto it forever. When the thing or the dear love one's missing then the heart holds onto the memories therefore memories never let us down in keeping us alive in the memories. Dreaming of a life in dreams is still a shadow of the life a reflactions of the past to make the future in another dream which is basically the hope! Dreaming or making a future by dreaming in future making plans means no facking actually a reality to move forward in making things ahead for future.

Very slowly love from life is disappearing while the survival of life costing a lot from us time, energy, the decaying value of a peace of mind, the stress we get in the way to acheive all the materials for living and which is now-a-days only the survival through the biological systems of our bodies where the souls die every day and each moment when we struggle hard for living. We don't think of love, passion, emotions and basically we don't have the break to look at the beauty of the creations of Nature anymore either at a beautiful woman or the beauty fo Nature itself and most of all we don't have the luxury time or the sensitive heart and mind to love someone or something while the mind and the soul only have to think and feel the urge of the running time to hurry to get into business for our very ownself for money only which keeps us get going through the survival of the life in making life desperately making only money meaning life by all means. Any ways, where was I? Yes! At the matter of the very human thing used to be once very human now only an optional fun? Possibly! When the body only feeds itself then it feeds the love by love making unlike the very falling in love kind love? And the matter of the memories of love in the pictures of some one as a couple which as a memory of the past also unable to come back in the future of our children when the present time is in the process of demolishing it through the damages of the old constuctions to build up the new? The monuments of the very Love thing in the picture of a couple or various couples are getting damaged at the same time for keeping no sign in the memories to remember Love as an very important issue of the human life generating heart to heart for the sake of humanity as being passionate and sensitive for giving and sharing the ever valuable emotion for the sake of humanity as well as for humans living in love or with love to value life and the living by some values abstract again for the good for human kind as opposite to the animal kind. it's not us it's the time which is making us to demolish Love banishing it from our heart for a better future in the best productivities in goods not for the welfare for the living for lives in hearts and souls, in sense and sensibilitiies for a healthy life for the sake of humanity again. But again, it's true when the humanity failed for the excessive emotions for possessions either for the body or for the love for the heart, either for the goods for the living or for the desperate trials for possessions out of a lot of struggles by killing the hearts, emotiond and devotions then no point to keep the abstract emotional thing in our lives to be very sensitive to kill ourselelves one way or other. This complex world holding the complex life in all comlexcities never ever was happy or right in a true sense. If I say we don't make the world it's the destiny which guides us urges us through the instincts, through the tiny tiny vains as a flow of the blood to the directions we can't really controll either by heart or by running through internally through the body for the next generatins most probably the existence of 'Love' like in the lives of Bulbuly and Basher. But still be the love loving for the life only by loving the family by making a family and friends, with kins and kittens, with pain and gain, in rain and storm, in luxury and reality. In love and hate, in luxuries and realities, in humanistics and techniques, with natural and artificial; by heart and mind, by body and the soul, in flesh and blood again in mechanism in a least pain.

Still the life's a blowing wind even though a little peeping through the gaps between stuctures what we build. The open sky up and the conjested concrete structures down on the land while the open sky is the limit for the limited land for peple as we can thrive, we can build to break through while the ventelations can't provide the freshness of the fresh air. All in all we're living in populations with the very poluted heart and the soul just like living in the polluted environment by inhaling the polluted air while exhaling the same the same ways our hearts and souls as loveless and heartless to live in the loss of love, the loss of humanity to inhumanity. The Polutions in our hearts and mind is the ways it's in the body to generate for humanity nothing but a life to be lived not knowing for what what's the destiny there and here after believing in some human values to practice by practicing all good for the good for our own societies, for the sake of humanity by proving or at least by keeping humanity after all! While the man made robots are insensetive robots then they are also cruel on commands or the still human robots are living for life by making a life while they have gotten no passions or emotions to generate through heart to heart. And when the 1st human value which's humanity can't provide a reparing for the lost love at least to protect the families from falling apart or to protect the families from falling apart or to wean a love in relationships when we are a mess to do any good to us the humans the very humanistic humans.

For me leaving behind the loveless and the careless west headed for the east to my birth place where I grew up in love and care in a family of mine of course mine also in blood and bondage together as a family in hope to revive me from the lost myself in the little loss of the peace in a little war of reality a simple and very nessessary inevitable reality of life in life for a short period of time still by causing enough loss of life living in life and instabilities as always caused by all the wars through the ages from the beginning of the human civilizatins and before causing deaths and the damages through the destructions as the tales of the history tell through all the natural human attempts of reconstructions by the destructions caused by the human wars or conflicts of interests between and for the aggressive nature of heading forward for possessions even by applying forces and foes towards humanity again to reconstruct through the loss in rebuilding or the reconstructions for a better building of a new civilzation by reviving or by regaining the lost ego in the regained refresed energies by building the old and the broken or the destroyed a brand new one. Sometimes it made better on the loss sometimes only the reconstructions on the dstructions but definetly had been making histories into the tendencies by building better civilization while making new places out on the broken one'. Civilizatons evolved as revolved through ages. For me leaving behind the loveless and the careless Well developed Land headed for my little country growing a little by little or trying to grow as a toddler to stand up with full might where I believe still the Love thing prevails about whom I have been talking about as my very concern to still live in love and care in some togetherness in a bondage with a hope to vevive my own self which already has gotten lost in the hopeless world of the machines and the mechanism. All souls really look like the lost world of the hopeless, aimless and the heartless humans of the new era of humanity neither feels nor bother anything anyone, neither holding a tendencies to hurt each other nor to support one another. Therefore, no help no support, no compromise no sympathy, no caring no looking in the eyes of another to read the language of the heart to hate or to regret. The man made man-machines are doing well in making machines while a lots are in wastage to reproduce the machine workers for the work making machines to remake machine and the goods for the machines again for the sake of the fast productions of the machines and the products again for the purpose of the same machines who only work and consume the same categories working as an consuming machines only for the work again. For example, parents reproduce children to grow them up just like themselves looking and behaving like machines to survive on consuming food and products fed and given by them to live and grow fast to do the same as becoming robotic human workers the very man made robot- people to do the same again by working for the sake of humanity again in non-humanity to serve the businesses or the organizations making work for the robotic generations as well as the products the need to consume or for the use while they are the same work force to survive to make or regenerate the same work force still through making relationships or making a couple for regerations. The question is, regenerating what and for what? I know I'm all cynical to my senses it's only the survival for the sake of survivals in making and producing the same people making people while at the same time by being productions in cosuming the same productions eatable non-eatables made or produced by the same humans live structures of the present robotic behaviored human body machines consuming the produces or the goods and goodies for the energy as to fuel them to proceed with the same repeatative systems in the man making man factory or in the other sense generating the workers making working man machines by the same man apparently almost out of the human values in order to run for the running life cycle machine' while living in the life itself the same time saving the same time consuming little little packet food consuming human body productions producing the same to keep up the life to keep up the God gifted the entire human community for good of humans while almost expiring in the expirations of the human values and understading? When the robots make robots then where do the human values stand to make people people? We have got not much time from work and our values left to sit and relax to think to feel to value the life as a life very alive in sense and sensibilities again in an easy trouble free and hastle free society in advanced robotic human generations.

Never mind, thats an exaggerated phenomenon of the whole imaginative scenario of the very near future of the mankind we are heading to as running out from a world of individual interest for some bondage in love and friendships can't really showing any repect in real sense to stay in hope. We have started to beleive in 'To earn life to live life' and at the same time as desperate as frustrated to put down the burdens of life either to destry it or to leave it behind' to stay in hope. Our home land is losing both home and the lands together at the same time. I lost my friends and my sister lost her love her dear husband her life partner still living in her heart to still dreaming of a real home. The small world is getting smaller now as almost came into a little cell phone we always carry to look at while sitting, driving, schooling or working inside home or outside home at work or on vacations. Our world is smaller now than the bigger from a huge one to a tiny one or brought the huge one into a tiny one actually to worry about the huge global globe. As the houses becoming smaller, apartments tiny to hold more people in quantities into a many story building to save lands in some cases to make rooms for the constructions for the housing to comply with the needs for people looking like making space for the little ants in one high rise housing constructions. Large families already broke into smalls with a couple only to live together in an apatments sometimes even a single person in an apartment. Looks when all the individuals thrive for living and accomating themselves individually then they only can bump with one another cant really make a real business, a real society or even a normal healthy living for them. Family ties are breaking apart each day by the pressure created out of the systems lacking in systems to discipline people or the streets or even in systems keeping in systems as an order feeling like no co-operations between co-workers or the drivers on the roads and on the busy streets to carry on the life vehicles by watching out for life.

As I intended to go out for a walk in the fresh air outside the aprtment building in the open air if there is any at the same time to look for a coffe shop or for a tea place for a cup of coffee or tea someone knocked at the door. It's nobody but my sister Simi herself coming back from work looked like very happy to see someone her own as a brother at home opening the door for the sister after a log long time as a family member with love and affection. She smiled and asked me 'How's the jetleg? What time did you wake up brother?'

'not long ago but still feels like a century passed in a deep sleep feeling good though! How are you today?' I asked and she answered very normal as if the work makes her no tired at all 'good! Time to work at home now! What a life!' she sighed and quickly entered the kitchen to take care of the dishes couldn't wash before going to work or last night said again,'work, work, work all day outside and home. We dont live now it's only work we live for!'

It's evrywhere!' I had to console her,'what can we do? We can't bring the old back by shading off the new!'

'and we can't fix the problems the old put in the new to make a new!' Simi's answer. I thought again 'when did she became so mature?' while she mentioned 'yes, we changed the world in progress in the need to do better but we still don't know how much to do for the real good to the running present society while we don't know whether it got real bad actually worse in better?'

'you mean progressing in the progress of the technologies?' asked me.

She jumped out of her joy finally to answer the old eager family company who's now very present in her home to make it a home again doesn't matter for a shorter time or for a longer saying, 'right! Yes! It made the life better and easy but we spend the time when we save it again to move forward in working more to progress in inventing more to make more, progressing more in better and better in the ever evolutionary process in technologies through the day to day updates thinking ourselves an innovative and progressive behaviour in making the life better in what sense we actually don't know while the dependencies on the machine' or electronic devices and all the everyday changing or progressive technologies basically taking us where in the way of the very near future while the time is money and the money is life then the fast living lives in the long working hours a lot more than before where it's taking us we can see and feel now as we all are making a motion in the lack of emotions and passions without figuring out what's next ;whether we are heading towards a society a very human society by converting ourselves into some robotic bodies or even worse as some manimals to be destroyed by nothing but by ourselves in the terror of man killing man in the form of robotic man or in the form of the mixed chacteristics as half of us in the mixture of the brutality of an animal together with hamanistic behavior good enough to destroy the world in man killing man in the form of robotic humans with better brain or intelligence and in the form of brutal manimals together with the ferocious nature of an animal and the very intelligence of a man.

When I intervene between her continuing complains about the life now by saying 'very good! Very good! and when did my little sister became very sensitive to be that much thoughtfull? I cant beleve it!'

'it's time now! It's actually a time that changes time by changing people and our life. Everyrhing is changing evrything!' she sighed deep as if for the first time since my arrival she poured her pains in emotions in the loss and the changes brought by that in the life now. I went close to her sometimes we all feel the same. In this present world of us we are trapped within ourselves while can't really pour out what we feel what we need in order to fulfill our hearts in desires while the dead's remaining inside and the life showing it's actvities as a slave to who we can't really figure out actually the modern advanced trend for life made and created by the life itself while requiring all these fast and vast mobility, mechanism, advancing life in advance process in making life for our comfort, in making our life in short life and in more productivities. The dead souls make little songs in little feel in composing songs from the heart. But still the good news is, the frozen souls still survive to revive in expressions just like Simi my dear liitle sister going like a machine on two wheels all day long for the sake of the survival guided by the to do lists each day everyday. We are all now know or trained by the situations or the trends and the already made up as well as set ups of the processes to carry on the life in the fast mobility while at the same time in fast activities. All we can say time made us slave to the time while the life makes the time in changes by changing it's nature and the routines to be followed by but still we don't know actually whether they are trapping us within ourselves to go and behave like a slave from the morning till night dreaming only about the next day routine to perform the life alive into a graph which keeps the consciense alive while the mind supposed to be resting in sleep at least for the night. In this modern world we're all actually working as some robotic slaves in life making life with no life! What an irony! when we fight with each other compit with one another in order to prove ourselves better than others we don't realize that we have gotten no ground actually. We're all groundless, lifeless lives very progressive through the inventions and evolutions by thinking, making a life where's losing the life itself every moment in making the life again on the groundless ground where it's all a lifeless life while the very baseless and groundless at the same time.

Very quickly Simi made a dish of rice and a dish of fish. She announced very happily that tomorrow we'll go out for shopping and more as tomorrow is the week-end. We talked, we ate together wandaring into the memories of the past lived as a family together with parents and all the siblings. Bulbuly and Bashar didn't show up yet as they had to go for some coaching from school will be late at night. I might not see them in the morning as they will be busy with the week-end's programms in doing some part time jobs as well as hanging out with friends for some free time after all. After a long time both of us went out again in the city of Dhaka in an insignificant small country while still having some significant distinct cultures and matters in passions and fashions both to charm the human hearts in some charming ways by pouring out the pure hearts of the people very unique while amusing by decorating them with the costumes demanding to be the universal to show off in the manners of the new to make it enough enchanting and charming over all. The aspects of the present materials and the goods and the subjects as well as the displaying contents of the show business took a new turn to amuse people. Me and Simi set off to go places to places and as usual I already started to watch every detail of what's on the banners, at the painted or photo images of the movies in the theatres as displayed up outside the theatres. The actors and actresses are all in the costumes in the mix and match manners most of the things are the mixture of the east and the west. Going complex in manners, cutures, behaviours and making things in the mixture of many made some displays looking somewhat between a combinations of two different kinds partly funny looking, partly out of the culture in the loss of the haritage in a shame. It's all the same as before with the huge crowds on the very conjested streets and roads and the people around made the phenomenon very chaotic with horns all around. People here know how to run by a making a way to the destinations for purposes without looking at each other minding their own businesses only made me see the picture as depicted in my imaginations about our life in a city where these chaotic people use no voice of their own to a way to go but by the loud horns to alert. Minding one's own means made them selfish rather than some robots with no feel at all. We are still in the show business playing human emotions but mostly in showing the excitements of life in attractions displaying by the beauty of the body, while the soul remains silent into the very souls by still holding people into dirty businesses which involve images of sex and the sexuality in the death of the dynasty of the love. People are running for their businesses and the destinations for their life by earning some life for life in the money making business. They are all tiny insects like the ants on the streets between the big big banners of enchanting displays of the shows, musicals, shopping places, restaurants, theatres with the paintings displayed up with some picture models of the monuments of present passions in the costumes very sexy wearing by the girls to sale at the same time costumes and the costume wearing people man or woman for the advertisements of some movies or the shows here and there. Some female models wearing nothing to display their beauty of the body to capture peples'eye sight only on them when wearing some cloth doesn't make business they try to make desperately by going back to primitivism. Simi's driving very tricky I looked at her from the side to ask, 'where did you learn driving?'

'time teaches everything.' Her answer.

Yes, how about the kids?'

'they won't have much patience to drive in the streets like this.' One thing is missing when I looked around to ask Simi, 'where did the Rickshaws go?.They are not in sight are they not allowed?

'They are not banned yet but got depleted by themselves as got discouraged by the heavy traffic on the streets to drive up in the midst of all this mess in little space causing accidents while drive. Time to time they got called off the busy streets get back as needed on the narrow roads as needed to sneak in easily.

I said, 'But I miss them!

'I know! missing the old of a culture once was someone'own heritage feels like a ban to be deprived off. Time changes all the old backs up or perished while the new take over. But we'll make a time to get a ride on a rickshaw any time.'

Tha fast moving vehicles don't really look at each other I mean at the people inside. The odds of the whistlers or the staring youngsters at the beautiful ladies in the streets have not been noticed. People mind their own business now. All the running vehicle's are very fast moving all in the speedy harmony in the speed life in the speedy carriers in the speed of life streets of the speedy modern civilization in the speed of life all together in a harmony the harmony which makes no song for the soul but make life in business. The running lives are in a harmony stopping and starting again by the traffic signals. Road side businesses big in the shopping Malls or small in the small stores are still there but the hockers are gone as not selling by sittting on the foot path or selling flowers through the short time stopping traffic windows for a quick access to the little business for life. The city looks a little more tidy and clean with not much crowd in comparison to the cities very developed in the developed countries around the world. The honking traffic in the narrow space for a small city like ours making no soulless soul yet as of a developing city like ours but the glass door barriers between the crowd of the people and the bunisses behind the shopping plaza's with all the lined up glass door stores making an shinny glass barrier images by separating people and the goods for sale making a difference between the honking traffic on the roads and merchandice are being sold kept in a safe distance makes a sense to the sensitive minds to think deeply about the desperate busy and honking crowd on the street are running desperately for work for business or for any purposes for earning or making money only for those merchandise awaited while kept in care only for the same crowd of people for those only. The good looking goods are coverd and kept carefully with the value they possess always as desirable for people desiring extra some beauty for life the business in the daily need for the survivals which always cost more than what we always need for neccesities in the daily life. The eye catching beauty of those products are all expensive enough each and individually as everywhere as they don't sell on a regular basis. For extra charms in life now costs a lot more as they increase the value in selling less. People look like not much interested or lost the interest in extra values of life in luxuries or for the fancy, for the beauty in life or caring for the beauty along with some luxuries in life. Life is now short cut, simple and fast moving for the fast forwarding life in the basics of the life. Socializations as well as the entertainments make not much room in time left for the hard working people. Wasting time in spending life is much more of a concern to utilize the time for more work and in less life in leisure and in rest rather than valuing time in earning money as spending in buying life in wasting energy even though for the sake of life while still killing life in killing time for the sake of a liitle spare time to get to spend at home together with the loved ones'or in some entertainments to be enchanted a liittle in the spare life left after all the life making hard life in work and in the soul seeking souless time. I have seen random deads left behind the walking or driven human traffic carried into the speedy vehicles leaving behind whatever gets rejected from the wastage of the contemporary human resources as a valuable potion of the very Natural resources. The industrious insects as the colony of the ants are moving forward and coming back in making moving traffic of the ants in no care, no fear only knows to move forward with guts as long to survive, while the fallen soldiers are left behind no time to look back to take a look at least at the fallen left behinds even to worry for themselves as a consequence. No free hands no pick ups nobody's there to offer a hand to pick up at least a waste. Life has become a recycling living industry by making a life in huge productions of goods and the people at the same time in raising people in making labours for the same for the productions of the goods needed for people again. We try to do better in productions for the betterment of the people to make more in shorter time at ease for the workers to make more at ease. The key trends for the life is no life but only an industry in making things for the working force as humans fascilitating themselves with better products needed for them for life in comfort in making or producing them by themselves. In a way the life cycle is basically an on going recycling process in making life for life. Comparing us as the humankind in the modern or should be said in the contemprary world to the industrious force of the trend in life makes more sense as we are neither human nor a robot or an animal to distinguish ourselves from the rest of the natural resourses in the entire universe as gifted by the Almighty after all and overall. Our life has become an industry to raise labours by raising people for better productions to live better in working more for more. Who dies who survives doesn't really matters anymore.

After almost an hour we reached the biggest mall in the whole city with many story high rise buildings high up. Simi's very excited said, 'Long time!'

'That means you didn't come for shopping?'

'Yes! I don't get motivation anymore to go shopping as I don't need much.'

'why?' because you don't have friends, no society to buy and show?' we both looked at each other to laugh loud with a full heart. She said,'Yes! a kind of!'

Simi looked into my eyes with a deep look inside hers said, 'Bhai! I miss all we had! Parents, brothers and sisters as a family together, bying new clothing at Eid, competing with each other for everything, competing in studies, in showing off ourselves in beauty and in things, in proving who's the greatest in wit in school credits, in friends making, in all kinds of credits and capacities to be the greatest.'

I stopped for a little while on the upward on the car in the street while excited to look back in her eyes to see how big her regrets and sorrows or the pain pining for the lost world in love. Are they deeper than mine or a little less. All in a sudden just felt a mild bump to jump out of the excellerating excelator for our floor to step on for now as 'time and tide wait for none.'

It's been a long time all got scattered in the family. Some of us left the country to live in some foreign places some stayed here in the origin. People go away from home to come back again now and then to look around the home land is not the home anymore. People behave the same like all others in the foreign lands. I looked around inside the big mall pretty nice even in comparison to those in the well develpoed countries with all the modern aspects and decorations even bigger and more luxurious than those in the land where I live not exactly though! Now my home land is not the home land for me anymore as living now in a foreign country for a long time together with another lived before.

The surrounding waliking people in the Mall are minding their shopping of course but still some of them in a group sitting in a place to get together. They all mind their business either in a group or as a couple or alone all mind their own intentions to be fulfilled either shopping or chatting by sitting in a corner or in the food court. There was a time as I recall the youngerters used to look at the beutiful girls or even looking for girls to have some fun in ifteasing in some ways. Now, looking like each individual has gotten enough mature to mind their his or her's own business as the busy life style changed the attitudes we got before. I believe lovers find their matches online to chat online in an intention to proceed towards making a relationship. So conceiling emotions in making a love relation leaving the space for the showing off the nudity of the 'love' thing between a man and a woman is becoming a business for public which is still good in a way as the beauty of the man-woman relationships in secrecy making it valuable in human values while the nudity of the same value has gotten dirty in showing good enough to spoil a generation who already lost faith in love while well experienced in falling in love and making love. So the selling of the body of the beauty has been categorized in the products and the good about it is under the vails should have been an open aspect of the very life in love should be the in the purity of the beauty in chastity which is the very beauty of the very sacred Love! To my views all the people look the same as dressed up the same but still a little a loof in behaviour.

We entered some stores where the shop keepers do not talk much with the customers to offer a Pepsi or a Fanta or even a cup of tea to sit and talk while burgaining for a merchandise. Prices are all marked at the products the cheaper products are kept on separate racks and the expensives on the different also the clearance is at the door to be seen easily. So again the introduction to the high tech world is visible here too buying time saving so does the selling with less words to waste in the wastage of the value of time as again while the time is money and money is life consequently saving time saves the money? In a business like this people still had some releif in socializing or in a relaxing luxury while shopping for the luxury items by being offerd by the shop keepers to have a sit and to have a drink to talk while seeing and buying and selling in some hearts in the matter of business for making money and spending money between the two opposite parties in relation to the business in selling products and buying products. The fact is who is winning in spending money for the products and who is losing or gainning in selling the products for the right price or not? So, in a matter of a business in exchange of dear money as the means of dear life in exchange in the value of it in money as well as in the value of the perchase there is a tention very mild but still a concern to be judged where there was a value offered to the customers by the offer to sit and relax in one of a kind socialisations even in a small businss. So all I wanted to say the very valuable time in the value of money exchange has been taking away our socialisations finally to drag us to the ground of the heartless human behavior to pour us finally into inhumanity.

Sometimes we look alike while wearing different costumes or clothing in a different country other than ours as sharing the same heart in different costumes and now here in my place all wearing the same regular desi dresses as for the same culture and the heritage while behaving different in different attitudes as for being strangers to each other in same language and in the same costumes of the same culture. Time has taken a lot leaving the generations in the lack of some very valuable values always make people people or even humans in humanity. Minding ones own business or the lack of helping each other means no human qualities. There are security systems at the entrance for the Exits and the entrance for everyone. Places like ours have differnces between status as high's, low's, middle classes and high classes in classifications just like the high and low rise constructions for accomodations as well as for the commercials and for the status to acommodate people according to the classifications. Costume's can't define the differenes as most of the time wearing same costumes covering the low and the down graded class of people looking the same in the same quality costumes. People can be categorized by social status but he heart and the soul of each individual remains the same as they do not take cocun to hide themselves they flow in the heart the way they feel, they desire as they dont aspire having dreams they only want to taste the life and to feel the life in all of the life as a common hearts and souls for all. In the leading progress of the tequenology for the sake of the comfort for the people there is something very important is missing everywhere even in the country like ours where there always was the feel in emotions and passions as in fight and might in love and hate both, in friendships, in love, in the family ties in all kinds of a relationship. The costumes, customs and the courtecies took the place of the hearts to flow spontaneously.

I got tired finally in the big mall as Simi wanted to buy me something but can't think of anything she intends to buy for me turns out to feel that it's even better in the far land where I belong now! That's true we fake most of the time in making the duplicate of the original of most of the products except some like Sari's and the other women things generally fancy and eye catching. So, finally Simi bought a pair of expensive Parkar pens assumed to be the best choice for me also let me know that if I was her sister she could buy me a lot of nice things like Sari's and jewleries. I smiled saying,'ok next time i'll arrive as an woman to be gifted properly by my little sister.'

As my legs started aching finally to take a place to be sitted to relax after all. We got to be sitted in the food court to have some snacks very traditional like samosa's as craving for them for a long time as the original one's are only here as I happened to beleive but Simi ordered a burger and some fries as just the opposite with a bottle of Pepsi while asked for a glass of water together with a cup of desi tea due to the snack crave. Simi started smilng seeing me having the hot tea in the hot season said later,'I know you're from the cold place must be enjoying the very heat with no tanning?'

'Simi! Sometimes you get very annoying!'

'never mind! Answered my dear little sister at least I could make her smile! Poor Simi! People sometimes need a break from the daily life while boring at the same time very monotonous in the motionless emotions. Casting the eyes at the beautiful things around made us no intentions to buy anything as they didn't tempt us to tend to buy things at the post young aged brother and the sister. Both of us got hit by the hard hands of the harsh reality. Destiny is cruel in some people's life, in some people's dumb brain to dump themselves into the trash of tremendous troubles pushed away by the lucky people to be unfortunate who didn't walk on the paths of life in careful steps. For both of us still some life ahead left with our next generations meaning our children for who we live now, thrive now and move forward with a good set of goals for their betterment as we walk through the life along by holding the lamp of hope in darkness and in despair, in the moonlight and in the bright neon light in shine but still failed to make our lives by make over. Here we're now both as single one's with two children another' not. After keeping us quiet for a long time Simi opened her mouth first,'why don't you come back here forever?'

'I will if I decide to marry find me a bride.' I thought I would answer just like every time she asks me the same question. But this time I asked her instead 'why?'

'just asking! I mean if you like.'

'that's true If I like! I really wanted to think about it by observing all by judging all at the same time and I also know it that the questions will remain unsolved as forever. We leave what we need to leave for better by leaving some good as well as some favorites also because the life pushes us sometimes to leave a place has gotten infavorable for some reasons we are not responsible for. Life is love for life being in love with live.

'falling in love with someone makes a better life too!' answered Simi.

'I know, I spent a long time in the foreign lands knowing a lot of people time to time in business also thought about to be with someone by a making relationship but didn't work out to be like that.'

'because you don't know what you want.'

I looked at my present mature younger sister wondering how she reads my mind?

It's true a soulless body always tends to get the lost soul into it where it belongs and when the body needs a favorable place then it gets used to it in the feel when a beautiful place gets as favorable as the life demands gets used to it in living in the comfort and the facsilities while the pushed away soul remains silent to decide which one should choose the soul or the body only to facilitate on the ground very favorable for the body itself only. And naturally a self tends to live in and with both while the body and the soul are inseparable then why is the irony of leaving in one while the other one is existing as the separate one and while it is very hard to keep both together in one place as together with the reality and the dreams, as the fascinations and the feels of the heart are inseparable. Our hearts stay and roam around in the past where we come from lives in the land in sweet memories unforgettable as much as the childhood memories are unique and pure to cherish in times of some breaks from hard work.

I looked into her eyes again very carefully to read her mind at least to know what's she is thinking about me. O, well! nothing must be very dangerous or dregading about me! On the other hand Simi also was trying to read what's on my mind so I answered propmptly so that she doesn't think anything bad about me 'it's just a life style a habit you built over the time. I know I've no personal life over there and no family, no personal life with a partner at least to share and care but I have life of my own with my views and visions as how I see myself and my life over my visions what pictures I depict in my mind about life itself to lead it along with leading generally at least a little to find a reason to live gracefully. Researches in Botany brings me to life in knowing Nature and the growing nature of Nature in plants. Their origins, their growth, their food, their breath and air just like us from the Sun making life everyday with new inventions and new theories. I grow everyday and mature myself as there's not much to worry.

'that's why you couldn't make a relationship may be you didn't go into deep to keep someone in fear of losing!' Simi's judgements.

I got very surprised to exclaim 'how do you know? You're a genius!' She joked then 'Yes! Because I'm your sister the very younger sister a little stupid to feel love to fall in love to lose what I expected in vain and now in pain for not acheiving anything! Simi smiled and said again, 'I wish I could be a tree to live on only food whatever it is matter for the sun in no bondage and no weakness at all.' I sighed to say,'I know!'

'how do you know?'Simi again.

'I know because I am not them the way you think I'm? I was born in a family loved and being loved by all mom, dad, you and Bony my brother. I miss you all the time and that's love in a pain I know very well also if the desire of making a life partner in love and romance that's a love too happens to be desired and dreamed off by everyone in their lives. Today or tomorrow I'll marry to be settle down don't worry!'

True! But loving someone as a soul mate or as the only life partner is the only love as in your own heart very different as it aches when that soul mate is no more or even apart for a reason. But when you think you are only a vegetable to live and grow on food and water only then you are better off with no regret, no pain inside the heart. When the body shares the self with a heart it just can't live in a proper sense without that inevitable portion which is called the 'Love'! I felt very sorry for my poor sister a deep sorrow grabed my heart feeling her heart in pain in the loss of her husband to live a life in reality with two children while can provide only some support for life for life for living in the struggle for survival only. I looked painfully at my sister as a struggling single mother with no support which only the spouse can provide with love and care and share. A mother is a part of the life force in an natural urge to take care of the children in all the struggle for the survival more for the children than for herself in taking care of them, in protecting them by feeding them, sheltering them, treating them well in love and care and with all the support dying hard when being a single parent. This Love is the greatest Love to me as the natural selection happens to be for the growth of the entire human kind as their mental and physical developments in health, in behaviours for all the good for life to be lived properly in health and education. Simi's true to her beliefs as I passed that age to be fallen in love with someone like at the age when Romeo and Juliet fell in love with each other but still the love remains in passions and emotions but over all the devotions dominates the relationships between men and women as a relationship of love. I believe this serious kind of love like Devdas & Parboti or Romio Juliet is becoming shorter and shorter in existence into a bondage once built up as the severity of this Love when it is decaying or even dying day by day through the harsh realities in the present life where only the survival remains as the main concern for life to live and to carry on for the sake of the survivals only as a law of Nature. Everything of the human emotions are getting less and less under circumstances because the sharp scissors of the harsh reality is get going by chopping off the emotion thing from the very flesh and the body lives after all. Life has become a shorter existence in life in love and emotions with passion even in fashion as cutting off the jewels and the frills from the fashionable designs for the costumes as our life in the heart and the soul wearing the costumes of love, passions and emotions to add the value and the beauty to it. We get less leisure, less time to relax, less breaks for vacations to vacate all our tentions and stress by pausing the work for a little while for the life only. We even make love in hurry as the mind tells 'the clock is ticking!' as 'early to bed early to rise' good enough to shut the eyes to the beauty of the loved one or even to things in beauty in Nature or from the very nurtured and man made things displayed in the show cases of the civilizations very modern as well as making enough time to see or explore the old in the monuments and the places from the history with outstanding beauty along with some values to be seen to be known to be viewed in the feel of the heart and the soul while lelaxing and sitting with the loved one's to enjoy a time good in the open air sometimes by the bank of a river or by the shore of the sea in some company we love to feel together with the heart in the feel of some romance while the souls are still alive! Time is running fast the way we all humans are running out of us. It's a time running time when the various vehicles carrying us in the high speed as well as the feet also walking fast forward carryng our hearts and souls into the bodies which can't stop a bit for the soul to feel or realize what it' has been going through in the life in mechanism fascilitated by the technologies with techniques taught while without the heart and mind to think and feel if the feet could stop for some fascinations about what's going on, what's left behind, what's even ahead to think ahead and feel ahead for pausing a bit for a passion. We are in less love and more in labour ; in less leisure while in more labour; we keep our bodies in the boundary; brains in the box; we keep our hearts and the souls stuck in the smartness; smart minds mind only business; we possess shortened pleasure looking for it here and there in no time as ever. All in all we thrive to live by pushing forward the round planatery which is a round global globe coming back to the same as all around. Basically we're heading towards the primitivity while losing humanity in the loss of love and the life in heart and the mind. Sometimes I also think why don't we put this Love thing aside or push it away? Then we might also lose the dignity as for the lost humanity living only biologically in the loss of the feel of the softness in the heart to kill each other in no mercy in zero tolerance for the grace of the conscience. I really feel that the kind of real love in us especially between a man and a woman. If the love kills a person while in loss of that then why is this love created by the Almighty if it can't keep the life in balance to live normal by doing things right and justified working as progressing in some passions for life it's hard to keep the 'norm' while we don't know what's actually the 'norm' as to what extent the nature of norm is. If we cut down the Love from our life we turn to animals if we keep it very close to the heart as never to lose it then we even die for love by losing the grip of life.

But still life prevails in majority only some exceptions who die for love in the same exceptions who die for love in the loss of their world now-a-days as becoming a vegetable or living like a vegetable only for the productions as for cultivations for more productions. Living together two different individuals or each alone is getting very common now even if people like to breed or to have children after living together two parents or each individually as its happening a lot now. Still the institution of the marriage is active people get married a man and a woman living together after to get separated again after even for a short period of time to get separated from each other to live individually as a consequences. While people are turning to vegetables in productions to serve the human society as being humans themselves meaning people being people serving people by turning themselves as the part of the entire productions for the survivals of humans. When people are considered as food as some consuming vegetables to grow to serve people considered as the same vegetables to serve meaning the people in serving people has been considered as man consuming man. Yes humans always serve humans in all different ways. All together we are nothing but the consumers by consuming products we produce by using all other different products available in Nature. All together we make a world man, animals, woods, plants, birds, soil, air, fire, sky and water all the five elements in creations of all alive or non alive all all together making the world by using and consuming each other. Looking like we came across the evaluations of love or passions to love our own selves to be provided love for life to survive only. Living together of two individuals or each alone is getting very common now even if people like to breed or to have children after living together two parents when they separate one of them with children basically the Mom who' the only one who cares the most. In this case we appreciate the Love actually the Mother's love in the Mother Nature like many other animals or birds after mating or making a nest together as a couple they separate to fly away with full freedom from place to places the other naturally the female one is to sit there in the nest to hatch the eggs to make the next generation in the love and care which no one other than the mother bird can do like all other mothers in Nature. So the pure Nature seems calling us back in Nature to live naturally by getting rid off the society and it's set ups in all the systems, customs, cultures, in the pride and the prejudices as when all and all have gone failed to go back to Nature where we belong either to the barbarism or to the pure Nature contains all natural love and hate, fear and the foe in the very natural flow of the basic human instincts as for example the hunger which urges people to hunt while also taught them to snatch some food from the others same ways to fight for a suitable place to occupy for the need for a safe shelter. All human needs and instincts made barbarians going arrogant on one another same ways also with the time some learned to make things for their need. This way when the human society proceeded through some evolutions it set rules also for things to share and care among themselves but on the contrary setting rules or making certain systems for the sake of better human societies made our lives complicated for our ego, for our pride and prejudice, for different beliefs and cultures, and for the different colors also which make a difference between people in different identities to carry on the life all over as life meant to be global on the created round globe to see each other, to make business, to socialize and most of all to lead and live the life all together directly or indirectly in sharing and caring for the sake of life again supposed to be an individual while have to live in a society for share for care for better for better.

And where I was? Yes, at the question of the chastity and the beauty of the human behaviour in the present civilizations on the ground when we are proceeding towards or going like the barbarians in the costumes of the very civilized civilization in manners while no manners remain in no manners now at all! Societies basically proceeding towards the naked nature in the show of all nudity of all the human instincts showing in even more nudity of our nature, our natural instincts and desires showing in the displaying exposers of the naked body of the very natural pieces of beauty either human body or the beauty by violating the beauty of the Nature or the natural human beauty in our appearances under the covering costumes aparantly used to be the beautifying beauty added to the appearances covering the nudity with clothings like the trees covering the hard rock trunks as the same way our behaviours by attitudes covering us our tendencies to be very selfish with a heart concealing hatered by being very smart through educations to gain or to fulfill some intentions as the modern educated humanity could do things in humanity ironically through hypocricy also the opposite when we try to be good in caring humanity tend to cover us by our attitudes in being nice behaved, in sharing and caring in chastity and in honesty. But mostly we tend to do the bad one' in the current situations in buying and selling to show human values in the value of money only while the instincts of the survival pushing us towards the limit to do the same like the primitive people to snatch, to kill, to deprive, to do all the things all wrong and odds and not right in the civilizations at this time or at the age of it's flourishment in human beauty in costumes, in cultures, in education, in arts and cultures into creativities, in descency, in behaviour, in rules and regulations in the law, in the settings concrete as well as the settings through the self developing systems settings. The primitive life showed natural instincts in the pure human nature happened to be expressed in the nudity in appearances as well as in the brutality and in the behaviour very gross in the ways to get whatever they wanted to get out of the instincts of all kind. So now, we the civivilians are by allowing all the human instincts to fulfill in the behavior very much like the primitives caring loving, helping each other, behaving well by being nice to each other while covering in no vails for a shame. We claim us to be civilized while we do not know what makes it a civilived till now. We do good and bad both in the same systems very legally set up by us. We still do pick on someone else's behavior as it never ends some times we care less sometimes we overe-act to some attitudes of some one else. But still some basics are there should be in vails to show some respect to the civilized human soceties which still exsist will always be. The contrasts between Nature and the nurture always needs a balance to make for the sake of the descent make-overs. We are pure out of Nature while that purity shows nudity in nature and in Nature there are guidelines told us to take and make shelters for safety for ourselves the ways through the human conscience the very primitive Adam and Eve happened to feel shame to cover themselves with some leaves. This way the primitivity began to cover it's shame in nudity in covering. So we were never totally a barbarian as we represent purity of Nature to take attempts to cover the nudity out of it when some parts of it looks odd to our senses as we have been given conscience to feel to care for better societies in cultures. Neither can we live as a pure naked nature in the lap of the very Mighty Nature nor in the restrictions of the societies' settings of a lot of the systems, rules and regulations to be abide by to revolt against the restrictions heard for our pure souls to live a life in the freedom of the choices or the in the extremes of all odds of our very instincts to need to fulfill them in a culture and in a behaviour through some extents by nurturing ourselves when we are wild or mild, when we are bold for the beauty, when we are only Nature tend to be nurtured, when we are bad try to be good or the vise vasa, when we are destructive while at the same time very creative, we work alone still we make together, we tend to be barbarian while at the same we like to be descent, we are animals in the human bodies while again we are basically very human in humanity by possessing the very important thing within us called the very 'human conscience' and the 'hearts' for being humans seems another animal in two feet in contrary to the four feeted wild animals while inside pretending to be human fitting ourselves into the costumes very human in the appearance, we are pure in innocence while again very polluted inside in evil intentions and thoughts and all together we are humans tends to be purified into perfections into the grace of humanity.

In this complex era of a huge diversities we are all confused and imbalanced. It's hard to follow only one path to go all all along the journey through life. Nature itself is wild in flowing both in good as well as in bad as it's spontaneous in every flow of Nature the ways it flow in fire in heat very tremendous when as a volcanic erruptions as the same way flows the very necessary cold water fall down the valleys or like waves into the river or in the oceans. And while the nessecities represent the mighty Nature in the flows of all good in the nature of something very aggressive as it's hard to nurture the natural flows of life in maintaining a balance which is why we are getting lost in between. The confusions arised when all the mix and the matches of things and beliefs in the current world when one global globe has become one together with all cultures in business as well as in beliefs and behaviors we take some of others while we discard some of our own not knowing what values we are losing and what wrongs are we allowing into ours. The confused societies make things confused as well. When the mango tree producing the mangoes only and the apple tree the apples only then why they don't sit in their own baskets separately to still mix together in their own identities? That's what has been going on but now through the generations going by some random mix and match in marriages in the new generations tend to sit together in making things together the ways they make their children in mix and the match of the both different color parents. The ways this generations behave in the confused mentality don't know what to take what behavior from which culture and in making a new one could be the same as in confusions to choose the right one by considering the other as a wrong out of it. But at the matters of the cultures people still tend to keep their originals while go with the present one. In a way these confusions make different people from different cultures helping them to learn other cultures for varieties in the beliefs of their own considering or keeping of their' as their own side by side going with the flow of the present one in which they presently live by Living in a different country still alowing people to keep their own heritages in making an especial day for the particular one while all others also make their festivals separately by making no comments on others. As long people are well educated and well understanding we make no problems in our daily life by making no mess just like the magoes and the apples in the different baskests by seeing each other similarly in one present culture and courtesies as all ethnicity celebrate' their days with or without inviting others and with or without attending others. People always have their choices to live together.

I like to believe that people are all the same flesh and blood as well as in the heart inside as it feels the same while having the same rhythms in the beats only their beliefs and rituals make the differences as we take some of other's culture, behaviors, and beliefs when we migrate to another places we tend to or need to adupt some of other cultures, courtesies and formal behaviors to co-op with them while living longer in another place adupting cultures of the people of the land we live presently which by getting ourselves along through them as becoming one when mix together time to time or a half of the day at work being all together. Consequently, what happens is we tend to talk in the same language making their's as a media to talk in the same language to be the common. Just this way the societies get very adupted by the other cultures and behaviors while slowly making the language their own by learning by heart the ever flowing hearts to make people feel and understand the same quite after a long time through educations as well as through adaptations while mingling together working together through migrations while by the globalizations. We are as a tribe or as a nation very distinct and small so we tend to adopt a lot of the big places we happen to migrate for reasons and purposes. While we are in the most developed and and the vast land to adopt their cultures in courtecies for good for business, for the manners we need to practice all in all kinds of an organizations for work and for educations to go together parallaly for the betterment of the societies all together. Human society already chose English as an international language to fascilitate all to live together as a whole on the same and on the only one globe for all to think and to do things all together globally while believing in the same heritage or the culture happens not to be possible to be accepted by all but at least facsilitating one another in the same language for the sake of the interactions can make things easier to understand to do things right to make things better for all. It happened to prove that the people doesn't matter from where they feel the same in the heart more or less while at the bottom line all thinks the same feels the same. Cultures or the different heritages in different beliefs covers people's bodies by the costumes weaned in and made with each distinct culture to make each of them looking and behaving different than one another while the hearts flow the same for all always very natural while spontaneous for all. Most people in common share some common thoughts while thinking the same, having the same ideas' that's how we on the globe have become global in oneness in thoughts, ideas, work, medias's and managements. The rest is all culture's remain aloof from each other while still keeping the traditions. We tend to keep our own identity in the different heritage and the traditions. We try holding onto the basics of our own as distinct as a culture and the heritage happens to be unique in it's own ways still let it go to mix in some of others eventually and naturally while mixing by allowing ourselves to see all other different people in contact in sharing and caring to adopt each others without a knowledge while accepting certain things from the other' own beliefs and identities very slowly with no reckoning that we have already have lost some of our own to the other's either in behaviors or in nature to do things accepting the fact as an universal in the long run. It happens mainly when we open our views to see things as common in a borader sense to see the world as one in the oneness. The ways the net and the internet made things easier in businesses, in communications, most of all in seeing and making things together by sharing different ideas all together again for the better for better. As a consequence our generations have been modified in nature and culture while happen to grow in the differences in the different culture'. At this point we can't insist to keep our distinct values or beliefs but only to compromise with the new as a part of ours by adopting them within us. In the fast and the vast societies together we're all becoming one in the same waves of life. It's mobility, technology, trades and the mixed up diversities into one to make a global one as one human society in cultures by adopting while shading off some of one's or by losing some to the other. The skin colors remain the same in distinctions so does the clothing. Basically while we start to talk, to think accepting at the same time the same to certain extentions we're good to go in peace and harmony as well as in understanding. Culture is now happens to be mostly in general now for some major factors in our lives as we made our lives easier automatically when some aspects of our normal behaviours or the materials we needed for our living with the flexibility in acceptance as when the judgements don't fail. For example, as we as Muslims allow ourselves to eat non halal birds as chicken when the halal one's not available but some people don't when they are very restricted or happens to be very strong believers in their customs and ethnicity.

Anyways, me and my dear sister stayed longer at the food court longer than enough while eating, chating watching the folks around. One thing definitely very noticible to me as for the clothing people wearing in varieties of our own and all the other's derived from the western, from another country in the same continent as I could see people in payjama' and Panjabi, in pants and shirts, in salwar-kameej, in saries, in tops above skirts, in long dresses to prove that we all got mixed up in beliefs and cultures in keeing some of ours own while taking some extra's to add and adopt with all of ours. This is how the global world of the same human kind in different colors is going with mix and match in cultures. People mix and match while still the differences remain as in their looks still carrying the differences even though with a slight difference sometimes even very subtle to notice still making the origin a distinct one than the other.

Time to leave. I felt a pressure for no reason when Simi asked 'why you rush when you are on a vacation now!'

'o, yes! I realized to say, 'that's true I cant believe that I don't have to rush for work. Ah! What a releife! Still life!'

Simi showed me what she bought this afternoon a sari for our other sister, a set of salwar kameej, also a purse for her too! And for all the children some sweet together with some snacks said' 'if you buy too much for kids they get spoiled to show no value to things we buy as easy to get from the market with some hard earn money.

'that's true! I answered to ask again the next question 'have they already made their boyfriend girlfriend things?'

'no, why you ask?'

I shook my shouders up a little to answer, 'just asking!' of course with a fear to be appreciated what I just asked. Simi took a breath to answer the unexpected question to my very sister living still in a country a lot different than mine said, 'I know why you ask. Here still some restrictions from the society as long the families remain with parents for parenting. Some people are in advance to follow what the westerners do most of us don't.'

'O, well! Good! Very good! Should try to keep this way.'

'I know about the lack of emotional bindings, prejudices, social and ethical barriers over there. But still I don't know the future of our children when they take some from there while like to keep most of their's as for beauty as still don't care about the barriers to restrict to some limit. And this way when all the mix ups then eventually our kids will stand on the gaps between both to be floating with confusions which's already there between cultures.' Simi siged again with her reactions in her answer to the fact arised just like this.

Seeing Simi so much in concerns I responded like, 'I know! In the mixed up of all the growing children happen to become confused in complex mentalities to get enough neive while behave as they don't know how to behave with their parents, their old friends and how to manage both to satisfy both parties in the differences in cultures. Looks like in a social gatherings they need to sort out the different guests in different categories to say 'Hi's and "Hellow's to the other. The ways they are floating in both or into many makes them very confused the same ways they might happen to be very rude behaviored while very confused choosing only one to go on at ease making a society in one for the sake of life and the living in flexibilities as well as in friendships to make it fair.'

'Yes! Replied Simi, 'in a free society young generations do whatever they feel like but unlikely here they tend to go beyond to free themselves by committing some conducts beyond their descency. They get either reckless or unnessesarily naieve or shy as not knowing the limits to perform a conduct or in keeping a conduct normal in some limitations. Sometimes they get violent while allowing themselves to stay out late to make a love relationship in having sex together to get violent to harm the social behavior in the society still keeps the barriers.

'yes people go wrong when it's too much of the restrictions religiously or socially. Those who behave going beyond the considered things as the violations of of the restrictions of the normal social behaviors which is basically now- a- days hanging between the normal and the abnormal as an unusual behaviors to be considered as a violations of the social conducts to look odd to the eyes of what is called a descency in order to keep up the self confidence to go along with the soceity itself to bring them up as good citizens for the betterment of the future in a broader sense for the future generations through all the efforts all along the ways. For the young generations when they aspire to be free when no one's free on earth but their problem is they cant figure out the limitations as they still don't like to take the truth that people never can't be as free as they born to be. Our freedom is in our choices as which one to choose in our lives our best coices in our lives also tend to be in some restrictions to ride the horse properly while the riddle is already in our hands if we loose control to let it go then we fall together with the horse. That's the limilations in our lives.'

Simi agreed to say more like 'we have retrictions in our lives from the society, by the religion, by the code of behaviors of life all through the life. Its always a challenge to keep the balance between what we wish to have and what we need to restrict for the good for life as 'excess of anything is always bad'. Our hearts go like a flow as the wind we can't put it in a bag to hold it for later. We wish, we feel, we desire, we pine and die at the same time as life'always is an irony nothing but an irony! We live a life by doing the corrections only at every turn by depriving our hearts while try to achieve values in achievements. We learn from our mistakes to do better next time. It's like writing a novel of our own life as a big manuscript to do the corrections at every chapter after learning things hardway while coming across the previous one chapter by chapters through modifications while all our wishes, desires, hopes and plans remain unfulfilled along the way to write our own life in a big novel reaching the end by hurting and depriving ourselves through some hard earned experiences to discard the feels and the desires of the heart all along the ways for the things needed for the modifications with some restrictions while along the long ways the ever wishing, ever pinining and ever desiring hearts die at the same time all along the ways.. And very ironically finally the novel ends in no finishing in the wrapping up with all the aceivements at least a good number of the fulfillments of the desires and the wishes of our hearts to be fulfilled till the end of the non-ending or non fulfilled life time life-novel of anyone among all of us. Life is an irony therefore, making our lives or writing about a lifetime live novel book as a life manuscript remains as a tragedy to be anunfinished lifetime long story ending in no endings to be submitted to the Almighty who gave us the life to live, to lead and to treat by understading to live properly according to the commands.

Anyways, where were we again? Me and my dear sister Simi! Yes! We spent the whole noon till the afternoon to approach finally through the evening to go somewhere else. I'm not tired at all neither does Simi as she asked me to see someone we know as a friend or also as a relative. I looked her into the eyes as if I never know anyone. After a little significant silence Simi said surprisingly, we didn't see them yet brother!'

'O, so you wanna go now? '

'why not if they are at home now?'

'O, well! ok!' I felt like I forgot everyone I knew even before the past five years. So far I recall the big brother came to see me off at the airport a very long time ago. I don't know how many centuries I have came across to see a sister or a brother as my own siblings from the same parents! Both of us looked at each other mutually to agree to see the known in unknown or the unknown in the known? We agreed to see our own brother with his family! What a misery! Am I loosing myself? What's wrong with me? Since when I started to feel that I'm all by myself? I felt myself after all in these two or three days that I'm riding a car all alone nothing left behind, no destination ahead and no one's around. I'm just driving and driving all ahead all alone on my ways ahead wherever in bindings in no attachments to any one else or anything at all wherever it takes me in no aims, in no feel of the loss left behind, no aim ahead, no destinations in the desire, no pain no regrets, no aspiring, desiring nothing with no heart in no hopes where there' no dreams as hoping no gain in pain. All in a sudden after a long time being away from the country of my origin, from my only family I was bron in when didn't make my own with a wife and some children in a bongade in love as well as in the very blood relations. Now living only a life by following the daily routine, by consuming food for fuel for the flesh and blood body to run throughout the day for work for earning life in money for life again. Fascilitating the self by providing it some entertainments also for the same purpose the survival only as if the Almighty Creator had set the alarm to keep going on whereas the stoppage the destiny has been decided already to when and where to be stopped. Along the ways someone like me got thrown up by some sort of energy deciding his own destiny in the beginning by the ambitions being aside from the rest of his own family as if an apple thrown up on purpose not knowing what the destinyhas been decided for it. One blow threw him up and out another brought him back down where it belongs time to time while already losing its own identity slowly by the very time changing time to come to this point where memories get faded, life becomes a time pass in some cases only a survival in loss of the heart and soul in no attachments to anything by the ever desiring soul where ther's no pain and pining for a loved one left behind long long ago. The man made thrown up rockets are metallic meant to be material only to be thrown out up to come back down as a ping pong ball by the commands of the time setting alarm whereas the humans made of emotions loose emotions also when no time to sit and think, to regret to look back missing something and someone leaving behind when time has no time to feel the past or the relations they used to regret in the beginning of their departure. The fast life in work going very busy making people the very humankind to take off their hearts from the mind to mind only business where there's no room anymore for regrets roaming into the previosly recorded memories which the brain doesn't recall anymore as there's not much memory time for it to recall while as busy as in the ever working self brain itself in the body to which it belongs occupying it into the continuing business of work.

Sorry! Got lost again. And where was I? O, Yea! Simi! Offered to go see the brother with his family. What an excitement! Suddenly after all I realized myself by discovering myself again. My Brother! Who loved me a lot all my life! What a day! I was even going to forget my own brother? I recalled Simi as she's always connected to my account in the social media. This is how the attachments to family and the friends remain upto date.

'O, No! Simi's voice.

'what? Simi? Yes, we are going to Bhaiya after a long time! As if I just woke up now from the very dreams in dakness saying, 'long time! How are they? How are Maya and Mashid?'

'they are good! Lets see them! Rally, a Long time!'

I wondered, 'you saying this?' why? I thought I got the list only!'

'time changes all and everything doesn't matter you stay close or far it's all about our motives and our wishes sometimes we need to make a time by force doesn't matter how busy we are! We have to make a room for our souls to feel in relaxations, in the memories, in the time taking off from work. As long the heart and soul and the flesh and blood bodies are awake we can do things while we can manage to feel also by making a time to feel in roaming around the past, the present and the future in dreams. It's all about being alive by all means not letting anything go out of sight and out of the mind while we are prsently in the present time very busy in our daily life.

Before Simi starts the car I asked 'how's the big brother and the family?

'They are good! Will be very happy to see you after all!'

As I was sleeping a while ago to imagine myself on a road all alone by myself now in reality it's all horrible and beyond expectations. Simi's car got stuck in the middle of the road surrounded by the cars and cars all sorts of cars the only vehicles all around to be seen when Simi started to feel uneasy as screamed, 'damn! Why even did I planned to go to that directions? Its all traffic and jam damn!' the driver got irritated not me. I'm all in content started to feel that its all my little sister' responsibility to show me the ways and to take me to places. After sitting for a 15 min wait with a mouth shut the car pulled forward with a force by the driver who's no one but my sister. Holding the breath of the evening air actually a nice and a cooling finally gave me a nice break after a long time of my suffocating condition in a city which is not anymore of mine as supposed to be mine as the old city belongs to me where I was born and grew up with an attachment of my heart, a heart to heart relation with the home land. A connection to the core of the heart which feels a real feel with the connections between a land the Mother Land portrayed the picture of it with the motherly love, passion, emotions and the natural attachments growing or living with hearts as the heart flows and the life goes. Life is the Biology, life is the living in keeping us alive or in another way only a surviving. Life*'s a soul given to us as a precious gift sometimes even as a misery to keep and suffer in no choice to keep going by holding onto it as a mission till the end to accomplish the tasks whatever it' as decided by the Divine while that heart gets attachments to the place with all it's beauty where it started to feel the beauty of life in the beauty of Nature as the most valuable part of Nature. The beauty of life consists in the beauty of people as while all get along in love, friendships and all sorts of relationships between people.* we get along, we socialize with each other, we grow up into the boundaries of Nature as an inevitable part of Nature all as the resources we are surrounded by basically all are for us. WE use them by manipulating them, we consume them by cultivating them, we grow them with our own efforts when the ready made materials or the produces are already used up so we find the ways to develop, to make, to produce for more according to our need when the apple tree is empty we find the ways to grow more on the tree. The land we choose to live has its own beauty in the surroundings a river, the green bounties around. The people all are our known and familiar since the childhood. The culture, the customs, the costumes, food, rituals, different events, the love for family with all the members in the family together. The ceremonies or the occasions, different events, the society people we happen to know for a long time in a relationship can't be forgotten very easily.

Still the river flows it's way a destiny ahead to the ocean or to the Sea as it flows following one direction only can't go back or flow back normally. Human lives move up as people have to move up if one place starts to float for a reason as the time doesn't carry all on it's shoulder to shift our life materials and goods along with us to flow us back to settle down there with the full might and right. The river flows up, time flows up never to flow back, similarly people move up taking some of the life materials only the memories remain as a whole for the whole life they spent in the past. The life of the humankind is always impressive as moving forward with a progress can't really go back where it started it take's a lot along the ways while the memories remain while proceeding along the ways educating a self, seeing, helping while getting along with each other helping and being helped by people.

This ways, along the way we built societies, different organizations, institutions, schools for education, for higher educations for law and managements for all different sectors in our lives to live a social and healthy life all together. We have been proceeding through evolutions evolving every time for better by doing some corrections. We humans are weak and fragile can't rebuild ourselves when collapsed but we can build concrete constructions with all our might and rights to make better society for the sake of humanity as well as for the comfort for our bodies. We are proceeding through constructing and reconstructing along the ways for a long time and ironically while we are living into the concrete constructions to fascilitate us our hearts happen to die on the day to day basis as life has gotten stuck inside while covered all around by the hard brick walls and by the hard cover of the roof over the head.

Life has gotten hard as it's hard to earn on the very set up of the life on a platform. Its hard to earn while living and earning go side by side. Memories are always sweet the present time remains in the process to make new memories for the process to make the future. Good to come back to the memories!

The sudden touch of the cool wind woke me up from a dead feel. Where am I? Oh! Yes! Dhaka! My city! Simi's still serious about driving as driving very clearfully as it's real hard to drive in the very crowd of the high populated city of Dhaka the capital of the significantly and insignificantly a very small city as the capital city of Dhaka in over populations in the small country called Bangladesh.

I looked at my little sister who's no more a liitle one anymore apparently much more matured sometimes I feels like much more maturer than me while well maintained after all. On the other hand the unfortunate me who was always in a foreign land remains in day dreams in fun as well as pretty much striken by the harsh and hard reality in contradictions to the other. In my place a little beam of life peeps through the heat of the burning sun in a cool breeze seems provided by the same Nature as breezing through all the sky down while in my left behind land of my own the hardships in life peeps as a little beam of light through all the loving caring hearts in emotins and passions for each other as the cool breeze blows very soft with a soft touch by touching the body through the hearts of all. Even when we get frustrated or in conflicts with each other we make it up very soon as our emotions drives us to love, to show sympathy, to provide care while share the hearts together. A jealous heart burns like the very heated sun to cool down at once in regret to love where the passions prevails. But in a strange land of opportunities to get the opportunities we get the sudden blows of harsh and hard realities to face in no time in making that opportunity basically on our own when there's no one's around stretching a hand out for you to be a part of it to make the work or the business or the opportunity didn't come by chance but through the observations of your capabilities to make something for the provider to perform with all your might basically to take risk while gain. The opportunity seeking people get the opportunity by getting overloaded by the work by losing time in life which put them in a situations as achieving something makes them lose the short lifetime life in a land where they land to live better in acheiving some acheivements as a sign for the progress. Successful people get ambitious to achieve success while working hard through a harsh lifelong- living which makes no sense at the aceivements when took a lot from the life in bitterness, sickness while almost packing for life for achieving for life. Having mere fun in smile and cry chronically finally make us rude when facing the hard and harsh reality. We lose more to gain less to blame us ironically finally as a consequence. When at the end we gain we are already in pain to feel the good we earned hard way. We work hard to buy the comfort when in the long run the comfort can't really provide you a comfort to feel while the pain is more. We fail and gain again and again to gain while we fail many times to gain only once. The opportunities come with a blow of hard tests and harsh realities which in the long run through the success makes no sense in real sense to hold onto it to be happy or to feel with a heart when the beauty of the heart has been lost into the process of gain through the blows of hardness on the body and the soul to lose the very soul in the process of being stiken by the bolws of sudden misfortunes or the hardships believing again and again in the beliefe 'no gain no pain' becomes an irony for the gain finally at the end when the particular body already lost the soul in the decaying or the slow sickening body to feel at the end all to be a mystry. Living a real life in the true nature of life as it goes with all of it's true feelings, by making some choices of it's own, with the feel of all good and bads as the life and the Nature provides time to time. We the humankind tend to live a life not to make a life in true senses. We make things for life we cant make life for the sake of things.

Simi's still driving with no complain at all as sometimes the breath taking heat in the hot weather inside created at the sametime by the crowd outside and the traffic as well by making a traffic jam as usual. Looking ahead giving no break to see anything good. No nice feel of a soothing touch of a fresh natural air from outside even when the windows are pretty open from both sides. If we breathe by taking breath from outside from the crowd then I guess the readers can imagine even can feel the real situations through their imaginations!

Any ways, I started to burn up to sweat as in those old days long time ago a long long ago on the other hand Simi's still consistent looking into her crefull driving over all. Better now the car is moving into enough cool breeze to breathe to feel myself alive in my land. Very soon the city lit it's night time lights as to rise and shine in the electric lights. Now's better ugly gestures' of the old and small city won't be seen to be seen by the eyes always love and care for the city as don't want to see it's decaying beauty as well as the dignity in the physical appearances as well as for the moral senses to care. My mind has been wondering back in the past with all it's sweat memories. Past feels good in the present as we feel the pain by seeing the pain only in the present by ignoring the pleasure we get sometimes in the present time because of the magnified scenario of the bads or the odds in our look to feel. The past was not without a bad but we remember the memories only to feel the good only about it for some reason. The past is a memory only to look at the good of it only in the memories as contray to the great poet,'our sweetest memories are those that tells of the saddest tells' this might be in the negative sense while the past feels the most in it's loss by over looking the odds from there. Any ways, it's good in a way to keep the positives in the memory to take life as a gift to live with life, to feel, to cherish all including the sweet memories. When memories make feel good by looking back into the past in all good like love, passion, a life in life in all the aspects to chrish in the glory of all the aceivements and of course into the memories of all the earned and gained through the refreshments of the soul as well as through the dedications of the soul to depict some pictures of the troffee's of some honour and dignity in the life left behind to still proceed holding the paddle with strong wills to go along the ways in the present towards the future holding the experiences very positive to proceed with a heart and guts when we believe that we lost the glory of life behind to regain it all along the ways. We are very much valued into our memories and that value makes us do better in the present to regain the value we think we lost in the past.

According to my little sister a few more minutes for Brother's home but I din't mind driving all the way through the city as still the open sky remained visible through my views ahead the road side views are nothing but all the big and small business held in some small big and small concrete contuctions in the shape of all the stores or the series of different size shopping complexes holding all the merchandise for men to sell. Night time vision only makes people dazzle in to the lights of all the commercials and restaurants. When during daytime people work like the colony of ants and the night time life feeds them, entertains them, where there's only the sparkling neon lights make a life short for short break of life for life at sunset of the Sun as the sun is all day light keeping the darkness all out while the life in the neon light still prevails in the very darkness. I knew this scenario in the human world is always like this way, day light is all clear and visible the night time vision is always also a vision inevitable when it still can see through a vision not that clear as in the day time light. But the enchanted city look still looks nice to me while it's covering a lot of the odds belong to the dark side. The combinations of the enchanted city wonders and the night time cool air in the summer night glory especially in the cool touch of the cool breeze in the night made me feel a lot better to see myself in the very familiar. The speed takes away some actually a lot of the charms of our life while leaves stills some of it behind when we still can find some beauty into the darkness which makes no odds or hides no odds in the beauty of the darkness.

In fifteen min we reached a narrow neighbourhood known to be our brother's house felt to be very dear as close to the heart as another wake up call from my stupid dear dumb heart of my own ever living in illusions to be lost in the non- real reality. I got worried at the same time about the car whether will be able to sneak in the narrow lanes running to and fro passing by towards the brother's. It had a name can't just recall at this moment. O, well! I cant name a name for the very love word'Love' meaning the reality the reality which it's possessing the most known unknown, the most mysterious passion and the emotion in our lives in the feel as the most dangerous feel in the heart possessed by the very human body which can guide and misguide a person at the sametime by taking control of the very human mind as urging and directing to follow it's flow as if in the flow of the wind sometimes cool and soothing, sometimes mind blowing in the mind to be guided by the heart to follow it's flow definitely most of the time towards the destructions, sometimes the very opposite for some people as only Love can guide towards the right path when a person already got into a wrong path to follow for the life making life when have already fallen into despair in the loss of the valuable "Love" thing. If it's really a "Loss of valuable energy' then why do we need this emotion to take over? Life is a mystery after all! Then living with love is better than Living in love while it takes life in the loss! The irony is, people ironically fall in love to lose life again to love eventually while at the same time losing both the love and the life together to love only. Simi after all still looks very normal managing all in holding the steering of the speedy vehicle of life towards a life living in life for love the love for the life and the life in the love. Reaching Habib Bhaiya's residence made me feel nothing either as entering like a stranger or like a very dear person as the younger in the elder' to bow and honor in the first place. Big brother came forward running in holding the breath out of sudden emotions and excitements to see the stranger in his own brother strangely appeared to be a guilty one to show up like a sneaky unexpected guest in the house of his own brother coming late to show a sign of his existence towards the relationship with his own brother happened to be out of sight while might have been out of mind also unfortunately! On the other hand the elder brother started to hasitate himself in contrary for being a criminal not to be in contact with me frequently as if my honorable brother committhed a big mistake for not inviting him to visit them. Both of the brothers felt the same to each other. Habib Bhai remembered those days he used to scold the younger one for being so inattentive to his lessons to complete on time and for bringing home a poor mark sheet in the year ends. That responsibilities made him feeling very proud now as for being an elder to the proud younger brother happens to be now an American citizen to be proud of. Habib bhai started showing his happiness in the appearance of me his younger brother by hugging now, smiling constanly looking at the both me and Simi back and forth not knowing what's to be done by him as an elder brother to show his happiness at their arrival together. His happiness knows no bound to make him very restless even to offer them both to be sitted. The elder brother got very annoyed as if didn't know where to let them sit. Out of excitements or finding himself all in a sudden in an unexpected situation. He's getting this chair by rejecting the other the next moment for a better one to offer especially to me as if after a long time I happen to appear as a stranger from another planet. For a moment I felt a severe pain into my heart for my poor elder brother already lost self confidence feeling so inferior to his own younger brother! I don't know how he felt seeing me running towards him just now by seeing him after a long time but I still can't believe that the time gap made this much gap between us? And also wondering to bring myself so close to him all in a sudden after a long time the time which almost wiped off his existence into my heart to bring the sense all at once! Anyways, I felt good to be good after all by looking at both of them all together we are three siblings together seeing each of us the happiness into each others eye to feel the old to be very proud after all we didn't lose the family bondage at all! while in the beginning I asked Simi as she proceeded to the brothes house 'where are we?" 'where could we be?'

'is this the Habib Bhai's house?'

'right!' smiled Simi. I knew but I could'nt remember all I could remember was there was a lane in the neighbourhood named after a Mughal Emperor's name which I couldn't recall at all. I didn't lose the image and the old look of the place also as a sign of our family love, family bondage, the friendships between us as an identity for the family. This same neibourhood looked different in the past in real connections through the heart to heart relations in the real family life and business which was very close to these present hearts belong to the three siblings together now. A family is an identity for the selves as it rises never to lose in love into a bondage again suppose to be very strong as a document fot the rest of the life as an identity to prove living in a society to be mentioned by giving a family a name of their own. Another thing is finally I felt very great and proud of myself for restoring the old heart of the family even though living a far and far away.

The old house is gone by making the room for the constructions of the new apartment building for the lodging in a boundary keeping it out of the crowd. Good to have a parking underbeath the seven story tall building. The place looked nice with some plants in the front yard as planted for beauty. I noticed only one eucalyptus in the corner on the right side of the of the building touching the highest floor of the building close to the gate to the highest floor to the gateway to the next buildings like that in the huge area of all apt building closed by the boundaries.

As we reached the 5th floor it is none but Selina bhabi opened the door to greet and treat us a mother of three old enough children for not to look pretty anymore but the Divine One didn't forget to keep her smile as pretty as before to greet us with the greatest gift ever to make the home a sweet home and as a very dear and near very close to the heart. Selina bhabi told us to sit by taking a chair for her also asking, 'I heard about your arrival. How's everything? Do you like it here after so long?'

O, yes! Why not after all it's our own place? And especially when visiting my brothers residence always a dear one to visit relaxing on a very reclining soul?' They all started laughing including the very elder brother who looked like almost forgot how to smile.'

'that's right.' A short answer from my elder brother. I looked at my dear bhabi lost all he beauty over the time. I don't see her long hair I don't see her pretty deep black eyes. She's as skinny as she was only the time and age changed her complexions as well as her distinct natural beauty of her own. A Mother of two a son and a daughter looking as elderly as she should be. Sima and Shaon both already are married with children living separately in their own apartments.

Simi got very talkative while as very excited asking this and that. My dear brother also got very elderly looking. Time is ever forwarding while we are ever reclining over the time. We count on time as when we say like, 'time is changing.' When we see things are changing as all including the changing society, the ever changing nature of all the aspects of life including the Nature itself the way we grow, we age, we get changed in our looks by changing all around us to be more and more modern and to be in advance unfortunately only we the humans and animals as for being a living thing like all other in Nature by declining in beauty and behaviors while slowly naturally declining in the dying process over the time we believe it's changing everything while it remains the same in nothing but for us to count on a media to measure how much more we'll be proceeding and how much we already came across leaving all behind including us among all other living and growing things as well as the concrete' as it also change like the stone hardening slowly from the soil to hard soil, from there to the hard core. Funny is, time is time as ever as it exists and all the creation including us the humankind the temporary one's on one planet to decline finally by fulfilling it's destiny whatever it is. Time is nothing we are something to grow first by making them improving and eventually by declining in the phase of time as believe to be to count on as a media for mesaurments for how long all the things will last as the limited living planet also be in the declining nature.

Anyways, what I was saying is that my Bhaiya and Bhabi are now at the aging stage of their age. Both of us me and my sister and the brother are individually carrying the burden of life on each of us' shoulders to be declined by the time set for life at some point generally counted to be from the of 60 to 90 at this time. They look very tired to still carry on all the boundless burdens of life on their declining shouders. The burdens of life also look & feels very heavy on them which they can't leave without the will of the one who created them with the precious gift of life very close to the hearts can't really try to get rid off by their wills even if they wanted to. When life is no longer precious still then no one likes to give it up. Actually life's never is a precious gift and never was. Young people are enthusiastic anything makes them to be curious about and excited to see and feel while hold. They go with no worries when they see things all beautiful as their heart and mind are beautiful therefore, they are the energy for all evolutions and revolutions for humanity. They do, they thrive, they have the energy to proceed in full energy to gain in pain while loving things seeing the beauty in them. They are the one's who bring life to life. They tend to grow, they tend to create, they are the one's makings up for the betterments for better as thery are the revolutionary force to bring a change to move up. They see the life only as they see the beauty of it, the propects of it. They go into no negativities, in no judgements thinking or questioning about life what's there in life what good in it, what makes a life good etc. They learn, they thrive, they struggle to gain things and the successes in whatever they are doing or working for. They have the freshness of the age to take things positively as they have the faith in life they thrive, they make things while they do things in guts. They possess the innocence to see things better in nature as the positive energy makes them enthusiastic to proceed. They don't look for the meaning of life or the meaning in the nature of certain things as they don't think ahead like creating something by thinking it's prospective or the future or the possibilities to be successful in future. They look ahead only to that extentions which makes them feel good about it for its use or the prospects for further use. They stay away of those questions like what?', what for?', for what use?' 'what meaning it carries?'. Philosophers look for the meaning for life, question the about good it holds, or why we are here?, why we hold onto something and for what? Sometimes people thrive for life thinking going in vain while struggling in pain to gain. Young generations live, love, thrive, have hope and faith while don't question why we're here and why we thrive in vain in no gain even by thinking like 'how about if things go wrong?'

The same people in their age lose hope, dedications to their duties, lose hope and faith at the same time to end up in less productivity. They dream including their day dreams, they pine and die to gain in might as thinking right. On the contrary, four of us the four elderly members in the family are now waiting while living very slowly in dreams, in doubts, in delays in everything by making our moves slow in the slow moving move in no hopes and no dreams.

All three of us one brother and two sisters took our sits on the chairs on the open space outside the living room wishing to see the open sky to get some fresh air from there and while we wish to see the open sky by getting suffocated living inside the small cubes of concrete feels to be trapped in but the contradicting irony is the sky itself is also pretty much trapped as being blocked the buildings, by the huge walls as could be shown only some separate portions of the huge open sky by the showing of a little part part by part from here and there between the gaps, through the gaps made by the high rises as lined up for their facilities by blocking the sky's open view to be witnessed from there where ever they wish to view. The sky only can show His huge existence in a little part as peeping as a piece of light or as the tiny tiny portions of His appearance in the showing of His invisible body in a little white or in blue just like the city people when they think they are all trapped into the holes of the constructions high and conjested to peep only a littlie from the open holes considered as the little windows, some broken gaps between the buildings or from a broken space on the walls or the cracks only happens to look like an open space hanging or even attached to the concrete' as showing and viewing. Showing is for the trapped people into the buildings by allowing themselves to show them to the open sky in the open air to get along with the open air and the free breathing of them. The ways they are captivated behind the small windows same ways the sky has been trapped behind all the huge and huge walls of the concrete lodgings of humans to see them as some little creatures into a little place. The human eyes got blocked the same ways for their open views to view the openness of the huge sky as the same ways the sky happens to be blocked in its huge openness to look through all in one Big open eyes to be as great as a creation as opening up His huge territory in the huge as a Vast and an Open existence for all.

All of us together didn't have much to talk about only to talk about our old selves separately all together under the same roof with our parents only loving and fighting, caring and hating each other at the same time, in togetherness and in separations by fighting once again while caring the same ways as always. While we grew up together in accuracy and jealousy at the same time to realize that it was our parents together provided all the love and care by taking care of us equally to be appreciated for all the time the ways we realize now. We recalled our old houses, old schools, old life as happy with all the little little things, to be proud of our good report cards as well as our village where we spent our summer and winter vacations in a different settings happened to be a rural one to be ruled by only the mighty Nature to be only natural in instincts to play, to jump, to climb up the mango trees, to swim into the ponds, to cook some stuffs apart from the mother' to enjoy a rural picnic all together while for about all the exams, all the home work to finish and all the big assignments for school to accomplish.

Habib Bhai smiled to comment, 'we cheat on our tasks as life cheats on us even though we're honest in the long run still not knowing who's cheating on who! Is it us cheating on our own or by getting ourselves to be cheated by our own negligence or intentions or it's the life itself which slips away from our own dreams for which we couldn't fulfill our jobs to sucseed. Simi took a break from us to go inside to help bhabi. Brother looked me in the eyes to ask the same question Simi asked me earlier and that is 'why still I didn't I marry yet? When I really don't know why then I guess I had no choice but only to look down to avoid the most annoying situation when I don't have the answer to the question which I have been very frequently asked. Habib Bhai looked me again into the eyes to say,' I'm worried about both of you. If Mom and Dad were alive you wouldn't have been asked by me or anyone else. My dear brother took a breath to say again, 'living a life without making a family is like riding a boat without the paddles no aim no destiny where there's no living in the grip of nothing. When we don't care about the life by possessing it then we don't care about the supports for it to lose it like holding onto a hopeless, selfless self as being like doesn't mind at all to destroy it as being careless while selfless.' 'Simi has two children while you have none.' Big brother reminded me also of the nature of life as mentioning, like 'Life's hard. Think about it.' I kept quiet for a bit then answered 'people now-a-days live to live all by themselves and in most of the cases they are forced to do that as for the situations they get into to have no choice but to be separated from each other both as a husband and as a wife. They don't like to marry, don't like to live together as they have to mind their own business by working faster and faster for the society where there's no choices to go other ways by the mix and match while putting enough efforts to balance the hard and fast present life with the relationships to keep theselves up when it doesn't do anything other than making complecations and chaos while time, place and actions all go individually in it's own direction. Habib Bhai kept quiet for a little while to ask, 'Do you like that? Do you agree to the present social as well the human behavior? And my answer was none but to say only,'no choice bro, no choice! At some point people always tend to mind their own life and own business as we always make life together together with a group of an individual person holding each his or hers' own concerns as we all individually basically responsible for our own self while living in a society very unfortunately!'

Poor brother sighed to say nothing but kept quiet once again knowing the fact. What can he do what can he expect other than admitting the facts happening right now. We make societies still we are the people responsible for break it up into different sections finally starts to feel the urge to isolate us from the group then eventually from the very partner the one and only to us a company a little support finally to break us up for our own interests and the time managements which is getting hard day by day for communications as well as for the sake of companionships.

Bhaiya said again out of frustrations,'I don't worry much about my children the way I worry for you two both of you are single to worry about the future of our next generations? A bondage free life is the life of an animal as goes like 'dosn't care doesn't mind. Hope you be better! Sometimes how you feel for your well being as you live all alone in a foreign land! He paused here to take a deep breath out of frustrations said, 'anyways, what did you plan next? Are you going to see all of your friends? How about Dipok? are you still together as friends?'

'no-------------- 'I answered loud because that's a long time ago he was a friend of mine. We stopped seeing each other when I left for the great America a dream land and a land of opportunities. My family was also going through some concerns out of realities which made me leave the country. Dipok and me were very close friends together from the universities. He chose journalism and I chose Economics. So we separated at some point when my family needed money to go along with the contemporary social and political and mainly economic conditions. My American friends tease me for being so feminine in having some woman like behavior and character as well as some feminine qualities. But I took off my own land with no hasitations at all or by panicking out of any kinds of emotional attachments which could give me a pain to leave my land, my friends living in my hearts with full of dreams and the mind full of ambitions. So, I left my family all together my parents, all my siblings in a chain of the family bondage in the very blood relations to settle down all at once all in a sudden while wishing and dreaming for a long time thinking to be settled better in all the good opportunities for life to live better by being somebody superior in a lot better position in the land of opportunities while man dreams and the destiny decides. Dipok felt the same way what can we do or think in a land of our own very poor and under developed which still is developing day by day each day.

The way I left my Mother Land same way Dipok too as a journalist from his country to another country eventually to shift time to time for the sake of his job which is one like a journalist to tour the places all around time to time for the sake of his job. He thinks he's happy by getting the opportunity to see and to feel the differences between different land settings, the people in different clothings as having different cultures, languages, different beliefs, different out looks, different ways of life in different situations social, political and environmental. But he certainly likes to fly around up and above not in his soul definitetely but on a job as a journalist to report. But I still don't know what makes him so happy. He got his mission and I got mine who's succeeded who's not not known yet but I believe thinking positive is enjoying whatever' in hand can make everyone happy. Time to time we got to chat with each other but didn't still talk about our life whether or not we are really happy or thinking ourselves to be settled down already or even to talk about our settlements for life in a particular place we think to be the best to decide to settle down for the final destiny ironically while we already have our own destiny as we have a land of our own which is actually our home to come back always as for the birds to fly back as always! Anyways, both of us Dipok and me are happy in our carriers findinding a suitable place also to live while long time we didn't see each other to talk, to make jokes out of fun most of the time humiliating each other whenever in contact with one another. Long time I didn't hear from him and I don't know where he is now!

Simi came out of the kitchen with tea to serve all and said, 'Bhabi's making dinner we can have some tea now.'

Seeing her I asked 'did you hear from Dipok recently?'

'Nope!' with a short answer very careless about anyone to be a little curious.

'Oh!' sighed me while at the same time didn't know what made me feel very deep to sigh from the very bottom of the heart. I know it's only a friendship. My heart might have been felt differently to sigh at a loss of something which it's pining very secretely for something from the core of its depth as deep as like a deep black hole very inside where no one has gone before? Nope! That's called love. Dipok is my boy friend for a boy friend only. A soul sometimes pine for a soul mate which's similar to it in pain, in the deep sorrows, in pining for something very similar to each other an ever struggling soul in pain coudn't find the same to share in care, in the perfect understanding with each other. I don't think about him much but I do remember him time to time. As a flying soul he also might be flying back to sit on the same branch? We are strange, we are great as we are all the same as humans feeling the same, seeing things the same, loving sharing all the same as the same life caring same for the same?

Brother reminded me of him again and me and Simi decided to visit his house sometime before I leave. The declining family of the three of us as a sister and two brothers with some children as our next generations are all under the same roof together to share and care for one another. All the children are on their time in their own business and three of us are sitting out on the balcony looking outside down on the roads the at the running cars carrying the running lives all together as merging together on the ways of the very modern city life of the very present time with all it's glory while at the same time I am wondering in the hearts whether there will be another time to be together in a moment like this to look back looking at us as on the previous ones to wonder, to flatter the souls by roaming into the memories while the sweetness of the past making us feel better on the contrary the developing life and the place which always stays into the heart as a piece of monuments holding all the old as in the gold furnished and nicely portrayed as by cherishing the memories. We don't know a time sooner or later will give us the same time and the place to be together to gain our old life in the memories all together as a family all in the same hearts dreaming the same, wishing the same viewing the same as the sweetest memories of the past in taste.

My heart started to ache in pain a bit while the mind thought for a little by worrying like this time might not be coming back like the same as it is still now full of sensitivities deriving some memories from the past of all of us in the same feel as a view through the windows of the past memories to view as a brand new as in the renewal. The same age friends being in the same time pattern to share all lovely, all the glories, all the childhood memories as all grew up in the same environments sharing together all the old time glories to glorify the new in the present together as one soul making out of the all three as still unforgettable getting the lost time back in the present with the feel of the old love, old passions and emotions in feeling the life pattern on the old set as in imaginations all together to feel it the real as the old to be the gold we lost in fun and love to be all alive in our hearts and the soul. Coming from wherever we are now this moments on the same ground might be a memory only remaining as a memory when presently making a memory for the future only to keep like some pictures for the future we have in our home sweet home just like Simi's as she's keeping with a heart the photo's hanging on the walls of her'together with her lost love her husband to remember only time to time by taking a look as always staying in the heart. This little camera as a device helping us to take pictures of our favorites as well as our memories to be a great favor from the creations of man by manipulating the creations of the very Divine in the man made electronic device' as a camera to still keep the memories in the present by His grace after all. The globe has come to the global to reach anything from home or communicating anyone from our own place by the favour of all the devices by the favor of the technology. We make everything from Nature by putting all the ingredients and the materials together derived from Nature by manipulating sometimes sometimes shaping or reshaping sometimes nurturing when we need to nurture. While we still praise the old the very Nature as pure as it is always when we could not progress without developing us through the evolutions of the technology and in advance we couldn't do much living in the lap of Nature deriving and using all its mighty resourses very natural without all the artificial intelligences and technologies to take advantage to do things in more ease and with more and more convenience also very quickly. But we still know that the old is gold as a solid and sweet from the heart of the Nature not from a Robotic body or a device copying very smartly possessing a brain artificial almost the same but not the as same talking the same but still not the same. There's no spontinity in the robots they do things correctly as programmed to do so as their life is given by the technology collectively each move is a piece of commands as a part of the whole capacities of a robot to perform accordingly when there's a command to do so. They are still not capable of doing things by making a descision performing in a quick reactions to help a situation or to fix a problem all by themselves as they have no human brain. They think but all from the collections of the data set in the programming to answer a question to a human as required. We humans are also like that we can answer to a question only from the prior knowledge but still unlike the robots our knowledge is vast to make things, to answer from the common sense to handle a situation as promptly as possible unlike the robots. It's a far reaching ambition to make a brain like humans which hold the whole collections of knowledge and memories performing into the vast activity of the human brain which is elastically very expanding beyond a limit as natural as God gifted. Human kind thinks while being very passionate at the same time to do more or think ahead when necessary.

We can only nurture that part of Nature which makes shapes to shape proportionately like making a garden in a limited land with some modern ideas to use the ferlitizers or the artificial fascilities by applying on the plants or the vegetables as modified as necessary.

So we pick an era which used to be neither very mechanical nor totally natural which is somewhat and somewhere in between to enjoy life in originality with some ease by the help of some technological advantages. We promised Bhaia and bhabi to see Mohan and champa another time to get together all together once again. But Bhaiya insisted to stay for the night a lot to talk and share as time flies very quickly. Bhaia and bhabi feel lonely also most of the time. Daughter and the son are better off with their own family. People are now like corps to grow for productions by producing the next produce to keep going as to keep up the production only. Mama tree and the papa tree get themselves empty as drying up to die by giving the earth their all the fruits and the produce and the productions for the reproductions to carry on the reproductions in growth and to fall both side by side. All the people as plants in a big garden serving each other to grow to be fruitful to each other once again to keep up the earth and the world of the planetary services provided by all are for all actually in a recycling process or by consuming by the ascending branches to hold the next. When the society is declining an individual is getting self centred he or she can only make love to bring another individual to live alone by consuming all the environment will collapse also. So the universe is going to loose all bondages, all morals, values, to keep up the spirituality or the Divinity or the beliefs which keeps people as humans to breed and live like Humans in humanity.

Bulbuly and and Bashar called Simi their Mom to say 'Good night' with all the wishes. I looked at Simi's happy face with a motherly grace of all by hearing from them all. I looked at the motherly beauty of a grace of all by hearing from her children. I also thought thinking by 'what a beauty! Still Motherly love and care prevail! We are still human after all!'

Next morning when I opened my eyes up the only thing I noticed through the window was the great sun again at the dusk creating a fire red phenomenon at the east in the sky by the Fiery rising sun itself in the east making a beautiful scenery on the sky campus down with the sun beam through the trees on the spot over the roofs of some low rises while the high rises can't really allow to view the nice view of the beginning of a day break with light in might. The early prayer call from the nearby Mosque from where around woke me up from the materialistic mind in some beauty around as the surrounding view of the still green beauty without any existing nearby garden to bring me up to the spirituality or bringing me back to the realisations of the Mighty Creator for His creations to see, to view, to greet and to enjoy with a full heart to pay thanks to the Great and the Kind One to be grateful above all we regret. Seeing and viewing all through yesterday as visiting a shopping place occupied my mind in reality in comparison to the west for business, for better constructions, for materials concretes around making a materialistic world of our own all around consisting in a social behavior, the systems and so on to get me carried away by thinking what we get where or thinking too much of a life style by forgetting or ignoring all about love, relationships, our sweet old memories, family bondage and values including all moral values to struggle to keep us up as before. The Azan from the Mosque somewhere called me back to the Divine feeling getting back to divinity as by coming back to myself or to ourselves as a result of our last nights get together. Brothe, me and Simi kept talking, joking as in our old time of our glory living as a family together into ourselves truly and originally by recalling the time in this time making in the old time by forgetting about all the harsh reality was brought upon us to bring us here now in the change by the ever changing society we live in. Above all, the elder brother who can still play an important role to keep us still together as a family in a bodage with a charm after all where the hearts never die.

It's Bhaiya kept us living still instead of sleeping last night the whole night. I slept a lot long way in numbness in the loss of all the sensitivity, emotions and passions in order to hold onto jobs, carriers heading hard towards a future with no foundations just kept going with no feel, no fantacy only a false one a faking desire very finely. We spent the night in remembrance of the childhood, found the picture's to remember the high school buddies in uniforms to chat on our noble teachers by faking the notes for the home work or a class work.

Simi's on duty to make tea for all three of us on the same board to bring back the old to hold in the loss. A day and a night might never be back. Even if it is back it won't be the same while looking same in the loss of all in the lost time back only to the memories of all the charms, the heart as well as the remembrance in the feel very different in present broken hearts and the frozen minds feeling and thinking the same. Moreover, when we recall the past it brings us sorrows only for the lost charms the time and age very innocent to die now in remembrance as we even can't see the lost beauty and the innocence of the present grown ups. I doubted to see Bhaia next time in the same health condition if I can come back on time to see all once again for the soul as a whole. The way we are losing the physical health the same ways also the spiritual health as if the air is getting polluted by the abuse of the use the same ways the hearts and the minds. Hearts get hardened through the hard pressure from all around so does the mind gets polluted learning all the inpurity and the complexities through the practices of all the hypocricies of all human tyranny and hypocricy as to go on into the conventional trends of the behaviors and the simplicities into all the systems and social behaviors in the present societies. We do now neither cry nor smile we all are now into our own individual movies made by our own identities each as a complex character hardly carrying on our role' into all the complexities of the heart and the mind to make the life even the daily life living in a poluted society already polluted by all the complex and comfused people as in the lack of honesty and the spirituality while our hearts are in the lack of purity. The hard reality hardening the life in the ever hardening souls it contains to make us enough comlex, confused, doubtful in a society mostly while all the different colors and ethnicity as well as the very cultures mix together for better for bringing actually no better in real sence which lead us to a life to be lived in a place other than our own for the betterment of the life to live basically in a critical and a complex situations where we turn to nothing but all confused, doublful and even sometimes a little scared and subtle thinking like losing ourselves or all of our origins finally to end up like an egocentric a subtle and abnormal personality to make us looking different than the old one, the old you and me ironically!

Anyways a togetherness in the family, a sharing and a caring memories of the past together as a family gave me something very precious and dear beyond all the concretes beyond the heartless even the selfless present time of our own. We talk. We work, we sleep, we rest, we eat, we drink, we entertain ourselves all for our body and the soul to keep us up to be alive as a soul and as a healthy body to go with the flow only as our passions and emotions die everyday every moment a little by little to replace the human inside us for the animal sometimes in the shape of a monster, sometimes in the nature of an animal, sometimes acting like a robot as all the natural and artificial qualities have gotten together as mixed up all together to behave a very strange being time to time in an ever changing role to play as for the requirements of the present human complex social behaviors to keep us up into the survival nature of the continuing life while doing our businesses and carrying out our lives as business. The river can flow with the spontinity of it'all natural water to flow ahead but for humans there are the hearts and the mind. The heart tend to flow but to look who binds it up, keeps it in restrictions like holding it in different boxes as an unit in each as still a flow in flowing doesn't matter if it's not in the whole range in an open space but still a liquid a flowing nature as a quantity in a cube into a bondage in it's own nature?

Time flew very quick with the blow of the wind to feel every moment here in the land of memories, in the land of cherishing all the childhood, the youth the adulthood in the growth with feel and cherishing in love with the time giving education, family-friends, love and faith, passion, devotions and emotions to all the attachments couldn't realize when the life experiences from the very reality in both kinds hardened the body and the soul like a piece of stone from the soft soil over the time by the blows of the wind and the rain, heat and cold side by side from the very opposite forces of Nature in contradiction to turn something into a stone which is the very invisible slouls of our own don't know when and how to act and re-act like people once we considered to be very rude or heartless in the lack of emotional entities. What I got in this one month in my Land is priceless and for all the life cherished in all good not in riches but in relying on relationships in all goods again not in riches which doesn't exist only but makes it melt the hard piece of ice into the tear drops melting through the pain the heart takes in storing it's cold to melt after to come out through the eye as it's tear drops to drip from the consentrations of the dark or the ash cloud of the cloudy heart couldn't see to melt the pain in tear drops after all.

The time of departure is on the shoulder. A few more days. Simi did all the packing for me I came with two suitcases to leave with four in total. She kept buying for me with the money I gave her for herself and the children but the stubborn sister my dear sister kept buying and spend the money on me only. I repaid her half of the amount she already spent which I gave her as a gift from me meaning we shared the expenses as a half and half as she thinks I'm losing my interest in living which means I'm letting the life go very slowly by loosing my interests in things I used to loved once very much.

She kept telling me, 'did you ever fall in love with someone Bhaiya?'

When I asked why she answered, 'looking like a lost lover in the battle of love.'

In answering her question I attacked her saying like, that's you! You couldn't and can't forget your husband. Take it easy girl! Life is not a very favorable to all! we have to accept whatever the destiny decides!' looking at her pale face which is trying hard to glow in the fading color of her actual complexions I mentioned next, 'life is hard for all this way or other. All the people together can't get or gain the same while together with the loss in the same ways. We set our goals for some gain while we always aim at something while the destiny decides and the goal we are about to reach remains empty as most of the time we miss the aim unfortunately or in the lack of our efforts.

Life goes very slowly by letting us lose interest in things we used to love while very slowly we proceed through aging till the end. We know we live in the dying process and very slowly over the time we proceed carring the burdens of our work, our duty bound duties always as a burden to empty from our shoulders to get enough hard experiences along the ways in hardships on the path of lifelong life in a pair of safety boots still to be harmed and hurt along the way with little of the charity pleasure break or we usually expect from it a happiness in life in order to refresh the soul and the body while in reality our souls get bitter, taunted and the body gets sick while at the same time the feet gets bruises walking on the path in all the ups and downs, time to time in pain and in pining, with the dragged out soles under the feet belongs to the body which is slowly getting sick, and a broken spirit, broken body as torn and taunted as a soul. Finally it's time to leave the very stage of life as the final call says, 'time's up!'. Life is gifted with all the Good and Bads along the ways but while the good is only a little break between the hardships of all kinds along the way then it's eventually a decaying system to die soon.

Whenever Simi complained like that I answered with a smile, 'I'm older than you a decaying body as aging while my soul is hanging in somewhere else.

She gets angry says,' how about me? Do you think that I'm alright?'

You are still half alive in your heart and soul in the existence of your children at least. You are living in the place which belongs to your family and friends as still in the heart and soul doesn't matter you all together have to take how much hardships through the life struggle. You live all together stepping on the same land which is your's a very familiar place with all the familiar faces in the same situations, under the same ciecumstances even a little or more but all the pain or happiness all are the same and common over all. you can share and care all together in health and sickness. In good time and in a bad time. Here it's all your own good or bad all all together you are a common one.

Yesterday my synicism made her sad to look me in the eyes only which broke my heart actually I didn't argue there by calling me back 'No, not now, not again!'

Anyways, I saved a day only a day not dead but dark. On the dark day when I went to meet Dipok the sun stopped to shine to hide Himself behind the dark cloud which held the breath within to give no air to feel with a heart into the breathless hard and a suffocating humidity. Simi was driving said, 'I hate a humid day of this kind! Uf! So hot!'

I remained silent in the silence of the natural environment which stopped it's movements in the humid humidity. It wasn't nice to view outside the window as no wind's blowing in the mind blowing mind while the heart the and the mind blowing with blowing hair to represent a little aspect of a living life as still as apiece of life. On a damn day like this we desired to meet a friend practically out of sight and not out of the mind. His existence was all around throughout the visit in my mind only didn't feel the urge to see him again ever since departed on the two different ways might not to be met. Time changes people a lot so does the life experiences. At this age humans become inhuman only with the loss of the passions for the passionate desires and the emotins of the heart more than the basic instincts. When a friend is far away becomes more dear to the heart but the passion which drags us down with an urge no more much of an active heart when we lose interest to feel, when we lose interest to water the plants in the doubt that whether or not they grow back or not. Trying for life to live dies when we get hit by the blowing winds of time hitting hard to move forward in the mind blowing time of a bad time ironically at that time we get to boost up to get what we wanted. At some point we do not try hard even though we lit a very thin light of hope to see that what the heart wanted to see with the loss of the courage to see what if it' already buried to look ahead!

Simi said that it was an half an hour drive to Dipok's house which might not be. So far I know he keeps himself flying or wondering in the curiosity to come to know the worlds of unknown. It's been two years he stopped contacting me and I'm in a doubt whether on purpose or just couldn't manage all along. We crossed some dirt roads by the side of some shallow water as dirty looking in the muddy water as covered with light green weed like plants looks beautiful in color. After crossing all the streets busy and business based on the side walks. The dirt roads are wide enough to give you a hope for a life a new life to make all along leaving the crowd of the core of the city life in the busy and fussy streets and the constructing constructions all around. After almost a 20 min. drive we entered a narrow dirt road again looked developing with some houses on both sides a residence in between an urban and rural settings. We crossed the narrow lane on the major lane on feet by parking the car there. Yes! It is the house no 15 a wide single house with a wooden gate in between with a single board written with **odipto** on the top meaning not lighted yet. A beautiful young lady opened the door or the main gate to the strangers looked with an wide open and wondering eyes asked with a shy and confused smile, 'who you want?'

'is this Dipok's residence?' asked Simi first not me. Then answered the young lady, 'yes, but I don't know you yet!'

I smiled with proper courtesy to answer, 'I'm Minar Dipok's very old friend.'

'oh!' The lady of the house 'I guess!'didn't look very happy as answered very short in a low voice as she doesn't want to know more to welcome us. I smiled in my mind to think, 'Dipok got married but didn't tell me at all! but why? Why he does'nt consider me as his friend?' may be he is no more my friend then what? I asked myself 'did he actually forget me totally? And how and why?'

Finally we heard a male voice from inside towards us might be Dipok? Yes! I heard his voice finally, 'who's at the door Maya?' Maya looked back to answer 'your friend Dipok.' Both Dipok and Maya looked back at the guests to say actually it's Dipok my friend my dear friend got actually very excited, 'come!come inside!'also asked Simi to join together. After a long time still I behaved the same with no regrets, with no pain in my heart to say very joyfully, 'um----- nice home! You got married without inviting me? How dare you!' and my old friend smiled the same to answer, 'if I did you would'nt be coming here to see me or I wouldn't be lucky enough to visit you in my own place coming to pay a visit after all and to see my beautiful wife all at once! What a nice day after so long!' Dipok talked a lot about a lot about politics, places he visited as a journalist etc. His living room walls were covered with all the photo's he took in different places around the world. He took a sit on the sofa in front of me to say, 'Time to sit and relax how about you?'

'I'm visiting but going back again in two days'.

'why, what do you like it there?'

'what you mean? You know all! why we like to live in a foreign country and what would we like it here?' I guess I put my eye brows up in wonder!

'Strange! It's your place, your land! Come on!'

'Yes it is! Holding the soul here while the body's working there?' my simple answer again this time is the very simple! Dipok looked me into the eyes again to say with a pause 'you'are still the same!' then sain loud as commanding 'then take me there too! to live? But why and how?'

I didn't know what to say and how to answer all those questions which even I don't know either? Human mind and the heart act-and react and feel in a lot strange ways they both consequently react very strangely as when the mind works the heart doesn't follow as when the heart flows the mind can't set on what it's asking for. Human relationships are as complex as the functions of the body and the soul or the heart. But I know him very well. He's a flying bird rests for a little while to fly back again from place to places and God knows how I got a bit of my friend's nature without any blood relation that I'm also not for the home only like a woman. I don't travel much but my mind does. I know all the places Dipok visited for work or for a mission when he used to call me from anywhere. I travelled with his vision too through all of his stories he told me on the phone. The last two or three years he didn't call me and I don't know whether he remembered me at all! Then I looked at Maya a lovely bengali wife happens to be shy and very simple in an ordinary cotton sari wearing some clear glass churies meaning Bengals on her lovely hands as if like some fairies' the red thin bangals on her white hands reminded me of the old time by remembering my mother'hands or my aunts' or even my Bhabi's as if a very simple ornaments made with clear glass each in a thin layer all together as set of ten or more makes the beautiful hand very beautiful as rich in ornaments made with very chip material to be as cheap as to be worn now-a-days by some poor people. But still it'an ironically that the people in our place rich or poor or middle class women all equally appreciate the kind of Bengals regardless as beauty doesn't need to be bought with a lot of money specially when people can't ignore the beauty of their heart as their origins. Beauty is pure and precious while value is only pride definitely doesn't belong to the heart.

I taunted Dipok now by saying, you got a beautiful wife!' then made a comment by saying to her'is he good?'

Maya got shy didn't know what to answer but took the corner of her sari to hold by biting the very corner of the red border of her blue sari with red lines constantly putting into her mouth when'very shy to talk while doesn't have some appropriate words to greet or to treat with her foreign bound flying husband'Desi foreigner friend coming out of her mouth very spontaneously while being so shy to look very shy to still sanding there holding the tray to serve some snacks with tea. She smiled to make an excuse to go back to the kitchen. Simi found her world already by staring at the t.v in the dining area a bit far from us and looked like watching something with full attention. Dipok and me came back to ourselves again. Dipok was smoking by looking out at nowhere as I said suddenly,'your world is very different in every different ways in every different places you visit you can learn a lot about life right?'

'and that's why you cut off our connections to sit home and relax to write a big book of all of your memories by cutting off our connections to connect your own soul to the journeys through the travel through the world of imaginations?'

'I knew I'll see you again'. His answer.'and that's how you'll see Maya coming to your own home after travelling a lot through your own interest?' my answer now!

Dipok took a big pause now to regret said, 'that's my job too!'

'yes! You found the right job.' Seeing him quiet upset I taunted him again, 'it's Ok. At least you are true to yourself but you should have been true to me also at least by calling me that you're going to marry to settle down for a life?' He kept gazing at me to read me through my eyes to find an answer for what I don't know that might have been to read the unspoken language of my heart which is why I'm showing myself a little but very deep in some sort of emotion or an agony in expressions to ask him about his identity of what sort which I myself also had been looking for.

Any ways not much to talk about a relationship which doesn't have an identity to mention other than by hiding it with no friendship as it to call.

Last days were busy and quick before seeing Dipok in shopping around, meeting friends and family at home or in a restaurant. In the meantime also managed to visit Cox-s- Bazar to pay a visit to the Sea with all big beauties, big water under the wide open sky, Big and Big waves to wave us their greetings with their big big waving lumps up in water to make us cool to feel cool at the sight of the cooling part of Nature.

The final visit left us alone for later to pay a visit to Dipok for the sake of friendship or might be for being together in friendship and love in a friendship with him my dear friend from the very young age when we used to be in the college before entering the University to depart again from each other to meet again my dear Dipok after a while once again as a married man as half of him already got occupied with his wife as the other part of him and then me who's still floating on the edge of the Bachelor' life to be settled down with a female buddy to live together as a married couple like Dipok who's half away half in his country and I'm still deciding to choose only one place to settle down as a married man if it really ever happens to happen by a man like me who can never ever take a descision to make by reasoning as always floating and

living in the same place by letting the heart and the mind fly up all around stopping for a bit up on the cloud to decide whether to descend on his own Land for love or on the land where he lives to live in a life meaning to be still in the reality far away from the reality of a kind hard to manage or even to tolerate by being in love in with the heart while stepping out into a harsh and hard reality neither can be avoided in all the sweet bondages nor can be tolerated whereas the loveless, heartless and the soulless surroundings under circumstancs can't be very pleasing while living in a un-pleasant environment.

Finally, last week I took off the Mother Land without the mother to come back to the land of opportunities again to replenish the reality and by the by, need to mention also that I left with two suitcases filled up with my love for everyone I care and came back with the double of that in buying back as on departure half of the load was loaded with my personal belongings and on the arrival double of that which I took for all in return for me as the 'gifts of Love and Remembrance!'